The Hope of Celi

The bard put his hands to Rowan's shoulders, pivoting him toward the fire. "Look into the flames, boy. Tell me what you see."

Rowan stared into the fire. The air crackled and flared around him, and for a moment he thought he had fallen into the fire itself. Pain erupted along his nerves, clenched the muscles of his arms and legs tight. His body stiffened and his eyes widened until there was but a thin ring of clear brown around the black pool of the pupil.

"I see a sword—no two swords—deep hidden and guarded. I see a king and his enchanter. And I see a Champion and warrior-bard, a Kaith. I see the swords rightly taken . . ." He shuddered.

"And what else?"

"Invasion and war. Such a war . . ."

BOOKS BY ANN MARSTON

The Rune Blade Trilogy
Kingmaker's Sword
Western King
Broken Blade

The Sword in Exile Trilogy
Cloudbearer's Shadow
King of Shadows
Sword and Shadow

Third Book in the Sword in Exile Trilogy

SWORD AND SHADOW

ANN MARSTON

An Imprint of HarperCollins*Publishers*

This is a work of fiction. Names, characters, places, and incidents are the products of the author's imagination or are used fictitiously and are not to be construed as real. Any resemblance to actual events, locales, organizations, or persons, living or dead, is entirely coincidental.

EOS
An Imprint of HarperCollins*Publishers*
10 East 53rd Street
New York, New York 10022-5299

Copyright © 2000 by Ann Marston
Cover art by Yvonne Gilbert
ISBN: 0-06-102042-7
www.eosbooks.com

First Eos paperback printing: November 2000

Eos Trademark Reg. U.S. Pat. Off. and in Other Countries, Marca Registrada, Hecho en U.S.A.
HarperCollins® is a trademark of HarperCollins Publishers Inc.

Printed in the U.S.A.

10 9 8 7 6 5 4 3 2 1

For Lesley

The Royal Houses of Cell, Skal and Tyra

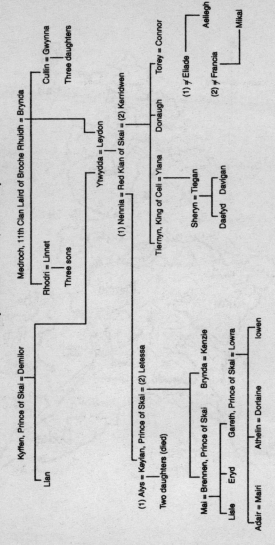

Prologue

Even in exile in the isolated high northern uplands of the Isle of Skerry, the yrSkai observed the Festival of Imbolc when Beodun of the Fires bestowed his gift of new fire on the freshly cleaned and scrubbed hearths and braziers, torches and carefully saved beeswax candles. Behind lay Winter Solstice and the dark, chill depths of midwinter; ahead lay Vernal Equinox and the promise of spring to come.

Imbolc represented the night of rebirth, signifying the return of light and warmth to the bleak world where snow piled high beneath a dark sky scattered with stars. On this night, the stars were so brilliant, so clear against the endless black of the sky, a careful listener might almost hear them crackle in the still, cold air.

Vivid garlands of dried gold and red flowers festooned the gray stone walls of the Great Hall where Athelin, exiled Prince of Skai, entertained his people. Fresh candles, smoothly pale and gleaming, clustered on the tables, the golden flames reflected in the golden mead. The massed torches sent shadows leaping across the floor to play among the guests dressed in unaccustomed finery. On the huge hearths, freshly scrubbed and cleaned, the first ceremoniously placed logs had already begun to crumble to ashes. Servants scuttled busily among the crowded tables, removing emptied platters, filling empty goblets with mead.

Some barely perceptible signal flashed through the hall. One by one, the gathered men and women began to fall silent until an air of quiet anticipation descended upon the Hall. In the expectant hush, a man who had been seated on a stool alone by the fire rose to his feet. A servant reverently unwrapped a bundle at the man's feet. A ripple of appreciative murmuring flowed around the room as the bard bent to take up his harp. Mioragh had only recently escaped from Skai on the Maedun-held main Isle of Celi and had made his way to Skerry. But his reputation as a bard had spread quickly throughout Skerry Keep.

He nodded in acknowledgment to Prince Athelin and the lady Dorlaine, who sat at the head of a long table to the bard's left. He nodded to Athelin's half brother Caennedd at Athelin's right, then turned again to face the room. He stood with the light of the fire and the massed candles glinting in his silver hair. His fingers delicately touched the strings of the harp, and a glissando of notes fell like a shower of sparks through the room. When he spoke, his trained and powerful voice filled the Hall like warm honey flowing into a bowl.

"My friends I give you greeting on this night of New Fire," he began. "And I bring you reminders of what we have lost. The Isle of Celi has always been a place where strands of magic wove through the fabric of the land like notes of music through the hall of a great lord." He touched the strings of the harp again. In the liquid fall of notes, a haunting melody began to take shape. "Many years ago, the Somber Riders of Maedun came to our land, and were repulsed by the bravery of a king and the magic of an enchanter only to be lost by treachery and sorcery. I shall sing of this bravery and this magic." He bent to his harp, gathered his *awen*—his muse—about him, and sang.

> *"Armorer to gods and kings*
> *Wyfydd's magic hammer sings . . ."*

Rowan knew the song by heart. He listened raptly as the bard sang, his own lips moving as he repeated the words. The story of how the swords were forged never failed to make his heart beat faster as he watched the magical scene in his mind's eye.

"Two sprung from a single seed,
Royal blood and royal breed . . ."

Like the awaited heros, Rowan and his brother Acaren,
who was the elder by eight minutes, were twins. Not the seed
of kings, mayhaps, Rowan conceded reluctantly to himself.
But twins nonetheless, and from the royal line. They were
sons of Prince Athelin, who was descended from King
Tiernyn's elder brother, Keylan of Skai.

Rowan blinked the tears from his eyes as the bard sang
of the defeat of the Celae army and the death of King
Tiernyn. Blood and treachery and a thread of hope. The
swords of Wyfydd lay hidden, waiting for a new king and a
new enchanter, who must take them to hand. And one day,
Celi would be free. . . .

As the last notes faded into memory, the two boys, who
had earlier been carrying pitchers of mead among the guests
in the Hall, wrapped themselves deeper into the warmth of
the woolen blankets on the bed of furs in a corner of the
Great Hall. They shivered, more in awe and delight at the
music than with the cold. Because it was Imbolc, and because
the bard Mioragh had come for the celebration, they had
been allowed to remain in the Great Hall long past their bed-
time for a rare treat.

"We would serve them," Acaren murmured as he always
did whenever he heard the "Song of the Swords." "We would
be their champions."

Rowan didn't reply. He lay watching the light gleam on
the bard's harp, and wondered about the magic in the music.

Near dawn, when the Hall was finally quiet, Rowan crept out
of the furs he shared with Acaren, leaving his twin curled
warmly in sleep. The bard slept, wrapped in his cloak, on a
soft pallet near the hearth. The fire, banked for the night, had
burned down to an occasional glimmering of flames on a
glowing bed of embers.

The harp, a wondrous creation of hardwood, ivory, and
gold, lay by Mioragh's hip, gleaming softly in the firelight.

Rowan went to his knees and sat back on his heels, his hands in his lap, looking at the instrument in awe. Unable to resist the temptation, he slowly, reverently reached out one hand and caressed the graceful curve of the top.

The harp, so sensitive a breath might draw music from it, whispered a hushed minor chord into the flickering dark. Guiltily, Rowan snatched back his hand. He wasn't fast enough. The bard's large hand closed painfully around his wrist. Rowan bit back a cry as he looked up into Mioragh's fierce brown-gold eyes.

"What are you up to, lad?" Mioragh asked mildly enough. "A bit of thievery on Imbolc Night, mayhaps?"

"No, sir," Rowan replied, shocked and dismayed that the bard might think him a thief. "It's just that the music was so beautiful . . ."

Mioragh's gaze never wavered, but it softened a fraction. "So you're fond of music, are you, lad?" he asked.

"Aye, sir. Very much." Rowan did not rub his sore wrist. Instead, he reached out to stroke the harp again. A small ripple of hushed notes spilled into the shadows of the Hall. "Is the magic in the harp, sir?" he asked.

Mioragh smiled. "Some of it," he said. "Some of it is in the hands and heart and soul of the harper."

Rowan felt a pulse of life in the glowing wood beneath his fingers. "It's so beautiful," he murmured.

Mioragh reached out and put his hand under the boy's chin. "Look at me, child," he said quietly. Rowan met his gaze and Mioragh smiled. "What's your name?"

"Rowan, sir. Rowan ap Athelin."

"The Prince's son?"

"Yes, sir."

"How old?"

"We celebrate our seventh Name Day tomorrow."

Mioragh's eyebrow rose fractionally. "Children of Beltane?"

"Aye, sir," Rowan said, nodding. "So it's said."

"Lucky and blessed all your lives," Mioragh said, and Rowan thought he spoke more to himself than to him. "Able to claim a goddess as a mother and a god as a father." Rowan nodded again.

"Which of you is eldest?"

"Acaren is, sir. By eight minutes."

Mioragh nodded. "I see," he said quietly. "A gift for a gift, then, Rowan Secondborn. What have you to bargain with?"

Rowan could hardly breathe, could not tear his eyes from the compelling, brilliant gaze of the bard. "I have nothing, sir," he whispered.

"Aye, you do." Mioragh sat up and put his hands to Rowan's shoulders, pivoting him toward the fire. "Look into the flames, boy. Tell me what you see."

Rowan turned his gaze toward the fire. He thought the fire had ignited in his belly, in his chest, in his head. The air crackled and flared around him, and for a moment he thought he had fallen into the fire itself. Pain erupted along his nerves, clenched the muscles of his arms and legs tight. His body stiffened and his eyes widened until there was but a thin ring of clear brown around the black pool of the pupil.

He stared into the fire. Slowly, shadows formed among the shimmering coals, and the shadows became blurred, indistinct pictures. Flashes and impressions. Glimpses of movement. He tried to look away, but the fragmented pictures held him spellbound.

"I see a fair, green land darkened and blighted," he muttered. "And a girl ..." He stared, his mouth drawn in on itself. "Just a young girl. She's looking at me, and she's so very sad. ... She says I've forgotten her."

"You'll know her when you meet her." Mioragh's voice came quietly and calmly, full of reassurance and certainty. "What more do you see, Rowan?"

"I see a sword—no two swords—deep hidden and guarded. I see a king and his enchanter. And I see a Champion and a warrior-bard, a Kaith. I see the swords rightly taken ..." He shuddered.

"And what else?"

"Invasion and war. Such a war ..."

Mioragh's hand under his chin forced his gaze back to

the bard's eyes. "Then it's true," he said softly. He released Rowan's chin and reached for the harp. "This instrument is yours, Rowan Secondborn. You'll find its magic in your heart."

Wordlessly, Rowan took the harp from the bard. It seemed to nestle into his arms. He had no words sufficient for thanks.

"Do you know your path?" Mioragh asked.

"Aye, sir," Rowan whispered. "I do. I'm to be the Kaith . . ."

"And for Acaren?"

"Champion."

"And hope of Celi," Mioragh said. "And hope of Celi . . . Together."

In the City of Clendonan on the banks of the Tiderace, Hakkar of Maedun, Lord Protector of Celi, awoke in a chamber that had once been the private quarters of the High King of Celi. He rose from the side of the woman he had chosen for the night, and went to the window. Hands behind his back, he looked to the north and west. His narrowly handsome face drawn into planes of thoughtfulness, he gripped the marble sill of the window for a long time, then sent a sleepy servant scrambling with a message for his son.

Horbad arrived within moments, dressed impeccably in unrelieved black, almost as if he had anticipated his father's summons.

"You sent for me, Father?" He stood, relaxed and at his ease, near the door of the room, elegant and slender as the black blade of a sword.

Hakkar turned from the window. "Did you feel it?" he asked.

"I felt nothing." Horbad took a step toward the window, his head cocked slightly as if listening. "No. Nothing. What was it?"

"Something . . . I don't know."

Horbad came to the window and looked out at the shuttered, sleeping city. Hakkar's spell shimmered darkly in the air, barely visible as a transparent haze.

"Something important?" Horbad asked.

"I believe so. Something happened. Some magic in the north. North and west."

"The Celae again?"

Hakkar put his back to the window. "Yes. It felt like it. A flash of powerful magic."

"But we stamped out the last of that magic more than eight years ago. How can there be more?"

Hakkar made a graceful gesture with his right hand. "I have learned never to underestimate the perfidy of these Celae," he said. He turned back to the window. "Look carefully. Can you see the glow of the magic up there?"

Horbad raised his eyes, looked north. "I see something, but I can't tell what it is."

Hakkar frowned. "Whatever it is, it's trouble. Send a troop of Somber Riders north. The best we have. Tell them they must look and act like Celae. Report to me when it's done."

"When it's done? What is done?"

"When the magic is dead."

"And how are they to find the magic? We have no more Tell-Tales. The cave in the cliffs on the west coast has been barren of them ever since we killed the man who called himself the Prince of Skai."

"Not quite," Hakkar said. "We have one more." He went to a chest of drawers standing in an alcove beyond his bed and took down a carved onyx box. He opened it slowly and reached inside. When he turned back to Horbad and opened his hand, a small, oval stone lay cupped in the palm of his hand. It glowed faintly blue-white, like the glimmer in the sea on a dark night as a school of silver fish passes just below the surface. A small crack marred the stone, a tiny dark line wavering across it in a hesitant diagonal. "There's this one. It belonged to my father's aunt Francia. This one glows only when it detects any magic not of our own making."

"The glow is faint," Horbad said.

"Aye, it is. But only because the magic is far away. As it comes closer to the source of the magic, the glow will become brighter. We shall give it to the leader of the troop we send north." He closed his hand, extinguishing the meager glow. "When they return, it should look the same as any ordinary stone."

"And the maker of the magic?"

"Dead. Of course."

In the southeast of Venia above the Verge where the living green met the burned, sere ashes of the Dead Lands, a solitary figure stood on the crest of a ridge watching the valley below. Ten armed men, bareheaded in the sun, rode at an easy pace beside the tumbling waters of the River Afon as it surged out into the foothills. The lone figure, small and dark, dressed in mottled green and brown that blended perfectly with the trees, brush and grass of the crest, moved silently as a shadow along the ridge above the riders, effortlessly keeping pace with them.

She was Valessa al Drustan. She was nearly twelve years old and the daughter of the man who was born to be Prince of Dorian. Because there were so few of them, and because they lived so close to the Verge where the Somber Riders of Maedun hunted men for sport, her people had learned to practice the same art of invisibility as the animals of the forests and meadows around them. From the shelter of her art, she watched the mounted men.

They looked like Celae, even to wearing their swords slung across their backs with the careless ease of long practice. They might have been men of Cai, exiled Duke of Wenydd, from the west by Laurelwater. Or men of Prince Athelin in the north on the island of Skerry. They might have been, but for one thing. They had come from the south, through the burned land beyond the Verge.

Valessa carried a bow and a quiver of arrows on her shoulder; she was swift and deadly in the use of them. But she made no attempt to unlimber the bow as she flitted from shadow to shadow along the ridge. It was said that the Somber Riders could not be killed, that the protection of the black sorcerer's spell would send the arrow back to seek the heart of the one who had launched it. Years ago, she had seen Goren try to kill a Somber Rider and die pierced by his own arrow.

She had no desire to die alone on a ridge above the River Afon. So she merely watched. When the Riders stopped for a meal by the riverbank, she crept closer in hopes that she might overhear something that would indicate where they were going. They acted like men with a purpose, and this time, because of the disguises, it seemed to be more than the mere sport of hunting Celae men and women.

Valessa wasn't surprised to discover they spoke the uncouth tongue of Maedun. She shook her head, marveling at the sheer arrogance of them. It would never occur to them they could be overheard.

She sat close enough, hidden by the light and shadow itself, to reach out and touch one of the Riders, close enough to smell the sour stench of horse and man sweat and something else emanating from them. Several times, she heard them speak the accursed name of the black sorcerer of Maedun. Two or three times she caught the word *magic*, heard the doubtful tone in their voices. Then she heard the word *kill*, accompanied by a short, abrupt, unmistakable gesture. At that, they all broke into laughter.

Like a wraith of smoke and mist, Valessa slipped silently away, mist melting into water. Drustan must be told of this, and messages of warning sent to Cai and Athelin. The behavior of these Somber Riders was strange and puzzling. It merited a much closer look.

Part 1

Lay of the Bard

1

The knock at the door startled Athelin. He looked up from his account books and ledgers, surprised that darkness had come while he was too preoccupied to notice it. Nor had he noticed when someone had obviously slipped into his workroom to light the candles. He glanced down. The ink had dried into an untidy knob on the end of his pen nib while he studied the figures on the page.

Survival over the winter was too often a matter of constant, relentless calculation—the number of mouths that needed feeding divided into the bushels of grain and the barrels of stored vegetables and fruit, or the number of hearths to light divided into the tonnes of soft coal and piles of dried peat or carefully selected wood. The day-to-day need exempted no one on the island, and even Athelin, his sons, and his wife worked in the fields during seedtime and harvest.

He put down his pen and rubbed his aching eyes as Ralf knocked again and entered the room quietly. "Your pardon, my lord Prince," he said, "but a messenger has come from Prince Drustan by the Afon."

"Where is he?"

"Downstairs, my lord. In the small workroom off the Great Hall. I've asked for food and drink to be taken to him, but he insists on speaking with you first. Shall I bring him up here?"

Athelin glanced down at the scatter of parchment on his desk and made a wry face. He'd had more than enough of this for a while. "No, I don't think so," he said. "Have them bring the meal to the small workroom downstairs." He stepped out from behind the table and went to the door. "He can eat while I read the message."

The messenger stood by the table in the small room, wrapped in a dark, hooded cloak, stained with travel and marred by snags from catching on branches and brambles. Athelin entered and saw weariness in every line of the drooping young body as the messenger turned toward him. The hood fell back as the messenger turned.

With a shock, Athelin realized that it was a young girl, not a boy, who faced him. The dark hair and brilliant blue eyes emphasized the pallor of the childish face. But if the thin, pale face was young, it also held the promise of beauty and strength. *Not much more than twelve or thirteen,* Athelin thought. *Certainly not yet fourteen.* Chilled, he wondered what dire emergency sent a child as a messenger.

Calling on some hidden reserve of strength, the girl straightened. Her shoulders went back and her head came up. Athelin almost smiled. There was no hint of subservience in this young Doriani.

"Prince Athelin, I bring you greeting from my father, Drustan of Dorian," she said formally. "I bear urgent tidings."

Athelin curbed his impatience to hear the message and pulled a chair up to the table. "Please sit down," he said. He went around behind the table and sat in his own chair. "It's a long and dangerous ride from Afon, and you must be exhausted."

The girl sank gratefully into the chair. "Thank you," she said.

"What's your name, child?"

The girl bristled. "I am no child but a woman nearly grown," she said stiffly.

Athelin hid his smile and lifted a placating hand. "I apologize. I meant no offense."

The girl inclined her head. *She has both pride and grace,* Athelin thought. *And a regal bearing that sits well with her strong, supple young body.*

"I am Valessa al Drustan," she said. "My father asked that I bring this message to you myself."

"I'm honored," Athelin said. "What is the message?"

"There are Somber Riders north of the Verge, my lord. I myself saw ten of them riding west along the Afon. They were dressed like Celae. I couldn't find out where they were going, nor why they had come. We kept watch on them until they were out of our territory. They didn't appear to be sport hunting. My father thinks they were heading either here to Skerry, or to the stronghold of the yrWenydd on Laurelwater. When I left the Afon, they were still riding north and west."

The last time Somber Riders had found Skerry, nearly twelve years ago, his older brother Adair had died in the skirmish, and he had nearly lost Dorlaine, his wife and bheancoran. A cold chill settled around Athelin's heart.

They come again, he thought. He came convulsively to his feet. "When was this?" he asked, unable to keep the tense alarm from his voice.

"A little less than a sevenday ago, my lord. Another messenger has gone to Duke Cai on Laurelwater, but my father believes the Riders were on their way here. If so, they won't be far behind—"

Athelin crossed the room in two quick bounds and yanked open the door. "Ralf!" he shouted. "Ralf, to me. Immediately."

Ralf appeared in the doorway, eyes wide, before Athelin finished calling his name. "I'm here, my lord," he said. "What's wrong?"

"Fetch Weymund," Athelin told him. "And Cynric and my brother Caennedd, too. Find Saethen. Tell him to double the guard around the keep. There are Somber Riders in the north."

Ralf wasted no time in replying. He merely nodded once sharply, then spun on his heel and sprinted off down the corridor.

Athelin went to the window, pounding one fist into the palm of his other hand. Above, the sky blazed with stars. The moon had not yet risen, and the starlight silvered the stark, bare branches of the trees, sparking back points of fire in the carpet of fresh snow in the carefully walled and hedged fields.

It had happened before that the Somber Riders of Maedun had come north of the Verge for more than just a sport hunt. That time, he had lost his elder brother Adair and nearly lost his wife. And now they were coming again.

"Hakkar will never lie easy until he knows for certain all traces of magic are gone from this poor island," he said, more to himself than to Valessa. "He'll never be content to let us languish in our exile here." Again, he saw the disguised black riders surging through the Great Hall of Skerry Keep, saw Adair lying bleeding on the polished flagstone floor, saw Dorlaine lying on the stairs, bleeding from a wound on her forehead. "Something important has happened. Something to make Hakkar risk sending his men up here."

Valessa's lip curled. "There is no risk," she said bitterly. "The Somber Riders cannot be killed."

Athelin turned. "They're only men, child," he said grimly. "They most certainly can be killed when they're out of the protection of Hakkar's spell or his warlocks. I've killed a few of them myself." He looked up as a serving boy entered carrying a tray of food and ale. "You must eat now, my lady Valessa. We'll find a bed for you. While you're eating, I must see to increasing the guard."

Valessa wasted no time tucking into the bread, cold meat, and cheese on the tray the boy set on the table before her. "Mayhaps they won't be able to cross the Skerryrace," she said.

"Mayhaps," Athelin said skeptically. "I don't think they'll know how to find the ferry that brought you, but there are others with little ships hardy enough to cross the race even in the dead of winter."

The boat was small and lay nodding lazily in the water alongside the jetty, which was little more than a pile of rock stretching a short way out into the sea. It was a natural formation, enhanced only slightly by the Veniani fisherman who had lived with his family in the low stone house on the headland rising steeply above the bay. The house was dark; it had been for a long time. It would remain dark forever now. The fisherman and his infant daughter lay in their beds, their throats cut while they slept. The woman had been spirited and had provided good sport for a while. When the Somber Riders eventually tired of her, they simply strangled her and left her in a tumbled heap on the floor beside the corpses of her husband and daughter.

Tran made his way carefully along the shore, conscious of the shadowy figures moving with him, all of them dark in the starlight against the light, drifting skiff of snow on the beach. There were only eight of them. Zerad and one trooper had stayed behind in the old stone cottage, Zerad to monitor the Tell-Tale stone and the trooper to tend to the horses. The horses would be needed again once Tran and his men had finished their business on the island.

He glanced down at the sliver of softly glowing stone that lay in the palm of his hand. He had been shocked and startled when the fragment split from the larger rock, but it hadn't seemed to surprise Zerad. Zerad had merely handed him the splinter and told him to follow its glow. When it was close to the source of the magic, it would shine more brightly, giving an unmistakable indication where lay Tran's target. Tran wasn't sure he understood how the stone worked, but it was enough that Zerad had given him orders. No one wasted time wondering how the lord Hakkar's sorcery worked, and certainly no one questioned an order from a superior officer.

The men climbed into the boat and released the lines that held it fast to the jetty. Tran took his place in the middle, crouching among the detritus of fishcatching, thankful that the bitter wind that scoured the northern crags during the day had finally died down. The sea was bad enough when it was calm; when it was turbulent and battered by gales, it was impossible.

Two of the men who knew sailing worked noiselessly, out of habit more than necessity, to raise the small single sail, and the boat began to move slowly. The man at the tiller leaned hard to his left. The sail caught the wind and filled with a muted snap. The space between the hull and the jetty increased rapidly.

The narrow channel between the main island and the islands to the north was a dangerous and turbulent stretch of water. Between ebb and flood tide, the current surged eastward, and between flood and ebb, the current moved west. When the tide changed direction, the current set the sea boiling and surging like a seething cauldron. With the wind blistering out of the north, the channel was impossible. Only in the few hours before dawn, before the tide turned, did the wind die down and the sea calm enough to make the crossing dangerous but marginally feasible.

Once the boat was moving well, Tran and all the men except the man at the tiller and the man handling the single sail huddled down out of the way as best they could in the cramped quarters. It was nearly ten leagues to the island across the Skerryrace, and Tran was certain it would not be an easy voyage.

They were not yet halfway across when his belly rebelled violently. Sick and dizzy, he crouched with his forehead against the cool wood of the wale, listening to most of the others being as ill as he.

But they made it. The sky had not yet grayed to the coming of dawn when they beached the fishing boat on a point of land on the south shore of the island. Tran led his small party ashore. They saw no one as they drew the little boat up beyond the high-tide line, up to the shelter of the low cliff among the salt-bitten furze. After cutting dead brown bracken and furze and stacking it around the boat to hide it from any casual observer, they staggered up the sandbank to the headland. They threw themselves flat in the snow and waited for their bellies to calm.

The firm, dry land beneath their feet acted as a tonic. Presently, more certain now of his own survival, Tran looked around carefully and located the three high peaks Zerad had told him to look for. He took his bearings from two of them and motioned his men forward.

The sentry surprised them as they climbed the frozen dunes to the winter-bare trees. Tran's heart leapt in quick fear in his chest. The sentry made a startled cry, then spun away to run. Drom's dagger brought him down, skidding bone-

lessly on his face in the icy sand, before he could raise any
alarm.

"What shall we do with him?" Drom bent to wipe the
blade on the Celae's breeks.

Tran glanced up at the sky. In less than an hour, it would
be full light. "Bury him in the snow under the trees," he said.
"In case there are more of them. We can't leave the body lying
around to give us away."

Drom bent to lift the body and grunted as he slung it
over his shoulder. He disappeared into the trees and returned
a few minutes later, dusting off his hands.

"They won't find him before spring," he said.

"Good." Tran drew in a deep breath and pointed to the
trees. "Let's go."

They set off and were quickly swallowed up by the forest, which grew thickly on the sheltered side of the island.
Tran pulled the glowing shard from his pocket and looked at
it again. It seemed to be brighter, indicating they were going
in the right direction.

Using all the stealth they had learned from years of
hunting Celae for sport, they crept along the forested lower
slopes of the mountain. By early evening, they lay in the protective cover of a bare hazel copse on the north slopes of Ben
Warden, looking down at Skerry Keep. They watched in
utter stillness, assessing the strength of the palace. It took
Tran very little time to decide they would not have to climb
the walls and overcome the guards. It would be much simpler
to wait until morning, and walk through the gates as if they
belonged there. Their quarry lay inside, unsuspecting and
vulnerable.

Shortly after she had broken her fast, Valessa received a summons from Athelin to join him in his workroom. He opened
the door for her himself and gestured to a deeply padded
chair by his worktable.

"Please have a seat," he said. "Saethen, my Captain of
the Guard, and Weymund, my Swordmaster, as well as Ralf
will be joining us in a few moments. I want them to hear what
you have to say."

She thought she might sink right into the cushions on that chair and never get out. She smiled and shook her head. "Thank you, but I'd rather stand," she said. She went to the window and looked out.

Below her lay the remains of the garden she had noticed from her window earlier that morning shortly after she arose. The courtyard itself looked as if a half-forgotten corner of the main house had been walled off and the garden planted to fill it. The only access to the charming little nook, only a little bigger than the Great Hall, was by a small iron-grille gate leading to the pastures and fields on the flank of the mountain behind the palace.

Someone had spent a lot of loving time and attention on that small courtyard. The long, brittle sticks, furred with thorns, clustered around the walls must be roses. In the summer, their fragrance would be thick as honey in the air. Carefully laid-out beds of what were probably herbs and flowers lined the gently curving walkways. Skeletally bare fruit trees stood against the walls, placed to make the most of the spring and summer sunshine. On an open area of wide, snow-covered lawn, a man worked with two small boys, teaching them swordplay.

Valessa drew in a quick, startled breath. The man looked Maedun with his tar black, curling hair and his dark eyes. She hadn't realized she had made a sound until Athelin stepped close to her.

"What is it?" he asked, alarm clear in his voice.

Valessa pointed. "He looks Maedun," she said.

Athelin smiled, the tense lines in his face relaxing. "He is," he said. "Or at least partly. He's Cynric, who was my sister's protector and friend until she died. His father was a Somber Rider, but his mother was a woman of the Summer Run, a Saesnesi. Cynric's been with us for more than seven years. I trust him as much or more than I trust any man on this little island."

"You trust him? A Maedun?"

"Cynric has proved his loyalty many times," he said. "A good man."

Valessa glanced up at him curiously. "It seems an odd place to find a Maedun," she said.

"Cynric is Saesnesi," he said. "Since my sister died, he's appointed himself guard and tutor to my sons." He glanced down into the courtyard and smiled. "Those two are Acaren and Rowan, the twins. Gabhain and Danal have outgrown his teaching and are with Weymund."

"My father speaks of Weymund," she said. "A talented man, he says."

"I agree," Athelin said.

Out of training and habit, she remained at the window, looking out at the forests and fields along the slopes of Ben Warden. The shadows made ever-shifting patterns along the flanks. "Watch the patterns," her father had told her. "Watch for changes in the warp and weft. You'll see a flaw in the pattern before you see an enemy."

She knew too little of the land around Skerry Keep to recognize an anomaly. Even in the short time she had been standing by the window, the sun had moved and the pattern had changed. Time, she thought. Time and familiarity would make her more knowledgeable. She frowned. But there was something out there. Something—

"Ah, here they are now." Athelin turned as three men entered the room. One of the men she recognized from the night before as Ralf, Athelin's Captain of the Company. He was about to introduce the other two, but she caught his arm.

"Look," she said urgently. "There." She pointed to a small group of men walking in a tight cluster toward the small courtyard gate. They had come, not from the town and harbor by the road that led to the main gate, but from the winding track that led into the hills and pastures on the lower slopes of the nearest mountain, Ben Warden. The subtle flaw in the pattern. She counted only eight of them, but instinctively she knew they were the same men she had seen riding through the Afon valley. Even as she pointed them out and tried to tell Athelin who they were, they broke into a trot, intent upon the gate into the garden and the boys just beyond it.

Athelin reacted instantly. He swore softly under his

breath and seized his sword, then spun about and ran from
the room, shouting to the men to go with him. She hesitated
only half a heartbeat, then leapt to follow them.

The small lawn in front of the courtyard gate seemed full of
men as Athelin sped across the snow. Cynric and two of the
guards had seen the danger and thrown themselves into the
midst of the attacking Maedun. He raised his sword and
waded into the middle of the fighting.

The sword Bane was a Rune Blade, handed down from
father to son since the first Prince of Skai. Crafted to defend
Skai and its people, it might almost have had a mind of its
own as Athelin swung it at one of the Maedun. In his mind,
Bane's fierce, angry voice howled and shrieked, and as
always, he felt as if the sword had become part of him, an
extension of his hand and arm.

The Maedun, not expecting an attack from the rear, fell
immediately to Athelin's sword. As Athelin turned to meet
another, he saw Ralf's blade cleave a second Rider nearly in
half.

"My lord, your back!" Cynric shouted hoarsely.

Athelin spun to meet the raised blade of a disguised
Somber Rider. He brought Bane up, parried the swing,
stepped sideways, and swept Bane in a rising arc. The blade
caught the man in the soft tissues below his rib cage. Athelin
didn't waste the time to watch him fall, but turned to meet
another enemy.

One of the Riders broke away, bounding in long strides
toward the gate that still stood open. Cynric turned away to
try to intercept him, leaving his back open to a foe. Athelin
cried out as Cynric staggered and fell to the snow, blood flowing from a wound in his side. The other Maedun leapt over
him without breaking stride, murderously intent upon the
open gate.

Blindly, instinctively, Athelin began to move toward the
gate, struggling through the wild mass of men fighting
around him. Only one thought burned in his mind. The boys.
The twins were in there. He had to protect the children.

Someone shouted a warning. Athelin turned, saw the

blade coming at his head. He raised Bane, but too late. His own blade deflected the descending sword enough so that it didn't cleave his skull, but the full force of the swing landed on his shoulder. The only thing that saved him from losing his arm was that the sword had turned in the Rider's hand. The flat of the blade slammed into his shoulder, not the cutting edge. He heard the bone break, a sound oddly like a dry twig cracking underfoot, and was vaguely surprised when he felt no pain.

The Rider danced back to raise the sword again. Something flicked past Athelin's cheek with a soft whispering rush of air, like the rustle of a small animal in dry grass. The Rider staggered forward almost into his arms, the shaft of an arrow, brightly fletched and gleaming, protruding from the back of his neck. Athelin twisted sideways, let the Rider fall to the trampled and bloody snow. On her knee at the edge of the small lawn, Valessa smiled grimly in acknowledgment and nocked another arrow. She looked up but there were too many bodies between her and the Rider who was already halfway through the gate. Even as she drew back her bow, Athelin knew she could not get a clear shot at the Rider.

Athelin threw himself forward, staggered against the gate. The Rider was already well within the garden with the unprotected twins. He knew—*knew*—he could not get there in time.

Even as he flung himself into the garden, he saw it happening, helpless to prevent it. Acaren and Rowan cowered back against the wall beneath one of the apple trees. The Rider swept his arm sideways, caught Acaren across the chest. The brutal force of the blow lifted the boy from his feet and sent him sprawling back into the stone wall. The Rider raised his sword to bring it slicing down on Acaren's lolling head.

2

Athelin's feet slipped in the snow and he went to one knee. Desperately, he lunged forward, blood from his shoulder wound flowing down his arm and spattering in the snow. He cried out in despair, nearly sobbing with pain and effort, and knew he could never reach the boys in time.

Shouting incoherently, Rowan threw himself against the Rider's legs, knocking the man off-balance. The descending sword struck sparks against the stone of the wall, missing Acaren's head by inches.

The Rider turned quickly and raised his sword again. Rowan stood his ground, a small, boy-sized sword in his hands. Not much bigger than a long dagger. Useless against the sword of the Rider.

Athelin shouted again, still too far away to help. The Rider laughed and swept his raised sword toward Rowan.

The sword flashed down. But Rowan was no longer there. He ducked, hunched down, spun away. He crouched in the snow beneath the Rider, almost between the man's feet. He brought his small sword up, plunged it into the man's belly just above the groin. The strain pulled his face into a pale, grotesque mask as he jerked the sword up with the whole of his strength. The Rider spilled forward, shock and surprise on his face, and collapsed onto his belly into the snow, nearly taking Rowan with him.

"Rowan!"

Athelin dropped Bane, staggered forward, and stumbled to his knees beside the child. Rowan stood trembling, his face chalk-pale, smothered in blood, mercifully none of it his.

Athelin gathered him into his arms, his relief leaving him light-headed and dizzy.

Still holding Rowan tightly against him, Athelin scrambled on his knees to Acaren. The boy sat up groggily, struggling to breathe. The Rider's blow had knocked the wind out of him, but had done little more damage. Athelin pulled Acaren into his arms, tight against Rowan, and buried his face against their hair, breathing a prayer of thankfulness over and over, and trying to control the wild, terrified beating of his heart.

"My lord?"

Athelin looked up to see Mioragh bending over him.

"My lord, you're hurt. Let me look at your shoulder."

Athelin glanced over his shoulder to where Cynric still lay in the snow outside the gate. Another coin of loyalty to add to his debt. "See to Cynric first," he said thickly. "I'm all right."

"Cynric will live," Mioragh said. "He took a blade in the hip, but there is no damage to his gut. You needn't worry about him. Let me see to your shoulder. You're bleeding quite badly."

"The Riders?"

"All dead, my lord."

Athelin let himself slump to sit on his heels. His shoulder felt on fire, the pain throbbing with each beat of his heart. He clung to the twins, eyes closed. Mioragh dropped to his knees beside him, put a hand to his shoulder. As if a cooling balm spread with the touch of the bard's fingers, the pain subsided to a bearable level.

"The children," Mioragh muttered, his attention on Athelin's shoulder. "The Riders were after the children."

"No," Athelin said through the weariness that spread through him, threatening to drown him. "Not all of the children. Just Rowan. They were after only Rowan."

Rowan stirred against him, pushing himself away. "Father?" he whispered, still pale as milk.

"It's all right, Rowan," Athelin said. "You're all right."

"But—" Rowan looked back over his shoulder toward

the open gate. "Back there." His voice trembled. "Behind the gate, Father. It's Danal . . ."

Cold fear gripped Athelin's belly. He let go of Acaren and climbed stiffly to his feet. One of the soldiers, seeing the direction of Rowan's glance, moved the gate.

A child's body lay in the midst of a wide, scarlet stain in the snow. Eleven-year-old Danal.

"No," Athelin whispered. "Oh dear gods and goddesses, no . . ." He fell to his knees beside his second son, but knew even before he touched the boy he would find nothing but the utter, unmistakable stillness of death beneath his hand. He gathered Danal's body to his breast and bent his head, his tears falling on the boy's still, pale face.

"No," he whispered again.

He hardly felt Mioragh's touch on his head. "Sleep, my lord," the bard said. Darkness closed about him, and he slept.

Athelin sat in his chamber, looking out over the neatly set-out fields on the lower flanks of Ben Warden. Snow still lay deep and drifted against the dry-stone walls and bare hedges. He rubbed his arm absently, even though the pain of the wound was little more than a memory. Mioragh's art had Healed the wound and knit the bone, but could do little to replace the blood he had lost. Rest, Mioragh insisted. Rest would bring the strength back.

But neither rest nor Mioragh's art could do much to assuage the tearing hole in Athelin's heart left by Danal's death. Only time might help that. Bleakly, Athelin wondered if there was enough time in the world.

A brazier glowed brightly near his chair, the warm red glow reflecting against the draperies on the window. Beyond the rippled glass, Ben Warden glowed brilliant white under a deep blue sky. Sunlight streamed through the window, striking blue sparks in Dorlaine's black hair as she sat near the bed with her needlework.

Two of the young guards at the garden gate had died with Danal. There had been three dead to bury after that skirmish five days ago. Grief still hung heavy in the hearts of

Skerry Keep and Skerryharbor, and would for many seasons to come.

Only sheerest chance had brought Danal to the garden. He had left the practice field and Weymund to return a whetstone he had borrowed from Cynric earlier that morning. He had been on his way back to the practice field when the Somber Riders burst into the garden, and had died before Cynric could so much as turn around.

"There are clouds in the west," Dorlaine said without looking up from her needlework. "I think we'll have more snow by evening. It will mean a green spring."

Athelin shifted in the chair and scowled. "It can snow until all the crows bleach white for all that I care," he said irritably.

Dorlaine let her needlework fall into her lap and looked at him levelly, her eyes bright with unshed tears. She placed her hand in an automatic gesture to the gentle swelling of her abdomen, an unconscious habit she'd developed since discovering she was again with child. The pregnancy hardly showed yet, and Athelin found the protective gesture touching.

"Athelin, your anger at yourself and the world can't bring Danal back," she said. Her own grief made her voice uneven and hoarse. "You can't blame yourself for his death any more than you could blame yourself for your sister's death."

Athelin looked at her. His eyes stung. "I should have been able to save him—"

"How?" she asked bluntly. "There were four guards and Cynric with the boys. The Riders killed two of the guards and very nearly killed Cynric. There was nothing you could do." She reached out and put her hand to his cheek. "Danal was my son, too, Athelin. I loved him as much as you did, and I shall miss him terribly, too. But you did everything you could to try to make all your children safe. Put the blame squarely where it belongs. On the Maedun. On the shoulders of the black sorcerer."

Athelin looked out the window at the high crags of Ben Warden. Beyond the mountain lay the Skerryrace, and

beyond the Skerryrace lay the main island—and the Maedun. "I wish I could take an army and kill him. . . ." he whispered.

A single tear spilled over Dorlaine's lashes and made a
silvery track down her cheek. "You can't," she said softly. "It's
not time yet. You know that."

Athelin closed his eyes, pain and grief churning in his
chest. "Aye," he said thickly. "I know that." He glanced up as
someone knocked on the door. "Come."

Mioragh came in, his face lined with fatigue. He pulled
up a chair and sat by Athelin's bed, a frown drawing the
shaggy, gray brows together above his eyes. "My lord," he
said quietly, "I have been thinking lately."

Athelin lay back in his chair and lifted one eyebrow.
"What's been through your mind, Mioragh?" he asked.

The bard looked up, his expression abstracted. "Did you
know that Rowan has strong magic?" he asked.

"It doesn't surprise me," Athelin said. "Strong magic has
always run in my family, after all."

"Of course," Mioragh said, nodding. "You are, in any
event, the nearest living kin to both King Tiernyn and his
brother Donaugh the Enchanter. None had stronger magic
than he, although your father certainly came close."

"What has that to do with Rowan and his magic? Or
with the Somber Riders in the garden?"

Mioragh reached into his pocket and brought out something that glared with enough brilliance to sear Athelin's eyes.
He blinked and turned away from it.

"What is it?" he asked, suddenly afraid he knew the
answer.

Mioragh put his other hand over the blazing sliver of
stone, shutting off the glare. "I believe it's a Tell-Tale, my
lord," he said. "Or a piece of one, at any rate. I found it in the
garden early this morning. I had gone to make sure all traces
of the Maedun were gone."

A cold chill knotted itself around Athelin's heart. Years
ago, Tell-Tales tuned to the magic of Rune Blades and carried
by Somber Riders had been the death of his parents, his
brother Adair and Adair's wife and unborn child, and had

nearly been his own and his sister's death. But surely those Tell-Tales had been destroyed.

But this one in Mioragh's hand was different. The ones Athelin remembered let off a painful, acidic green glare. This one burned with a clear, blue-white light.

"It brightens when Rowan is nearby," Mioragh said. "I believe it might be tuned to his magic. Or mayhaps Celae magic."

Dorlaine had gone pale. Her needlework slipped unheeded to the floor. "Can you do something about it?" she asked. "Hakkar will surely send more Somber Riders here to try to kill him."

"I think I can help." Mioragh rose and went to the window. He stood looking out at the garden for a moment, then began to pace, his hands clasped behind his back. "Once he's older, I believe he can learn to control his magic. Right now, he radiates it like heat from a flame. Hakkar can't help but feel it, so strong as it is. I believe I can work a charm, a masking spell. It may be enough to make Hakkar believe his Riders were successful and the magic is dead."

"Then by all means, you must work this charm," Dorlaine said. "Immediately, if possible."

Mioragh inclined his head in a sketch of a bow. "Of course, my lady," he murmured. "With your permission, I shall do it now."

Athelin looked up at him. The bard's silver hair glinted in the sunlight streaming through the window. Mioragh's gifts for Healing and music were strong, but his gift of magic was not.

"Have you the strength, Mioragh?" Athelin asked. "We've already lost too much. We can't afford to lose you, too, my friend."

"I shall have to find the strength," Mioragh said. "Rowan's life depends on it."

"We could send him to Tyra," Athelin said. "Our kinsmen in Broche Rhuidh would protect him."

"The Tyrs were little protection to your father and mother," Mioragh reminded him gently.

Athelin was silent for a moment. Finally, he nodded.

"Very well, then," he said gravely. "Go ahead, Mioragh. And thank you."

"Do you need help?" Dorlaine asked.

"No, thank you, my lady," Mioragh said. He smiled. "Not yet, at any rate."

Dorlaine watched Mioragh until the chamber door closed behind him. Slowly, she reached down and picked up her needlework, but merely held it in her lap. She held out one hand, and Athelin took it in his own.

"Can he do it?" she asked.

"I hope so," he said. "I truly hope so."

Nearly an hour later, Mioragh returned. Deep lines of fatigue and pain etched his face, which was the color of old parchment. His eyes were dull and filmed, and his hands trembled. Dorlaine leapt to her feet and took his arm to lead him gently to a seat.

"It's done, my lord," Mioragh said hoarsely. "Hakkar will not be able to sense any of Rowan's magic now. The only thing that can break my masking spell is Rowan's own magic when he learns to control it."

"Have you done yourself harm?" Athelin asked, alarmed at the bard's lack of strength.

Mioragh managed a smile. "It was not easy," he said. "But I shall recover, given time."

"Be careful," Athelin said, his worry making his voice sharp. "One day, you might push yourself too far."

"I might, my lord," Mioragh said. "But not, I think, this day."

Rowan was alone in the chamber he shared with Acaren. He sat on the padded bench under the window, knees drawn up to his chest, arms wrapped around his legs. His cheek rested on his knees, face turned to the window. He didn't look up as Athelin entered the room.

My quiet one, Athelin thought tenderly, looking at the young face so like his own, remote now, and withdrawn. Of the two of them, Acaren always seemed to be the leader. He was the boisterous one, the one who dreamed up the schemes that very often landed the twins in difficulties. But if Rowan was the follower, he never simply blindly followed Acaren's lead. If it was Acaren who got them into trouble, most times it was Rowan who extricated them from it. Athelin often thought of him as the shadow to Acaren's brilliant light. Yet it was Rowan who had killed the Somber Rider and saved them both.

Mioragh was worried about Rowan. The boy had been neither eating nor sleeping well since the morning the Somber Riders had invaded the palace. He had not touched his harp, usually a joy for him; nor had he gone with Acaren to Cynric for sword practice.

"Something sits dark on his soul, my lord," Mioragh said. "Something more than just the death of his brother, his slaying of the Rider."

So Athelin had gone to him. He crossed the chamber quietly and sat on the end of the bench. He curbed his desire to hold the boy and comfort him. Rowan had to come to his own terms with this thing. He was young for it, come to it sooner than most men. But in this, Athelin could not lead him. He could only offer the guidance of his own experience in the hope that it might help Rowan find his own way through.

Rowan didn't look at him. "I tried to help him," he said. "I tried, but the other Rider was trying to kill Acaren. And Acaren's my twin . . ."

"You saved Acaren."

"But Danal—"

"Grieving for Danal is proper," Athelin said softly. "But he knows you could do nothing to help him. We know it, too, Rowan. Nobody blames you."

Rowan closed his eyes, still not looking at Athelin.

"I haven't heard you practicing on your harp lately," he said.

Rowan raised his head and looked up. His face was pale, his eyes very dark in contrast, still focused inward, contemplative and introspective. He said nothing.

"Nor have I seen you go with Acaren to practice with Cynric."

Rowan shrugged and turned his face back to the window. Athelin sat quietly, waiting for the boy to take that first step. After a long while, Rowan turned back to him and reached out to touch Athelin's shoulder beneath his tunic. It was a gentle touch. Athelin barely felt it.

"Does it hurt, Father?" Rowan asked softly.

Athelin smiled. "A little, yet," he said. "It won't kill me, though. Mioragh assures me it's healed well."

Rowan frowned thoughtfully. "You looked so terrible when you came into the garden. You looked so white beneath the blood. I thought you were dying."

"No," Athelin said. "Not dying. But very much frightened."

Rowan's eyes widened. "You, Father?" he said. "You were frightened?"

"I was," Athelin said gently, beginning to understand. "I was terrified."

Rowan looked out the window again. Athelin saw him considering the information, integrating it and reconciling it with his own feelings. Finally, the boy said, "I was very afraid, too."

Athelin said nothing, merely waited.

Rowan turned, met Athelin's eyes. "I thought I might be a coward," he said candidly.

Athelin wanted to smile, but he kept his expression grave. "No man but a fool would not feel fear in the teeth of death," he said. "The difference between a coward and a brave man is what he does in the face of his fear."

"But I was very much afraid. I thought I might die of my fear before the Rider's sword even touched me."

"Yet you still slew the man who killed Danal and wanted to kill both you and Acaren. Your fear didn't make you helpless before it."

Rowan nodded, seriously considering that. "But I couldn't help Danal."

Athelin let his grief for his second son wash over him. "No," he said. "You couldn't help Danal. Sometimes, Rowan, we can't help. Sometimes, people we love die, and we can't do anything about it."

Rowan frowned. "I see," he said, but clearly he didn't see at all.

Finally, at last, Athelin reached out to the boy, placing his hand on Rowan's head, almost a benediction. "I'm well pleased with you, Rowan," he said. "I'm proud of you, indeed." The relief on the boy's face was almost painful. Athelin smiled. "Will you not play something on your harp for me?"

Rowan grinned suddenly, his whole being lighting with it. "Acaren says it always sounds as if I'm torturing the poor harp when I take it up," he said.

Acaren was in the outer chamber when Athelin came out. He looked up, then came to join Athelin, and they walked together into the corridor.

"I heard the harp," Acaren said. "Is Rowan better then, Father?"

"Yes, I think so."

Acaren nodded. "He was very afraid in the garden there," he said. "But he still killed that man." He looked up at Athelin. "I would have helped to kill him if he had not knocked me down. I think Rowan was very brave to do it alone."

"He was." Athelin smiled down at the boy. "And I think you might well learn wisdom one day, my young scamp."

In spite of himself, Acaren smiled. "Do you think so?" he said. "That would be so awfully tiresome, Father."

Hakkar of Maedun sat slumped upon the throne of Tiernyn, his long fingers tented before his face, and stared at the magnificent stained-glass window above the high, arched doors at the entrance to the Great Hall opposite where he sat. Once, it had been famed throughout the known world. Now, even with the afternoon sun streaming through it, the colors seemed drab and dingy, somehow diminishing the Great Hall of the dead king rather than enhancing it.

But this was a drab and dingy land, stifling in the summer, cheerless in the winter. Were he to lift the spell that dulled both the people and the land, it would still not come near equaling Maedun. He ruled a dead and wasted land when his heart yearned for the broad fields and cool, sprawling forests of his home.

He had come here as a young man, back when *he* was Horbad and his father had been Hakkar. He had not the vitriolic hate of the Celae that his father had worn all his life like a cloak, but he well understood the need for maintaining the spell. Not for the first time, he wondered if he would be able to pass the name on to his son. He strongly suspected that Horbad was flawed in some subtle way. Perhaps the taint of that strain of Saesnesi blood in his mother, the stain that Hakkar had been unaware of at the time he got the boy upon her.

Hakkar rose to his feet and moved restlessly to a window. He looked to the north, his black brows knitting together above his eyes. The faint, silver thread of magic he had detected was gone now, snapped as abruptly as a sword blade slicing through a vine almost a sevenday ago. Confirmation was on its way. Here now, in fact.

He turned as two Somber Riders strode into the Hall, their dark cloaks, still travel-stained, swirling around their tall, bespattered boots. He recognized Zerad, one of the men he had sent north. He moved back to the throne and beckoned them to approach him.

Both men dropped to their knees before the throne. Hakkar waited, and Zerad held out a hand to him. In his open palm like a precious offering lay a gray, oval stone, the size of a flattened pigeon egg. Its surface appeared granular and rough. Hakkar would have been surprised to see it gleaming.

"The Seeker Stone, lord," Zerad said.

Hakkar said, "Where is Tran?"

"Lord, he took a fragment of the stone with him to the small island. Only a few days later, the stone became as you see it now. Tran did not return, nor did any of those who went to the island with him. Jak and I returned to bring you proof Tran had fulfilled his duty."

Hakkar picked up the Tell-Tale from Zerad's hand and

closed his fingers tightly over it. It felt cold and dead against his skin.

"And had its gleam not dulled?"

"Lord, then I would have gone to the island and Jak with me, and seen to its dulling."

Hakkar smiled grimly. "You have done well. I shall see you rewarded for your diligence."

Zerad bent his head but said nothing.

A wise man, Hakkar decided. One perhaps ready for more responsibility and authority than he had previously carried. "You may go," he said. "Tell the Captain of the Guard to send my son to me."

3

Athelin moved restlessly in his sleep and muttered something Dorlaine didn't hear as she sat wakeful in the bed beside him. Ever since the morning the disguised Somber Riders had invaded the fragile safety of Skerry Keep, his sleep had been disturbed by dreams. His mother had been Tyadda, delicate and fey, which meant that, very often, Athelin dreamed true. Mayhaps he walked with Danal when he slept. Or with his sister.

Dorlaine knew nothing of what he dreamed when his sleep took him to those far places where she could not and would not follow. He never spoke of the dreams the next day, but morning always found him pale and withdrawn. She had learned not to ask about the dreams. In a marriage where they shared everything, this was the one inviolate area she could not intrude upon.

He moved again, his face twisting into lines of pain. As if in response, the child within her moved for the first time, a small, fluttering tremble. She pressed her hand to the gentle swelling of her belly to assure the child of her love and protection, and smiled as she had smiled at the first quickening of her sons. But this child would be the daughter for whom she had yearned for so many years—a girl in whom Athelin would take much delight.

He cried out softly, a sound halfway between a moan and a sob, and his hand moved as if to ward off a blow. Dorlaine put her fingers to his temples and began to massage them softly. One must not waken a person who dreamed true, but one could try to ease the pain of the dream.

For a long time, her fingers moved in small, gentle circles on her husband's temples. He had quieted, but he dreamed still. In the light of the late-winter moon streaming at full through the window, his face was pale and etched with lines of pain and grief.

Again, the child within her moved as if she shared her father's dream. *Take ease, little one,* Dorlaine thought. *Take ease and grow strong. There's time enough yet for you to take up that burden. Right now, your task is to grow and become strong and beautiful.* In her womb, the child subsided into rest.

Tears seeped slowly between Athelin's closed lashes and trickled down his cheeks, gleaming like pearls in the pale light. "Oh, Iowen," he said clearly. "Oh, Iowen, my lost beloved . . ."

Dorlaine bowed her head, tears stinging her own eyes, and she folded her hands together on the quilt above her belly. This was only the second time since her death a little more than seven years ago that his sister's name had passed Athelin's lips. The first time had also been from within the depths of a dream. His grief at her loss, his wretched sense of guilt, was so great that, even now, he could not bear to speak her name aloud.

He blamed himself, and Dorlaine could not convince him that the fault did not lie with him. There had been so much confusion that night, and no one had realized that Iowen was in danger until it was too late to prevent her death. Now, every Imbolc morning, Dorlaine placed two hoops representing the unbroken cycle of birth, life, death, and rebirth onto the cairn marking the graves of Athelin's sister—and the tiny, unnamed girl-child.

"Please don't fret so, beloved," she whispered. "Her death was not your fault. She wouldn't want your agony. How could you know? How could you possibly have known?"

His eyebrows twitched as if in pain, and he muttered something she did not understand. She looked up at the silver face of the moon. In moments, it would be out of the square of the window, the Huntress Star close behind it, as always in pursuit. When she looked at him again, he was awake, his face calm now, his dark eyes on her. He caught one of her hands in his and pressed it to his cheek, then turned his head to kiss her palm.

"Thank you," he whispered.

She said nothing. She smiled.

"You always guard my sleep for me, my love," he said.

"I am bheancoran," she said, knowing she needn't remind him. "My place is to guard you."

"For the sake of the child, you should be resting instead."

"For the sake of her father, I will be wakeful when it's needed," she replied, placidly certain of her right and duty.

He looked up at her. Even the pale light of the moon couldn't mask the pain and grief and remorse that filled his eyes. She wanted to look away because she felt his sorrow as deeply as he, but she held his gaze firmly. Their grief for Danal had settled into an ever-present ache in their souls, but Athelin could speak of his son, and even smile at his memory. Not so with his sister.

"You can't blame yourself, Athelin," she said. "No more than I can. When you did what she asked you to do, you didn't know—you *couldn't* know she was dying. How can you blame yourself?"

"I didn't know what to do," he said, anguish twisting his mouth. "Had I not lost her, I would have lost you, and I don't know which would be worse."

"She's told you she doesn't blame you."

"In the dreams, aye. She's tried to." He looked away for a moment, up at the window, then back to her. "When I dream true," he said.

"I know." Then, not a question but a statement. "She walked for you again tonight, didn't she?"

He hesitated, then smiled. "Yes," he said softly. "Yes, she did." He sat up and drew her into his arms. She rested her head against his chest and listened to the calm, steady, reassuring beating of his heart.

"I think," he said slowly, "the time is now past when we will not speak her name. And when our child is born in the spring, we will call her Ceitryn."

For the first time, she asked a question about his dream. "Did she say this to you?"

"She did." He answered with no hesitation, quickly and surely and gladly. He reached for his night robe and got out of bed, belting the heavy woolen robe around himself. It was yet a few days until Vernal Equinox, and the nights were still cold. "Come," he said and picked up her night robe. She slid across the bed and sat on the edge. He wrapped the thick, soft robe around her and held out his hand.

"Come," he said again. "I want to look at the boys."

She took his hand, and he led her out into the corridor. Lanterns set into high brackets on the walls lit the hallway. Their shadows fled before them, then retreated behind them as they passed the flickering lights. Still holding Dorlaine's hand, Athelin pushed open the door of the chamber where the three boys slept with their nurse.

A dark shadow moved against the glow of the brazier and resolved itself into a man carefully stacking peat onto the dimly glowing coals. He looked up as Dorlaine and Athelin entered the room. The faint light flickering in the brazier limned his high cheekbones and his thin-bridged nose, but drew no highlights from the tar black hair and left the dark eyes in deep shadow.

Even after all the years, the unexpected sight of Cynric caused Dorlaine's heart to give a startled thump in her breast. His mother was one of the Saesnesi of the Summer Run, whose people so long ago had come as raiders but stayed as allies. But his father was a Maedun Somber Rider, one of the soldiers of Hakkar of Maedun, who styled himself Lord Protector of Celi. He looked Maedun with his tar black hair and nearly black eyes, but had taken his place firmly with the Saesnesi and Celae nearly eight years ago. He spoke little of his past, a quiet, reserved man who seldom smiled and even less often laughed. Self-appointed guardian of the three boys who slept so soundly in the room, he took the responsibility seriously indeed.

He inclined his head respectfully. "My lord," he said. "My lady. The boys are asleep and safe. You have no need for concern."

"You guard them well, Cynric," Athelin said. "Thank you."

A shadow passed through Cynric's eyes, and he looked away. He was thinking of Danal, Dorlaine knew. He mourned Danal as strongly as she or Athelin did. For more than seven years he had never been far from the boys, as he had never been far from Iowen's side when she was still alive. He had given all of the boys their first lessons in swordwork, and still worked with the two youngest.

"We came to make sure they were covered and warm," Dorlaine said.

"It's very late," Athelin said. "You should be in your own bed, Cynric."

"I was just about to return to it, my lord Prince," Cynric said. He inclined his head. "Good night."

"Good night," Dorlaine said. "Sleep warm, Cynric."

"And you, my lady." He stepped into the shadows and was gone with no sound to mark his going.

Athelin put his arm around Dorlaine's shoulders as they went quietly to stand by the bed where the eldest slept. As usual, Gabhain slept neatly and tidily on his back, the coverlet drawn up to his chin, his breathing slow and measured. He was thirteen, dark-haired and blue-eyed like Dorlaine, and like Athelin's father, Gareth.

She smiled as she smoothed the quilt unnecessarily across his shoulder, and Athelin brushed his hand gently across Gabhain's forehead. Gabhain was almost a man and, awake, would have been painfully embarrassed by the tender gesture from his father. He was only a little more than two years from his first hunt, which would mark his first step into manhood. After that, he would move to chambers of his own, as befitted a young man, rather than sharing quarters with his younger brothers.

The twins, Acaren and Rowan, lay tangled together in the middle of their bed like a pair of puppies on a hearth, identical faces close on the pillow. Both had Athelin's dark gold hair and clear brown eyes, and bore the stamp of his features. As dearly as he loved Gabhain, Dorlaine knew the twins occupied a distinct and unique place in his heart. She credited him highly with the fact that none of the children had reason to suspect his special feeling for the twins.

Athelin did not reach out to touch the twins as he had done to Gabhain. Instead, he stood by the bed and let his love settle over them like a warm blanket.

"They will go to Weymund in the spring," he said quietly.

Startled, Dorlaine stared at him. "But they're only seven," she said. "Gabhain and Danal went early to the Swordmaster, but even they didn't go until they were ten."

"They've learned all they can from Cynric," Athelin said almost absently. "They need Weymund's instruction. I believe there are events shaping even now . . ."

His eyes blurred again, as if he still dreamed true. She put her hand on his arm and looked up at him in concern. "What events?" she asked, but he shook his head. His eyes cleared, and he looked down at the twins again.

"They'll need all the skill they can master," he said. "And the sooner they begin, the easier for them to learn."

Dorlaine looked searchingly into his face. In the soft glow of the brazier, the shadows of his troubled dreaming moved darkly through his eyes. All she said was, "Loisa will grieve to lose the last of her chicks."

Athelin smiled. "Come spring, she'll have another to nurse and spoil." He smiled again, then kissed her and led her gently back to their chamber.

Caennedd drew back into the shadows of the corridor as his half brother and kin-sister came out of the room where the children slept and moved unhurriedly back to the door of their own chambers. He waited impatiently, the jewel at his shoulder glinting furiously in the torchlight, until they had closed the door firmly behind them. He stepped out into the corridor and began walking swiftly in the opposite direction, toward the narrow staircase that led to the battlement walk. He paused outside the children's room, a slender, dark-haired shadow dressed entirely in midnight black, the single red jewel again glinting at his shoulder. By habit, his hand moved absently to caress the jeweled hilt of the dagger on his hip as he thought of the boys asleep behind the door.

Three sons, he thought bitterly. *Three more to huddle in fear on this island and rot away in exile while the black sorcerer and his Somber Riders rule over our stolen land.*

The wrong son had inherited Gareth's coronet and torc eight years ago. Mayhaps, had Gareth's elder son Adair survived to become Prince, things might be different. But Adair had died in a Maedun raid even before he could be invested as Prince of Skai, leaving no heir but his brother Athelin. And Athelin . . .

Caennedd beat a fist against his thigh, hard enough to hurt. Athelin contented himself with ruling only these two scraps of islands rather than the land that was rightfully his. Even after the Somber Riders had come to his very door and murdered his son, he would not lead an army south across the Verge to take back the stolen lands.

Had he, himself, inherited all those years ago, he would not be at all hesitant in raising an army to retake Skai from those accursed invaders. He might be ten years younger than Athelin, but he knew where his duty lay. He would have been ten times the Prince.

Something moved in the thick mass of shadow filling the recessed door of the boys' room. Caennedd managed to swallow his startled exclamation before it voiced itself as the darkness resolved itself into Cynric. Iowen's black dog, they used to call him before she died. *Cat, more likely,* Caennedd thought bitterly. He moved like a wraith and showed up where he was least expected. Or wanted.

"Do you need something, my lord Caennedd?" Cynric asked quietly. "Mayhaps I might assist you in some way?"

"No," Caennedd said more harshly than he intended. "I'm just stretching my legs before I retire for the night."

Cynric inclined his head. "Then I bid you good night," he said. A moment later, the doorway was empty.

Caennedd turned away and moved swiftly toward the staircase, silent as a shadow in his soft boots. He wiped his palms against his trews. Any encounter with Cynric unnerved him more than he liked to admit. Sometimes, it seemed the man could actually read his thoughts.

The door to the battlement walk opened noiselessly, and

he strode out into the night. The air was cool and scented faintly with the first breath of spring. Equinox was still a fort-night away, but already the deeply piled drifts of snow were visibly smaller, shrunken under the tentative warming of the sun as the days progressed slowly toward the Night of Balance and the coming of spring.

He found his favorite lookout and leaned his shoulder against the rough stone of a slender turret that soared above his head to four times his own height. He looked south. Just to his right, the huge bulk of Ben Warden shouldered the sky. To his left, the gentler dome of Ben Aislin loomed against the stars. North, towering over the cliffs plunging into the sea on the northwest coast of the island, the jagged spires of Ben Roth stabbed into the night sky and seemed to impale the set-ting moon on its crags.

Caennedd had no eye for the beauty before him as he stood leaning against the turret. Instead, he thought moodily about the swelling belly of his kin-sister, and the unfairness of the accident of birth.

"Bastard," he said softly, aloud.

Naming himself gave him a bitter satisfaction. He was a child of Beltane, supposedly blessed by the Duality and lucky. But he was also the only known by-blow of the old Prince. His birth resulted from the coming together of Gareth and the daughter of the Captain of the Company on Beltane night in a year when Gareth's wife Lowra was ill and did not attend the Beltane fire.

Caennedd's mother had died when he was eight. The Prince had acknowledged the child and taken him to the Keep to be raised along with his trueborn children, Adair, Athelin, and Iowen. He had been taught how to read by the same tutor who oversaw the elder children's education. He had gone to the practice field to Weymund the Swordmaster when he was twelve and worked hard to earn respect as a brilliant swordsman. When it came time for his first hunt, he had returned in triumph with an eight-point stag, easily as big as the stag Athelin had killed on his first hunt. He had gone to his first Beltane shortly after he turned sixteen to complete his becoming a man, and had been given a company of soldiers to command when he was eighteen. He had proved that, bastard or not, he was certainly a worthy son to Gareth, and the equal of both Adair and Athelin in everything.

Except that first Adair became Prince when Gareth was killed by raiding Maedun eight years ago, and Athelin inherited when Adair in his turn fell to raiders only a short while later. Athelin became Prince, and Caennedd became the bastard son of a dead prince, a half brother of the new Prince toward whom the new Prince had no obligations.

If only Iowen still lived. She was the only one who had really loved him. She was the only one to whom he could talk. Had she not died, everything would have been different now.

Caennedd shifted against the cold stone of the turret wall and drew his cloak closer about him. The moon had set, leaving only a pale glow that silhouetted Ben Roth's pinnacles, and the bright blaze of the Huntress Star, as ever diving down toward the dark horizon in pursuit of the moon. He looked up and saw that the Warrior Goddess now stood cold and clear above the Keep, the red star of her diadem glittering like the ruby on his cloak clasp. Four of the five stars of her sword glittered just above the turret, the fifth hidden by the turret's roof. He walked backward along the battlement walk until he could see all five of the stars.

The Sword . . .

He frowned as he gazed up at the line of stars. Surely there was something about a sword he had heard lately. Then he shivered as he remembered. Yes, of course. The bard Mioragh had sung a tale of the twin swords of Wyfydd Smith at the Feast of New Fire. Rune Blades, both of them, crafted with magic and music. The swords of a king.

If he were king, he could lead an army into Skai and take the country back from the black sorcerer's men. If he had the king's sword, there would be no man living who would not follow him. Then let Athelin be free to waste his life away on this meager little island.

4

Five days after the Vernal Equinox Celebration, Athelin made arrangements to take his sons south on a pilgrimage to the Verge, as his father had taken both him and his brother Adair. Danal's absence caught painfully at his heart as he supervised Gabhain's, Acaren's and Rowan's preparations. The loss weighed heavily on his spirit and put permanent shadows in Dorlaine's eyes.

Two days before they were to leave, Athelin sought out Caennedd and asked him if he wished to accompany them.

"I've seen the Verge," Caennedd said indifferently. "I've no wish to see it again until I lead an army across it to take Celi back from the black sorcerer."

Athelin suppressed a surge of annoyance. The same argument had recurred every spring since Caennedd turned sixteen. Athelin saw little sense in repeating it once again. Caennedd would not believe it was death to venture into the blighted lands bordering the Verge—the Dead Lands, deep under Hakkar's spell. Nor would he believe that any army led against the black sorcerer would by sorcery be prevented from joining battle with the Somber Riders.

"No," Athelin said. "We cannot."

"How can you say we cannot kill them?" Caennedd demanded hotly. "I've killed them. You've killed them yourself. Not one Somber Rider who managed to find this forsaken island has ever lived to return to the main island. They can be killed."

"Outside the protection of Hakkar's spell, yes," Athelin replied, striving for patience. "But on the main island—in

Skai—the spell is deadly. It might do you good to refresh your memory."

Caennedd's mouth lengthened into a grim, tight line. He turned swiftly and walked away, leather heels clattering on the polished floor in a swift, staccato rhythm.

Athelin curbed his exasperation and watched him go, then took a deep breath to calm himself. Caennedd may have come into the family as a sideslip by-blow, but he certainly inherited all the legendary stubbornness of any of Red Kian's descendants. He sighed, shook his head, then went on with his preparations for the journey.

Heavy in the last season of her bearing, Dorlaine came to the courtyard to see them off and bid them swift journey and safe. Then she climbed back to her dayroom to watch them from the terraced balcony as they rode to the harbor where the ship waited to take them west and south to the mainland.

As Athelin's bheancoran, she should have gone with them. But she could not risk the child she carried on such an arduous journey. Gabhain was thirteen; it was time for him to see what the black sorcerer had done to Celi. But the twins were only seven. She worried that they were too young to make the pilgrimage. The hazards of the journey were great. But Athelin's taking the twins when he took Gabhain would save another journey when the twins turned thirteen.

Athelin took only four men with him, among them Cynric, who stood silent guard over the boys as always. Athelin's friend Ralf, and Ralf's son Rhan rode beside Athelin, and with them, young Howel to look after the horses. The small procession moved down the track to Skerryharbor, Gabhain straight and slim as a sword riding at his father's side. The twins galloped madly about, playing tag and shouting until a quick gesture from Athelin brought them back to decorum. Just before the party crested the hill leading down to the village, Athelin and one of the twins—Rowan, she thought— turned in the saddle to wave to Dorlaine.

Even though she knew they could not see her, she lifted a hand in reply. "Safe journey, heart of my heart," she whispered. She put her hands to her swollen belly, cradling the child within. Athelin had promised they would be back before her time came, and she was sure he would be. But that didn't stop a wave of sadness and loneliness breaking over her as she watched her husband and her family disappear.

Excitement ran like summer lightning through the three boys, and Athelin's control over them was only tenuous as they boarded the ship. It was only natural, Athelin supposed. The boys had never before been away from Skerry, and the natural ebullience of children made them unable to carry grief very long.

He was about to scold the boys in an attempt to subdue their effervescing excitement but caught sight over their heads of Cynric's faint smile. He relaxed and allowed himself to smile, too. There was no harm in letting the boys treat the beginning of the voyage as a holiday. Time enough later for them to realize its seriousness.

"Is this the same *Skai Seeker* that brought Grandfather Brennen to Skerry, Father?" Gabhain asked.

"It is," Athelin said. "The ship serves us well. Before we return here, we'll sail along the coast of Skai and Wenydd and try to pick up any Celae who wish to come back with us to Skerryharbor."

Acaren clambered up the rail and leaned far over, peering down at the water beneath the hull. "And one day, she'll take us all back to Skai."

Cynric whisked him off the rail and set him firmly back on the deck. "Perhaps," he said drily. "But if you're not careful, you won't need the ship. Fall in, and the current will take you all the way to the Pointers and beyond."

After a few stern threats of dire consequences and physical mayhem if they got in the way of the sailors, Athelin turned the boys loose in Rhan's custody and went with Cynric to stand with the captain in the stern. A moment later, Ralf joined them.

"The horses are safely secured for the voyage, my lord Athelin," he said. "Young Howel is turning out a fine hand with them."

A slight smile twitched at the corner of Cynric's mouth.

He pointed to the main deck, where Rhan had just plucked one of the vigorously protesting twins out of the rigging as he attempted to swarm up the ropes in the wake of some of the seamen. "As Rhan may turn out a fine hand with the boys. That would be Acaren, I'd wager."

In spite of himself, Athelin smiled. "I'd not risk losing that bet. I think you know the boys rather too well."

"They'll settle soon enough, my lord," the master said. "The Western Sea will be rough this time of year. That should dampen their enthusiasm a little. It won't be much calmer until we enter Laurelwater."

Athelin glanced at him quickly. The master's face was blandly noncommittal, and Athelin remembered being dealt with when he himself was not much older than the twins, and just as exuberant. The master had certainly called the turn correctly then. Athelin wondered briefly how he would weather the pitching and rolling of the ship once they had left the sanctuary of the islands. Better than his first pilgrimage, he hoped. He had been sick from the time the ship rounded Marddyn until it anchored in the shelter of Laurelwater, where the green River Laurel emptied into the sea. Clearly, the master remembered that first voyage, and just as clearly, the memory amused him.

By nightfall, the combination of sea wind and excitement had tired the boys enough so that they went to their beds without protest after the evening meal. The next morning, the ship rounded Marddyn and entered the Western Sea.

Five days later, the *Seeker* dropped anchor in the deep green of Laurelwater. The twins were leaning on the rail in the bow with Gabhain and Rhan as the master ordered the sails lowered and furled.

While Howel brought the horses ashore, Ralf packed the gear in the cabin. Athelin, Cynric, and the boys would stay the night on the ship while Howel and Ralf exercised the horses and let them recover from the voyage.

Athelin came to stand beside the boys in the bow, looking up at the high crest of mountains. He could make out the narrow cleft of Thoren's Pass. He pointed.

"Up there, see?" he said. "That's where we'll be going tomorrow. The Pass will lead us to the River Afon, and we'll follow that until we can turn south for the Verge."

"Is it far, Father?" Gabhain asked.

"Three days' ride," Athelin said. "Mayhaps four for a child."

Acaren, who tended to be the spokesman for both twins, turned to him indignantly. "We ride as well as Gabhain," he said. "You'll not have to wait for us, Father."

Athelin smiled and put his hand on the boy's shoulder. "I never doubted it," he replied.

Spring had already traveled north as far as the River Laurel. They rode out the next morning with the new grass lush and green beneath the feet of the horses. Banks of young bracken massed pale green against the black and gray of the rocks. Soft gray furred the willows along the bank of the river, and the tips of the aspen trees held fat, red buds readying themselves to burst into leaf.

It was colder at the top of the pass where they stopped for the midday meal. Patches of tired snow lay in corners of deep shadow, and above them, the peaks in their caps of snow and ice gleamed red and gold in the setting sun.

As twilight fell, they picked up the River Afon and followed its tumbling surge, turned brilliant turquoise by glacier melt, down the mountains. That night, they camped at the mouth of Tiernyn's Way, the pass that would lead them down to the sharply defined edges of the Dead Lands, where they crossed the land like a noose around the throat of the Isle of Celi. They spent the second night in the wild Afon valley beneath the shelter of the towering overhang of a granite cliff.

The third morning found them only two leagues from land known as the Verge, where the strip of blighted land met the green, living high country. As they neared the Dead Lands, the sorrowful grief of the land physically overtook Athelin. He remembered his first sight of the wall, almost twenty years ago, riding beside his father. He had been only a little younger than Gabhain then. It had seemed to him that the day itself darkened as they approached the blight. Tears welled up in his eyes even before he had seen the sere and burned vegetation to the south.

"The princes of Skai are deeply attuned to the land," he remembered his father's quiet voice saying. "It's in our blood and our bone and our spirit. We come here to remember what was done to us, and what we have lost."

The boys felt it, too, Athelin saw. They drew closer to him, very quiet now, as the devastated land came into view.

They followed reluctantly as he led them right to its boundary.

Rowan was crying openly as he slid from his saddle to the ground, his face twisted in pain. "Oh, Father, it hurts so," he whispered, pale and frightened.

"I know," Athelin said gently. "But we come here to remember. You will never have to come again because this will stay with you for the rest of your life, Rowan."

"And we'll bring our sons to this place one day," Gabhain said softly. "So that they'll remember, too."

Athelin helped the three boys scramble up to the top of a tumble of rocks and they stood looking out over the ruin of what had once been the fair, green land of Celi. After a moment, Cynric and Ralf joined them on the little ridge, followed hesitantly by Rhan and Howel.

The sharp, painful contrast between the sere and ravaged land to the south and the living green behind them brought tears to Athelin's own eyes again. A dark haze hovered over the blight, hiding within it the creatures of the Pit Hakkar had called forth—creatures that fed on men's spirits, drove them first to madness, then to death. Men had once or twice returned from that blighted land, only to die raving within days.

Behind him stood an ancient oak. Its branches should have been readying to burst into leaf, but instead the tree remained dry and barren. Athelin glanced over his shoulder at it and frowned. Surely that tree was at least a hundred paces from the blight when he had come here with his father a little over twenty years ago. Trees and people seemed to become smaller as one grew, but could a distance that once looked like a hundred paces to an adolescent boy look like a little over thirty paces to a grown man? And had this low ridge been at the boundary between the Dead Lands and the living, free land?

He shivered and looked again to the south, drawing the boys closer to him. He stood surrounded by his sons, immersed again in his sorrow and loss. Acaren and Rowan both turned and buried their heads against his waist, and he held them as they sobbed aloud and clung helplessly to him. Beside him, Gabhain stood with tears flowing down his face.

Athelin felt Cynric's hand on his shoulder and turned to smile before he looked back at the desolation in front of them. There was no color there, only the burned and bitter gray-brown of ash.

"Is it all like this, Father?" Gabhain asked quietly. "Is it all this burned and dead?"

"No," Athelin said. "Beyond this blight, the land is still green. There are still farms where they grow what Hakkar and the Somber Riders need to live. The forests still grow, but now only the Maedun hunt and ride there. The people are enslaved and have little life in them, I'm told. They live, but the spell is capable of killing them if they try to take arms against the Somber Riders."

"Skai, too?" Acaren asked.

"Skai is still green," Athelin said gravely. "Skai is high-land country. Hakkar's spell cannot reach into the Highlands, and it cannot reach north past this spot. That's why the rock is here—to mark the beginnings of the north Highlands."

"The land is green and fresh everywhere else but another strip like this along the eastern foothills of the Spine," Cynric said. "I've ridden through the Dead Lands there, and it chilled my spirit."

Acaren looked up at him, marked curiosity clear on his face. "But you're part Maedun. You're immune to the spell."

Cynric nodded. "Partly immune," he said. "But even Hakkar's Somber Riders dislike riding through the Dead Lands."

"But there are still Celae in Skai," Acaren said.

"There are," Athelin agreed. "But the ones not under the spell are hunted through the mountains like animals.

Hakkar's spell cannot reach into the high country, but the Somber Riders are men, and men well armed and skilled in the ways of death. Every summer, we send ships to bring as many Celae as we can find to Skerry and Marddyn. Each year, we find fewer."

Rowan moved away from Athelin and wiped his eyes with his sleeve. "It wants to be free and green again," he murmured. "Don't you feel it, Father? The land wants to be free." His voice broke. "It hurts so much . . ."

"Yes, I feel it," Athelin said gently. "But there is no way to fight Hakkar's spell except by the magic of an enchanter, and Celi has had no enchanter since Donaugh fell by treachery to Mikal's sword."

Acaren reached out a hand so that it stretched beyond the edge of the sharp line of demarcation. He snatched it back immediately. "It's cold," he said, startled. "It's cold, but it burns."

"That's the spell," Cynric said. "What you felt is cold death from the Pit."

"Is there no way we can enter there?" Gabhain asked.

"Those who have Tyadda blood are immune for short periods to the spell, even in there," Cynric said. "For longer periods, if reinforced by a warding charm. Perhaps up to an hour, I've been told."

Acaren looked up at Athelin. "We have Tyadda blood through Grandmother, don't we?" he asked.

"Yes," Athelin said. "But there simply aren't enough of us—of people like us with some immunity—and it is useless to try to fight Hakkar without an enchanter. To die to free one's country is a sad but a noble thing. To throw one's life away for nothing is greater than mere folly; it is a sinful and shameful waste." How many times had he said that to Caennedd? A dozen? A hundred? And how many times had Caennedd stormed away, convinced Athelin was wrong?

"What can an enchanter do?" Gabhain asked, turning away from the sight of the devastation.

"He could break the spell that kills if Celae fight against the invaders," Athelin said. "Without the spell, our swords would then be protection enough."

Rowan pressed his face against Athelin's waist again. "Oh, it hurts, it hurts, it hurts," he wailed. "I wish I were an enchanter. I wish I could help it. It wants me to help it."

"I shall help it," Acaren muttered. He said it so softly, only Rowan, who stood next to him, heard.

With a last, anguished look south, Athelin ap Gareth ap Brennan, Prince of the Royal House of Skai, gathered his sons, and prepared to take them home again, home into exile on Skerry.

That night as the boys slept, Athelin lay wakeful in his blankets. Finally, restless and uneasy, he got up and went to the bank of the small stream, where he could see the land falling away to the south. A shadow moved beside him, startling him until he realized it was Cynric.

"You can't sleep either, my lord?" Cynric asked.

Athelin shook his head and looked southward again. "Did it seem changed to you? The Dead Lands, that is?"

Cynric hesitated. "Aye, my lord," he said at last. "More powerful. More malevolent, mayhaps."

"And moving farther into the high country."

Again, the hesitation before Cynric spoke. "I think so," he said quietly. "It seems so."

"I had hoped it was my imagination," Athelin said. A flicker of despair caught in his throat. "But it seems the spell *is* moving higher. If it moves as much in the next while as it moved since I was here last, Hakkar will push his spell into the high country before too very long, and all will be truly lost."

5

The last vestige of Athelin's temper shivered on the edge of evapora-
tion. It was becoming a familiar sensation lately whenever he
tried to deal with his half brother. Tight-lipped, he leaned
back in his chair and took a deep breath, reaching desperately for control.

"No," he said quietly. "I forbid it."

Caennedd exploded out of his chair, sending it skittering
backward across the smoothly polished flagstones and crashing into the paneled wall. He slammed both fists down on the
table and leaned forward intensely, his eyes blazing blue fire
in his fury. "You *forbid* it?" he shouted. "*You* forbid it?"

Athelin took another deep breath. "Caennedd, sit down
and listen to me."

Caennedd smashed his fist down on the table again. One
of the tall candlesticks toppled, dribbling hot wax across the
back of Athelin's hand. He bit down an exclamation of surprise and pain, and calmly set the candlestick upright again.

"I said sit down and listen to me," he said.

"Curse you," Caennedd cried. "Curse you, Athelin. I'm
twenty and a man grown. Don't treat me like a child."

"If you have no wish to be treated like a child," Athelin
said coldly, "then stop behaving like a child. We've been
through this too many times to count already. You will not go
south of the Dead Lands. And you will *not* take a company of
soldiers on a fool's errand like that. I absolutely forbid it."

"You can't stop me—"

"I may not be able to stop you galloping madly off at
full speed to your own death, but I certainly can prevent

you taking a company of my soldiers to their deaths. I forbid it."

"They are my soldiers—"

Athelin folded his hands together on the top of the table. "No, Caennedd," he said carefully, each word coming out sharp and distinct and emphatic. "They're not your soldiers. They're mine."

Caennedd went white, then scarlet with rage. "Ask them," he shouted furiously. "Ask them and see whom they would follow. Or are you afraid my men would deny you and show loyal to me only."

Athelin's control slipped another notch. He rose to his feet and went to the window. Carefully, deliberately, he peeled the cold wax from the back of his hand. It left behind an irregular, reddened welt. He rolled the wax into a precise ball and set it in the exact center of the sill. "Then perhaps I shall relieve you of command and the question becomes moot."

"You wouldn't dare—"

The anger Athelin had been desperately trying to suppress bubbled in his chest and belly. He turned to face Caennedd. "Oh, wouldn't I? Don't force my hand, Caennedd. I'll not see men of Skai die on a foolish mission with no hope of success."

"You have no right!" Caennedd shouted. He brandished his fist in Athelin's face. "No right—"

"I have every right. I'm your brother."

Caennedd snorted in disgust. "My brother," he snarled derisively. "You never cared about me. The only one who ever cared was Iowen, and she's dead. To you, I'm just your father's Beltane by-blow."

Athelin's mouth tightened into a thin line. "Nevertheless, I'm both your elder brother and your Prince. As such, I command your obedience, if not your respect."

"But you're wrong, Athelin. Can't you see that? You're wrong about not going south of the Verge to fight the Maedun. Criminally wrong!"

"You push me too far," Athelin said, his voice soft but

dangerous, the cutting edge of steel just barely below the surface.

"Mayhaps I can push you into doing your duty and ridding Skai and Celi of that abomination in Clendonan."

"By the horns of Cernos, Caennedd, *think*! How can you ask an army of five hundred to fight an army of nearly ten thousand who are backed by sorcery? That's sheer and utter folly. Even Brennen admitted that."

"You said it yourself," Caennedd cried. "You saw it. The Dead Lands are growing. Soon the spell will be all through the mountains. Skai is high country. Mountains. There is no sorcery there yet. If we go now, we can stop it ever getting there."

"Not all of Skai is mountains. How will you survive in the low country where the spell is heavy? No, I say. The time is not ripe yet. Soon, mayhaps. When the boys are grown—"

"When the boys are grown?" Caennedd turned to slam his fist against the wall, then spun back to face Athelin. "When they're grown, I'll be an old man. Like you! I want to do this now. While I'm still vital and alive! I will do my duty now."

"Your duty? Or do you seek only to glorify yourself with no regard to the cost?"

Caennedd's hand went to his dagger. Athelin stepped forward quickly and slapped his brother's hand away from the ornate hilt. "Don't even think of that," he said softly. "Treason and treachery won't get you what you want." He turned away, took a deep breath. "Caennedd, try to listen to reason. I promised our sister—" The memory of pain caught at his throat. "I promised Iowen I'd look after you."

"The same way you looked after her? You *buried* her, Athelin. Both her and the bastard she died giving birth to. Would you bury me, then, too?"

Athelin's control broke with a nearly audible snap. He spun around. At the last moment he opened his fist, else he surely would have sorely injured his brother. His palm connected with Caennedd's cheek in a stinging crack. Caennedd blinked in surprise, and his mouth fell open. He put his hand to his cheek, where the imprint of Athelin's hand glowed angry red against the tanned skin. Then he dropped his hand. His eyes narrowed, and a cold smile stretched his mouth.

"Quite a reaction," he murmured. "There was gossip seven years ago that the bastard was yours. How well did you love our sister, Athelin?"

Cold and trembling with fury, Athelin stared back at Caennedd. "I loved her well enough to want to kill any man who would offer her so deadly an insult," he said tightly. "Even you. Get out. Get out of here before I lose what control I have left and forget that you're my brother. And hers, also."

Caennedd seemed to realize he had gone too far beyond the boundaries of propriety. Pale and shaken, he tried to recover his poise. He sketched a mocking bow. "Enjoy your hunt, Athelin," he said. "I wish you luck. Mayhaps you can slay deer even if you can't or won't slay Somber Riders." He turned his back and stalked out.

Athelin leaned both hands on his worktable and stood, head drooping, while he tried to gather in the scattered threads of his temper. He had almost told Caennedd the one thing he promised Iowen he would not do; he had almost betrayed the last promise she had wrenched from him as she lay dying. He had almost said the name of her child's father.

Dorlaine sat quietly on a bench across the garden from her women. Rowan sat cross-legged in the grass at her feet, his back against her knees while he unhurriedly practiced chords on his harp. She let her needlework fall to the bench beside her for the time being. Her hand strayed gently to Rowan's sun-warmed hair and he turned quickly to smile up at her.

She was working on a dress for the baby, embroidering blue roses around the hem of the gauzy skirt. She smoothed her hand across the pale, delicate fabric. Both it and the silky blue thread had come from the Continent by way of Tyra—their only contact with the rest of the outside world now that the Maedun held most of the Continent. The fabric and the thread were dear, but the child she carried was worth the trouble and expense.

The close and exacting delicate work made her head

ache this afternoon, so she put it aside to rest her eyes for a while. She was content to let herself drift and dream in the pleasant warmth of the garden.

Above her, the apple blossoms clustered thickly on the old tree, their fragrance thick as haze in the air around her. Across the garden, petals fell from the cherry tree and drifted like pink-tinted snow in the green velvet of the grass. And in the background, like a benevolent guardian, loomed the towering bulk of Ben Warden.

The bright notes of Rowan's chords blended with the soft sounds of the afternoon surrounding her—the musical, industrious yet oddly sleepy drone of bees among the branches, the laughter of the women as they talked among themselves. Somewhere, gulls called to each other as they circled in the air above the rising tide. It all combined to relax her for the first time that day.

It was two days after Beltane, and an afternoon that seemed borrowed from midsummer rather than late spring. The warm breeze caressed her face and lifted her hair gently as she sat with her eyes closed, her face turned gratefully to the welcome heat of the sun.

She had awakened that morning with just the suggestion of a dull ache in her lower back and a nagging sense of undirected restlessness. It had worried her a little. She was still more than a fortnight from her time. Above all else, she wanted this child to be safe and healthy and strong. It hadn't been a particularly difficult pregnancy, but she had found herself with less energy, and she tired more easily than she had when she carried her sons. She supposed she wasn't really that old to be bearing again, but she was thirteen years older than when she had carried Gabhain. She'd had to be more careful with this child. She wanted to give it every chance for survival, and carrying it as long as she could was important.

The sound of the women's laughter roused her from her reverie, and she picked up her needlework again. Within her, the child kicked strongly, and Dorlaine smiled. She had been pummeling the walls of the imprisoning and protecting womb all morning, beating unmercifully with fists and feet.

"Soon, little one," Dorlaine promised in amusement. "Have patience. Your time is soon now."

The faint, chiming sound of a horn came from the southwest, from the slopes of Ben Aislin. Athelin was up there this morning, hunting with Ralf and Mabon the Seneschal. The larder needed meat, and she had wanted fresh pork or venison for the table tonight. The horn sounded again, not the warbling cry which signaled a kill, but the eager yelp of a sighting.

Pain ripped through her abdomen, catching her by surprise. In spite of herself, she made a small, dismayed sound. Instantly Rowan dropped his harp and leapt to his feet, bending over her in concern.

"Is it the baby, Mother?" he asked urgently.

Dorlaine could not speak. She nodded.

He beckoned frantically to Loisa. "Take my mother to her chambers," he commanded. "And send someone to fetch my father. Quickly."

"No," Dorlaine gasped. "No, let them finish the hunt. There will be time enough later to call him."

She had to lean heavily on Loisa and Marlynn as they helped her up to her tower chamber. Rowan snatched up his harp and followed them, his face pinched with anxiety.

Bent low over the shoulder of the horse, a pounding terror he dared not name in his heart, Athelin hurtled down the slopes of Ben Aislin and skirted the shore of the loch. Clods of earth spun high in the air behind him from the flying hooves of the madly galloping horse. Spatters of lather streaming back from the horse's straining chest stained his clothing. He had far outdistanced Ralf and Rhan, could no longer even hear the thunder of the hooves behind him.

Young Howel had just brought down a stag when Rhan had come tumbling off his horse into the clearing to deliver the message that the Lady Dorlaine had been brought to bed with the child. It was early for it, only a fortnight, but for some reason, Rhan's words caused a cold lance of fear to impale Athelin's heart. Motioning Ralf and Rhan to come with him, he left the others to see to the stag and leapt to his horse.

They had left the courtyard gates open. Athelin did not slow his horse until he was through the gates and well into the courtyard. A servant—he had no time to see which one— ran forward to catch the reins of the horse as he brought it to a sliding halt and vaulted to the ground, hurling himself into the Great Hall. Gabhain and Acaren were in the hall, sitting quietly by the hearth with Cynric, Acaren frightened more by the tense attitudes of the adults than by what was happening in the room above them

Athelin turned tensely to Gabhain. "Your mother?" he asked.

"In your rooms," Gabhain said.

"Where's Rowan?"

"With the lady Dorlaine," Cynric said. "He flatly refused to come when I went to fetch him. I thought it best to leave him until you came."

Loisa met Athelin halfway up the stairs. She caught his arm as he tried to brush past her.

"My lord, you are not going to enter a birthing chamber like that," she said quietly.

Athelin stiffened with anger. "You forget your place, Loisa," he said coldly.

Loisa refused to give way, not releasing her grip on his arm. "I most certainly do not, my lord Prince," she said firmly. "You're covered with mud and dirt. For the sake of the child and your wife, you must change and wash before you go to her."

She spoke only the truth, he realized. He acquiesced and nodded. "Of course," he said. The sound of a cry of pain, forced out between clenched teeth and bitten lips, came from above. He went white.

"Is she all right?" he asked.

"It's a difficult birth," Loisa said gently. "Hurry. She's asked for you."

Dorlaine lay sweating and pale upon the bed, her fine dark hair matted and tangled around her head on the pillow. The skin of her face appeared stretched taut, too close to the delicate bone structure beneath. Slowly and with great effort, she turned her head as Athelin entered the chamber. Her dark blue eyes were blurred and dazed with pain. She smiled, and his heart twisted in his chest as he saw what it cost her.

He went to his knees beside the bed, caught her hand between both of his. He kissed it, then pressed it against his cheek. "I'm here now, my very dearest," he said.

She smiled again, then closed her eyes. Athelin turned to the midwife, who stood by the end of the bed, wrapped in a white apron.

"Tell me," he said.

"The child is positioned badly," the midwife said. "Twice I've turned it and twice it's moved back. The lady Dorlaine is not so young as she was the last time I delivered her. The birthing pangs are draining her strength too quickly."

"What are you doing for her?"

"Poppy," she said. "To quiet both her and the child and ease the pain. She needs to rest to gain strength, and if the child is calm for a while, perhaps I may be able to turn it again for the delivery."

"Will it work?"

"I pray it will, my lord. It is for the Duality to say."

"Athelin . . ." Dorlaine's voice was the merest whisper of sound, a breath of wind stirring in dry leaves.

He turned quickly back to her. Her eyes burned feverishly bright in her bloodless face. He smoothed the tangled hair back from her forehead and smiled. "Hush, dear heart. Save your strength."

"Athelin, tell them . . ."

"Hush, sweetling. Please."

"No." Dorlaine moved her head back and forth painfully. "No. Tell them, at all cost, they must save the child. *At all cost.*"

He shook his head, unable to speak. She clutched his arm, and he nearly wept at how translucently pale that normally slim, brown hand was now.

"Promise me," she said. "At all cost, save the child. I will *not* lose this daughter. . . ."

He bent his head, pressing his forehead to her shoulder, tears blurring his vision. "I can't promise that," he cried. "Dorlaine, forgive me, but I can't." Seven years ago, he had been unable to make the same promise to his sister Iowen. Then, even the best efforts of the midwife had failed, and he had lost her. Hearing Dorlaine repeat those same words sent a cold dagger of fear and pain through his heart.

A wracking spasm of pain tore through her body, and she writhed on the bed. The midwife stepped forward and put her hand to Athelin's shoulder. "You must leave now, my lord," she said gently.

Athelin nearly stumbled over Rowan as he turned to leave the room. The boy sat huddled between the bed and the small table holding the lamp and an ewer of cool water. He clutched his harp tightly to his chest, hardly looking up as Athelin's foot grazed his knee.

"Will she be all right?" he whispered. He was nearly as pale as Dorlaine.

Athelin reached out to take Rowan's hand and drew him gently. "Yes," he said with far more confidence than he felt. "Of course she will. Come with me now, and let's get out of their way."

Rhan had taken Acaren up to his chambers. When Athelin came down to the Great Hall with Rowan, only Gabhain and Cynric remained by the hearth. Cynric gently herded Rowan back up the stairs to the rooms he shared with Acaren.

Gabhain was old enough to understand what was happening. He had refused to be swept out of the way with the twins. He stood as his father approached the hearth, taut and pale, his worry etched into his face.

"My mother?" he asked.

"It goes hard on her," Athelin said.

Gabhain closed his eyes briefly. "Duality help her," he said, and turned away to look into the fire.

Athelin sat on one of the low stools, his back against the stone of the hearth wall. He felt limp and drained, more weary than he had ever been in his life. Gabhain stood, one hand on the mantel, staring fixedly down into the fire. *He's so tall*, Athelin thought abstractedly. *It won't be long before I have to arrange a hunt for him*. He closed his eyes, random thoughts flitting through his mind. A hunt. A first kill. First Beltane night. The process of becoming a man.

From the tower room above came another cry of pain. Gabhain turned to look, then silently clenched his fist and pounded it against the mantel.

He looks just like Dorlaine, Athelin thought. He wondered if Gabhain would be all he had left of her after this night. He had already lost Danal. . . .

Much later, Cynric brought him something to eat. Without looking at the food, Athelin pushed it away.

"My lord, I insist," Cynric said quietly.

Athelin looked up, met those black, fathomless eyes. Cynric shared his memories of that terrible night when they had lost Iowen. She was Athelin's sister, and more dear to him than his life, but she had become Cynric's soul. She never knew it. Or if she knew it, she never acknowledged it. But Athelin knew. And he appreciated Cynric's presence.

"I can't eat now," he said. "Thank you anyway, Cynric. Later mayhaps."

Cynric inclined his head and took the plate away.

Then, finally, without warning, came the high, thin wail of a child. Athelin catapulted off the stool and took the stairs three at a time in his rush. He hardly noticed Mioragh the bard in the corridor outside the door of the chamber. He burst through the door to see Loisa wrapping a tiny child in soft blankets and the midwife working over Dorlaine on the bed.

He came quietly into the room and looked down at his wife. She lay still as death, waxen pale, against the pillow. Cold fear clutched at his heart for a moment, until he noticed the slow, quiet rise and fall of her chest. The midwife turned to look at him.

"You have a daughter, my lord," she said. "Healthy and strong, and very beautiful."

"And the lady Dorlaine?"

The midwife shook her head bleakly. "It's a far journey she had to go to bring back this life. It may be that she cannot find her own way back."

Athelin went to the bed. Dorlaine lay quietly, her arms

still by her side. The color of her eyes showed through the almost translucent lids, making them appear bruised. But a faint smile curved up at the corners of her bloodless mouth.

Loisa came to him and placed the child in his arms. Athelin looked down. His first impression was of ivory and cherry blossoms and ruddy gold. The midwife was right. It was a beautiful child. Then the baby opened her eyes, and he looked down into clouded blue that might one day pale to a soft, clear gray.

"Ceitryn," he murmured, and bent to kiss the tiny forehead. "Do everything you can for the lady Dorlaine," he told the midwife. "Everything. I will be close by if I'm needed." He handed the child back to Loisa.

"Duality grant you won't be needed, my lord," the midwife said.

Mioragh reached to touch his arm as Athelin emerged into the corridor. "Pardon, my lord," he said. "I might be able to help. Would you permit me an hour with your lady wife."

Athelin looked at the singer speculatively. Dressed in the long, pale tan robe of a bard, he carried a strength and a force that Athelin had not noticed before.

"You can Heal more than wounds?"

One corner of Mioragh's mouth lifted. "Yes, my lord. I believe I can help the lady Dorlaine."

"If you can save my wife, harper," Athelin said quietly, "you have but to ask anything of me, and it will be yours."

Mioragh smiled thinly. "Don't make rash promises, my lord," he said. "You may find the cost is more than you are able to pay. If I help the lady Dorlaine, I do it for love of her."

"Please. Then do it."

"Give me an hour, mayhaps less. Then we will know for certain, one way or the other, how the Duality decides."

Athelin remained in the corridor. The women came out of the chamber, clucking indignantly, then left quietly when they looked at his face.

It was only slightly less than an hour before Mioragh came out of the chamber, leaving the door ajar behind him. His body drooped with fatigue and his face was gray with exhaustion, but he was smiling. "Please enter, my lord," he said. "I must go and rest now."

Dorlaine lay smiling on the bed. Most of her color had returned, and the dull film had gone from her eyes. She was radiantly beautiful. With tears suddenly blinding him, Athelin stumbled to the bed and laid his head against her shoulder and held her tightly.

"Isn't she a beautiful child?" Dorlaine asked softly. She raised her hand to stroke his hair.

"The most beautiful," he agreed, his voice broken. "Truly the most beautiful child ever born to the Celae." He caught a flash of movement out of the corner of his eye and looked up. Rowan stood by the cradle, looking down in awe at the carefully swaddled child. He raised his head slowly and met Athelin's eyes. Suddenly he smiled, a brilliant, joyful smile, then reached down and gently brushed the baby's cheek with his finger.

6

Two generations past, when the people of Skai first fled to the Isle of Skerry under Prince Brennan, they had raised the graceful, circular structure of the shrine and its slender columns on a ridge of land that thrust out from the foot of Ben Warden. When it was done, they found and transplanted twelve sturdy oak trees in a ring around the building—twelve trees for the three sacred numbers, two, three, and four. Two for the twinned Duality which was neither male nor female but both, three for the Presence and the Power and the Love, and four for the earth, wind, fire and water of the world. Around the roots of the twelve trees they planted ivy, which twined and grew around the trunks, and hung from the branches so that, in summer, the ivy leaves formed a cooling green shade around the shrine, and dappled the walls of the building with an ever-changing tapestry of light and shadow.

On this morning of spring, the shrine was hung with banners of blue and green, shot with ribbons of red and yellow. Flowers braided into ropes twined the columns of the balconies. More blooms cascaded in a riot of color in celebration from the ledges which held votive candles. The precious scents of sandalwood and cinnamon drifted in the air.

The twelve priests and priestesses stood awaiting the arrival of the child whose naming ceremony they were about to enact. The High Priest and Priestess, bound left arm to right, left leg to right, enveloped in one robe that left only one arm apiece free, represented the combined essence of male and female in the Duality. They stood a little apart from the rest as they watched the brightly colored procession winding its way down the road from the Keep. Overhead, the sun shone bright and warm, and a small breeze played with the trailing curtains of ivy around the shrine. It was a good day for a Naming.

Loisa al Morvyn, dressed in a simple gown of blue, led the procession, carrying the child in her arms. Behind her, arm in arm, came Prince Athelin and the lady Dorlaine, both also dressed in blue. The sun flashed on the gold torcs about their throats, the only jewelry they wore except for the gold bands on the heart finger of their left hands that bound them as man and wife. Directly behind them walked Gabhain, Acaren, and Rowan, and following the boys were the men and women of the court.

The six priests formed a line to the left, the six priestesses a line to the right, all of them smiling, to guide the procession to the altar where lay a stone bowl of water, scented with oil of violets, mauve and yellow petals circling lazily in it.

The High Priest and Priestess moved smoothly to stand before the altar and face Loisa. They held out their hands. Together, in practiced and harmonious unison, they intoned, "Who brings this child to the presence of the Duality?"

Loisa gently placed the child in their hands. "I bring this child to the presence of the Duality," she said quietly but clearly. She stepped aside and went to stand behind Athelin and Dorlaine. In the background, the twelve priestesses and priests began a soft, nearly inaudible chant of thanksgiving.

"Who gives this child in offering and blessing to the Duality?"

Dorlaine stepped forward. "I do. I, Dorlaine al Keagan, give this child, born of my womb, in offering of love, and ask blessing upon her until the number of her days are counted and totaled."

"Who gives this child for protection and guidance to the Duality?" The chant wove through the sound of the priest's and priestess's blended voices, adding joy to the solemnity of the words.

Athelin moved to stand beside Dorlaine. "I do. I, Athelin ap Gareth ap Brennan, give this child, born of my seed and my blood and my line, to the Duality, and ask protection and guidance for her until the number of her days are counted and totaled."

"And who gives the name for this child for the Scrolls of Annwn?"

"I do," said Dorlaine. "I give her name Ceitryn so that she might be so written on the Scrolls of Annwn, and recognized by the Counter at the Scroll when the number of her days are counted and totaled."

"Then shall the Duality accept this gift and offering, and return it to you in joy and twice blessed. In return for the gift of the child Ceitryn al Athelin, the Duality shall ask of you that, in its name, you give her love and protection and guidance until she returns to the Presence and the Power and the Love. Will you accept this burden and responsibility, in the name of the Duality."

The song rose in a delicate crescendo, and the first notes of a triple flute joined with the voices, threading an ethereal counterpoint through the voices.

Dorlaine dipped her hand into the bowl of water and sprinkled it on the baby, then on her own breast. "In the name of the Duality, I accept this charge gladly and freely."

Athelin sprinkled water on the baby, then himself. "In the name of the Duality, I accept this charge gladly and freely."

"Then to you, in the name of the Duality, I give this greatest of all gifts, and charge you to keep your vow made this day in the presence of the Duality, and in the presence of these witnesses. May your days and the days of Ceitryn al Athelin be counted joyously like bright tokens until they are totaled. Go in peace, my children."

A second triple flute, its note slightly higher than the first, braided a graceful descant to the song in a joyous final chorus as Dorlaine accepted the child from the hands of the Priest and Priestess, and the royal party turned to leave the shrine.

There was feasting that night in Skerry Keep. All day servants had bustled and scurried around the palace making ready for the celebration. Rows and rows of tables were set up in the Great Hall, fresh candles and torches were set into the brackets along the walls. In the kitchen, a whole ox and a whole pork roasted on spits turned by kitchen boys whose faces glowed red from the heat of the fires. Great platters of sweetmeats and honey cakes, guarded by fierce kitchen girls from the determined raiding of children—led by the sons of Prince Athelin—stood ready to present once the feast had begun.

By late afternoon, the guests had taken their places. The spillover filled the courtyard, where great kegs of ale had been tapped, dispensed by servants to all comers. In the Great Hall, the laughter and happy voices of the guests ebbed and flowed like the tides.

As they prepared to descend the stairs to the Great Hall, Athelin turned to Dorlaine. "Are you sure you're feeling well enough for this?" he asked.

She laughed. "I'm very well," she said. "And I'm very happy."

He took Ceitryn from Loisa and held her cradled in his left arm. He offered his right to Dorlaine, who laid her hand upon it lightly. "My lady . . ." he said, and smiled as he made her a small bow.

Silence fell over the Great Hall as they entered and took their places at the high table. Gabhain sat at Athelin's left tonight, Acaren and Rowan seated at Dorlaine's right. A servant stepped forward and poured wine into Athelin's glass. Athelin handed the baby to Dorlaine and stood.

He spilled a few drops of the wine for the lesser gods and goddesses, then raised his glass. "My friends, I give you Celi," he cried. "I give you Skai, that we might one day return to our home."

When the toast had been drunk, he bent to take Ceitryn from Dorlaine and, holding her snugly cradled in his left arm, once again raised his glass. "My friends, I give you my daughter, Ceitryn al Athelin."

The toast brought cheers from the tables crowded with guests. When they had drunk and called out wishes for joy

and happiness for the child, Athelin returned the baby to
Dorlaine's arms and gave the signal to the servants to begin
serving the meal.

Ceitryn stirred in Dorlaine's arms and opened her eyes.
She seemed to be staring straight at Rowan. Dorlaine glanced
at him and saw he was looking at the baby. He smiled, a
small, secret smile, and Dorlaine could have sworn Ceitryn
smiled back. But it was ridiculous to think that a child less
than a fortnight old would smile in response knowingly.

She remembered the night the boys had come to see her
and make the acquaintance of their new sister. The baby had
been fussing, hungry and eager for the breast, when the boys
came in. Gabhain, old enough to realize the miracle of new
life, had quite simply been awed. Acaren assessed the baby
critically, then accepted her with a broad smile. Rowan, without hesitation, fell in love unconditionally at first sight. He
approached the bed, smiling, and reached out a gentle finger
to trace the line of the baby's cheek. Ceitryn quieted, and her
tiny hand had wavered up to clutch tightly to Rowan's finger.

"She's very beautiful, mother," Rowan said, delighted
and charmed. "But I knew she would be."

It was late now, and the throng in the Great Hall of Skerry
Keep had thinned until only the determined revelers were
left. Dorlaine had taken Ceitryn and retired to their chambers, and most of the other women had left the feast with her.

Determined to stay awake to the bitter end and enjoy the
feast as princelings at the high table for the first time, Acaren
and Rowan drooped in their chairs, but had not quite fallen
asleep. Relaxed now and smiling in his high chair, with Gabhain to his left, Athelin beckoned them onto his knees, where
they leaned sleepily against his chest and earned a scornful
glance from Gabhain, who was intensely wide-awake, and
superior in his advanced maturity. The twins ignored him.

Finally, came what they had been awaiting since the
remains of the meal had been cleared. Mioragh arose again
from his seat at the table nearest the high table and went to
his harp. Immediately, silence descended over the Hall. With
only a few introductory chords plucked from the harp, the

Bard launched into the tale of how Cernos of the Forest had been fooled by the woodcutter Bran into finding the son of a noble house to marry his daughter Mearna. The twins laughed as much as everyone else at the delightful gambits and schemes of the woodcutter.

When the song was done and the laughter finished, Mioragh ran his hands across the strings of the harp, and it seemed to Rowan that the Bard looked straight at him.

"This next story will tell the tale of Anwyr the Champion and Avigus the Kaith, and how they came to the Court of Tiernyn," Mioragh said, still watching first Rowan and then Acaren. The boys sat up straighter on their father's knee, focused attentively on the bard. "Listen carefully. This is how it begins."

And so it was in the fifth year of Tiernyn as High King of Celi, together with his brother Donaugh the Enchanter, that the brothers, Anwyr and Avigus, came out of Wenydd in the west. Anwyr carried on his back the great sword Slayer, crafted they say by Wyfydd Smith at the ford on the River Eidon where Cernos of the Forest guarded the road and Adriel of the Waters sheltered travelers. As long as the blue jewel shone from Slayer's hilt, no man was more powerful or skilled in battle than Anwyr.

Beside him rode Avigus, the sword Singer at his side and the harp Songmaker slung on his back. His skill in wielding Singer was exceeded only by his skill at coaxing music from the golden strings of Songmaker, and in all of the land of Celi, he had no equal as a bard.

The fame of these two, as Champion and Kaith, had gone before them so that when they came to Dun Camas on the River Camm, Tiernyn himself, with Donaugh as always beside him, descended to the courtyard to greet them, and Queen Ylana herself offered them the guest-cup of welcome.

When the guest-cup had been drained, Anwyr and Avigus went to one knee before Tiernyn and Donaugh, and offered service.

"We ask but a humble place with your Companions, my lord King," Anwyr said, "for surely we are the least among those who serve you."

"Not so," replied the King, and he raised them up and bestowed upon them the kiss of brotherhood. "Your sword, Anwyr, will be welcome at my left in battle."

And Donaugh stepped forward, and he, too, bestowed upon Anwyr and Avigus the kiss of brotherhood. "Your sword and your harp, Avigus," he said, "will be welcome beside me, for I love music as much as I love a loyal man."

"My lord Prince," Avigus said. "For all time, the whole world may be sure that one sword will guard you and one harp will sing the praises of Tiernyn and Donaugh his brother."

And so it was that Anwyr and Avigus came to the Court of Tiernyn. It is told that they found for Tiernyn the great sword Thirster, but that is another tale for telling on another night.

Athelin noticed that Mioragh seemed to be telling the story for Acaren and Rowan alone. As the boys settled drowsily back against him, he watched the Bard, a thoughtful and speculative expression in his clear brown eyes.

Caennedd slouched in his chair as the bard's words rang through the hall. His fingers toyed absently with the stem of his goblet as he watched Athelin closely though narrowed eyes. He drained the mead cup and held it out as a servant appeared at his elbow to refill it. He frowned thoughtfully, his mind circling something he could not quite fit together, something to do with how Dorlaine had looked, her head bent over the child in her arms. He looked at his half brother again, sitting in his high chair with the twins on his knees. The two young faces were identical, and they both strongly resembled Athelin.

But there was something — Yes, definitely something, Caennedd thought, his mead-furred logic still worrying at the amorphous knot. Then Acaren moved his head, held it to one side as he looked up at his father to tell him something. Caennedd froze, and everything suddenly clicked, crystal clear, into focus.

The twins resembled Athelin. Of course they did. But they resembled Iowen, too. Could it be possible . . .

The twins had been born the same night Iowen died in

childbirth. It was said the distress of her kin-sister's death brought on Dorlaine's own labor, nearly a season too soon. A little more than two fortnights. Far too soon.

Caennedd sat up straighter and studied the twins. Yes, they could easily be Iowen's children. They could be Athelin's, too. There had been much confusion in the palace that night. Could two live children born to a dying woman have been substituted for one dead child born too soon?

The fascinating conjecture dissolved almost as quickly as it had sprung to life. There was no doubt that Dorlaine loved her husband, but would even an extraordinarily loving wife accept, raise, and obviously love the bastard children of her husband's sister?

And what if his angry, hurtful thrust were actually true? Suppose the twins really were Athelin's bastard children by incest with his own sister? He had meant the cruel remark only as revenge. But what if it were true?

The thought left him with a chill knot of disbelief in his chest. Iowen wouldn't do that. He had looked up to her, admired her, respected her. She loved him as much as he loved her. She certainly wouldn't betray him. . . .

Still, the secret exchange could have happened. It mattered little who had actually fathered Iowen's child. But would Dorlaine know? Caennedd bit his lip, frowning again. Would it be possible for Athelin to switch the dead child for the living without Dorlaine's knowledge? Caennedd sighed and let that concept die. Could any woman who had given birth to only one child be persuaded she had given birth to two? That was too unlikely. Highly doubtful, even if the woman were stunned by poppy. Women knew.

He remembered that first Imbolc after Iowen's death. He had seen Dorlaine go to the burial ground with two hoops of ivy to place on her kin-sister's grave—one normal-sized hoop woven with holly, mistletoe, and scarlet silk ribbons, one small hoop woven with dried flowers and white silk ribbons. A hoop for a child. She had knelt and placed both hoops on the cairn, but it was the small hoop she had reached out a tender finger to stroke, tears making her cheeks glisten in the wan, winter sunlight.

Caennedd drained his cup again and let the fanciful notion go. It was too absurd, too complicated. There were women in attendance at both births. Had a switch been made, tongues would have wagged. Even if the story had not flashed around both Skerry and Marddyn more swiftly than the gulls moved between the two islands, unquellable rumors would have surfaced periodically. And there had been no rumors. Not once.

Still . . . Caennedd considered his construction in a different light. He stared down into the shifting pattern in liquid gold the mead in the goblet made as he swirled the cup, hardly listening as Mioragh's story came to an end. He looked up at Athelin again through narrowed eyes, watching his half brother as he handed the sleep-slackened bodies of the twins to Rhan and Cynric.

Rumor was a powerful tool, Caennedd decided. It could possibly be used to gain him what he wanted most.

7

The sound of a harp being inexpertly plucked came from one of the small chambers off the Great Hall. Curious, Athelin pushed open the door to see Rowan sitting on a low stool, his head bent over a small harp, the sun from the window turning his hair to bright gold. Beside him, patient and smiling, sat Mioragh, intent on guiding the small, unpracticed hands in finding the notes. So absorbed were the two of them, they did not see Athelin in the doorway. As he watched, Mioragh murmured something, and Rowan's hands moved in response. A sweet, clear arpeggio came from the harp. Rowan laughed in delight as Mioragh nodded in satisfaction.

"Yes, that's it," he said quietly.

Pleased and elated, Rowan said, "Shall I be a Kaith, Mioragh? Like Avigus?"

"Time will reveal that, child," Mioragh said gravely. "Now, try this . . ."

Athelin moved quietly away, letting the door close gently behind him. Again, his face was thoughtful and grave as he ascended the stairs to the family quarters above the Hall.

The evening meal was done, and the children safely abed. Servants moved quietly through the palace, lighting the lamps and torches along the corridors and in the chambers. Athelin left his own chamber and made his way quickly to the guest wing, where Mioragh had been given a spacious suite of rooms. He hesitated before the door, then lifted his hand to knock.

Mioragh himself opened the door. He was Tyadda, one

of the strange, fey race that had inhabited the Isle of Celi since long before the Celae came, when the island was called Nemeara. His hair still showed the dark gold of youth threaded among the shining silver of rapidly encroaching old age.

When the Celae came to the Isle of Celi, the Tyadda were a fading race, their once-strong magic slowly dying away. Intermarriage between the Tyadda and the Celae strengthened the magic, but it would never be as powerful as it had once been.

The Celae didn't conquer the Tyadda; they married them. But there were very few trueborn Tyadda left, and those few for the most part still remained in their concealed fastnesses deep in the mountains of Skai, well hidden from the invading Maedun. Their dark gold hair and startlingly dark brown eyes tended to show up in the descendants of the Celae who intermarried with them. Athelin had inherited his mother's Tyadda brown eyes and her dark gold hair from her, along with his great-grandfather's powerful build.

Mioragh held the door wider for Athelin to enter, and inclined his head respectfully. "You do me honor, my lord," he said. "How may I help you?"

"I would speak with you, Bard."

"Of course." Mioragh gestured toward two comfortable chairs, a table between them, which sat by the window alcove. "Please, take your ease, my lord. May I offer you some wine?" He went to a cupboard and drew out a flask and two goblets. "I have here some of the apple wine the people of Wenydd make by Laurelwater."

Athelin took a seat and sat back, relaxed and comfortable, as he watched the bard pour wine into two tall goblets. Mioragh brought both glasses to the hearth and sat opposite Athelin, handing one glass across the table.

Athelin lifted his goblet. "To Celi, that we might go home one day," he said. He spilled a few drops, then drank sparingly. "I saw you with Rowan this afternoon."

Mioragh smiled. "The child has the magic of music in his heart, my lord. I do my poor best to help him bring it from his heart to the instrument."

"I rather thought you were the one teaching him. How long has this been going on?"

"Since the Feast of New Fire, my lord. Do you object? If you do, I will cease teaching the child."

Athelin waved a hand. "No," he said. "No, I have no objections. If Rowan wishes to learn, then he shall learn. Is he able to command his *awen*—his muse—yet?"

Mioragh smiled again. "He is more commanded than commanding right now," he said. "If he is to be a bard, the control will come. But surely you didn't come to discuss music and the command of *awens*, my lord."

Athelin sat back in his chair. "I've been watching you closely this last while," he said. "You say you've placed a masking spell about Rowan to hide his magic from Hakkar's searching. What else are you teaching my son?"

"Whatever he might learn, my lord."

Athelin smiled thinly. "By the horns of Cernos, I think you are no ordinary bard, Mioragh of Wenydd," he said. "Are you an enchanter, then?"

Mioragh shook his head. "No, my lord. When I stretch myself to the limits of my poor ability, I have nowhere the ability that even your father's aunt Brynda had."

"Yet, you Healed my shoulder, and you saved my wife's life, both of which took the art of a powerful Healer."

The bard raised a depreciating hand. "The lady Dorlaine has some magic of her own," he said. "With mine, it was enough."

"The lady Dorlaine lay very near death. She could invoke no magic."

Mioragh frowned thoughtfully. "It was indeed a strange hour, my lord," he said softly. "When I entered the chamber, the fires of life in your lady wife had dwindled to a very faint spark indeed. I tried to establish a link so that I could transfer some of my strength to her." He rose and went to the cupboard to fetch the flask of wine back to the table. Before he continued, he refilled his goblet and offered more to Athelin, who shook his head. Mioragh took his seat again, leaving the flask on the table.

"For a long time," he went on, choosing his words carefully, "I appeared to make no headway. It was almost as if I met that terrible emptiness that signifies a mortal wound, one that no Healer can mend. Then it seemed that there was someone else there, helping, and my strength flowed into the lady Dorlaine. I felt as if someone had taken my hand to help. Someone small. Mayhaps a young boy."

Athelin looked up quickly, a small frown drawing his brows together above his clear brown eyes. "Rowan, mayhaps?" he asked quietly. "He was there in the room with you all along, I think."

"Was he? I didn't see him come in."

"Nor did I. I was by the door every moment while you were in there with Dorlaine."

"Rowan?" Mioragh frowned thoughtfully. "Mayhaps. At the time, I thought it was some of the lady's own magic I met, my lord," he said quietly. "But the more I think about it, the more likely it seems that it was Rowan's magic, called by her own."

"It may be that it did," Athelin said. "She has some, as you said. Enough to speak with the child while it was still in the womb."

Mioragh smiled. "A magic many mothers have." He slanted a sharp glance at Athelin from beneath his shaggy, gray brows. "Your own mother was Tyadda. Your grandfather was known to have the Sight, and your father had a powerful magic. Have you any, my lord?"

Athelin's brow quirked, and one corner of his mouth lifted. In answer, he blew out one of the candles and waited until the thin wisp of smoke had dissipated. Then he touched his finger to the cold wick and flicked it back to flame. "A little," he said. "Enough to resonate with the Rune Blade I carry. Enough to amuse children. A few tricks, that's all."

Mioragh sat back. He sighed heavily. "There are far too many of us with too little magic to be of much use," he said softly.

"Were you thinking of weapons against the Maedun?"

Mioragh smiled bitterly. "We all know that gentle Tyadda or Celae magic can't be used to harm," he said.

Athelin raised an eyebrow. "Red Kian of Skai used it as

a weapon. So did Donaugh the Enchanter. And my father, come to that."

"No, my lord," Mioragh said. "They used it to assist them, but they couldn't use it as a weapon. It was their own strength and intelligence that they used to win against the Maedun. Not the magic itself."

Athelin looked up, his head held to one side, watching the bard closely. "Why did you come here?"

"I don't know," Mioragh said slowly. "I believe I was sent."

"Sent? By whom?"

Mioragh shrugged. "By Celi, perhaps. By the very *darlai* of the land itself. Its very heart and spirit." He looked up. "You told me in the corridor after your daughter was born that anything I asked of you would be mine."

"And you said that the cost might be more than I was willing to pay. What price are you asking, Bard?"

"Your sons."

"My *sons*!" Athelin lurched forward in his chair, hands gripping convulsively to the carved oaken arms. He came halfway to his feet, his face pale. On the table before him, the wine in the goblets sloshed, nearly spilled.

Mioragh smiled. "For two hours each day, my lord," he said mildly. "I would teach them."

Athelin settled back into his chair. His color had returned. He reached for his goblet, ran his finger lightly around the rim. "What then would you teach them?" he asked.

"Do they read and write, my lord?"

"They do. Even the twins."

"History? Languages?"

A bleak pang snatched at Athelin's heart. "Not since Iowen died. She had a gift for teaching languages and history. There's been no one to take her place since she died."

"Then I expect I can be of much assistance. I shall teach them mathematics and history and philosophy. And the youngest . . ."

"Rowan? What would you teach him?"

"As you saw, he would play the harp, my lord. I believe

he has the magic of music in his heart. But he has the magic of the land in his blood and bone, the same magic your father had. As Donaugh the Enchanter had. Mayhaps even enough to help defeat the Maedun."

Athelin raised an eyebrow. "As Kaith?" he asked softly.

Mioragh met his gaze with only a hint of a smile. "Mayhaps. Or mayhaps in another way."

Athelin regarded him gravely for a moment. "Sometimes, Mioragh," he said softly, "I believe you know far too much."

Mioragh inclined his head respectfully. "Sometimes, my lord Prince," he said, "I'm afraid I know far too little."

His mood abstractedly thoughtful and introspective, Athelin retraced his steps through the deserted, torchlit corridors to his chambers. Mioragh's talk of music and magic had been disturbing. It resonated strongly with what Athelin could remember of the strange dreams that had troubled his sleep since the Midwinter Festival, but he could see no clear connection. Perhaps there was none. Or perhaps the time was not yet ripe for the meaning to be revealed. The meaning of dreams, even when the dreamer dreamed true—or perhaps especially then—was never easy to interpret. Too often, the message of the dream was ambiguous, decipherable only *after* the event.

Athelin's steps slowed. He frowned, trying to recall the images of the dreams. It always seemed that he walked the green mountains of Skai, the presence of his sister Iowen very close to him. Yet, even though awake he hungered to be in Skai, back in the homeland of his people, in the dreams, his heart hung heavy with grief and loss. In the Great Hall of Dun Eidon, where his father was born before the invasion, empty places at the banquet table gaped like bleeding wounds. And always, in the dream, Iowen's voice: "The day is coming, Athelin my dear brother. And both of us shall both rejoice and regret it."

Athelin sighed and shook his head. There could be no victory without its price. Was it the terrible cost that troubled his dreams so?

He realized he had walked past his own chambers and stood outside the door to the chamber where the twins and his daughter slept. He put out a hand to push open the door, hesitated, changed his mind. It was late. It would be unfair to chance waking Loisa, who slept in Ceitryn's room, or Rhan, who served the twins. He turned back to his own rooms.

He did not see Caennedd in the outer chamber until his half brother rose from the chair near the hearth. As usual, Caennedd wore black, unadorned except for the red jewel set in the brooch embossed with the white falcon of Skai at his shoulder. Caennedd at sixteen had sworn to wear only black in imitation of the usurper in Clendonan until Skai was once again free of the galling presence of the Somber Riders of Maedun. Athelin thought the gesture to be overly dramatic.

Masking his irritation at finding Caennedd uninvited in his private chambers, Athelin flicked two candles on the table to flame and turned to his half brother. "The hour is late," he said, "but how may I help you, Caennedd?"

Caennedd sat down again, slouched in the chair, his legs stretched before him, ankles crossed, his arms folded across his chest. He smiled thinly. "You may authorize the outfitting of my company of soldiers for an expedition south of the Verge. . . ."

Athelin turned the other comfortable chair to face Caennedd and seated himself before replying. He leaned back and drew one leg up to cross his ankle over his knee. Elbow resting on the arm of the chair, he brought his hand up to his chin. He took a deep breath. "I believe we've had this conversation before," he said calmly. "The answer then was no. It has not changed."

Caennedd inclined his head. "So you say." He paused, half smiling, then: "You're certain there's nothing I can say to persuade you to change your mind?"

"Nothing. You know the reasons. The time isn't yet right."

"Again, so you say. I have no choice but to accept your opinion." He unfolded his arms and tented his fingers beneath his chin. "Did I remember to congratulate you upon the birth of your daughter?"

"You did. Briefly."

"Our father's line has always produced many sons, but very few daughters. Only one per generation, I believe. The child our sister died birthing was also a daughter, wasn't it?"

Athelin regarded Caennedd through narrowed eyes, wondering where the conversation led. "You know it was."

Caennedd shrugged. "I paid little attention to events like that seven years ago," he said. "I was, of course, little more than a child myself, then." He looked up and smiled again. Not an expression of amusement. "The lady Dorlaine, though, if I remember aright, seemed to grieve for the loss of the girl-child. More than one would think necessary for the child of a kin-sister." Abruptly, he changed the subject. "The twins are certainly growing quickly now," he said slowly and thoughtfully. "I noticed at the Naming feast how Acaren especially more and more resembles Iowen than you in that certain way he holds his head at times. I thought it very curious." He left an odd, expectant little pause at the end of the sentence.

Athelin held himself very still, allowing no change of expression on his face. "Why should that be strange?" he asked quietly. "Iowen was, after all, my full sister."

"One could almost draw the conclusion that she was the mother of both twins rather than their aunt." Again, that odd little pause, as if he were considering some significant scrap of knowledge.

"Caennedd, you tread dangerous ground—"

"I suppose it would be possible that Iowen might even be both their aunt and their mother, were you the true father." He looked up, still smiling. "What I cannot decide is how you convinced the lady Dorlaine to acquiesce to your command that she pretend they were her own."

Athelin shot out of the chair. "That's monstrous—" he cried.

Caennedd lunged to his feet to meet him. "Is it?" he demanded. "Monstrous it may well be, but I challenge you to prove it is not the truth." He leapt back hastily as Athelin, white with fury, took one long stride forward. "Do not touch me, *brother*," he snarled. "Lay one hand on me, and that interesting and titillating little fable will race across both Skerry and Marddyn like Beodun's own wildfire, and I myself will fan the flames."

Athelin had to exert every ounce of his strength to control his outrage. "Speak one word of that to anyone, Caennedd," he said, his voice thick with anger, "and I will personally rip your tongue from your filthy mouth. Do you understand me?"

"Give me my company, send me south of the Verge. You have my word that I will not mention this if—"

Athelin turned abruptly on his heel. "Ralf!" he called.

The promptness of Ralf's appearance at the door of his small room off the main chamber made it clear that he had not been sleeping. "Yes, my lord?" he asked mildly.

"Ralf, my brother Caennedd is under arrest. He is to be taken to his chambers and confined there. You will see that the doors are guarded, and that he speaks to no one until I have decided what I will do with him. Is that quite clear?"

Ralf did not so much as glance at Caennedd. His face expressionless, he said, "It is, my lord."

"You, yourself, will escort him to his chambers. Report anything he says to me."

"To you, and to you alone, my lord," Ralf replied, and Athelin realized he had heard everything Caennedd had said.

Crimson fury suffused Caennedd's face. "Athelin, you can't do this—"

Athelin turned to him. "Can I not?" he asked coldly. "You've crossed the line from mere insolence to approach very close to treason. I'll deal with you when I'm less inclined to let anger govern my judgment. Take him away now, Ralf."

It was after midnight, but Athelin was still wakeful in his bed. He had finally sloughed off the blinding rage the incident with Caennedd had aroused, and now tried to contend with the aftermath of the intensity of the emotion. For one instant, he had been less than a hairbreadth from becoming a kinslayer. That he had come so close to losing control of himself frightened him. A prince often had to endure worse than what Caennedd had done and retain both his equanimity and his judgment.

Gradually, he calmed his ragged breathing, quelled the last of the residual tremors of rage. Bleakly, he wondered if he still loved his half brother. As a child, Caennedd had been bright, outgoing, and cheerful, an easy child to love.

Iowen had welcomed him to the family. Her demeanor had made it obvious the addition of a young brother had delighted her. And it had been patently obvious that Caennedd adored her. The relationship between the two of them was as close in its way as the relationship between Iowen and Athelin. Young Caennedd had basked in its warmth and had flourished.

Iowen had that sort of effect on everyone around her, Athelin reflected.

It was not until Caennedd was well into adolescence that the obsession with returning to Skai to oust the Somber Riders had taken root. It had altered his personality completely. The charm was still there, but now assumed or discarded at will—used more as a weapon than anything else.

Athelin sighed and wondered grimly how he would deal with this latest manifestation of Caennedd's obsession.

8

The outer chamber was spacious and comfortably appointed, if not luxurious, but Caennedd had no patience with the trappings of luxury. He had spent little time in his own chambers since assuming command of his company of soldiers at eighteen, preferring to be with his men. The windows overlooked the training field to the south of the palace, where Caennedd could see a group of boys, including Athelin's three sons practicing with swords, bows, and spears. Weymund appeared to be absent, the training now supervised by three young assistants. And, oddly enough, there was no sign of Iowen's black dog, either.

Caennedd's blinding fury at being confined to his chambers had finally dissipated sometime during the early morning. He had been a fool, he decided at last. He should have known Athelin could not be coerced by a threat of blackmail. And he should have known Athelin would tolerate no hint of scandal to touch their sister's name.

In spite of himself, he was relieved his ploy had not worked. He wanted more than anything to be the man to free Skai from the murderous Maedun, but he knew he could never bring himself to besmirch Iowen's name. Her memory meant too much to him. He could threaten Athelin, but he could not carry through on the threat. And Athelin probably knew that as well as he himself did, he thought sourly.

There must be some way to convince Athelin of the necessity of sending men back to Skai, Caennedd thought as he watched without seeing the boys on the practice field. There *had* to be a way. How could Athelin not see that now was the time? He himself had said many times that the Somber Riders became only men when in the highlands where Hakkar's spell could not protect them. If an army of Celae returned to Skai, even if the black sorcerer himself came from Clendonan to face them, the mountains of Skai would protect the sons of Skai. Surely Athelin could see that. They could win back Skai, and once Skai was free again, the rest of Celae would follow. It had to be done now before the blight engulfed the high country, the only place immune to Hakkar's spell. If the spell was allowed to take over the mountains, in only a few years, there would be no one left to fight.

A small group of five mounted men left the palace and rode toward the village. Caennedd noted it automatically. Part of the guard going off duty. Probably headed for the inn and some relaxation. Most of his own soldiers were probably at the inn. He wondered if they were angry about his arrest.

Caennedd moved away from the window, frowning thoughtfully. In one respect, he had told the truth to Athelin. His soldiers were loyal to him. Loidd, his lieutenant, held the same opinion as he about going to Skai. So did most of his soldiers. He had spent the last two years quietly exchanging the men in his company who did not agree with him for men who did. If he went south of the Verge, they would follow.

Caennedd slammed one fist into the palm of his other hand. Very well, then. If Athelin would not authorize the foray south, there were other ways. He went to the locked door that led to the corridor and pounded on it.

"Send me my servant," he demanded. "Send Tadwyr to me now. I require his services."

One of the guards opened the door and stood stolidly blocking the doorway. "Prince Athelin said no one was to enter," he said.

Caennedd caught a glimpse of Tadwyr huddling in the shadow of a recessed door halfway down the hall. He gave the guard his coldest stare. "He most certainly didn't mean to deprive me of the services of my servant," he said. "Send my servant to me. Go and ask my brother first, if you must. But send Tadwyr to me."

The guard hesitated, then beckoned to young Tadwyr,

who still hovered anxiously in the corridor. A moment later, Tadwyr slipped into the room and stood, eyes downcast, waiting for Caennedd's instructions. Caennedd stared at the guard until the man stepped back and closed the door.

Caennedd smiled. "Don't be ashamed for me, Tadwyr," he said quietly. "We'll show every man on Skerry and Marddyn who's the better man between my half brother and myself."

"He shouldn't have put this humiliation upon you in the first place, my lord," Tadwyr muttered.

"That's of no matter now," Caennedd said. "I've a plan. You're the only man I can count on to help me."

Tadwyr's hand went to his sword hilt. "My life is yours, my lord," he said. "You know that."

Caennedd smiled. "Yes, I know that, Tadwyr, and your loyalty is appreciated." He went to the carved chest that sat against one wall and went to his knees before it. The small vial he wanted was buried near the bottom beneath an old cloak. He got to his feet and turned back to Tadwyr, holding out the vial. "This will get me out of here," he said. "Put this into the ale the guard will be drinking with their evening meal. It will make them sleep for a few hours. While they sleep, it will be easy for us to slip out of the palace."

Tadwyr took the vial, but bit his lip doubtfully. "It will not harm them, will it?" he asked. "My brother—"

Caennedd shook his head. "No, it will not harm them. Only make them sleep. See to it that you do not drink any of the ale once you have emptied that vial into the cask. When you have done it, go to Loidd and tell him I will meet him by the inn two hours before dawn. Tell him to have my horse ready."

Tadwyr bowed. "Yes, my lord," he said.

When he had left, Caennedd went back to the window. Outside, shadows lengthened quickly as the sun slid lower in the west. The training field was now empty of boys.

The little garden overflowed with bright roses, their scent hanging in the air like smoke. Petals of red, pink, and yellow rode the gentle breeze like snowflakes and scattered themselves in drifts along the green velvet of the grass. Against the wall, the pleached and pollarded trees held out small, hard, green fruit to the nourishing rays of the sun.

Rowan had avoided the walled garden ever since the afternoon the Maedun raiding party had invaded Skerry Keep. It still occasionally filled his nightmares — nightmares from which he had little difficulty awakening. Finding himself standing in the midst of the riotously blooming roses surprised him, even though he was completely aware that he was dreaming.

Behind him, someone said his name. Startled, he spun about and nearly lost his balance. The girl who stood in the shelter of the roses appeared to be about his own age. She wore a simple yellow gown that exactly matched the roses behind her. The fabric held the quiet sheen of silk. Not a dress to be worn by a serving girl. She had kilted up the skirts so that her bare feet and ankles showed plainly below the hem. Her hair, red-gold as fresh-minted copper, tumbled around her shoulders and down her back, held only by a pair of shell combs. Her eyes, large and wide-set, were the color of rain clouds in spring, a clear and luminous gray. She regarded him gravely, unsmiling, her hands held clasped behind her back.

"You've forgotten me," she said.

"Your pardon, my lady?" he asked, puzzled. He had not forgotten her because one could not forget someone one had never before seen.

She sighed and rolled her eyes. "This always happens," she said. "And it will happen again. You'll forget me again."

She was quite the most lovely girl Rowan had ever seen. "I could never forget you," he said gallantly.

"Ah, but you will," she said. "You will. But there's no time for that now. You must come with me." She held out her hand. "It's very important."

"Where do you want me to go?" he asked.

"I've something to show you that you must know. That Athelin must know. Come."

He hesitated only a heartbeat, then took her hand, again surprised to find himself trusting her completely. Her hand was warm and strong in his, the skin sun-browned to a golden tan. He let her pull him out of the garden, out into the fields toward the lower slopes of Ben Aislin. It never once occurred to Rowan to marvel at the speed they ran across the island.

"There." She pointed. "See the boat?"

He shaded his eyes with his hand. Against the glitter of the sea, a small boat bobbed, its single sail belled out. A Veniani fisherman's boat. He recognized the configuration instantly. Not something that spelled danger.

"It's just a fishing boat," he said.

"Is it?" she asked. She held out her cupped hands. Startled, Rowan watched them fill with sunlight like liquid honey. She formed the light into a globe and held it out. "Is it?" she said again. "Look here. Look harder."

Rowan bent forward, peering down at the glowing translucent globe in her hands. Dizziness swept over him. Light-headed and giddy, he tried to draw in a deep breath, but his throat closed on the air. He thought he heard her voice saying, "You must tell Athelin." Then he fell into the globe.

The bottom of the small boat scraped softly against the sand of the beach. Five men jumped out and pulled the little boat across the sand to a thick clump of sea pink. They cut the stiff stalks to cover the boat, then turned and made their way swiftly into the forest covering the lower flanks of the nearest mountain. In an hour, they had found themselves a hiding place overlooking the palace on the harbor below.

They waited as the sky overhead turned from radiant turquoise to luminous royal blue. Several men who were obviously soldiers left the palace and rode to the village by the harbor. The guard at the gates and in the watchtowers changed.

Presently, the light of torches and candles in the upper windows began to go out, one by one, and stars glimmered in the eastern sky even while a faint glow remained in the west.

The waiting men spoke quietly among themselves and agreed that what they wanted lay in the upper floors, probably the second story. They decided it would be best to wait until shortly before dawn, when sleep was heaviest and the will to resist would be at its lowest ebb in any guards still awake.

A few of them slept lightly as they waited. Some of them merely watched the darkened palace, fingering the keen edges of their swords to test their readiness. They had already chosen the place they would climb the wall, a spot halfway between two guard turrets with the roof of the bakehouse directly below on the other side. They expected no trouble. The Celae they had hunted like rabbits in the highlands of the

*west were stupid—almost as stupid as the Celae under Hakkar's spell.
They were beneath contempt. These Celae, for all their brave display of
posting guards, would be no different.*

Rowan snapped awake, gasping for breath. Sweat
streamed down his face. Nausea swirled uneasily in his belly,
and his heart seemed bent on tearing itself out of his chest.

"They're coming," he whispered aloud, then held his
breath, listening for something that might betray an
intruder's presence. The only sound in the room was Acaren's
untroubled breathing.

Rowan threw back the bedclothes and struggled out of
the bed. A wave of dizziness swept over him, nearly knocking
him to his knees. He steadied himself against the side of the
bed for a moment and tried to swallow the nausea clogging
his throat. Pain split his head and blurred his vision.

He had to find his father. He had to warn Athelin.

The polished wooden floor felt like ice beneath his bare
feet. He staggered against the walls of the corridor. The distance between the door to his room and his parents' chambers
seemed like miles.

He raised a fist that felt as if it were made out of lead and
banged on the door. The movement took all of his remaining
strength, and he could only lean against the wall, waiting for
Athelin to come into the corridor.

He didn't see the door open, but Athelin was suddenly
there, strong hands gripping his arms, holding him up. From
somewhere within the chamber, Dorlaine asked who was at
the door.

"It's Rowan," Athelin said. He put his hand beneath
Rowan's chin and lifted the boy's head so Rowan had to look
into his eyes. "What is it?" he asked. "Rowan, what's wrong?"

"Raiders," Rowan gasped. "Maedun raiders. They're
almost to the palace. They've come again . . ." He closed his
eyes, swallowing hard, afraid he could not contain the nausea.

Athelin took Rowan's shoulders in his hands gently to
steady him. "Where?" he demanded. "Where are they,
Rowan? Tell me where!"

"On the mountain," Rowan gasped. His head was about

to burst with the pain, and his skin burned with fever. "On Ben Warden. In the hazel copse."

"What is it, my lord?"

Mioragh's voice. Rowan had not heard him approach.

"Raiders," Athelin said. "Take care of Rowan."

"They're almost here," Rowan whispered. But Athelin was already gone. Rowan let himself sag into Mioragh's arms as darkness swirled around him and took him away.

The muted click of the key turning in the lock of the outer chamber door sounded loud in the stillness. Caennedd pulled the quilt higher around his throat and turned his back to the bedchamber door. He concentrated on making his breathing slow and regular despite the surge of his racing heart. If it was the guard checking on him, he must appear to be sleeping soundly.

He listened intently, straining his senses, but could not hear the door opening. The servants kept the hinges well oiled. But a moment later, he heard the soft sound of a careful footfall in the outer chamber. He tensed, every nerve in his body screaming.

"My lord?"

The quiet whisper was Tadwyr's. Caennedd flung back the bedclothes and leapt from the bed. He was already fully dressed down to his boots. He reached for his sword and cloak.

"I'm ready, Tadwyr," he said softly. "Is all clear?"

"Aye, my lord." He reached up to help Caennedd fasten his cloak. "The guard in the corridor is sleeping. I made sure he got a flagon of the same ale as the other guards. I've no doubt they're sleeping soundly now, too."

"Good. We won't be stopped?"

"No, my lord." Tadwyr stepped around to Caennedd's back and adjusted the sword harness. "There's no one to raise the alarm."

"Good man. And my soldiers?"

"Waiting for you, my lord."

"Then let's hurry." He strode to the main chamber and opened the outer door. The guard sat on the floor, slumped against the wall, hands resting slackly on his thighs and his chin lolling on his chest. Nothing moved but the flickering shadow cast by the torches along the walls. Caennedd stepped quickly out into the corridor and beckoned Tadwyr to follow.

The palace was so quiet, he could hear the hiss and flutter of the torch flames. He turned away from the main corridor, toward the other end of the hall and the servants' stairs that led down to the kitchens and the kitchen gardens and the small postern gate.

The kitchens were dark and deserted. They did not catch a glimpse of even the boy who tended the fires overnight. Only a sliver of moon hung in the sky above the craggy tor of Ben Roth, giving barely enough light to distinguish shadows. In less than an hour, the sky would begin to lighten toward dawn.

Keeping to the shadowed darkness beneath the overhanging currant bushes, they crept along the path to the little gate hidden among the fruit trees and berry bushes. Caennedd placed his feet carefully, hoping the faint crunch of gravel beneath the soles of his boots would not give them away if the guards were not as soundly sleeping as the one in the corridor outside his chambers.

Something moved ahead. Caennedd froze, peering intently into the gloom. *Something tall,* he thought. *A man?*

He put his hand to Tadwyr's arm and pulled the young man deeper into the shadows.

"I thought you said all the guards had some of the ale," he whispered.

"Aye, and they did, my lord," Tadwyr said.

Caennedd stared hard ahead, trying to penetrate the gloom. He watched while he counted off nearly fifty heartbeats. But nothing moved now. A gentle hint of breeze ruffled the leaves of the bush around him. It might, he conceded to himself, have been only a branch moving quietly in the breeze that he had seen. Not wishing to take any unnecessary chances, he waited another twenty heartbeats, just in case.

Nothing moved. He took a deep breath and again slipped out onto the little path. He was just about to reach for the latch on the gate when a man stepped out of the dense shadow by the gate, sword drawn and ready. Caennedd's heart leapt in his breast like a terrified deer. Before he could step back and reach for the sword across his back, another man came out of the shadow and a hand like an iron band closed about his sword arm just above the wrist. Horrified and startled speechless, his breath rasping in his throat, he realized he was surrounded. Surrounded and helpless.

9

Rowan hung limply in Athelin's arms, pale as death, his face twisted in real pain. Athelin hesitated for a moment, watching the boy intently. A true warning? A boy's nightmare?

But could he take the chance the warning was not a true one?

"Go, my lord Prince," Mioragh said. "You must. I'll take care of the boy."

Athelin nodded. "Of course," he said. He turned to find Dorlaine behind him, her sword strapped across her back. She held his own sword out to him and quickly helped him into the harness. By the time he was finished, Ralf and Cynric had joined them. On their way to the courtyard outside the Great Hall, Athelin explained what had happened.

"Get twelve men from the guard barracks and meet us at the postern gate," Athelin said. "No torches. No light at all. We can't take a chance of warning them we're coming after them."

"Aye, my lord." Cynric sketched a gesture with his hand toward his forehead, then he and Ralf ran together toward the barracks on the east side of the courtyard. Athelin and Dorlaine sped up the narrow stone stairway to the battlement walk along the curtain wall.

But no one challenged them as they approached the first turret; nor did anyone answer when Athelin called out. For a startled second, he thought the turret empty. Deserted. Then he realized the sentry sat slumped on the floor, back to the wall, chin down on chest, snoring gently.

White fury blazed in Athelin's chest. Sleeping on duty

was tantamount to a charge of treason. He aimed a kick at the sole of the sleeping man's boot.

"On your feet before your Prince, you imbecilic insect." He kept his voice soft, but anger turned his tone harsh and grating.

The soldier didn't move.

Athelin went to one knee and slapped the sentry. The open-handed blow snapped the man's head to one side, but still he didn't show any sign of feeling the blow. He clearly did not realize Athelin stood before him.

"What's wrong with him?" Dorlaine asked from behind him. "Is he dead? Poisoned?"

"Not dead," Athelin said. Frowning, he bent forward. A bitter, astringent odor rode on the sentry's breath. Not poison, then. But mayhaps a sleeping draught, and a powerful one at that.

Dorlaine bent down and sniffed. "Quillberry," she said. "Probably in his ale." She glanced at Athelin, her face a pale oval in the dim light. "Deliberate, then, but not his own idea."

Athelin got to his feet and ran to the next guard turret. Another sleeping, oblivious guard. And yet another in the next turret. Grimly, he glanced along the battlement wall. The pale light of the quarter moon picked out silvery angles and black, shadowy planes on the row of turrets. No doubt he would find only soundly sleeping guards in all of them.

"Caennedd," Athelin said.

"Caennedd?" Dorlaine repeated. "Surely not, Athelin."

"It was Caennedd," Athelin said. "Or it's his doing." He wasn't sure how he knew, but he had never been more certain of anything in his life.

"He wouldn't stoop to treason and treachery, would he?"

"Mayhaps not deliberately," Athelin said. "But I can see him doing it if he thought it would make it easier for him to slip away and take his troops over the Verge against my orders." He turned away, leaving the sleeping guard lying where he was. "We can deal with Caennedd later. Right now, we need to see what—or who—is on Ben Warden."

Only Cynric, Ralf, and three officers stood waiting for them at the postern gate. Cynric gestured toward the barracks.

"My lord, I can't —"

"Waken the guard," Athelin said. "I know. All the turret guards are asleep, too."

"Treachery?" Ralf asked, startled.

"Betrayal?" Cynric asked, his voice overlapping Ralf's.

"Not deliberate, I hope," Athelin said. "But we'll deal with that later. We've no time now."

"There are only seven of us," Ralf said. "How many men did Rowan say were on Ben Warden."

A brief flicker of amusement flashed through Athelin as he realized how completely Ralf had accepted Rowan's dream as a true Seeing. "Eight," he said.

Dorlaine smiled grimly. "And we have surprise with us," she said. "As good as five extra swords, I'm thinking."

A small sound broke the stillness. A footstep? Athelin threw up his hand. "Someone coming," he said. He stepped with Dorlaine back into the shadows of the wall. Within the space of two heartbeats, Ralf, Cynric, and the three officers had also vanished into the shadows.

The tall, shadowy form by the gate stepped forward and resolved itself into a man carrying a sword at the ready. He spoke in a harsh, angry voice. "Caennedd! Just how in the name of the Duality did you get down here?"

Caennedd prevented his heart from leaping straight out of his chest and through his teeth only because he recognized Athelin's voice even if he could not see his half brother's face in the dark. He took a deep breath to calm himself. His mind racing, he cast about desperately for a reasonable, logical-sounding explanation.

"We — we heard you hurrying out here and thought you might need some help," he said breathlessly.

"I see." Skepticism and sarcasm filled Athelin's voice. "And what happened to the guard I posted at your door? Did he obligingly step aside and let you through because you asked politely?"

Caennedd thought rapidly. "He —" he began, then changed his mind. Behind him, Tadwyr drew in his breath sharply in apprehension. Caennedd went on swiftly. "Isn't he with you? There was no one at the door when we came out. Was there, Tadwyr?"

"No, my lord." The lad's voice shook uncertainly. "No one there at all."

"I see," Athelin said. "Well, in any event, mayhaps it's as well you found us. We've word of raiders in the hills."

A cold chill settled around Caennedd's heart, clutched his belly in an icy grip. "Raiders?"

"Raiders," Athelin said. "Maedun. It would seem that all of the guards were otherwise occupied and didn't see them in time to give earlier warning."

"Then who—" Caennedd had to clear his throat. "How do you know there are raiders?"

"Rowan told us. He dreams true."

"I see." Caennedd shuddered. Magic was one thing he wanted no truck with.

"Come with us." Athelin turned and opened the small gate. Before Caennedd could protest or try to turn back, Cynric and Ralf fell in behind him. Their presence hung heavily over his head. Trying to escape with both of them behind him, and Athelin ahead of him, was hopeless. He might have a chance of making good his escape once the raiders had been taken care of.

If there were raiders in the first place. It was incredible that Athelin would put so much faith in a young boy's ridiculous dreams. It seemed too much of an amazing coincidence that the raiders would come on the night he had told Tadwyr to drug the guards. While there had been attempted raids before from the mainland, none of the raiders had made it past the shore guards.

He bit his lip. Of course, the guards had not been drugged on the other occasions. He shivered again, and followed Athelin at a swift jog-trot toward the fields along the bottom slopes of Ben Warden.

The battle was bloody, vicious, and shockingly brief. Guided by Rowan's dream, Athelin led his small troop along the hedgerows and low stone walls up the slopes of Ben Warden. They came upon the small hazel copse from above and took the Maedun raiders completely unaware, coming from an entirely unexpected direction. Nevertheless, the Somber Riders put up a grimly creditable defense.

Athelin had time only to note that the raiders wore the black uniform of Hakkar's soldiers—not a disguise, a uniform—before he had no more room for outside thought and lost himself in the concentration and effort of the battle.

The sword Bane, one of the fabled Rune Blades crafted uncounted generations ago by Wyfydd Smith for the first Prince of Skai, sang in his hand as he swung it. Its wild, fierce song reminded him of the primitive, keening wail of the pipes of Celi. It drew him in until he was one with the sword and it became as much a part of him as his arm or his breath.

Dorlaine fought solidly at his side, guarding his left as was her right and her privilege and her duty as his bheancoran. He didn't have to look to know she was there. Her presence danced and shimmered along the bond between them, alive in his heart and spirit. The bond of prince and bheancoran now, not man and woman or husband and wife. They had no need of speech or even conscious thought to move together like two dancers, two pieces of a matched set.

It ended abruptly with no warning. Athelin dispatched one raider, then turned to face another and found none. It startled him to see that dawn was a glow of royal blue and pale azure against the eastern sky. He could make out quite clearly Dorlaine's face, runnels of sweat trickling through the smear of blood on her left cheek and temple. She put her hand up and smudged it over a wider area as she tried to wipe it with her sleeve.

"Not mine," she said in reassurance. "But that's yours."

He looked down. A wide strip of fabric from the left sleeve of his tunic hung down across his wrist, sodden with blood from a wound on his upper arm. It had already stopped bleeding, and the blood had congealed into thick ropes along his forearm. He didn't know when it had happened; hadn't felt it at all until Dorlaine pointed it out. As he looked, it began to throb with each pulsebeat, painful but bearable.

Ralf stepped forward, leaning on his sword, using it as a staff to help keep himself erect.

"Are you hurt?" Athelin demanded.

"No, my lord," Ralf said. "Just winded. I need to spend more time with Weymund on the practice field, I think."

Athelin allowed himself a small smile. "I, too, I think."

Ralf glanced over his shoulder. "It's too late for Tadwyr," he said quietly. "The lad's dead. He took a mortal wound in the chest and died in my arms."

Athelin closed his eyes, resigned grief washing through him. Tadwyr had been a promising young man, and his father was a good friend. "May his soul be shining bright so the Duality find him quickly," he said.

Ralf bowed his head, then glanced up. "He told me before he died that he had put something in the guards' ale," he said, his voice too low to carry beyond the small circle of himself, Dorlaine, and Athelin. "He said Caennedd gave the bottle of sleeping potion to him. He wanted my forgiveness. Said he didn't want to die with that on his soul."

"It comes as no surprise," Athelin said wearily.

"I smelled quillberry in the guard turrets," Dorlaine said. "We thought it was Caennedd's work. I didn't want to believe it at first. It would appear we have little choice now."

"My lord?"

Athelin turned at the sound of Cynric's voice. Cynric knelt beside a crumpled figure in the wan light, his hand at the man's throat.

"Your brother, my lord," Cynric said quietly.

Athelin looked down at the wounded man. He could find no grief or sorrow in him at the sight of his brother's body. "Will he live?" he asked coldly.

"I'm not sure," Cynric said. "It's a bad wound. Mayhaps Mioragh's arts can Heal him. In any event, he's still breathing."

"Then bring him back to the Keep. And find Mioragh and bring him to me. I'll be in my chambers."

His hair still damp from his bath, a pad of clean, white bandage on his arm, Athelin went to the window of his chamber and looked out at Ben Warden. From where he stood, the hazel copse was little more than an anonymous blotch of darker green against the gentle green of the upslope meadows and pastures. He could hardly distinguish the dark figures of his men moving among the foliage. The bodies of the dead Somber Riders would be buried in an unmarked grave farther up the slopes of Ben Warden. Tadwyr would be brought down to the shrine for burial, attended to by the High Priest and Priestess.

He turned from the window as the door opened. Dorlaine slipped quietly into the room, her skin still glowing from the scrubbing that had rid her of the stains of Maedun blood.

"How is he?" Athelin asked.

"Rowan's sleeping peacefully," she said. "He seems none the worse for his dreaming true. I was worried about him. He looked so ill when he came in here."

He ran his hand through his hair, then shook his head. "Dreaming true isn't supposed to be that hard on the dreamer," he said. "It doesn't make me ill. I don't ever remember it making my father ill, either."

"But both of you had found your magic, and Rowan has not." She crossed the room to join him by the window. He put his right arm around her, and she rested her cheek against his shoulder. "Rowan is still so young. Only seven."

"At seven I had a fair sense of my magic, such as it is," he said. "Not strong, as my father's was, of course. But enough to resonate with Bane now."

"But your father didn't come into his own magic until he was a grown man," she said. "Mayhaps Rowan won't, either."

"But it's there," he said. "His magic is there. My father never knew he had magic until he found it suddenly. Rowan's is there, and we all know it, especially him. He just can't seem to manage it yet. Not his fault. Nor Mioragh's. Something will happen to give him the control he needs."

"But what?"

"I don't know. And neither does Mioragh. I wish we did." He traced the line of her jaw with his thumb. "If he—"

A knock on the door interrupted him. Dorlaine left the shelter of his arm and went to answer it. Mioragh came in, his robes snagged, burrs and twigs still clinging to the hem. Athelin turned to meet him, frowning.

"Well?" Athelin demanded. "What did you find?"

Mioragh plucked a cocklebur from his sleeve and flicked it into the fireplace. "Nothing, my lord," he said. "I searched all eight of the Somber Riders thoroughly, and went over the whole area using my fingers as a rake." He held up grass- and dirt-stained hands. "Nothing. I found no trace at all of anything even remotely resembling a Tell-Tale stone. Nothing."

"You're certain?"

"Absolutely, my lord Athelin. As certain as I can be." He brushed his hands together and regarded the broken fingernails in patent disgust. "One of the Maedun was still alive. We—that is the soldiers you sent and I—questioned him. He knew nothing of a Tell-Tale stone. He had never heard of one. They came across the Skerryrace only for the sport of the hunt, he told us."

"Sport? You're sure?"

"Aye, my lord. Reasonably. The man was only a common soldier. Not an officer. Granted, an officer might not have mentioned anything about a Tell-Tale to a common soldier, but the man said they had all come only for some sport. Hunting, he said. There's a bounty paid for killing any Tyadda."

"Bounty," Athelin said in angry revulsion. "Sport. By all the seven gods and goddesses. Sport! Paaah!"

Mioragh nodded grimly in agreement. "Nevertheless," he went on, "I made sure the masking spell was still strong around Rowan."

"And the Somber Rider?" Athelin said. "What did you do with him? Bring him down to the infirmary?"

Mioragh gave him a bland, unreadable glance. "My lord, he died," he said without expression.

"I see." Athelin got to his feet. "Then come with me, Mioragh. We have dealt satisfactorily with the Maedun. Now we must deal with my brother."

Caennedd lay in his bed, unmoving, attended by one of the priestesses from the shrine. His face against the pillow slip was an unpleasant gray, his lips a bloodless blue. His eyelids appeared nearly transparent. The rise and fall of his chest was nearly indiscernible. The coverlet came up only to his waist. Strips of bandage swathed his chest and left shoulder, blindingly white against his skin.

The priestess sat in a chair by his head, watching him, while her fingers moved quietly in her lap making the sign of the Unbroken Circle of birth, life, death, and rebirth. She glanced up as Athelin entered with Mioragh and shook her head slightly.

"No change, Mioragh." Her voice, trained since childhood, sounded incongruously musical and sweet in the sickroom. "It's almost as if he's given up."

"I shouldn't wonder," Athelin said grimly. "Thank you, Meaghan. You may go now."

She rose and inclined her head in a polite and gracious acknowledgment to Athelin, then slipped gracefully out of the room. Athelin stepped forward and looked down at Caennedd.

"Is he dying, Mioragh?" he asked.

"He shouldn't be," Mioragh said, mild exasperation creeping into his voice. "He won't let me help him. He flatly refused to let me try to Heal him."

"We'll see about that," Athelin said. He sat in the chair the priestess had vacated and leaned forward. "Caennedd, can you hear me? Caennedd, it's Athelin. Wake up. Wake up and speak with me."

Caennedd didn't answer, but his eyebrows twitched as if in pain.

"He can't hear you, my lord," Mioragh said.

"I'm sure he can," Athelin said. "Caennedd, wake up. I must speak with you now."

Slowly, Caennedd turned his head on the pillow to face Athelin. He opened his eyes as if even that tiny movement was torture. He put his tongue out to try to moisten his lips.

"Where's Tadwyr?" he asked, his voice sounding like the whisper of the breeze in dry reeds. "Where is he? They wouldn't tell me where he's gone."

"To Annwn," Athelin said bluntly. "He's dead, Caennedd."

Again, the shadow of a grimace of pain flashed across
Caennedd's face. "I feared as much."

"He died because you were stupid and self-centered and
arrogant," Athelin said. "It was only sheerest luck that everyone in the Keep didn't die with him."

Caennedd turned his head away. "Then go away and let
me get on with this dying of mine," he said. "Tadwyr will be
revenged."

"Tadwyr is already avenged," Athelin said. "All the
invading Somber Riders are dead, including the one who
killed Tadwyr. Come to that, you're avenged, too. But you
won't need it."

"I'm nearly dead now."

"No, you're not," Athelin said. "And there's only one reason you're not dead, and that's because I'm not sure if order-
ing you executed as a traitor would make me a kinslayer." His
carefully controlled anger squeezed into his voice, making his
words harsh and grating. He took a deep breath to calm himself. "I have no wish to arrive at the Portal of Annwn with a
kinslaying on my soul, so you live."

Caennedd's chuckle was thin and bloodless. "So you'll
just let me die by myself, is that it?"

"No," Athelin said. "I don't think so." He glanced up at
Mioragh. "Can you Heal a man against his will?" he asked.
"If he doesn't and won't cooperate with you?"

Mioragh frowned thoughtfully, doubt tracing deep lines
in his cheeks. "I'm not sure, my lord," he said. He raised one
eyebrow, obviously intrigued in spite of himself. "It's an interesting question. I'm not sure anyone's ever tried it." Black
humor twisted the corner of his mouth. "Most people are
rather anxious and grateful for the services of a Healer." He
frowned again. "I'm not sure if I have enough strength to do
it without his cooperation."

"You can Heal an unconscious man," Athelin said.
"Unconscious men don't cooperate."

"True." Mioragh stepped closer to the bed and bent to
place his hands on Caennedd's chest above the padding of
bandage. Caennedd tried to twist away from the touch, but
had not the strength. Mioragh pressed both hands hard down

on Caennedd's chest, his face blank and rigid with the strength of his concentration. Athelin thought he saw the Healing power, like threads of translucent green-and-blue ribbon, flash down Mioragh's arms, curl around his wrists, then plunge down into Caennedd's chest.

Caennedd cried out. His body convulsed, back arching to raise him off the bed. His eyes stared wide and startled, then he collapsed back onto the bed, shuddering and gasping for breath. Mioragh stood up, his face as gray as Caennedd's had been, drooping with fatigue.

"It's done, my lord," he whispered.

Athelin put a hand on Mioragh's shoulder. "Thank you, my friend," he said quietly. "Now go and rest. You've nearly exhausted yourself. I need to have some private words with my brother."

Mioragh nodded, and shuffled to the door. Athelin waited until he had gone, then turned back to Caennedd. Caennedd lay on the bed, breathing like a man who had been winded and was trying to recover his breath. Color had returned to his face, but his lips still retained a little of their blue coloration from the blood he had lost. While Athelin watched, he managed to get his breathing under control and turned his head to look at him. The movement seemed easy and painless.

"Now what, brother?" Caennedd asked, a trace of his old disdain and derision in his voice.

"Now," Athelin said very quietly, "I think I'm about to grant you your heart's desire, brother."

Caennedd's eyes went wide. He tried to sit up, but Athelin pushed him back on the bed.

"To Skai?" Caennedd asked. "You mean I'm to go to Skai to fight the Maedun?" He laughed, half in triumph, half in disbelief. "I knew you'd come around to seeing reason, Athelin. I knew it." He laughed again and raised his hands to his face, cupping his cheeks in wonder and delight. "Oh, Deity, this is marvelous."

"You'll fight Maedun," Athelin said. "Oh, yes, for certain you'll fight Maedun. But not in Skai."

Caennedd raised himself up on one elbow and stared at Athelin. "Not in Skai? But—"

"You'll go to Tyra," Athelin said. "This isn't a granting of a boon, Caennedd. Make no mistake about that. This is a banishment. I want you gone. I want you as far away from Skerry as is possible. I want to give you no more opportunities to betray us in our beds. You'll go to Tyra, and you'll be attached to one of the Laird of Glenborden's companies of soldiers. With a little luck and some skill, mayhaps you'll raise yourself to the rank of an officer in a couple of years. And I promise you, you'll have all the fighting against Somber Riders you can stomach, and then some. You'll most certainly come face-to-face with the sorcery you claim is only a fable."

He got up, ignoring Caennedd's protests, and left the room.

"They grow up so fast," Dorlaine said. "Gabhain's nearly a man and the twins have grown a handbreadth since Imbolc."

"They'll have to grow faster," Athelin said. "Early to Weymund. Early to their first hunt."

She glanced at him, startled. "So early—" She stopped and put her hand to her mouth. "Oh, no," she whispered. "It's not time to tell them, is it? Not yet, surely."

He closed his eyes and shook his head. "Soon," he said. "We can't hold it back much longer. They have to know."

"Of course," she said. She looked away for a moment and he thought he saw a flash of pain cross her face. Finally, she turned to him. "Ceitryn must go to Tyra," she said. "To keep her safe. The raids will continue, and I can't take any chances that she'll be hurt."

"She'll be safe with us—"

"No," she said. She looked up at him, her eyes bright with tears. "Don't you see, Athelin? I'm your bheancoran. I belong beside you; it's my duty and my privilege to guard your left. I—I can't do it as I should when I'm worried about Ceitryn."

"But you worry about the boys, too."

"Of course I do. But the boys will be warriors. Ceitryn will be a Healer. We can't afford to take any chances with her. It would be different if she were to be bheancoran, but she won't be. And I can't split my heart like this again. It will break it to send her away for fostering with Rhuidri and Peigi, but I'll know she'll be safe there."

He took her into his arms. "Soon, then," he said. "We'll go when Caennedd goes."

The gate of the small garden hung open in the clear silver light of the moon. Running as hard as he could, Rowan flung out his hand to catch the gatepost and catapult himself through the gate and into the garden. He tried to call her name, but nothing came to his lips.

The garden stood empty and abandoned. The perfume of the roses drifted in the air, and the leaves of the fruit trees whispered quietly to themselves in the faint breeze. No figure in a yellow gown stood by the rosebushes.

"Where are you?" he called.

No answer came to him in the night. He pulled in a deep breath to steady himself, and looked around. On the stone bench where Dorlaine often sat with her needlework lay a single rose, its petals limp and withering. Rowan picked it up and studied it, frowning.

It should mean something to him, he knew. But for the life of him, he couldn't remember what it was. Like the lyrics of an old ballad, words echoed in his head.

"Forget me not, beloved. . . ."

It was eight years before she came again to his dreams. By then, he had all but forgotten her completely.

10

Acaren's voice, low and struggling against laughter, came out of the darkness in a near-perfect imitation of the High Priest Nemwd's consciously sonorous tones.

"There are eight hinges of the year."

Rowan chuckled, and replied with the same inflection in his voice: "And there are eight hinges to life."

"Vernal Equinox."

"Conception and quickening."

"Beltane."

"Birth."

"Summer Solstice."

"Childhood." Rowan muffled another laugh. "Acaren, we ought not to be making sport of this."

"I know. But Nemwd invites it so much. Lammas."

"Adulthood, upon which we are about to embark."

"In great trepidation." Laughter bubbled thickly in Acaren's voice. "Autumnal Equinox."

"Marriage. . . . Speaking of marriage. I'll wager you anything that Gabhain and Valessa pair off at Beltane this spring."

"He's been mooning over her for six years now. She may well be his bheancoran, but I don't think she's quite as smitten as he is. Samhain."

"Parenthood. Oh dear, I hope not yet."

"Shh. Keep your voice down. If Loisa hears, we'll scandalize her and she'll faint dead away. Midwinter Eve."

"Old age and wisdom. Oh, Acaren, really." Rowan sat up. "Old age. Ugh. And wisdom? Us?"

"Better it should happen first to Gabhain. Imbolc."

Rowan made a strangled sound, a perfect imitation of a long, gargling death rattle. "Death," he moaned, with all the dramatic, chilling hollowness he could put into his voice, and flopped back bonelessly onto his bed.

Acaren tried to muffle his laughter in his pillow, but failed dismally. "Do you think the High Priest has any idea how pompous he sounds?" he asked.

"Likely not," Rowan replied, remarkably lifelike for someone who had just passed the portal into Annwn. "We should try to sleep. We have to be up with the dawn."

Acaren sat up suddenly, struck by a stupefying thought. "Rowan, suppose we don't make a kill—"

"We will."

"But suppose we don't?"

Rowan refused to entertain the idea. "Acaren, belt up and go to sleep."

She was waiting for him as he began to dream. Not in the little walled garden this time, but on a wide and empty plain. Behind her loomed the vast, soaring bulk of a cone-shaped mountain, taller by half again than the surrounding mountains. It seemed to reach up to scrape the clouds. Rowan found himself gazing up at the mountain, smiling. So that was what Cloudbearer looked like, he thought. All his life, he'd heard of the massive mountain, sacred to all the seven gods and goddesses of Celi and Skai. Somehow, it didn't surprise him to find himself beside it in his dream.

"So, finally you've come again."

He turned. The girl stood ankle-deep in the dew-soaked grass. This time, she wore her hair long and straight, and instead of the shining red-gold, it was a gleaming, nearly white-blond. But her eyes were still the soft gray of mist on an autumn morning, and she carried her supple body in the familiar, confident manner. In spite of the changes, he knew her. As if he'd seen her only yesterday and not eight years ago, he smiled at her.

"You've forgotten again," she said, mildly accusatory, as if she expected nothing less.

"No, I haven't. I remember you."

"But only in dreams."

"Of course," he said. "You're part of my dream."

"Oh, of course," she said with exaggerated patience. "Well, time enough for that later. You'll forget me again. But do you remember this?"

She waved her hand in a sweeping gesture to take in the whole of the plain around her. He followed the movement of her hand and saw for the first time the massive Dance of stone silhouetted against the glow of the sky.

He had arrived in that mystic, transitional time between sunset and dusk, when the sky was still streaked with light and color. Bands of red and orange flamed in the west, illuminating the triple ring of standing stones set in the center of the flat plain. The imposing menhirs of the outer ring stood starkly black against the luminescent sky, crowned in pairs by massive lintels to form trilithons. The middle ring of stones bulked slightly smaller, gracefully joined all around by capstones, polished like jet to reflect the incandescent glow of the sky. The inner ring, standing alone without lintels, was not really a ring at all, but a horseshoe of seven menhirs enclosing a low altar stone that reflected the burning sky like a mirror. It reminded Rowan of a jewel cradled safe in cupped and loving hands.

"Do you know this place?" she asked.

"The Dance of Nemeara," he whispered, touched with awe.

"At least you don't forget that," she said. "Well, don't just stand there. Go in."

He turned to her, his heart suddenly beating too fast. "In there? Are you jesting?"

"Of course not. You must go in."

"But I don't want to. I—I can't."

She folded her arms adamantly across her chest. "How do you ever expect to know anything if you won't go in there?"

He looked over his shoulder at the Dance, and shuddered. The forbidding bulk of the stones both repelled him and called irresistibly to him.

"No," he whispered.

"Yes," she said gently. "Please, Rowan. You must. You know you must."

He took a deep breath, knowing she was right. No matter what awaited him in the Dance, he had to go in to find out for himself.

The moon rose, full and clear. The Dance became a place of hard, black shadows and pale, washed silver. Rowan sat cross-legged, his

*back against the residual warmth of the polished black altar stone. As
the moon lifted behind the shoulder of Cloudbearer and climbed into the
black, star-dazzled sky, he watched it, envying its serenity. A dreamy
lethargy crept through his body. He wasn't sure when Acaren had
arrived to take his place beside him, and wasn't even sure that it was
Acaren who sat there with him, but he was barely aware of his twin's
soft breathing where Acaren sat with his legs drawn up, forearms
propped on his knees. They had been quiet for a long time now. Rowan
had no idea how long, but there was no sense of strain in the easy
silence.*

*The moon cast a strange pattern of light and shadow on the seven
pillars of the inner horseshoe. Startled, Rowan studied them with
renewed curiosity. How had he failed to notice the deep carving in the
stones before this? It looked for all the world as if the figures of men
and women had been cut in bas-relief into the stone. They appeared
queerly alive.*

*As he watched with growing interest, he suddenly realized they
really were men and women. They stood quietly, still as stones, but
relaxed and at ease in the moon-shot night. One by one, he recognized
them.*

*They were all there. Rhianna of the Air, her long, moon-silvered
hair floating like a veil about her body. Cernos of the Forest, with the
tall rack of stately antlers rising from his brow. Adriel of the Waters,
carrying her enchanted ewer. Gerieg of the Crags, with his mighty
hammer that smote the peaks and shook the ground, spilling great
landslips down the crags. Beodun of the Fires, carrying in one hand the
lamp of benevolent fire and, in the other, the lightning bolt of wildfire.
Sandor of the Plain, his hair blowing like prairie grass around his
face. And the darlai, the Spirit of the Land, the Mother of All, smiling
in compassion and tenderness.*

*They waited in companionable silence. Rowan felt a mild amaze-
ment because he wasn't startled or frightened. Something not quite
audible broke the silence, something just under the threshold of hearing. A new shadow spilled across the silvered grass. The tall figure of a
man stood framed by the gateway trilithon. Silently as a shadow, he
moved to stand between the capped menhirs of the second ring of standing stones. Acaren—or the young man who might or might not have
been Acaren—scrambled to his feet as the man stepped between the*

stones and approached the altar. Rowan rose more slowly, staring as hard as Acaren.

The man wore a long robe, pale in the moonlight, girdled by something that glinted like gold. His hair and beard, silver as the moon itself, framed a face carved into austere planes and hollows, the eyes shadowed by silver eyebrows. In his hands, he carried something long and narrow, and the flash and sparkle of stars blazed at one end.

Quietly, the man crossed the grass toward the altar, his feet making no disturbance among the young, green blades. He gave the impression of vast age and wisdom, but moved with the lithe grace of a youth.

Rowan's muscles tightened convulsively. The Guardian of the Dance. This was the man who inhabited myriad tales and ballads. But if he was dreaming the Dance, surely he would dream the Guardian, too.

The robed man stopped, facing Acaren, close enough to reach out and touch him. "Acaren Firstborn," he said, his voice akin to the whisper of the breeze in reeds.

"Aye, my lord?" Acaren's reply came hoarse and raw from his dry throat.

A smile caused a ripple to shimmer through the white cascade of the man's beard. "I am called Myrddyn, and I am the guardian of this place. I have a gift for you."

"I have no need of gifts, my lord," Acaren said, sounding breathless.

"You will very shortly have need of this." The Guardian stepped forward, the long bundle held before him. "Hold out your hands then, Acaren Firstborn. Accept the sword of Wyfydd Smith."

Acaren held out his hands. The Guardian placed the bundle across his palms. It was a sword in a worn leather scabbard. The hilt, bound in stained leather, was unadorned except for a faceted crystal gem on the pommel.

"Draw the sword," the Guardian said.

Acaren grasped the scabbard in his left hand and drew the sword with his right. Runes glinted along the blade, flashing shards of light like the points of a gem.

"Can you read the runes?" the Guardian asked.

*Acaren held the blade closer to his face. He dropped the scabbard and reached up to trace the carved figures with two fingers. **"Take up the Strength of Celi,"** he murmured in surprise.*

The Guardian turned the blade in Acaren's hands. "And these?"

Acaren traced them, frowning, then shook his head. "No," he said at last. "These I can't read."

The Guardian smiled. "You will when it's time," he said. "Do you know its name?"

"Surely not Heartfire," Acaren said doubtfully.

The Guardian smiled. "Mayhaps," he said. "Mayhaps not. You'll know soon."

Acaren held the sword up to the light of the moon and stars. Rowan had the strangest sensation of merging with Acaren, becoming one with his twin. Acaren's awe quivered in Rowan's chest, and he saw the sword through Acaren's eyes, felt the ridged leather wrappings of the hilt against his own palms.

The sword began to resonate in Acaren's hands. Softly at first, then faster and faster, until Rowan swore it was alive. He became aware of a high, clear, sweet tone singing in the air around them, like a note plucked from a harp string in the highest register. At the same time, the blade began to shimmer, then to glow. At first, like the musical note, softly and gently. Acaren's hands on the hilt trembled, and his whole body quivered like the air just before a lightning strike as the vibration traveled from the sword into him, but it was Rowan whose skin shivered with it.

The musical note increased in pitch and volume, wild and keen, sharp and distinct as shards of crystal in the circle of the Dance. Overtones of triumphant jubilation sang in the note with shades and subtle nuances of burgeoning power. As the harmonic tone increased in pitch and intensity, so did the gleam of the blade. It moved swiftly through red to orange, then to yellow until it was incandescent white, burning with a radiance to rival the sun, too painful to look at directly. The whole spectrum of the rainbow swirled and spun in wild patterns, edging the looming standing stones in flashing patterns of coruscating color. The joyous chord rang wildly in the air. Rowan had the distinct impression of something awakening and stretching after a long sleep.

The runes blazed bright and clear, flashing silver fire back to the gibbous moon. The words ran like liquid flame along the length of the blade with a life of their own, searing their eyes with unbearable brilliance.

Surrounded by a brilliant corona of light and color, Acaren spread his arms wide, brandishing the sword with a flourish around the *inner horseshoe. He cried out in a strange mixture of elation, triumph, and fear.*

Acaren stood transfixed, staring at the sword he held. A faint twinge of envy pricked at Rowan's belly. Even if Acaren was not yet aware of what the gift of the sword meant, Rowan knew. He wanted desperately to know Celi needed him as much as it needed Acaren.

A woman's soft laughter behind him spun him around, startled and breathless. She had stepped from her place in the center of the horseshoe, tall, graceful, but obviously no longer young. Her dark hair, streaked with silver, hung down across her shoulders and framed a face more kind than beautiful. She reached out to touch his cheek, and a rich, quiet sense of peace filled Rowan's heart.

"Why do you long for a destiny not yours, Rowan Secondborn?" she asked, her tone whimsical. "Do you hunger after glory and fame?"

The heat of shame climbed in Rowan's cheeks. "No, Lady," he said. "I know whose is the glory. I've always known."

"Yes, you have. You're very like him, do you know?"

"Like who?" he asked, startled.

She laughed softly. "Your ancestor, Donaugh the Enchanter. But do you know who I am?"

"You are the Mother of All," he said. "The darlai of the land."

"I am the living spirit of Celi, Rowan Secondborn," she said. "I am Celi herself, and my gift to you will make itself as apparent as the sword your brother carries. You will be mine again as you were before, and my gift will be with you always."

"With me? But I have not the wisdom, Lady. . . ."

"Wisdom I cannot grant you, my child. But you will know the path Acaren and the sword must take. Search your soul, and you will know." She touched his cheek once more, and her fingers scorched his skin with a stab of pain hardly distinguishable from ecstasy.

She stepped back. Rowan stumbled forward and reached out to her. "Lady . . ."

But there was nothing around him but silent megaliths, thrusting upward from the spring carpet of grass. Even the moon was gone, and the first pale hint of dawn stained the eastern sky.

Rowan came out of sleep, gasping for breath, fragments of his dream swirling around him. He sat up and swung his feet over the side of his bed, trying to control his breathing.

A dream. Another dream. Of a tall mountain. And a girl. And the Dance of Nemeara. He scrubbed his hands across his face. Yes, the Dance of Nemeara. This time, he was certain he had been speaking with the gods and goddesses.

The last of the dream shards glittered, then slowly faded to nothing. He drew in a deep breath, let it out slowly, and smiled to himself.

How very odd. He believed in the gods and goddesses, of course. But he wasn't sure they actually appeared as men and women to anyone with offers of help. That was fine for ballads and stories, but certainly it couldn't be real. He honored them, but he thought he might prefer not to share their company.

Acaren lay oblivious in sleep in the other bed. Rowan lay down and pulled the coverlet up around his shoulders. He needed sleep. In the morning, he and Acaren would be on Ben Aislin, each seeking game on his own. A harsh test, hunting alone. But worth it. Well worth it.

As he closed his eyes, he remembered—or thought he remembered—the face of a young girl. Blond hair and gray eyes? Or red-gold hair and gray eyes?

He couldn't remember, so he dismissed her from his mind as negligible. He needed sleep now more than he needed to remember what a girl in a dream looked like.

Alone in the forest on the slopes of Ben Aislin, Rowan followed the tracks of the deer. Beneath the high cloud, the air was so cold and so clear, he thought he could hear it ring like tapped crystal as he moved. He was very cold. No residual warmth remained in his belly from the heated wine he had drunk with Acaren before they set out, each to a different side of the forest. His short cloak was little protection from the biting cold. Within his boots, his feet grew numb, and he worried the dry squeaking of the snow beneath them as he moved would warn the deer of his approach. He didn't know if he could bear the disgrace of returning from his first hunt without a kill.

The deer he followed was in no hurry, picking its way carefully around the trees and high drifts of snow. Rowan shifted the strap of his quiver to a more comfortable position on his shoulder and looked ahead. He saw no flicker of movement through the bare trees to indicate he was any closer to the deer than he had been when he found the trail. He began walking again, careful how he placed his feet.

As he entered a small clearing, the sun flashed out from between the clouds for a moment. Against the sudden bright dazzle of the sun on the snow, he saw something move. He froze next to the dark bole of an oak and squinted into the glare.

Above a thick copse of bare hazel trees, he saw the antlers of a stag. His breath came out in a long, slow hiss. He counted nine points on each antler. A huge stag. Keeping his movements slow and deliberate, he nocked an arrow and drew aim at where he thought the stag's chest would be.

"Stay," a voice commanded.

Startled, Rowan spun around. His breath caught in his throat in wild astonishment as he saw the woman who stood behind him.

She was naked in the bitter air, her skin like warm ivory against the blue-white glitter of the snow. Her hair was also white, the white-silver of moonlight rather than age, and it hung about her body like a cloak to her knees. Her eyes were large and wide, the same green as the glacier-fed Afon and her lips the delicate pink of cherry blossoms. She seemed to glow with a soft radiance there by the dark trunk of the oak. She was the most beautiful woman Rowan had ever seen.

"Stay your arrow, Rowan Secondborn," she said again. "See who your arrow would have pierced."

Rowan tore his gaze from the woman and looked across the clearing. A man stepped out from behind the copse of hazel. He stood taller than any man Rowan had ever known, and he was as naked in the cold as was the woman. From his forehead grew the great rack of antlers Rowan had seen. Stunned, Rowan fell to his knees.

"Cernos of the Forest," he breathed.

The woman came to stand in front of him. Her slender

bare feet appeared barely to touch the ground, so lightly did she move. She shimmered before him, and he knew her at last. He bowed his head. A deep, hard shuddering began in his belly; a shiver that wasn't entirely from the cold.

"My Lady," he said softly. "Do I dream?"

The woman smiled. "In a way," she said. "You know me now, Rowan Secondborn?"

"Rhianna of the Air—"

She reached out and put her long, white fingers to his forehead. Her delicate touch burned like fire and froze like ice, yet was gently reassuring and soothing. Rowan's shivering stopped abruptly. "You are mine, Rowan Secondborn," she said. "If you meet my tests, the time will come when I will claim you. For now, know only that I have provided for you. And for your brother. Listen."

From far across the forest came the trilling warble of a horn announcing a kill. Its ethereal fluting echoed off the cliffs above the forest, like drops of silver in the air.

"A stag for Acaren," said Rhianna of the Air, smiling. "For you, this . . ."

Rowan heard a crashing sound as something very large blundered through the trees. He scrambled to his feet, reaching for his bow, fumbling for an arrow.

A huge boar the size of a half-grown deer burst out of the trees on the other side of the small clearing. It paused for a moment, its tiny eyes blinking in the sudden brightness. It shook its head and broke into a lumbering run straight for Rowan, its red mouth open. The tusks, sharp and deadly as spearpoints, to either side of that evil mouth, were as long as Rowan's forearms.

The boar was incredibly fast for an animal with its bulk. His heart pounding louder than the thunder of the boar's hooves on the frozen ground, Rowan loosed his arrow, saw it sink into the dark, thick skin covering the mound of flesh on the boar's shoulder. The animal stumbled, but didn't fall. Rowan leapt aside as the boar swept past. The point of one of the boar's tusks scraped against his thigh, slashing through his breeks and slicing deep into the skin and muscle below.

Rowan felt the hot blood pouring down his leg as he nocked another arrow.

The momentum of the boar's charge had carried it a good distance beyond Rowan. It turned, shook its head and charged again. An icy calm descended over Rowan. He drew back the arrow, took careful aim, and let fly. The arrow went straight and true to its target, piercing the heart of the boar. Dead but not knowing it, the boar continued to run. Rowan leapt back, his calm shattered, and prepared to shoot again. But the boar stumbled and fell, its tusks only inches from Rowan's booted foot. It grunted once, then its enraged little eyes glazed over and it was dead.

Panting, Rowan ripped a strip from the bottom of his tunic and quickly bound up the gash in his thigh. When he had the bleeding under control, he looked up.

There was no sign of the woman, nor of the man with the stag's antlers. When Rowan looked around, he could find no trace of the tracks of the stag he had followed to this clearing. Nor had the woman left any footprints in the snow. Nothing at all broke the clean surface of the snow in the clearing but the trampled path of the boar and the bright blood that had spilled from Rowan's thigh.

"I dreamed," he said aloud, wonderingly. "I was so cold, I dreamed." But the dead boar was real enough. Rowan limped over to the oak and leaned against it, still panting. When he had his breath back, he put two fingers to his mouth and whistled shrilly. All he had to do was sit back and wait for his father's men to find him and blow the horn to announce his first kill.

Somewhere in the back of his mind, he knew he had not dreamed. The vision of Rhianna was as real as the boar's blood mixed with his own in the snow. He thought he heard a girl's sweet, distant voice, laughing at him in tolerant amusement.

11

Rowan stood quietly in the chamber he shared with Acaren and let Rhan adjust the folds of the plain white short tunic around him, a tunic identical to the one flung carelessly across Acaren's bed, awaiting his return from the bathhouse. Identical to the tunic worn by Rhan, and by every man and woman old enough to take part in the rites of Beltane. On Beltane night around the fire, every man was an incarnation of the god and every woman the goddess. A serving girl could offer her cup of mead to a prince, or a queen to a stableboy.

Rowan clenched his hands behind him as Rhan fussed with the drape of the light wool fabric. He wondered if an incarnation of the god on this night was supposed to feel this hollow with despair.

He stepped away from Rhan. "Thank you, Rhan. That will do nicely, I think. Best you go and see to your own preparations."

Rhan bowed. "Thank you, my lord Rowan," he said, formally accepting the dismissal. Then he grinned. "May you drink deep of the golden mead tonight."

Rowan managed a smile. "Thank you," he said. *But it wasn't the mead*, he thought. *It was the magic.* Beltane Eve glittered with magic. The threads of power, strengthened by the music of the joyous celebration, moved through the air and earth like the tides of the ocean, powerful and soul-deep. The threads he could sense, he could feel were there, but he could not touch them. Could not use them.

Rowan went to stand by the window. Twilight had deepened to dusk. On the slopes of Ben Warden, the last logs would be now laid upon the firebed. The young priest and priestess whose dance would begin the rites had been sequestered in the shrine since midnight yesterday, undergoing the secret rituals of preparation. Within the hour, they would lead the procession up the mountain to the oak glade, sheltered beneath the green silken canopy.

Rowan remembered other Beltane nights when he had stood by this window, able to see the glow of the fire against the dark flank of Ben Warden, able to hear the eerie wail of the pipes of Celi, but unable to see much else. His imagination had provided enough detail then to leave him breathless and light-headed, a turgid churning in the bottom of his belly.

This Beltane night, he was a man, able to participate in the festival. No longer a youth, but a man in his own right. His grandfather Gareth had not come into his magic until he was a man. Even Donaugh the Enchanter had not come into his own magic until he was sixteen. But the fire feast of Imbolc marking his own sixteenth Name Day had come and gone, and not brought him any measure of control over his magic.

He had expected something to happen after the coming-of-age rite of his first hunt. He had, after all, dreamed of Rhianna of the Air, and of Cernos of the Forest. But nothing more had come of it except that he had spent several painful hours having his wound attended to by Mioragh, who berated him for being careless.

He remembered the clear, clean slice of the arrow through the air as it left his bow, and the bonelessly final sprawl of the boar, nearly at his feet. Then came the haunting warble of the horn announcing his first kill only moments after the horn had declared Acaren's stag. There had been feasting and overflowing cups in Athelin's Great Hall that night, and the sun the next morning was far too bright for a head filled with wine-sickness.

But no magic. Never any magic for him.

Year after year, the blight was growing, moving inexorably farther north, higher up the slopes of the mountain, turning verdant dales into burned, gray wasteland. And every year, he continued to disappoint Mioragh and his father by failing to control the magic he knew he had—the magic he felt flowing through his bones and blood and through the land and air around him.

Surely there must be magic for him. . . .

He took himself firmly in hand and took a deep breath. Brooding over the perennial question of his magic was going to get him exactly nowhere. How many times had he heard both Mioragh and his father say that the gods and goddesses gave their gifts in their own time? Neither man nor woman could hurry them beyond their own pace.

But surely . . .

Determinedly, he turned his thoughts elsewhere.

Who would offer him her cup of golden mead tonight? A vision flashed briefly across his eyes of the gleaming hair and blue eyes of Eliene al Saethen. Would she choose him, or would she choose Acaren? Or neither of them? Next autumn, she would declare herself as bheancoran to Acaren. There had never been any doubt of that since the day she had announced herself with a calling. But the bond of bheancoran and prince didn't always mean that a bond of man and woman would follow. Not always.

Rowan turned as Acaren stepped to the window beside him, hair still damp from his bath, his skin glowing. Subdued laughter glinted in his eyes, and something else, as he looked toward the slopes of Ben Warden.

"Truly, Rowan," he murmured, "I almost wish my arrow had gone wide of the mark."

Rowan nodded. "Far easier to kill the boar than this, I'll wager," he said glumly.

Acaren laughed. "Ah, Rowan, but it was such a splendid boar."

"And such a magnificent stag."

The two boys exchanged solemn glances. Then Acaren laughed again. "We might as well go and get this done with," he said. "The procession will be starting any moment. Offer me your sword to fall upon if I look to be making a fool of myself."

Rowan stood a little apart from the rest of the men as the god and goddess incarnate for this night threw their torches into

the pyre to begin the festival. A quick murmur of relief and
approval rippled through the throng like the soft sound of
water as the fire caught immediately and flared brightly into
the night. It was an auspicious beginning when the wood
took eagerly to the flame. Rowan watched the cloud of sparks
rise like new stars into the sky, then looked around to see if he
could catch sight of Acaren. He had lost track of his twin
shortly after the procession came into the glade. He found
Gabhain, tall and straight among the men, but he found no
trace of Acaren.

The first drone of the pipes began, like the distant murmur of the sea. Overhead, the stars blazed like beacons in the
dark vault of the sky. The crowd fell silent as the god and
goddess came together by the fire in the first graceful, stylized
steps of their dance.

The skirl of the pipes grew louder in the flickering dark.
The god and goddess stepped lightly around each other,
miming the chase. Darting first right, then left, first one pur-
suing, then the other, they whirled and leapt through light
and shadow. Then suddenly, both turned at the same time,
caught the other in eager arms, and swirled together like
fallen petals caught in an eddy of rippling water. Their bodies twisted and gyrated with the quickened beat of the music
as the chase ended and the offering of each to the other
began.

The young god and goddess incarnate danced higher
and fiercer than the flames themselves. Then hands and bodies came together and locked in the glitter and shimmer of the
light that flowed like water over their golden skin. There
were drums now, Rowan realized dimly, but he had no idea
when they'd begun.

Then it was over. The two ran quickly, hand in hand,
into the depths of the surrounding glade. A cry of joy and elation rose triumphantly from the shadowy figures clustered
around the blaze. The pipes stopped like a sword cut for a
long, timeless moment, then began again in a soft, haunting,
seductive refrain as men and women swirled like leaves into
the circle of light cast by the flames, and began their own
dance, the mead cups of the women held high and carefully.

Fortunate and blessed was the woman who spilled no mead this night.

All around him, mead was being offered and accepted as Rowan moved lithely with the changing rhythm and cadence of the pipes. But he saw no trace of Eliene's glossy blue-black hair and blue eyes as he searched among the dancers. He saw Gabhain moving gracefully among the dancers searching for Valessa al Drustan. He smiled. He would collect his wager from Acaren on that, he thought. A little farther from the fire, he found his parents. Dorlaine's mead cup was gone, and she held tightly to Athelin's hands. They were completely absorbed in each other. Gabhain swept past them, said something, and was rewarded by a smile from his father.

A laughing couple, arms twined about each other, nearly stumbled into Rowan as they hurried to the shadows of the trees beyond the glade. Rowan sidestepped them deftly, and as he spun, he finally caught sight of Eliene al Saethen. But even as he began to cut his way through the dancers toward her, she held up her silver goblet in offering, and Rowan saw who bent to accept it. Acaren's face, flushed with the excitement of the festival, fairly sparkled with laughter and exhilaration as he drained the goblet and hurled it, empty, to the ground.

The hollow, barren ache under Rowan's heart surprised him. But he truly hadn't been expecting Eliene to do anything different. In bitter disappointment, he turned away from the sight of their hands and mouths coming together in the ritual of the dance. When he looked back some moments later, they were gone.

So was the fire. And the rest of the dancers. Not certain how he had arrived there, Rowan stood in the midst of the small stone circle above the shrine on Ben Warden's lower flank. Above him, the spark of the Beltane fire glowed among the trees, flickering as dancing figures moved between it and his eyes.

"So you came when I called you."

Startled, he spun about, nearly losing his balance, and stood gaping. She stood for a moment between two of the stones, her gown glowing faintly in the wan light. For a moment, he thought he could see the outlines of the trees behind her through the shimmering fabric and her body.

"Rhianna?" he asked, his throat dry. He shook his head. "No, not Rhianna," he amended. "I know you. But who are you?"

"I have had many names, beloved," she said. "As have you." She smiled. "But tonight, you can call me Cat." She came to him across the dew-wet grass, her hair floating about her head in a pale cloud of red-gold. She held out her hand, and he reached out and took it in his.

"Do I dream again?" he asked.

"Mayhaps. Look. Do you remember this?"

The standing stones had disappeared. They stood at the edge of a clearing in a grove of mixed oak and ash. Two huge fires burned brightly in the warm night, flaring brilliantly in the center of the clearing. Beyond the fires on three sides loomed rank after serried rank of steep, savage mountains, and on the fourth, the eternally restless surge of the sea glimmered faintly in the starlight.

Two fires? How very odd. . . .

Laughing men and women danced around and between the fires to the unbridled skirling of pipes, meeting and parting in swirling patterns of light and shadow. For a moment, Rowan could not sort out what was different about them. Then he realized that the men wore kilts and the women wore long, flowing white gowns rather than the simple white tunic he wore. But as he looked down, he saw that he, too, wore a kilt.

No harps or flutes softened the wild keening of the pipes. Rowan had just time enough to wonder where he was before familiarity swept over him. The empty goblet he held in his hand still retained the warmth of her fingers; the taste of the Tyran heather ale it had contained tingled on his tongue.

Rowan laughed and flung the goblet high into the air. The silver chasing on the cup flashed and sparked in the firelight, then disappeared into the dark as the goblet fell unheeded to the ground. Rowan reached to take her outstretched hands and pulled her close to him. She came to him joyously and led him through the stylized steps until he caught her up in his arms and carried her between the trees, away from the fires to a secluded place beneath an overhanging ash tree.

As they sank down together onto the deep grass, he cradled her face between his hands. "My soul is cupped in the palm of your hand, my Cat," he said softly.

"Ah, beloved," she whispered. "Your soul has always been sheltered safe within my hands and my heart."

The bond they shared drew them together, one soul in two bodies. Rowan lost track of where he ended and she began. The wild music of the pipes of Tyra sang in his blood the same way the rapturous magic of her love played like music along his skin and nerves. The world shattered and spun for them, and as it subsided into sweet lethargy, he held her close against him, her head cradled on his shoulder. He closed his eyes and breathed in the fragrance of her hair. She smelled of apple blossoms and clean, crisp herbs.

The sky was graying toward dawn when Acaren returned to the room they shared. Only just returned himself, Rowan was in bed, but awake. He raised himself on one elbow as Acaren sat on the edge of the bed.

"Rowan, I *am* sorry," Acaren said softly.

Rowan felt only the smallest twinge of envy, the last before it all slipped away and vanished, and no bitterness at all as he smiled at his twin. "It was her own choice to make," he said softly. "And she made it. Who can gainsay a woman's choice made freely?"

"She truly loves both of us, you know."

"I know. But she chose you. I'm content with that, Acaren. Truly I am." And Rhianna of the Air had warned him that Eliene was not for him. His heart and soul lay bound somewhere else. With the strange woman of the stone Dance, mayhaps?

Acaren put his hand to his twin's shoulder and squeezed lightly. He went to his own bed.

"Acaren—" About to mention the strange encounter,

Rowan bit down on his words. He wanted more time to think about what the goddess had said to him. Disturbing and exciting at the same time.

"Yes?"

Rowan hesitated. Then, "I won the wager. Did you see Gabhain with Valessa?"

Acaren laughed softly. Then, sleepily, his voice came through the dark. "Did you ever before notice just how knobby Gabhain's knees really are? But then, one doesn't usually see them, does one?"

Part 2

Song of Rowan

12

Rowan stood leaning against a tree, his sword hanging loosely in his left hand while blood from an arm wound flowed down his wrist and across the back of his right hand. The early-autumn sun had broken through the dissipating clouds, and he sweated freely in its fading heat, his breathing ragged with exertion.

In the clearing beyond Rowan's chestnut tree, Acaren writhed and twisted like a living flame, sword flashing diamond-bright sparks into the early-afternoon air, as he defended himself against three armed and determined young men. The air reverberated to the clash and slither of tempered steel against steel as thrust met parry again and again. It had been raining all morning, a slow, fine drizzle, and the grass was still wet and slippery, affording poor footing for the combatants. Around the clearing, the leaves on the trees blazed in gold and scarlet, the red berries on the ash trees clustered thickly on their stems.

As Rowan watched his twin brother, he knew almost what he himself must look like wielding a sword. But although they shared the same deftness and speed of reflex, Rowan knew he had not the wild, vivid grace that burned brightly around Acaren whenever he moved, and especially when swinging a sword. It was the same deadly grace of an expertly fletched arrow, sent in flight from the bow of an adept archer, and it was uniquely Acaren's, his personal trademark.

For five minutes while Rowan watched, the balance of the battle hung precariously as Acaren reluctantly gave ground, step by step, to his three opponents. The fight could have gone either way. Rowan wondered idly if he had strength enough to go to his brother's aid, and if he would ever be forgiven if he *did* go.

Then, in movements very nearly too swift for the eye to follow, Acaren swept the feet out from beneath one adversary, smashed the second onto his back on the damp grass with his shield, and had the point of his blade hard at the throat of the third.

"I yield!" cried the young man in the teeth of the sword point, very real fear adding fervency to his tone as he dropped to one knee.

Rowan untensed and leaned back against the tree, laughing softly. Acaren sheathed his sword on his back and reached out a hand to help one of the soldiers to his feet.

"The boy will do." The voice behind Rowan held grudging approval.

Rowan swung around in astonishment on Weymund the Swordmaster. "Do?" he cried indignantly, stung. "Only just do? He was brilliant. He was—" He stopped as he saw the hard glint of amusement and pride in the stocky man's eyes, in spite of the mouth held grimly level.

"Aye," replied Weymund. "He'll do. And you're nearly as good. A pity the pair of you weren't whelped carrying a little more capacity for respect of your elders."

Acaren, chest still heaving with effort, joined them in the shade of the chestnut tree in time to overhear the remark. He made a fierce expression for Weymund. "Whelped," he snorted. "You speak disparagingly of our lady mother. Whelped, indeed."

"No man has more respect for the lady Dorlaine than I," the Swordmaster said mildly. "But as for you pair of insolent pups—"

Acaren grinned and turned to Rowan. He pulled a scarf from his pocket and quickly bound up Rowan's wounded arm. "You were careless out there, Rowan," he said.

"No." Rowan wiped the back of his hand against his thigh and sheathed his sword. "Today Deyr was uncommonly quick."

Weymund grunted, unimpressed. "Go down and get

Mioragh to take a look at that arm," he said. "You'll be no use to me if you lose it to wound fever. Acaren, back to the field."

Athelin stepped out beside Weymund, sheathing his sword as he watched Rowan make his way swiftly toward the palace. He, too, was sweating from exercise, but he was smiling.

Weymund turned to Athelin, smiling, too. "I love all those sons of yours," he said softly. "But oh, Athelin, my friend, the two youngest. They glow brightly in my heart like the flames of my own youth."

"You drive them hard, Weymund," Athelin said. He looked across the field to where Gabhain stood patiently practicing the same lunge and thrust maneuver over and over in dogged determination to master it. Valessa watched him critically, offering advice now and then, her brow puckered in concentration. Gabhain would someday make only an adequately competent swordsman, but he would make a wise Prince. Behind him, laughing as usual, Acaren swung his sword exuberantly, passing the hilt from hand to hand, making the spinning steel blade look like a flashing mirror around his head and shoulders, while Eliene al Saethen, her own sword stilled at her side, watched in fascination.

Both Acaren and Rowan had already proved to be more than a match for the best swordsmen among Athelin's men. And between them, Acaren was the more brilliant swordsman. But while Acaren always seemed to rely on the blaze and dazzle of his genius, Rowan used his intelligence to seek out and exploit his opponent's weaknesses. In a match against each other, each could fight the other to a draw. Fighting back-to-back, in tandem, they were almost invincible among trainees their own age.

Athelin watched Eliene as she tried the twirling of the sword that Acaren had done so effortlessly, a frown of concentration furrowing her brow. She did it slowly and cautiously, mindful of the keen cutting edge of the blade, but her determination to master the exercise showed in the intense focus that blotted out everything else.

She most certainly had a calling as bheancoran. But she would not serve Gabhain, who would one day be Prince of

Skai. At the feast of Samhain, she would declare for Acaren. It had surprised no one — with the possible exception of Gabhain himself — when Valessa, daughter of Drustan, Duke of Dorian, had declared for him in early spring. For as far back as anyone could remember, the Prince of Skai had been served by a bheancoran who acted as soul's companion, guardian, and confidante. Not often had the bheancoran been of other than yrSkai or Tyadda stock, but it wasn't unknown.

The bond between prince and bheancoran was soul-deep, lasting a lifetime. Athelin had Dorlaine. Not every prince married his bheancoran, but many had. His father had. The lady Lowra was both Gareth's wife and bheancoran.

But Eliene — Eliene seemed to be proof that something had been set in motion. Something that began even before the twins were born, before Athelin's sister Iowen had become bheancoran without a prince for whom to declare herself. Eliene's emergence as a bheancoran had startled Athelin, but he had said nothing when she began training nearly nine years ago. He said nothing now. But he wondered. And worried. And watched in silence.

"The boys need hard driving to keep on the edge of their skills," Weymund said.

Startled, Athelin looked at him. He had almost forgotten what they were talking about. "I suppose we all need that," he said.

Weymund laughed. Then, a different tone in his voice, he said, "Do you suppose they're really the ones?"

"The ones?"

"In the song," Weymund said. "The legend."

Athelin shrugged. "So says Mioragh the Bard. The Champion and the Kaith. Who knows? But there's time. They're young yet."

"Tiernyn was not much past eighteen when he was raised first to Corrach and then to High King of Celi to battle the Saesnesi. Donaugh, too, of course, when he became King's Enchanter." Weymund shrugged again. "If there be a man out there who is trueborn High King of Celi, Acaren and Rowan will be ready to serve him well."

A shadow clouded Athelin's heart. "If . . ." he murmured. "Weymund, old friend, I've dreamed of the day I can come out of exile and return home to Skai, but I will not do it through their blood."

"If they choose to give their blood, who are you to gainsay them, my lord?" Weymund shook his head. "No, not even a father has that right once a boy becomes a man." Then he laughed. "You talk about returning to Skai, my lord. You've never seen Skai. When your grandfather brought your father here, the lad was too young even to know how to get you upon your lady mother, and your lady mother was not yet even born."

Athelin fixed the Swordmaster with a stern, reprimanding gaze. But the two men had known each other far too long. Athelin's not inconsiderable skill with his own sword had been hard-won under Weymund's unrelenting tutelage. He laughed and shook his head in amused exasperation.

"I'll grant you you're right," he said. "You seem to have one student here yet, Swordmaster. Best you go and earn your keep, which costs me so vastly each year."

Weymund looked across the field to where Eliene stood, her hair gleaming like a raven's wing in the sun. "It's been many years since the yrSkai produced two bheancoran," he said quietly.

"Not really," Athelin said quietly. "My sister Iowen knew she was to be bheancoran from the time she was six, even though Dorlaine had already begun her training. Eliene's doing well?"

"At first, she did as any young one new to the sword," Weymund replied. "Clumsy to begin with, but better each time she picked it up. She's deft and agile with it now, and still improving daily, and I'd wager she's better with the bow now than Gabhain."

Athelin smiled. "A bitter blow, perhaps, for Gabhain, but we all three know the bow was never his strength."

Weymund shrugged helplessly. "I would that I had been able to teach Gabhain more skill."

"Gabhain has skill enough," Athelin said. "And he'll always have Valessa beside him, and loyal men with swords ever ready to serve him. His strength lies elsewhere. He has the ability to inspire trust and loyalty, and he understands the minds of his people better than any other man on this forsaken island."

"Except perhaps for Rowan," Weymund said.

"Yes, except perhaps for Rowan," Athelin agreed. He was watching Eliene again. "She's got the strength and the grace to handle a sword well," he said.

Across the field, Eliene sheathed her sword. She was dressed as the men were, in soft boots, cross-bound breeks, and a short tunic. Her bare arms were slim and brown. On her left wrist, she wore an archer's deep leather cuff. She had secured her hair in a long plait behind her neck with a bright green scarf, to keep it out of her way.

As Athelin watched, she picked up her bow and drew an arrow from the quiver at her hip. She nocked the arrow and drew back, the young muscles in her arm corded and prominently delineated. She let fly. The arrow went straight and true to the target hung on a tree across the clearing. She turned, saw Athelin, and smiled at him.

He smiled back, but he found it unsettling. First Mioragh's certainty of the path the twins were to tread, then the emergence of a second bheancoran. And he remembered another bheancoran who apparently had no prince to serve. His sister Iowen, who had gone to Skai and returned to die in childbed.

He shook his head to clear the sorrowful memories and looked again at Eliene. Her emergence echoed too strongly with his dreams. They had been given the time they badly needed to prepare, and they had used it well. Every man and boy on Skerry could use a sword or a bow, and each of them had a sword forged in the smithy within the Keep's walls, or a bow shaped and crafted by a master. Even the women had trained with Weymund's archers.

The events foreshadowed by Athelin's dreaming seemed to be crowding in closer now. But his dreaming still had not given them any shape or form, and he could not tell what to expect.

He smiled again at Eliene, then turned as Ralf hurried into the clearing.

"My lord, a messenger arrived," Ralf said. "We are to expect Drustan and his party by evening."

"Have we word yet from Cai?" Athelin asked.

"Yes, my lord. He'll be wintering at Laurelwater, but is sending his son Thaine as he says his old bones can't take the sea voyage in this weather."

"Then we had best go and tell the lady Dorlaine there will be a few more guests for Samhain," Athelin said.

13

Drustan of Dorian arrived in time for the evening meal. He swept into the Great Hall, his cloak of subtly checked greens billowing behind him, his son Bryand on his left, and ten of his men trailing in his wake. He was a big man, tall and broad, and his full, dark beard was shot with gray, yet he moved as gracefully as any youth and trod the ground as lightly as a dancer.

Dorlaine came forward, smiling in greeting, to offer him the guest-cup. He took it, drank half the ale in one long draught, then handed the cup to Bryand, who finished it. Drustan swept Dorlaine into his arms and kissed her forehead with high good humor.

"Athelin, my friend," he said, turning to the Prince, "I swear your lady becomes more beautiful each time I see her. And your sons grow another handspan." He grasped Athelin's arm in greeting, then looked around. "Where is Gabhain? And my daughter?"

"Practicing with Weymund," Athelin said. "Valessa is determined to teach Gabhain how to use a bow." He smiled fondly. "She may be a long time at it."

"The meal is ready," Dorlaine said. "Shall we go?"

"I've asked Mioragh to join us," Athelin said. "He'll already be above stairs, I think."

The meal was served in the family quarters above the Great Hall. When it was finished, Acaren took Bryand off to the stables to inspect the colts to be broken in the spring. Rowan, Gabhain, and Valessa sat quietly at one end of the table.

"What news from the southeast near Afon, my lord Drustan?" Rowan asked.

"The blight is still growing," Drustan said heavily. "Faster now, if we can believe the evidence. I hate to think that Hakkar is growing stronger each year." He turned to Mioragh. "Is it possible that he might learn to use Celae magic against us?"

Mioragh hesitated. "Ten years ago, I would have given you an unequivocal no," he said. "Now— Well, now, I'm not certain. The Verge is moving higher and higher into the mountains. He might be learning to use our magic. I hope not, but I don't know. We need to strengthen our own magic to stop him."

Rowan clenched his fist. Mioragh had not looked at him—had not in any way indicated disappointment or disapproval—but Rowan could not help but think both the disappointment and disapproval were there. He tried to control his magic. No matter what he did, the wisps of magic around him refused to come together into a coherent, usable thread. Neither his frustrated anger nor his despair made any difference.

"As for the rest," Drustan said. "An early winter. The snow is already high in the passes. We had a difficult time coming through the last one before reaching the coast. Any more snow up there and the mountains will be impassable until spring. The sentinels were preparing to come back when we saw them. What magic do you use here to soften the bite of winter, Athelin?"

Athelin laughed. "Mioragh says the bard lore tells of a warm current of water in the Western Sea that flows around Marddyn and Skerry," he said. "It protects our small islands. Is there any more news of activity south of the Verge?"

Drustan sat back, playing with his wineglass, his expression grave. "It isn't good news, I'm afraid," he said. "The Maedun are becoming bolder and more arrogant. There have been more parties of Somber Riders north of the Verge this last summer than ever I've seen before. And larger parties, too. We found one place where they'd surprised a village of perhaps forty Veniani. All dead, every man, woman, and child, and left to rot. Even the dogs and horses had been slaughtered." He shook his head, his eyes filled with pain. "I've heard it's much the same all along the Verge."

"Then it must be the same in the highlands of Skai and Wenydd," Athelin said. "No, that news isn't good."

"Why are they so restless?" Drustan asked. "What is it that's set them off like a hawk among the pigeons?"

Athelin glanced at Rowan, then quickly looked away. "Mayhaps Hakkar senses magic again somewhere," he said. "You know how terrified the Maedun are of the prophecy that says an Enchanter will come from Celi to destroy all of Maedun."

Drustan grunted. "They've been using that excuse ever since the first Maedun army went out and captured Falinor. How many years ago was that? It was in Red Kian's time, surely? A century ago?"

"Nearly that," Athelin said. "We've taken a leaf from your book, Drustan. Every man, woman, and child on this island, and on Marddyn, has been trained in weaponry. The men and boys all know how to use swords and bows, and the women all know how to use bows and throwing knives. All the young men and women serve a season each year as sentinels in the mountain passes. We've been lucky. Most raiding parties we've stopped on the shores. They haven't reached the village." The line of his mouth thinned and lengthened. "Danal's death taught us a painful and costly lesson. We shan't be caught out like that again."

"A terrible lesson," Drustan said softly. "At a terrible price." He paused for a moment. Then, "Is there word from Cai yet?"

Athelin shook his head. "Thaine will be wintering here with us. He's due here soon. But I expect his news won't be much different than yours."

Drustan took a sip of his wine. "It appears the time we prayed for is about to run out," he said quietly.

Athelin looked again at Rowan, who was watching Drustan fixedly. Rowan looked up and met his father's eyes. For a moment, father and son merely looked at each other. Then Rowan smiled slightly. Athelin turned back to Drustan.

"We'll have the winter, in any event," he said. "The

Somber Riders aren't about to come north in the snow, and the seas will soon be closed by the winter storms. It's a little more time."

The morning of Samhain Eve brought the first storm of the autumn season. Under a heavy, lowering black sky, the sea, gray as the granite cliffs of Ben Roth's forbidding flanks, heaved and writhed, flicking grayish white foam and spray into a mist high above the water, even over the sheltered strand of Skerryharbor. The ship carrying Thaine ap Cai of Wenydd came skittering into the harbor under half sail at midmorning, blown in by a gale strong enough to bend her soaring masts like saplings before it.

Drenched by spray and rain that was almost sleet, and half-frozen, the crew made the ship fast to the pier and disappeared into the welcome warmth of the nearest tavern while the escort sent by Athelin took Thaine and his small retinue, including his wife and daughter, to the palace. Fires and braziers blazed in the rooms that had been prepared for them the night before, and they gratefully settled into welcome warmth.

Shutters were drawn early on homes and taverns that evening. No man or woman willingly went abroad after dark on Samhain Eve, the night when the dead walked the earth and the Wild Hunt was likely to thunder through the sky seeking the souls of the lost. The heat and light made the Great Hall a snug refuge from the cold and dark.

Rowan could well believe the Hunt rode this night as he listened to the wind screaming around the eaves and towers of the palace. He closed the book Mioragh had given him to read when Rhan came to the door to announce the evening meal.

Mioragh dismissed him with a wave of his hand and Rowan got to his feet tiredly, knowing the session had not gone well again. The books were difficult to understand, and Rowan was beginning to despair that he really had as much magic as Mioragh thought he had. After all the years of study and effort, Rowan could no more control his magic than he could that first night Mioragh had commanded him to look into the fire and relate what he saw. Rowan despaired of ever learning how to use the power that flowed around him, thick and solid as spun gold or honey.

"Will you come down for the meal?" he asked.

Mioragh shook his head. "No. I'll ask Deyr to bring something up to me later."

"Mioragh, I'm sorry . . ."

Mioragh smiled wearily and shook his head. "The fault lies not in you, Rowan," he said. "Part of it is with me. It's difficult to train someone to do something one doesn't know how to do oneself."

"But you have magic—"

"Not enough, I fear," Mioragh said. "And not the kind of magic we're in need of. I'm Tyadda, as was your grandmother, lad. I don't have the Celae blood that seems to strengthen Tyadda magic. It's not your fault I've only small tricks to use for my own amusement. I cannot teach you what I do not have."

"You had enough magic to save my mother. I was there. I saw you working. You have enough to be a Healer."

Mioragh smiled and shook his head. "Being a Healer is quite different from being an enchanter, lad. Donaugh himself had not the gift of Healing, even though both his mother and father had it. And his sister."

"My grandfather Gareth had both."

"Yes, your grandfather Gareth had both. As did Red Kian. But it's rare that both gifts appear in the same person. And as for the magic— You know we could never use our magic as a weapon. Even when the Saesnesi came, we relied on our swords and the bravery of our men, as we tried to when the Maedun came. We were successful with the Saesnesi. Tiernyn forced a truce with them, and they lived as neighbors to us in the Summer Run. But you yourself know how dismally we failed against the Maedun and their sorcery."

"Donaugh was a great enchanter, though."

"Donaugh simply built a curtain of powerful enchantment around the Isle of Celi that the Maedun sorcerers couldn't penetrate," Mioragh said. "When he fell, we had no

defense against them. There were men and women who had
magic in the overrun lands, but Hakkar tracked them down
and killed them when he found them. There are too few of us
left now, and any who might have taught you properly are
gone."

"It's not your fault I can't command my magic, Mioragh," Rowan said miserably. "I just can't seem to grasp it
properly, no matter what I do. I'm trying—"

"I know you are, Rowan. But I think something is going
to have to happen to bring your magic to strength, some
event that I can't foresee now."

"What happened to Donaugh to give him his magic?"

"I'm afraid no one knows. Not even the bard lore speaks
of it. Go and have your meal, Rowan. I'm tired, and I must
rest."

When the boy had gone, Mioragh held his hands out
over the heat of the brazier to warm them. He sighed.

The art of magic, he had discovered long years ago, is
not easily learned, nor was it easily taught. Even with a student with a vast amount of potential such as Rowan ap Athelin, it didn't go as well as Mioragh had hoped it would. One
did not choose to follow Rhianna of the Air; one was chosen
as Mioragh himself had been chosen on that night in the oak
grove on Laurelwater he would never forget. Some event
must herald that choosing, and when it happened, then the
dimensions of the gift could be tested and measured. But not
until.

So few, Mioragh thought. Sometimes he came close to
despair. *We are so few, and the task is so immense.*

Athelin's magic was only a small gift. Even after years of
training, it was not very strong, nor would it ever be. There
was a world of difference between merely lighting a candle
and calling down Beodun's own wildfire from the sky, something that Mioragh himself was incapable of doing, but
Donaugh the Enchanter had more than once been seen to do.
Dorlaine's magic had proved to be useless as any but a
mother's magic, potent in its way between her and her children, but not what Mioragh needed.

Of all the yrSkai on Skerry and Marddyn, many had

Tyadda blood, enough to give them some protection against Hakkar's spell. But none were potential enchanters. From the yrWenydd of Laurelwater, had come only two—one mage, an old man frail in body but strong in mind and magic, and a youth with potential that proved to be as difficult to bring to flower as Rowan's potential.

Mioragh sank into his chair, staring at the brazier. Misgivings grew within his breast, and he raised one hand to rub his weary eyes. Tiernyn and Donaugh had come from the Royal House of Skai, younger sons of the same Prince who had been Brennen's grandfather. Brennen's son Gareth, Athelin's father, had possessed strong magic, but not as strong as Donaugh's own. Mioragh wondered if all the magic in the line, the real magic, had culminated in Donaugh and ended there. Was there no way to bring it back?

It was hot in the tavern. Flushed with the heat and enough ale to raise his spirits, but not impair his faculties, Acaren had shed his cloak and his heavy vest and undone the top fastenings on his tunic. He knelt among the circle of soldiers, waiting for Lluddor to make his throw with the dice. Before him on the floor lay the small pile of his winnings.

He had taken to spending a lot of his time with the men in his troop of soldiers. Being the second son, he didn't have to maintain the reserved partial detachment of the heir to the Prince's throne, which suited him very well. He loved his brother dearly, but he sometimes thought Gabhain could be overly stuffy and far too conscious of his dignity and position.

The soldier threw the dice, crowed with triumph, and raked in half the pile of silver coins in the middle of the circle. He passed the dice to Acaren. "You may have the rest, my lord," he said, laughing. "I've won back what I lost."

Acaren grinned and shook the dice. He looked down at the coins in front of him, then concentrated and threw the dice. A star, an ash tree, and a seven. Neutral. He neither won nor lost. He laughed and passed the dice to the next man.

"That's it for me tonight," he said. He gathered up his small pile of coins and one set of the hexagonal dice, then got to his feet.

One of the soldiers looked up and made a jesting remark about giving him a chance to win back what he had lost.

"Eight silvers?" Acaren asked, feigning astonishment. "Marto, that's barely enough to pay for the ale." He laughed, passed the coins over to the tavern keeper, and assumed an expression of stern authority. "Now, as your commander, I'm giving you all a direct order to have one last flagon of ale with me, then I must go."

He made his way slowly back to the Keep. There was nothing else for it, he supposed. He had no choice. He had to see Mioragh tonight. He could put it off no longer.

The sentries at the doors of the Great Hall recognized Acaren and stepped back to let him pass, giving a slight bow of sketched reverence. Acaren wished them a good night, then bounded up the stairway at the far end of the Great Hall to the family quarters.

At the head of the stairway, he paused, looking down at the three hexagonal dice that gleamed in his hand with the light of the torches. Then, finally, knowing there was little else he could do, he turned toward the guest wing.

Mioragh's servant, Deyr, answered the door, rumpled with sleep and mildly indignant at being roused in the middle of the night. His expression became only marginally less ruffled when he recognized Acaren.

"I know it's late," Acaren said, "but I have something I must show to Master Mioragh."

"It's past midnight, my lord Acaren," Deyr said.

"Master Mioragh . . ."

"Is awake." Mioragh's voice came from the inner chamber. "Please bring him in, Deyr."

As Acaren entered, Mioragh rose from the table and the open book. A brazier glowed on either side of the long table, and a fire burned in the hearth near the bed. The only other light in the room came from two candles in tall holders on the table. Mioragh smiled a greeting. "May I offer you some wine, young night owl?" he asked.

Acaren shook his head. "Thank you, but no. I've had my share of ale and wine tonight, I think."

"Then take your ease and tell me what brings you here so late."

"I want to show you something," Acaren said. "I know it's late, but I was certain of this only tonight, and I thought you should know as soon as possible."

Mioragh took his seat behind the table again. "What is it?" he asked.

"This." Acaren shook the dice in his hand and threw them onto the table. Without looking at them, he said, "There will be a star, a falcon, and a seven there."

Mioragh bent forward and peered at the dice, then looked up at Acaren. "There are," he said. "Seven falcons under a star. Not a bad throw."

"This one won't be as good." Acaren gathered up the dice, threw them again, his eyes closed. "A one, an ash tree, and a hare," he said. One hare under an ash tree. Always a losing throw.

Mioragh looked again. "Once more, as you said, it is," he said quietly. He looked up at Acaren. "What does this mean, Acaren? Can you see them without looking?"

"Not exactly," Acaren said slowly. "What would you like me to throw? Anything . . ."

"A crescent, a stag, and a seven," Mioragh said.

Acaren shook the dice and threw them onto the table. The pale light of the candles picked out the distinct shapes of a crescent moon, a stag's antlered head, and seven dots on the faces of the dice. Mioragh leaned back, the candlelight emphasizing the sharp planes and deep hollows of his face, drawn into thoughtful lines.

"Can you do that every time?" he asked.

"Every time," Acaren said.

"What are you doing?"

Acaren held up his left hand, the dice held in his right. He made a swift, complicated pattern with the fingers of his left hand, then threw the dice. A seven, a star, and a sun showed. Seven stars around the sun. The top winning combination.

"Where did you learn that?" Mioragh asked, intrigued.

"I don't know. More by accident than design, I think. It

just suddenly came to me one night in a dice game when I was losing rather badly."

Amusement brimmed over on Mioragh's face into a smile. "And you used it to strip your soldiers of their last copper?"

Acaren shook his head and grinned. "Well, no. Not exactly. Just enough so that I didn't leave in embarrassed penury." His grin faded and he took a chair, leaning forward intensely across the table. "Mioragh, is this any help to you? Do I have magic?"

Mioragh nodded slowly. "Yes, I believe you do," he said, his voice quietly pensive. "I don't believe I've seen magic exactly like this before."

"I know it's not much magic," Acaren said. "Will it be helpful?"

"All magic will be helpful." Mioragh reached out and touched the dice thoughtfully, one by one, with the tip of his finger. "We need all we have. Will you work with me and see what we can do with it?"

"Of course." Acaren grinned suddenly. "What a pity," he said. "This probably means I'll never be invited into another dice game."

14

Rowan awoke from a chaotic dream feeling agitated and feverish. His head pounded with pain intense enough to blur his vision and send a coil of nausea twisting through his belly. Gasping for breath, he sat up, then had to brace himself with both hands as a wave of giddiness swept through him. He closed his eyes until it passed, then raised a hand to his brow. It came away slick and wet with the sweat that streamed down his face.

A fragment of his dream drifted tantalizingly clear through his mind. A woman, silver-haired and naked, danced slowly in a graceful turn, hair floating about her body in a shining cloud, green-turquoise eyes filled with some emotion, some message he could not begin to decipher.

The thumping pulse of pain in his head shattered the ephemeral image, and he closed his eyes again. *I'm ill,* he thought fuzzily. *I must see Mioragh. . . .*

He stumbled from his bed and staggered into the corridor. The fever and the pain in his head made it difficult to balance properly. The feeble, wavering light of the torches seared his eyes, and the polished parquet floor of the corridor felt like ice beneath the soles of his bare feet.

He clutched at the doorpost of Mioragh's apartment for support, leaning hard against it, and lifted one hand to knock. Mioragh himself opened the door immediately. In Rowan's fever-muddled state, he thought the bard might almost have been expecting him.

"Rowan," Mioragh exclaimed. "Are you ill?"

"Head hurts," Rowan muttered.

Mioragh brought him into the inner chamber and drew up a chair for him by the brazier. Rowan tried to explain about the dream and how he had awakened feeling ill, but found it difficult to speak. Mioragh crossed the room quickly to a small chest under the window and went to his knees in front of it. He opened it and searched through the contents while he listened. When he came back to where Rowan sat, he carried a small bundle of leaves.

He paused, then bent to take a closer look at Rowan's face. "Look at me," he said.

Rowan lifted his head with an effort and looked up at Mioragh. The light from the single candle on the table hurt his eyes, and they began to sting. Tears formed along the lower lashes, and his vision blurred again. He had to close his eyes tightly and turn away from the light.

Mioragh put his hand to Rowan's forehead. "I know what's wrong with you," he said in a softer voice. "She is not making it easy for you, is she? Sometimes, she is not a gentle mistress, Rowan."

Confused, Rowan tried to ask what Mioragh meant, but the bard shook his head. "You dreamed of Rhianna of the Air." He made it a statement, not a question.

"Twice," Rowan said. "Once tonight. Once on the day of my hunt. And another woman . . ."

"Who?" Mioragh asked, his voice suddenly harsh.

"I don't know. I've dreamed of her since I was a child. She's very lovely, and she haunts me." The light suddenly seemed to become brighter. He could not see through the stinging tears. He put up his hands to cover his eyes and heard something metallic scrape across the floor.

Then Mioragh put his hand to his forehead again. In a stern and commanding tone Rowan had not heard since that night so many years ago in the Great Hall at the Feast of Imbolc, Mioragh said, "Look into the fire, Rowan Second-born. Tell me what you see."

Rowan opened his eyes. Mioragh had pulled the glowing brazier close to the chair. Rowan looked into it, the brightness making his eyes water again. He began to shiver—deep, hard, shuddering waves that he could not stop. He clasped his hands hard together on his knees to stop their trembling, clenched his teeth to control their chattering. The embers in the brazier blazed and grew fiercely brighter as he looked into them, until they filled his eyes and his head, and the heat threatened to consume him. He was afraid he would fall into them and be swept away in a bright blaze of flame.

It was very dark. A cave. He sensed rather than saw the damp rock walls crowding close around him, smelled the dark, earthy scent of moist soil beneath his feet. A cooling breeze, faint as a whisper, came from ahead, from deeper in the cave, and he knew it must open to the sky again farther in. He heard the faint, musical sound of water dripping into water coming from somewhere near, but could not tell the direction because of the myriad echoes all around him.

The quiet sound of a striking flint came from behind him. A soft light glowed as the torch flared. Rowan saw a figure ahead dressed in white, a brilliant red cloak thrown over his shoulders, clasped by a round gold brooch emblazoned with the white falcon of Skai. He stood, motionless and waiting, in the narrow confines of the cave passageway. For a moment, Rowan thought it was himself. Then the figure moved, and he knew it was Acaren.

Or was it? The young man's features wavered in the torchlight. Sometimes, Rowan was certain it was Acaren, then the light flickered, and the man looked as old as Athelin, or older. And sometimes, he looked like a young woman with her hair in a thick braid falling over her shoulder beside the hilt of the sword she wore across her back. Then, in the next moment, it was Acaren again.

Acaren began to walk deeper into the cave. His shadow leapt and twisted ahead of him, flowing over the uneven floor of the cave, growing and shrinking, advancing and dwindling, with the movement of the torch behind him. Between Acaren and the torch, Rowan realized without surprise that he himself cast no shadow. Acaren was alone in the cave with the blurred, indistinct figure holding the torch.

The narrow passageway opened suddenly. Rowan sensed the vastness of the cavern ahead, but could see nothing of it. Acaren stepped into the cavern and paused, waiting for the torchbearer.

The torchbearer did not move in front of Acaren, but stopped at the mouth of the small cave behind him and held the torch higher. The light from the torch illuminated tall white limestone pillars where water dripping over centuries had built them up from the ground to meet the stone icicles descending from the ceiling.

The torch flashed and flared brightly. As if each pillar were made of crystal gems, the light streaked from one to the other, glittering, leaping, growing, running like liquid fire from pillar to pillar, striking sparks of green and red and blue and violet. One pillar after the other caught and erupted into evanescent light until Rowan thought he was trapped within a crystal that caught the sun and sent it sparking in shimmering rainbows of color and light to all corners of the immense gallery.

A table, an altar, carved of crystal or ice, stood alone beside a massive pillar, its shadow looming tall and dark against the glistening white of the limestone. Two tall, slender golden goblets stood on the altar, supporting between them a sword. The steel of the sword blade shone brightly in the scintillating light, the jewels in the hilt pulsed with living fire in green and blue and red.

"Take up the sword," a voice commanded.

Acaren walked confidently toward the altar, his shadow leaping to advance before him, climbing the pristine white of the limestone pillar with the shadow of the altar and the sword. He reached out, closed his hand about the hilt of the sword, and lifted it. On the gleaming pillar, his shadow, so sharply defined it looked three-dimensional, raised the sword as Acaren did, and Rowan felt the perfect fit of the hilt in his hand.

The magic burst through him, igniting his heart and his spirit. All around him, it sizzled and crackled, dancing around the arm holding the sword like the dancing lights in the northern sky. Or the blue ropes of witch fire that played in the rigging of a ship. Searing and cooling at the same time, it flooded through him, turning him into a torch that gathered the magic all around the light-filled cavern and threw it back, brighter, stronger, fiercer.

Rowan cried out, pain and ecstasy combined. . . .

"Rowan, drink this."

Rowan opened his eyes. He lay on Mioragh's bed, propped up by several cushions. Mioragh bent over the bed, a goblet in his hand, the liquid in it gently steaming. He held it to Rowan's lips. It was wine with some bitter undertaste to it. Rowan took a few swallows, felt his headache fade away.

He no longer shivered. He lay back and closed his eyes. The illness had left him, but he felt extremely weary. A warm lassitude crept through his body, and he wanted to sleep.

"Do you remember what you saw this time?" Mioragh asked.

Rowan nodded. "Yes." He dragged his eyes open. "Did I tell you?"

"Yes, you told me." Mioragh made him drink more of the wine. "Try to finish all of it. It will help you to come back."

"I was a long way away," Rowan murmured drowsily.

"Yes, you were. Your great-grandfather Brennen had the Sight, too. As did your grandmother Lowra. Did you know that?"

Rowan frowned. "It is not an comfortable gift," he muttered a bit crossly.

Mioragh smiled. "No, it sometimes is not. But it will be easier for you next time, I believe."

Rowan tried to keep his eyes open, but failed. "Do you know what it meant, Mioragh?" he asked. He was almost too sleepy to care.

"I believe I do. Go to sleep now, Rowan. We will have to speak with Athelin tomorrow. Right now, the best thing you can do is sleep."

Horbad was with a woman when the summons came from his father. The messenger was out of breath and in some distress, a good measure of the urgency of the summons. Reluctantly, Horbad resettled the spell on the weeping woman, left the bed, and dressed quickly. He wore the black uniform of an officer of the Somber Riders, unrelieved by anything but the small silver insignia at his collar and the small badge on the shoulder of his shirt, but the dagger at his belt was jeweled, the blade etched with power signs.

Hakkar was in his apartments, standing by the window, looking north, his hands clasped behind his back. He did not look around when Horbad entered.

"I have warned you before about lifting the spell from the women you take to your bed," Hakkar said.

The mild tone did not deceive Horbad. He had heard his

father give execution orders in that same uninflected voice. "I always resettle the spell when I've done with them," he said, his tone matching Hakkar's. "Making love to a woman under the spell is like making love to a straw dummy. I like them a little more lively."

"You spend entirely too much energy in your bed, Horbad. You have little left in reserve to serve me."

"I serve you well enough, Father," Horbad replied. "Did you send for me merely to give me another reminder of my duties?"

Hakkar turned, his dark eyes burning in his narrow face. "You are perilously close to insolence, my son," he said quietly. "Do you wish to test my wrath?"

Horbad suppressed a shiver, then turned away and flung himself carelessly into a chair to hide his nervousness. "There is precious little else to amuse a man in this forsaken land," he said. "As long as I'm careful to resettle the spell, you should have no objections. The women are only a small thing. This woman tonight gave indication of enjoying my attentions."

"I command your attention now, Horbad. You would do well to listen."

"How may I serve you tonight, Father?" Horbad asked.

"I gave you command of the western garrisons. When were you planning to travel west to take charge, or were you planning on staying here all winter?"

"My preparations are all but finished," Horbad said. "I leave in three days' time."

"No," Hakkar said. "You leave tomorrow. You must be well settled in before the snow becomes too deep for travel. You will encourage your men to hunt down the renegade Celae in the west, and you will mount a campaign against the northern Celae."

"Of course. Come the first sign of spring, we'll —"

"No, not spring. Now."

"In the winter? Father, the snow in those mountain passes is better than man-deep in the winter. You can't possibly expect an army to get through to the north."

"You will think of something, Horbad," Hakkar said with a grim smile. "You have a fertile imagination, or so your servants assure me. The time has come to wipe out all traces of opposition."

"Has something happened then?" Horbad asked. "Have you sensed any magic from the north?"

"We have left the renegade Celae alone for too long. It is time to remind them of Maedun's strength." Hakkar turned away. "You had better see to your preparations."

When Horbad had gone, Hakkar left the window and went through a door in the corner of the room. The narrow spiral stairway led upward to a small, round room. The tower room was dark except for a faint blue glow emanating from a table in the center.

Hakkar walked slowly to the table and frowned as he reached out one finger to touch the rounded stone that lay there. The Seeker Stone was no longer gray and rough. It had taken on a pearlescent sheen and glimmered very slightly in the complete darkness of the room. *So, not strong magic,* Hakkar thought. But magic nonetheless. The stone had detected it even if his own senses could not.

He picked up the stone and held it cradled in the palm of his hand. Slowly, he turned in a complete circle. The glimmer was strongest when he held the stone to the northwest—the same direction that first hint of magic had come from nearly nine years ago now.

He placed the Tell-Tale carefully back on its bed of black velvet and watched it abstractedly for a few moments. In natural light, the glow of the stone would have been undetectable. Only in complete darkness, as now, was it discernible.

"What are you telling me?" Hakkar murmured.

Another child born with magic? Or, after all these years of waiting, the emergence of the enchanter of the prophecy? The man who would be the destruction of Maedun itself?

It would be best to act as if the Tell-Tale announced the advent of the enchanter, Hakkar decided. It was time to complete the campaign started by his father more than fifty years ago. The Celae in the north must now be wiped out. The first step, a campaign he had planned even before Horbad's birth, would be carried out this winter. The next step might take several years, but this winter would be the beginning. The emerging enchanter would be found, and he would be destroyed.

Hakkar smiled. The Celae in the north had been lulled into thinking they were safe after more than fifty years of being left more or less to themselves. Now they would discover differently.

And perhaps, just perhaps, assuming the responsibility for this campaign might strengthen Horbad. The link between them enhanced Hakkar's power, but it had not brought Horbad's own power to fulfillment. This campaign might be the remedy Hakkar had been seeking for close to thirty years.

He reached out one finger and traced a thread of pale light down the center of the stone. The line of his mouth lengthened grimly. Horbad must be strong enough to assume both his name and the power should something happen to him. With discipline and effort, Horbad could overcome the slight taint of foreign blood he had received from his mother's Saesnesi great-grandmother.

15

The winter wore on, a hiatus of rest between the hectic activity of the harvest and the beginning of labor to prepare the fields again for planting in spring. It was a time to repair and mend equipment, of long evenings by the hearthfires with hot mulled wine to help ease the chill of the air, and of telling and retelling of tales so that even the youngest children learned the history of Celi and the glories of her heroes.

In cottages and Keep both, women spun wool and wove it into cloth for clothing and blankets, telling gentler stories of the gods and goddesses who were on Celi to greet the Celae when they came. Stories of Adriel of the Waters, or Rhianna of the Air were favorites to tell children, as these were the less wrathful of the pantheon who ruled under the Duality, and the goddesses who were kindly disposed toward women and well-behaved children—this last phrase always subtly emphasized with a meaningful glance toward those who might benefit most from the lesson. They told stories of Beodun of the Fires and his twin nature of warming hearthfire and wildfire from the sky. There were stories of Cernos of the Forest, Sandor of the Plains, and Gerieg of the Crags, too, because all children loved to be thrilled into delightful terror by the stories of the wrath of these potent gods at the transgressions of men.

Midwinter Eve came and went, marking a bright spot in a cold and bleak season. There was laughter and song in Athelin's Great Hall and the exchanging of small gifts.

A fortnight after Midwinter Eve, an unprecedented event took place. A ship, its rigging sheathed in ice, its sails

ragged from the fury of the winter storms, limped into Skerryharbor. It carried nearly fifty people, mostly women and
children, all of them half-frozen and near death with exhaustion and cold. The whole village turned out to find warm
places for them by hearths and braziers and most of them
were quickly settled with hot food and the generous comfort
the people of Skerry could offer them.

One man, a youth of about nineteen, clutching two chil-
dren by the hand, insisted on being taken immediately to
Prince Athelin. He had grave news, he said, news both the
Prince and Thaine ap Cai needed to hear as soon as possible.

Silence fell immediately over the Great Hall as the
young man and the children entered. With a soft cry, Loisa
rushed forward and gathered in the children. The young man
released them gratefully to her and managed a reassuring
smile when the children looked doubtfully over their shoulders at him as they were swiftly rushed upstairs to warm
baths, beds, and food.

Athelin rose quickly to his feet, Thaine ap Cai at his side.
The young man paused at the entrance, his face haggard and
pale. He seemed to gather a last reserve of strength about him
like a cloak, and straightened as his eyes found Thaine. He
stumbled forward and went to one knee before Thaine, his
head bowed, his eyes closed. The pain etched into his face
made him look like an old man.

"My lord Duke—" he whispered.

Thaine went white. He reached out a hand and raised
the young man to his feet. "I know you, Dafydd ap Glenyr.
What news do you bring?"

"Your father, Duke Cai is dead, my lord," Dafydd said.
He swayed on the very edge of his endurance and strength.
"He is dead, and we are destroyed at Laurelwater."

There were twelve of them—a full war council—assembled
in Athelin's workroom above the Great Hall, and they filled
the small room to the point of overflowing. Athelin sat at the
head of the long worktable, his back to the window where
snow piled high on the sill against the ice-frosted pane. Dorlaine sat to his left with Gabhain, Valessa, Drustan, and Cyn-

ric to her left. Opposite Athelin at the other end of the table sat Dafydd ap Glenyr, fed now and rested, but still pale and worn-looking. Thaine ap Cai sat on Athelin's right and beside him, Acaren, Eliene, Rowan, and Mioragh. Ralf moved smoothly and adroitly around the table, pouring hot mulled wine for everyone, then, without fuss, took his place beside Cynric.

Rowan glanced around the table. A grim assembly, he thought. The news from Laurelwater was bad news indeed. Cai, Duke of Wenydd, was a kinsman, descended like the princes of Skai from Red Kian of Skai, but through Red Kian's daughter Torey. The kinship grew more distant with each generation, but neither the dukes of Wenydd nor the princes of Skai ever forgot it or dismissed it as negligible.

Thaine ap Cai spoke without rising. "Dafydd ap Glenyr is the son of my father's Captain of the Company. Both of them I've long known and trusted completely. Dafydd, please tell us what happened."

"Somber Riders, my lord Duke," Dafydd said hoarsely.

Rowan's gaze flicked to Thaine. Thaine winced almost imperceptibly as Dafydd addressed him by his father's title. Rowan glanced quickly at Athelin, then at Gabhain. As Gabhain would if something happened to Athelin.

"Five companies of Somber Riders." Again, deep pain etched Dafydd's face. "They came up the coast the day after the Midwinter Festival, my lord, and fell upon us before we could gather to defend ourselves."

"No warning?" Drustan asked.

"None at all," Dafydd said. "And, of course, we weren't expecting an attack at that time of year." He looked at Thaine, mute entreaty and pain in his eyes. "We've always been safe in the winter. The snow has always protected us before."

"Of course," Athelin said. "Please go on."

Dafydd ignored him, his attention unwaveringly on Thaine. "I would have stayed and fought them to the death, my lord, but your father himself charged me with the safety of your young brother and sister. I took everyone I could find to the ship with me. We barely made it out of the harbor alive, and some didn't survive the voyage here. Your lady mother was among them, my lord."

Thaine's face spasmed again, and his lips thinned. Then he looked up. "They came over the mountains?" he asked incredulously. "Through the passes in the middle of winter?"

"No, my lord. Along the coast. Horbad himself led them. I saw him. His sorcery must have given them a path through the snow and ice along the coast."

Cynric shifted in his chair, nodding. "It's low country there, after all," he said, his arms folded across his chest, his heavy brows drawn together in concentration. "I know that country to the northwest of the island. Hakkar's spell and Horbad's sorcery would work there very effectively, I'm afraid."

Dafydd made a helpless gesture, blinking back tears of frustration and grief. "They were an army of five hundred, my lord. We were helpless before them. We stood no chance at all." His fist clenched in a harsh spasm around the stem of his goblet, the knuckles white against the dark, glossy glazed pottery. "But the Somber Riders died in the snow under our swords. My father and his men sold their lives dearly."

"Were there any other survivors?" Dorlaine asked gently.

"I believe some fled into the high country, my lady," Dafydd replied. "I don't know for sure. There was no time to gather them before we were overrun. I doubt there were many."

Athelin sat back, his mouth a thin and level line. Rowan had never seen him look so bleak. "The loss of Cai and his people is tragic news indeed," he said. His voice was soft, quiet, nearly uninflected, but Rowan could see the iron control Athelin exerted to keep it that way. Overcoming anger and outrage and grief, not fear. He turned to Thaine. "I can only offer my sympathy to you and your family, my lord Duke. And offer you what shelter we have in Skerry Keep for as long as you need it."

A bitter half smile twisted the corner of Thaine's mouth. "There's not much else you can do," he said. "We can't attack Hakkar or Horbad in return."

"We may have to," Athelin said.

Mioragh, who had been staring down into the wine in his cup, stirred restlessly in his seat. "Hakkar must be mounting a campaign to wipe out all the Celae not under his spell," he said quietly without looking up. "With the loss of Cai's men, we have not much of an army left to us."

"In any event, we couldn't survive a war of attrition," Gabhain said. "We are too few to begin with, and even the loss of one man would be felt drastically. Hakkar has an unlimited amount of men at his disposal. If he sent them against us, it would be only a matter of time before he destroyed us all."

Drustan shifted in his seat, frowning. "We should have seen this coming," he said. "The Doriani saw what was happening all along the Verge this past summer. I should have known Hakkar was mounting a campaign against us. Even the Veniani, who have never lived south of the Verge and never opposed Maedun, have been slaughtered."

Athelin looked at Mioragh. "What say you, Mioragh. Will Hakkar send his troops against us here on Skerry?"

Mioragh lifted one shoulder, let it fall. "I don't know, my lord. We've been fighting off raiding parties at the rate of one or two a year for the last nine or ten years. Is this any different?"

"This was an army," Athelin said. "Not a simple raiding party. An army and an attack that amounts to the beginning of a serious campaign."

Mioragh frowned. "Hakkar doesn't rule the sea, and the sea is the only way to Skerry and Marddyn. He may be content with the destruction of Cai's people on the Laurelwater. I know of no way of finding out for certain."

"What do you say, Cynric?" Athelin asked.

Cynric leaned forward. "I'm of the opinion that Hakkar still thinks he's destroyed the Prince of Skai and all his family. We took great pains to make it look that way." A spasm of grief, quickly mastered, crossed his face. "But the sliver of Tell-Tale we found after the raid when Danal was slain still disturbs me."

"I've masked Rowan's magic," Mioragh said. "I believe it's working to hide him from Hakkar."

"I believe it, too." Drustan turned to Athelin again. "It's difficult to say at this time, my lord. I would agree with Mioragh, though. Unless we can find someone who's privy to Hakkar's orders, we have no way of finding out what his intentions are."

"I would beg to differ, my lord Drustan," Cynric said. "I believe Athelin is right. Hakkar has begun a campaign to destroy all of us."

"And our magic?" Drustan asked. "Where do we stand with that? Is there any way we could raise a curtain of enchantment around both Skerry and Marddyn as Donaugh did around Celi itself?"

"I doubt it, my lord." Mioragh turned to Dafydd. "I assume that Haelwd and Loth were not among the people you brought to Skerry?" he asked.

"Haelwd is with us," Dafydd replied. "I myself saw Loth fall to a dark sword."

Mioragh raised his hands, palms out. "In that case, we have only myself and three young men with potential," he said. "And we are pitifully little defense, I fear."

"We have one weapon we might use," Athelin said slowly. "A weapon the Maedun both loathe and fear greatly."

Rowan looked up quickly. There was something odd in Athelin's tone, and Rowan suddenly knew exactly what he would say. Beside Rowan, Mioragh drew in a deep, unsteady breath.

"Is it time, my lord?" he asked.

Athelin glanced at him, then nodded. "It is," he said. He looked around the table, meeting every pair of eyes. "We have weapons. If we can find them in time. The Swords of Wyfydd Smith. And the enchanter of the Maedun's own prophecy."

Acaren leapt to his feet. "We will fetch them back, Father," he said. "Rowan and I will go to Skai and fetch the swords back."

His heart beating hard enough that he was sure the others must hear it, Rowan stood. "First to Tyra," he said quietly. "First to Tyra to ask the Council of Clans for an army to help us take first Skai, then Celi, back from the Maedun."

Acaren's eyebrows rose in surprise, then he frowned. "No. Skai first. Skai is the most important."

"Believe me, Acaren," Rowan said. "In this, I'm right. Tyra first. An army to back the King and the enchanter, once we find their swords. We can't do it all by ourselves. Even with the swords . . ."

"Nor can you do it yet," Athelin said firmly. "I'll not risk anyone, especially any of my sons, to the seas in winter. The seas won't be safe until at least Beltane."

"But, Father," Acaren said. "We can't wait that long."

"We have to wait that long," Athelin said. "The Maedun aren't good sailors. They'll not be risking themselves to the winter gales. Even Hakkar's sorcery can't control the winds and ice storms."

Rowan sat down slowly and drew in a deep breath. "The swords of Wyfydd Smith," he said softly. He glanced at Acaren's face, lit from within by excitement. "You will be Champion after all, Acaren. And I shall be Kaith. . . ."

"We'll see," Athelin said, his voice strained. "We'll see."

Horbad rode slumped in his saddle, his thick cloak wrapped tightly around him, letting the horse have its head as it plodded south through the driving snow. The cold wind seemed to find every slight opening in his clothing, poking its chill fingers down against his flesh as if determined to pluck the last warmth from his body.

He hated this accursed country. He hated the snow that swirled up as thick and choking around his mouth and nose in the winter as the ashes in the desolate country did in the summer. He hated the high, arrogant mountains in the west and north, and he hated the spiritless, half-alive people still mindlessly working the land where his father generously allowed them to eke out their pitifully wretched existence. He couldn't believe that it was these beaten people his father, and his grandfather before him, had feared so greatly that they had virtually destroyed the island.

The men of Laurelwater in the north had proved to be no match for his soldiers. On the other hand though, he reflected, he had left over three hundred of his five hundred men dead and dying in the snow beside the bodies of the Celae. But there was no longer a settlement of Celae on Laurelwater. He had burned their squalid little village, razed to rubble the rude pile of stones they called a palace. In the whole settlement, he had found only one old man who gave off even the faintest emanations of magic, and he personally had separated the old wizard's ancient head from his feeble body. Not one spark of magic had been thrown against him.

The prophecy his father always harked back to told that an enchanter would come from this forsaken island who would obliterate the power of Maedun, extinguish the power of her sorcerers like water quenched a candle flame. Horbad couldn't believe that. He had seen what these people were like. Mindless and soulless and spiritless. Even the ones who called themselves free in the north had nothing that could cause even the slightest troublesome ripple in his own magic, and his own was not nearly so powerful as his father's. What could Maedun possibly fear from men such as that? Hadn't Maedun conquered most of the known world? How could one insignificant little island threaten her?

Horbad had wanted to go to the Continent for the winter. There were places in the south where the orange trees grew, the grapevines were thick on the hillsides, and the sun shone warm even on the day of Midwinter. The crisp, tart wines of the southern provinces flowed freely there, and the women were more lively than these sullen, dispirited Celae bitches who had been known to let their own children starve if that child had been sired by a Maedun soldier, one of the celebrated Somber Riders of Maedun, a father any woman should be proud of for her child. What kind of a woman would do that? Obviously, his father had to do something about that alarming trend, or soon there would be very few Celae left to work the land and produce the gold and iron and copper Maedun needed.

Horbad drew his head down deeper into the folds of his cloak and muttered a curse. Instead of letting him winter in the warmth of the southern provinces, Hakkar had insisted he mount this winter campaign against those lamentably weak Laurelwater Celae. It was completely unnecessary in

Horbad's opinion. Hadn't the only gleam of magic his father had ever sensed out of the north been extinguished years ago? And not a glimmer since. Perhaps his father was getting old, and becoming fearful with it.

Now there was a possibility, Horbad decided. Perhaps his father was becoming too old to keep his hold on this accursed land. When Hakkar died, his full power as well as his name would come to Horbad. Were he Hakkar, he could see no reason why he couldn't spend the coldest season of the year in the south. Some lesser warlock could certainly hold the spell in place for just one season, especially since it didn't have to be held so firmly over the land in the cold. Almost any warlock could hold the spell over the people for a short while, and it was the people who needed quelling more than the land.

It was an intriguing thought, anyway.

16

Storm after winter storm roared out of the northwest and rampaged its way across the Isle of Celi, whipping the surface of the Western Sea into a churning mass of ragged foam and freezing spume. The Cold Sea between Celi and the Continent seethed with violent currents clashing with the winds, making the sea itself as impenetrable to all ships as solid stone. Knowing that any ship with a master and crew foolhardy enough to try the seas would end up shredded and blown away like chaff before the wind, mariners retired to homes and taverns. No ships would brave the seas until well past Vernal Equinox.

In Rock Greghrach on the west coast of Skai, Horbad closed the doors of his fortress against the blizzards and spent his time before the blazing hearths in his private quarters, content with the knowledge that he could not possibly be expected to lead an attack on the Celae during the appallingly inclement weather, and that no messenger from his father could get through the passes to tell him to try.

Unless necessity forced otherwise, the people of Skerry Keep stayed indoors. They huddled by brazier and hearth, and listened to the wind howling and grumbling around the eaves while they spun wool and flax into yarn, wove fabric, or mended tack and tools, and retold the old tales and legends.

Rowan spent his time studying with Mioragh, with as few results as ever, and planning the expedition with Acaren and his father. Acaren had little patience with the detour to Tyra. He argued that the swords should be found and retrieved as soon as possible.

"We can't waste the time," he said. "We need to find the king and enchanter to give them the swords immediately. What if the Maedun attack Skerry again while we're in Tyra?"

"What if we fetch back the swords and have no army to fight the Maedun?" Rowan countered. "Even if we do find the swords, and find the king and the enchanter, you and I and the small army we have here stand little chance against the whole of the Maedun army."

"But we'll have the enchanter—"

"The enchanter may keep Hakkar and Horbad busy, but how are we to fight an army of thousands with a mere handful?"

Acaren turned to Athelin for support. "Tell him, Father," he said.

Athelin shrugged and smiled. "I agree with him," he said quietly. "You could do worse than listen to his counsel."

Impatience and exasperation showed plainly on Acaren's face, but he eventually agreed that the trip to Tyra to speak with the First Laird of the Council of Clans was, indeed, essential.

A fortnight before Imbolc, Athelin gave a feast and announced that the twins were to go questing for the swords of Wyfydd Smith. As cause for celebration, the announcement fulfilled its purpose. Conversation in the Great Hall was about little else.

Eventually, the hall grew quiet. Two servants brought Mioragh's floor harp into the Great Hall and put it down near the high table. Mioragh bowed to Athelin and Dorlaine, then took his seat and settled the harp against his shoulder.

"For this auspicious night," he said in a voice that carried to all corners of the Hall, "I have a story of hope that I learned a few years ago. It's a new story, one that will go into the bard lore. I sing it for the young men who will venture forth on an important mission a season hence. May this story give them and all of us hope and strength. It is the story of Daigwr and Ganieda." He struck a few rolling chords on the harp and began.

Some say that when Tiegan, son of Tiernyn, fell in the Battle of Cam Runn, so fell the last of the line of the High King of Celi. I tell to you that this is not true, for Tiegan's wife Sheryn who was of the Tyadda people, bore within her womb the seed of Tiegan, even as he fell. Tiegan's loyal bheancoran, Brynda al Keylan, granddaughter of Red Kian of Skai, and her brother Brennen, Prince of Skai, bore the lady Sheryn away to a fastness known to the Tyadda in the heart of the western mountains even as the dark armies of Maedun overran the green lands of Celi. There she gave birth to Tiegan's child, a son whose name in secret she called Daigwr, which is to say Avenger.

In the hidden fastness, Sheryn raised her son, teaching him such lore as the Tyadda knew and teaching him the history of his royal lineage. Daigwr had magic from his mother's line, and he had skill with a sword not seen since Anwyr wielded his great sword on the fields of battle against the Saesnesi.

When Daigwr was a man grown and in his prime, near unto thirty years, he went forth from the Tyadda fastness to look for his people. He had his magic to protect him, and a charm fashioned by his mother. For ten years and more, he traveled the high country as an itinerant bard, hiding his true nature, but found too few Celae with magic enough to protect them in the blighted lands under the hand of Hakkar.

Daigwr was sore at heart, and thirsted after vengeance for his father and his land, but he was such a king that he would not lead his people to certain death on the desolated fields of Celi. In all his travels, he met no man or woman with more magic than he himself possessed, no enchanter as had been his grandfather's brother, Donaugh.

Then one spring, Daigwr came to a place that was like a golden island in the midst of the desolation. It was the morning of Beltane night, and the people were deep in preparation for the festival to take place that night. Daigwr presented himself to the Prince of the place as a traveling bard and was made welcome. Daigwr's heart lifted for he saw there was great magic at work in this cove sheltered at the foot of great mountains that held back the spell of the black sorcerer of Maedun.

That night at the fires of Beltane, Daigwr met his love —

Ganieda, whom some called Gwynfleur and some called Cerrid-wylt. She was the daughter of the Prince, and her unbound hair like the blaze of oak leaves in autumn hung down her back to her hips.

Her beauty shone like a precious gem among the women at the fire, and Daigwr was charmed and bewitched by her. And she, finding him to be graceful and entrancing, sought him out among the dancers and offered to him alone her cup of mead.

Their love flamed brighter than the fire around which they danced as they came together in joy and celebration of the festival. As Daigwr bore her away to the shadows, they pledged their love forever beneath the stars and the sheltering leaves of the sacred oaks. And when Daigwr slept, Ganieda twined her hair about him to bind him to her for as long as he might live.

But Daigwr dreamed in Ganieda's arms. It seemed to him that Tiernyn and Donaugh walked with him beside a wide river that gleamed silver in the moonlight, and Donaugh told him that Hakkar would be defeated in single combat by one of Tiernyn's line and blood. Hearing this, Daigwr was reminded of his vow of vengeance, and arose before dawn in determination to vanquish the black sorcerer. He took a silver blade and severed the strands of golden hair that bound him to Ganieda, and laying a kiss upon her sleeping lips, he slipped into the darkness to seek out Hakkar.

In answer to Daigwr's challenge, Hakkar left his stolen fortress in Clendonan and met Daigwr on the plain near the Dance of Nemeara. The very standing stones of the Dance shivered to the clash of their swords as they fought each other for two days and two nights. But when it seemed that Daigwr's magic was a match for Hakkar's, Hakkar's son Horbad rose in treachery and loosed an arrow at Daigwr that took him in the thick of the thigh and his blood flowed into the soil of his people and he gave a great cry in anguish.

Thus weakened, Daigwr fell back and was slain by the dark sword of Hakkar. And it is said that, every spring, even among the burned and bitter ashes of the desolate country, the red anemones bloom where Daigwr's blood nourished the soil of his beloved land.

When word of Daigwr's death was brought to Ganieda,

who was then heavy with child, she cried out a loud lament and fell senseless to the ground and soon died in grief for her lost love.

But before she died, in secret she gave birth to the seed of Daigwr, taken in love on that Beltane night.

So I say to you now that there lives in this land the true-born High King of Celi. And there will arise an enchanter to stand by his side as Donaugh stood by the side of Tiernyn. There will come out of the high country a Champion and a Kaith such as were Anwyr and Avigus, and once again, the land of Celi will be free.

Mioragh struck one last chord on the harp and let the echoes fade slowly to silence. He got to his feet and beckoned the servants to remove the floor harp, then went to receive the silver ring and the cup of wine Athelin held out to him.

Athelin's eyes narrowed enigmatically as he looked into the bard's eyes. "Mioragh," he said softly, "sometimes I think you know far too much."

"My lord, sometimes I am just as certain that I know far too little."

Unable to sleep, Acaren tossed back the quilts and got up. He glanced quickly out his window. The heavy clouds had broken and scattered, but the wind still sent snow driving horizontally across the fields and coarse gravel shingle by the harbor. He shivered. It was not a night to wander the terraces or the battlements of the curtain wall. He went instead to the solar where the windows looked out over the harbor.

The room was deserted and frigid. No residual warmth remained in the hearth, and the charcoal in the braziers lay cold and dark. Acaren drew his heavy house robe around himself and looked out over the water of the harbor. The full moon tossed restlessly among the broken shards of cloud, and the Huntress Star, as ever in pursuit, winked on and off as the scud raced across the sky.

"You're awake late, Acaren."

Acaren glanced over his shoulder at the sound of his father's voice, then turned back to watch the sea. "All the bards sing about how difficult it is for young men to sleep peacefully, don't they?" he said.

Athelin came to join him by the window. "It's quite possible that's true," he said. "I believe I remember being young once."

Acaren grinned. "Sometime around Red Kian's time, wasn't that?"

"Don't be flippant," Athelin said, but took the sting out of the words with a smile. "I also remember that it's in spring that young men are supposed to have trouble sleeping." He made a sweeping gesture to include the frozen scene outside the window. "That's hardly spring, I'd say."

"No," Acaren agreed. "Hardly spring at all."

"Rhan tells me you've not been sleeping well at all for a while now. Is it something I can help with?"

Acaren watched the sea. The moon path on the water's surface seemed to lead from the jetty straight out through the mouth of the harbor to the Western Sea. For a moment, he watched it in silence, then turned to Athelin.

"I want to go to Skai now," he said, unable to keep the emotion from quivering in his voice. "I don't want to wait until spring. I know I must wait, but it rankles."

Athelin merely waited.

"And I don't want to go to Tyra before we go to Skai. Rowan insists, but I can't see it doing any good at all."

"You'll need the Tyran army."

"So Rowan says. And I suppose he's right. But still it rankles." He stood for a moment as the moon slipped closer to the horizon. He turned to meet Athelin's eyes. "All our lives, Rowan and I have taken for granted that we would be Champion and Kaith to the king when he comes. Now that it might actually be happening, I have no patience with waiting."

"Patience is hard to learn," Athelin said. "It comes with learning wisdom." He smiled. "And wisdom is one thing you've always told me you despaired of ever learning."

Acaren didn't smile. "All my life I've joked about the things that meant the most to me," he said. "I even joked about discovering that I possessed a spark of magic." He shook his head. "But I can't joke about this. Not about this."

"Don't disparage a spark of magic," Athelin said. "I have only a little magic, but it's enough. It's enough to resonate with the Rune Blade I carry. So will yours be."

"A Rune Blade? I'll carry no Rune Blade. Gabhain will someday carry Bane. But none for me—"

"We'll see what happens when you get to Skai," Athelin said neutrally.

"But first Tyra," Acaren said.

"Aye. First Tyra."

"It's a good plan, my lord."

Acaren swung around to see Cynric standing just inside the door of the room. Athelin turned more slowly. Cynric crossed the room to stand beside Acaren, looking out across the harbor.

"It's a good plan," he said again. "And I shall accompany you when you go. Especially to Skai."

"Your sword would be welcome," Acaren said. "But—"

Cynric said. "I have no doubt the Tyrans will be eager to join you and Rowan, once Hakkar and his sorcery are neutralized. However, it won't hurt our cause to have a small army already in Skai and waiting for a signal to attack the Maedun."

Acaren frowned "Who are you talking about?"

Cynric smiled. "Athelin knows, I think."

"The free Celae in the mountains," Athelin said. "Enough to form a small army, agreed. But scattered."

"Aye, they're scattered wide," Cynric agreed. "But I think there's a man in Skai who could gather them quickly enough."

Intrigued, Acaren said, "And who would that be?"

"A man named Devlyn Wykanson," Cynric said. "Devlyn Wykanson is the seed of Aellegh, son of Donaugh ap Kian, and Celwalda of the Saesnesi. I knew his father, Wykan."

"Where—" Athelin said, then broke off, frowning in deep thought. "Ah, of course. Before you came to us here in Skerry."

"Aye. When your sister and her husband went in search of the swords all those years ago."

Athelin studied him, speculation and consideration in his eyes. "Yes," he said slowly. "Yes, I see."

"I think I can find Devlyn's people quickly," Cynric said. "And Devlyn will be able to raise the support we need right there in Skai."

"And the king?" Acaren asked. "Does Devlyn know where to find the king and the enchanter?"

Cynric shook his head. "No," he said. "But they both will be ready when they're needed."

Acaren pulled his house robe tighter around him in the chill of the room. A detour to Tyra might be a necessary delay. But an army of yrSkai —

He laughed a little breathlessly. For the first time, the expedition felt like a reality rather than just a cherished dream.

17

Imbolc came, the time of New Fire. The ships were back from the shores of Laurelwater with the last of the survivors of the Wenydd colony that had flourished there since the invasion over fifty years ago. The yrSkai of Skerry and Marddyn made room for them, welcoming them to share the meager bounties of the small islands.

On the eve of the Feast of New Fire, Rowan closed the book he had been studying and went to the window. All around the harbor, light blazed in windows as the people of Skerryharbor made the last preparations for Imbolc. He turned away and looked down at the book on the table, running his fingers across the worn leather binding.

Learning magic from a book was an impossible task. But he had no idea how to obtain the knowledge without the books. When he asked Mioragh how he had learned his magic, the bard could not say precisely. "It was just there one day," he said. "It came to me in the oak grove near the shrine."

"But how did *you* learn to control it?" Rowan asked in frustration. "Surely you can tell me what worked for you. It might work for me, too."

Mioragh held out both hands helplessly. "From the start, my magic was biddable. Not strong by any means, but biddable."

Rowan looked down at his own hands. Not strong magic and most certainly not biddable. Surely after all these years of studying with Mioragh, he should have more control of the incipient magic Mioragh assured him was his. Surely, it should be there. . . .

"Rowan, we're just about ready to start. Are you coming?"

He turned to see Eliene al Saethen peering around the door of the room. She laughed and held out her hand.

"Come on. You don't want to be late."

He hurried forward to take her hand, and realized that Acaren, still in the corridor and calling to someone farther down the hall, held her other hand. Rowan caught up her hand, and she glanced happily from him to Acaren.

"I have the two best-looking escorts in the Keep," she said, laughing. "Let's hurry or we'll be late. It's nearly sundown."

As the sun set, all the fires in the Keep and in the village were left to die until there was nothing left but cold ashes in all the hearths. The people of Skerry Keep and Skerryharbor, dressed in robes of coarse, gray homespun, gathered in the Great Hall. The women carried large bowls made of unglazed earthenware, and the men carried small ash shovels and whisk brooms made of straw from last autumn's harvest.

The priest and priestess from the shrine above the village, bound together as always to symbolize the male/female nature of the Duality, mounted the dais at the head of the hall and began to intone a prayer. As they finished, silence fell over the Great Hall. The priest and priestess raised their arms and smiled.

"Let the cleansing and renewal begin," they said.

In pairs, the men and women went to all the hearths in the Keep. Rowan found himself partnered with a young serving girl who smiled shyly as he swept the ashes from one of the cooking hearths in the kitchen and filled her bowl with the pale, powdery ash.

He had always loved the quiet ritual of New Fire at Imbolc. While he drew water and scrubbed the hearth until it gleamed, he listened to the women singing as they walked out into the night with their bowls of ash to spread them on the gravel shingle along the harbor. Their voices, high and clear and sweet, chimed in the night, filling it gently with music.

When Rowan's hearth was clean, he returned to the Great Hall. Gradually it filled again as the men finished their cleansing tasks and the women returned from the harbor, their bowls empty. The priest and priestess slowly circled the room, extinguishing the candles one by one as they went. As the last candle went out and darkness descended with a rush, an expectant hush fell over the room.

In the stillness, the priest and priestess's voice seemed loud. "Let now the doors be thrown wide to welcome in any wandering gods of the night."

Rowan carefully made his way through the crowd to the door of the Great Hall, then down the stairs to the Keep gates. Gabhain and Acaren joined him, and together they opened the massive gates wide. No lights at all showed in the village. Overhead, the moon and stars gave a faint illumination to the world.

People streamed out into the night, gathering the wood that had been stacked in readiness for the new fires. Laughter rang out, and snatches of song.

Rowan carried new wood to the kitchen and carefully laid a new fire on the hearth he had scrubbed, then returned to the Great Hall. The darkness made it difficult to see. Muffled giggles and whispering made it clear that some were taking full advantage of the dark. Quiet descended again as the priest and priestess called for attention.

"Beodun, Father of Fires, hear us!" they cried from their place on the dais.

"Hear us, Father of Fires," Rowan responded with the crowd.

"Father of Fires, bless this house with your New Fire, and bless the people herein. As the hearths are cleansed and made ready for your needfire, called from the heavens themselves, so cleanse the hearts and spirits of those gathered here. All praise to you, Beodun, Father of Fires."

"All praise to you, Father of Fires."

A rustle of movement shimmered through the Great Hall. Rowan reached under his robe to bring out the special candle, made of beeswax from a wild hive. On the dais, the priest and priestess had already raised their candle.

"Send us your fire, Beodun," the priest and priestess cried in practiced unison.

Out of the dark came a bright arrow, a hissing lance of flame. The wick of the candle the priest and priestess held sputtered, then flared up brightly, casting flickering shadows across their faces, turning their gray robes red with reflected fire.

"Children of Beodun, share his gift with us," they said, offering the flame to the gathering.

One after the other in a long file, the men and women in the hall stepped forward and touched their candles to the flame of the candle the priest and priestess held, until the Great Hall was ablaze with light. Dorlaine went to the hearth beside the dais and knelt, slowly reaching out with her candle to light the wood newly laid there. The flame caught immediately, a good omen, and a ripple of satisfaction shimmered around the room. The kindling crackled and popped, then smoke curled up and was swept up into the chimney.

New Fire had come to Skerry Keep. The god's gift was accepted with gratitude.

Rowan went to the kitchen to light the fire he had made. Music sounded in the Great Hall, then filled the whole house. Women laughed as the men formed and baked the flatcakes. The women brought the honey they had gathered from the wild hives during the summer for just this purpose. The men spread the cakes with honey and handed them around amid much good-natured laughter and bantering.

Dancing had already begun in the Great Hall when Rowan returned. Acaren's bright, dark gold hair stood out sharply under the newly lit candles and lamps in the Hall as he danced with Eliene. Athelin and Dorlaine stood by the dais, giving greeting to the people.

Rowan stood in the shadows by the entrance to the Great Hall and watched. Beodun's gift of New Fire blazed in the hearths, at the tips of the candles and lamps upon the tables, and in the massed torches along the walls. The light glittered and sparked on silver brooches, jeweled combs in the hair of the women, and gold bracelets and chains. The people of Skerry Keep had turned out in all their finery to honor the god's gift.

Rowan turned his back on the blazing gaiety in the Great Hall and made his way toward the kitchens. He pulled on his woolen doublet and his fur-lined cloak. Unseen, he slipped out into the night.

Overhead, the moon rode high among shreds of leftover cloud and turned the skiff of new snow into a glittering carpet of gems that crunched and squeaked beneath Rowan's boots as he made his way up Ben Warden's lower slope. He passed the shrine that stood in the midst of its twelve oak trees, the lifeless strands of ivy hanging stiffly like frozen strings from the bare, skeletal branches. The path he followed led around the shrine and farther up the mountain.

The small circle of stones stood in a shallow bowl sheltered on three sides by stands of cedar, fir, and delicate traceries of white birch and silver-leaf maple. The seven stones themselves stood only half again as tall as Rowan himself, and were arranged in a circle that would have been completely symmetrical had there been eight stones. The stone that apparently should have stood at the east end was missing, leaving an opening—an entryway—into the circle.

Rowan paused just outside the circle. The stones, each representing one of the seven gods and goddesses, stood smooth and tall in the moonlight, casting indigo shadows across the glittering, unmarked snow. To his left, Beodun of the Fires, Adriel of the Waters, and Sandor of the Plains. To his right, Cernos of the Forest, Gerieg of the Crags, and Rhianna of the Air. And facing him, the *darlai*, the Mother of All. The very Spirit of the Land.

He shivered, but not from the cold. He thought he had once dreamed the stones had come alive. But tonight, they were only stones. Tall and smooth and polished. But only stones.

He stepped into the center of the ring and made a deep obeisance to each of the stones in turn, and lastly to the *darlai* stone. He went to one knee and looked up at the sky. The stars blazed fiercely in the black of the sky, and not even the light of the moon approaching full could dim their fire.

If he closed his eyes, he could feel the currents of power flowing around him, through the air, in the earth beneath his knee. They were so strong, so vivid, he felt he could trail his fingers in them as if in the bubbling water of a swiftly flowing brook. If he held out his cupped hands, the moonlight itself seemed to have weight and substance. And in the day, with his eyes closed, the sunlight streaming across his hands felt thick and warm and viscid as honey.

But he could do nothing with any of it. Not the streams of power, nor the moonlight nor the sunlight. Every time he tried to pick up a strand of the power or to cup the light in his hands, it evaporated to nothing and was gone.

"What am I doing wrong?" he asked the silent circle. "Why can I not use this power if I can feel it?"

The circle had no answer for him.

"My grandfather didn't come into his power until he was a grown man," he said aloud. "And tonight, I am a man. In the morning, Acaren and I will celebrate our seventeenth Name Day. No longer youths, but men." He raised his hands to the stone representing Rhianna of the Air. "Twice I've dreamed of you, Lady. Twice in my dreams, you've told me I am your man." He looked down at his empty hands and bowed his head. "I can serve neither my father nor his people without your gift," he whispered. "Nor can I serve you, Lady." He held his hands out in entreaty to the *darlai* stone. "I can feel the power. It's so close, yet so impossibly far away. How can I become Kaith to Acaren's Champion if I have no magic?"

No answer came to him through the night. The circle remained silent.

Despair ran through him. His eyes stung with unshed tears. The moon moved in its stately progression across the sky and dipped below the rocky crags of Ben Roth. Rowan didn't move. Cold seeped into him, and his breath plumed white around his head, rising to turn his eyebrows and hair white with long strands of hoarfrost.

He hardly noticed the sky in the east beginning to pale. The deep black lightened, and the stars overhead dimmed. The wan light grew until he realized he could see the trees behind the stones quite clearly. Stiffly, he climbed to his feet and stamped his feet to bring some feeling back to them.

As the light strengthened, he bowed deeply to each of the stones and turned his back to the *darlai* stone. Slowly, he made his way back to the Keep. The gates were closed, and the hunched shape of sleepy guards showed in the turrets. The guard at the postern gate greeted him with a tired smile and stepped aside to let him through.

Acaren was already asleep when Rowan entered the room. He added another handful of charcoal to the brazier, then stripped and climbed into his own bed.

Very faintly, he heard a voice—a voice he recognized as belonging to the young woman who haunted his dreams.

"Soon, beloved," she said quietly. "Soon now."

"Soon," he repeated hopelessly. "Aye, soon. Half my life has gone while I wait for *soon*."

Rowan dreamed. Again, he saw the Beltane fires leaping high against the spring green of the oak grove. Two young men stood in the shadow of a shrine, arguing fiercely. There was something hauntingly familiar about them. For a moment Rowan thought the young men were Acaren and himself. They were twins, but they were younger by several years, and subtly different.

He watched them for a moment, intrigued, then realized he knew who they were. Donaugh the Enchanter and his twin brother Tiernyn, who would become High King of all Celi.

But Tiernyn wasn't High King in the dream. Not yet. He was still only Tiernyn ap Kian, a young man who burned to lead an army against an enemy.

Rowan stepped forward, but the hanging curtains of ivy twined around him and held him back. But he heard what they were saying. Fascinated, without self-consciousness, he listened.

"Watch," Donaugh said. "Watch closely." And for a moment, Rowan thought he was speaking to him. But as he leaned forward to hear, it seemed to him that he had slipped into Donaugh's body and merged with him. Rowan ap Athelin became the dream, and Donaugh ap Kian became the reality under the shadows of the ivy.

Donaugh reached out and grasped a thread of power flowing through the earth beneath him. He let the magic build slowly. He felt

*light and airy as a bubble in a wineglass. The music sang in his blood,
and crackled along his nerves. Behind Tiernyn on the wall of the
shrine, their shadows wavered and shimmered like water sheeting down
the sheer rock face of a cliff. As the shadows re-formed, they built a pic-
ture of a man wearing a crown, standing tall and straight as one of the
twelve sacred oaks, the sword in his raised hand glowing with a radiance that lit the trees. But where Donaugh stood, there was nothing—
only a slim wisp, smoke or mist in the moonlight.*

"There," Donaugh whispered, his voice rough and hoarse. "Do
you see?"

The king-shadow stood sharp and clear on the pale wall of the
shrine as letters painted on parchment. Wordlessly, Tiernyn nodded.

Donaugh let the magic go. It snapped and cracked like a cable
breaking under tension. Pain whipped at Donaugh, and he caught his
breath.

And Rowan was himself again, watching the two young men as
they turned away from the shrine and made their way to join the procession up the mountainside.

He stepped back, trying to see where they went, but the trees and
the mountain and even the Beltane fire faded into a drift of mist.
Rowan blinked, and found himself standing in a room, a small-scale
Great Hall, where a fire blazed brightly in a hearth to ward off the
severe chill of winter.

The room held two men and one woman. One of the men, tall,
blond, bearded, stood with his back toward the fire, frowning in disbelief and anger. He was Saesnesi. Startled, Rowan recognized him. Elesan, the Saesnesi Celwalda who fought against Tiernyn. Rowan
wasn't sure how he knew, but didn't question the knowledge.

The other man—again Rowan knew Donaugh instantly—sat
at the table, the woman beside him. Tension filled the room, tangible as
the smoke that rose from the fire. The antagonism of ancient enemies
lay between Donaugh and Elesan. And a desperation that Rowan was
certain Elesan couldn't see hung like a mist around Donaugh.

The woman turned her head and looked directly at Rowan where
he stood invisible in the dream behind the table. The woman, her wheat
blond hair held in place by two gold combs that were a darker gold than
her hair, watched him levelly for a moment. Her image wavered for a
moment, and Rowan saw he was mistaken. Her hair was a flowing
mass of red-gold waves and curls, not straight and shiny blond. Those

eyes were gray, though. As gray as spring mist. She raised one eyebrow, then smiled very slightly and turned her complete attention back to Donaugh and Elesan, and her hair was, after all, very blond.

Shocked, Rowan stepped back a pace. She had seen him. She was as aware of him as he was of her.

Elesan said something angrily. Rowan looked at him quickly.

Donaugh made an exasperated gesture and drew in a deep breath. "I will show you what I saw," he said quietly. "If you won't believe what I say, believe what I show you."

Again, Rowan let his own awareness sink into Donaugh as, for all intents and purposes, he became the Enchanter.

The lines of power flowing in the earth beneath him, through the air around him, were thinner here than in Skai, more tenuous and fragile. Donaugh settled himself with an effort and began to gather power. He wasn't sure if he could do this, wasn't sure how to go about it, wasn't sure if it had ever been done before. He muttered a brief prayer to the darlai and to Rhianna of the Air for support and assistance. If he were to convince Elesan of the absolute necessity of working together, it had to work.

He looked into the fire, concentrating on the power flowing around him in living streams. Sweat rolled down his forehead and into his eyes, stinging. As he had done at the shrine in Dun Eidon when he showed Tiernyn the king-shadow, he wove the power together. But this was infinitely more difficult. He must bring forth images stronger and sharper than mere shadows if Elesan were to believe him and help him.

Painfully, straining with the effort, he built pictures against the blaze of the hearth, brushstroke by agonized brushstroke. The battle scenes appeared before the flames, thin and nebulous as shadows, but recognizable and ghastly in their silence.

Donaugh bent his head, closed his eyes, concentrating to bring every nuance of his vision clearly to Elesan. His head throbbed and pounded, and his breath, dry as sand and ash, rasped like a file against the back of his throat. Elesan watched silently. Only his tense breathing and the whitened knuckles of his fist on the polished wood of the table betrayed his tautly stretched nerves.

Donaugh faltered as he struggled to build the last of the vision in the air before the fire. The scene wavered as the Celae captain's soldiers pulled Elesan's son Aelric to the center of the ring of Celae soldiers, blurring and fading behind Donaugh's closed eyes. Eliade rose and *placed her hands on his shoulders. The strength of the bond between them steadied him. He felt her tremble as she pressed against his back. Fighting for control of the power, he brought the last details of the scene to life. The captain's sword flashed down, and Aelric vanished behind the wall of Celae soldiers.*

Elesan made a strangled sound in the back of his throat. He lurched to his feet, his hand reaching out to his son. But even as he did so, the fire rose up to consume the island. The images of blood and trampled snow vanished in the leaping flames. Ash and cinder . . .

Elesan cried out in anguish. "Enough," he shouted. "That's enough. I will watch no more."

Exhausted, Donaugh slumped in his chair. He released the magic. The threads of power snapped, cracking like a whip, lashing him with pain as they sprang back into place in the earth and air. The images in the air crackled, then shattered like fragile glass. They flickered briefly, glinting in the firelight, then vanished.

Rowan came gasping out of sleep, wincing with the pain of released magic. He wrapped his arms around his chest, trying not to cry out with the agony. It faded eventually, flowing away like water into parched earth, leaving him aching and sore.

Mayhaps, he thought, *if that's magic, I don't really want it.*

A woman's faint laughter came to him. "We'll see . . ."

18

*Rowan awoke to the sunlight streaming through the window and flow-*ing brightly across his bed, golden as new honey. He put his hand out and trailed his fingers through the river of light. It tingled and fizzed against his skin like water bubbling from a mineral spring. But when he cupped his hands and tried to let the light fill them, it became only ordinary light, nothing but bright air with a few dust motes like sparks floating gently through it.

He let his hand fall back to the coverlet and sat for a moment studying it. It was merely a man's hand, lean and brown and strong. Deft and skilled enough when holding the hilt of a sword, passably adept on the strings of a harp. But only a hand. Not a vessel to contain magic, nor a tool to shape it or command it. Just a man's hand.

He clenched it into a fist and lay back against his pillows. He had dreamed of Donaugh the Enchanter. From what he had read of history, and from what he had learned of the bards' lore, he knew one of the things he had seen was Donaugh trying to convince the Saesnesi Celwalda Elesan that the Celae and the Saesnesi had to work together in order to defeat the coming Maedun menace. Tiernyn's army had captured Elesan's son Aelric. In the vision Donaugh had reconstructed for Elesan, the Celae army had beheaded Aelric, and because of that, the black tide of Maedun swept across the land.

Donaugh had succeeded in preventing Aelric's death on the field of battle. But he hadn't been able to prevent his murder at the hands of one of Tiernyn's most trusted captains.

And while Tiernyn and Donaugh had succeeded in driving back the first Maedun invasion, the Celae army went down in defeat before the second invasion some thirty years later, but only after Donaugh himself fell to treachery at the hand of his own son by a Maedun sorceress. So, even as he had succeeded with Elesan, Donaugh had sowed the seeds of failure in the end.

Rowan wondered if Donaugh had paid the price demanded by his magic. Treachery at the hands of kin, the loss of everything he'd held dear. The loss of his life's beloved. It might be that the cost of magic was too dear. Tragedy. Loss. Defeat.

But there was hope of redress. There was a promise of salvation—the swords that Wyfydd Smith had built for Donaugh's use in defeating Hakkar the black sorcerer. If Rowan could not command his magic, he could certainly go with Acaren to raise a Tyran army as allies, and find the almost mythical swords for the coming king and his enchanter.

He threw back the covers and got out of bed, following the streaming river of light to the window. Outside, the wind blew a mist of snow in a blinding white swirl across the fields. Waves crashed on the ice-glazed rocks of the breakwater, sending freezing spume two or three man-heights into the air. Ice turned the surfaces of the jetty and the wooden piers treacherously slippery. Rowan sighed, and turned from the window. There would be no ships venturing forth to the Continent this day.

Imbolc wore on toward the Vernal Equinox and storms continued to batter the small islands. The combination of a wind that blew incessantly from the northwest and a sea current that flowed from the southwest set the water to churning violently and dangerously, even when the sky was clear.

Eventually, the wind direction eased around from northwest to southwest, and blew across the land, carrying a hint of warm air with it. First along the south slopes of the mountains and in the southernmost pastures and meadows, the snow turned first grainy, then slushy, then melted. Glowing white blossoms of snowberry began to appear between the tired patches of snow. The winter-dead grass of the practice field turned sodden with mud underfoot. Rowan went every day to practice with Weymund and tried not to think of either Tyra or the magic he felt surging through the gradually awakening land all around him.

A little less than a fortnight before Vernal Equinox, when the soggy brown grass in the fields seemed to be beaten to death by the rain and the stark trees dripped moisture into the sodden ground, Athelin called them together. The Master of the *Skai Seeker*, he announced, thought two days hence in the morning would be a good time to begin a voyage to Tyra.

The snow-covered peaks of Ben Aislin and Ben Warden blazed gold and pink as the sun slipped down through the clear sky toward the western horizon. Since Athelin's announcement, Acaren had been doing a creditable imitation of a finch flitting from one uneasy perch to another, unable to settle for more than the space of a few heartbeats before skittering off to somewhere else. On this evening before the journey was to commence, his excitement and almost feverish agitation burned within him like a visible flame. Just trying to watch him made Rowan tired. He took himself off to his chambers to see to his own last-minute preparations.

He was trying to decide whether or not to take a second pair of boots when Cynric entered the room. Rowan beckoned him over to the bed where he had laid out the equipment he thought he would need.

"What do you think, Cynric?" he asked. "Have I everything I need here?"

Cynric looked down. "You'll need a small mess kit," he said. "You should be able to get one in the barracks. They'll be light enough. Remember, you'll be carrying all this yourself."

Rowan frowned down at the array on the bed, then resignedly removed the second pair of boots. Cynric reached out and ran a hand over the smooth contours of the small harp.

"Do you plan on taking this, too?" he asked.

Rowan gave him a hesitant, slightly embarrassed smile

and leapt to the harp's defense. "Well, where I go, Songmaker goes," he said. "He's not very heavy. I can put him in his carry case and sling him over my shoulder easily enough."

Cynric smiled. "I wasn't going to suggest you leave him," he said. "I wasn't sure you'd want to take such a beautiful thing into harm's way."

"It's stronger than it looks," Rowan said. He laughed. "Like a lot of people I know."

Cynric smiled, then said, "Your father is waiting for you in the solar. He asked me to fetch you there."

Rowan looked up, met Cynric's eyes. The irises were as dark as the widened pupils, and, as usual, gave away nothing of what Cynric might be thinking. Rowan found no clue there to tell him what Athelin wanted. He folded the carry case around the harp and secured the laces.

"I'll come now," he said.

Gabhain and Valessa were already in the solar when Rowan came in with Cynric. Athelin and Dorlaine sat in their comfortable chairs by the hearth.

Both Athelin and Dorlaine looked uncomfortable, almost ill at ease and worried. Rowan glanced quickly at Cynric, but found no answers there.

"Are you all right, Mother?" he asked. "You look a little pale."

Dorlaine gave him a smile that was strained a little at the corners. "I expect I'm just a bit tired," she said. "It's been an eventful few days."

"Indeed it has," Athelin agreed. "Please sit down, Rowan." He looked up as Acaren and Eliene entered the room. "Both of you, too. Please have a seat." Cynric turned to leave the room, but Athelin called him back with a quick gesture. "Please stay, Cynric," he said. "This concerns you, too."

Acaren looked from Athelin to Dorlaine and back to Athelin. "If you're worried about us, I wish you wouldn't be. We'll be perfectly all right in Tyra. And in Skai, too."

"I'm sure you will," Athelin said. "I have complete confidence in all of you. This family conference is about something else entirely. Something everyone needs to know before you and Rowan leave here."

Athelin leaned back in his chair, but the knuckles of his hands where they rested on the carved wood of the arms of the chair were white. Rowan glanced quickly from him, to Dorlaine, who was almost as pale, then to Gabhain and Valessa. They sat quietly, almost identical quizzical expressions on their faces, halfway between worry and puzzlement. Cynric, as always, appeared calm and composed and noncommittal.

"Before you embark upon this momentous journey, there is something I must tell you." Athelin spoke slowly, his tone deliberate and precise, as if he were choosing each word carefully. "There is something you must know—all of you."

Rowan watched him, an odd, unsettled sensation simmering under his rib cage. Athelin met his eyes briefly, and Rowan's breath caught in his throat. He could not read what emotion lay in Athelin's eyes, but whatever it was sent a chill shivering down his spine.

He knows why I can't use the magic, he thought in shock, then immediately realized that was wrong. *Something else, then.* Something that had haunted him since childhood.

Gabhain spoke for all of them. "What is it that we need to know, Father?" he asked quietly.

Athelin took a deep breath, then looked to each of his sons in turn. "First of all, you know I love you all."

Acaren laughed a little nervously. "That," he said softly, "has never been in doubt."

"There is no easy way to say this," Athelin said. Blindly, he reached out with his left hand and Dorlaine took it in hers. "Bluntly, then. Acaren and Rowan. As much as I love you, as much as I've looked upon you as my sons and raised you as my sons, the time has come to tell you that you are not my sons. Nor are you Dorlaine's sons."

Rowan leaned back in his chair and let out the breath he hadn't realized he was holding. He seemed to be sitting in the midst of utter stillness, every detail of the room limned in a clear, lucent light. Candlelight glinted in a curve of Dorlaine's hair, sparking back a blue more brilliant than sapphires into the room. The folds of her creamy woolen gown might have been carved out of ivory. Across the room, Acaren leapt to his feet, each separate movement of each individual muscle clearly and precisely defined.

Fascinated, Rowan watched his twin. Unable to sort out his own spinning thoughts, he saw the same confusion, consternation, and disbelief reflected in Acaren's face. Acaren stood, one hand on Eliene's shoulder as if for support, and stared at Athelin, his mouth open but no sound coming from him.

Athelin's words hung in the air, echoing in the stillness, nearly visible in the dancing light of candle flame and blazing hearth. There was a certain inevitability about them, Rowan realized. They had certainly shocked him; but had they surprised him? Strangely enough, he didn't think they had. *How very odd*, he thought. *And how very interesting.*

Neither Gabhain nor Valessa had moved. They sat staring blankly at Athelin, unable to speak. Eliene sat with her hand clutching Acaren's where it rested on her shoulder. Valessa had moved protectively closer to Gabhain. But of all of them, Gabhain looked the calmest and most thoughtful. His mind was busy, Rowan realized, calculating exactly what Athelin's announcement might mean to the future of the yrSkai of Skerry Keep. Gabhain was, first and foremost and always, heir to the throne and torc of Skai, and he never forgot it. Rowan admired him for his steadfast singleness of purpose. Skai would need a Prince like Gabhain to help the province recover once the Maedun were vanquished and gone from the land.

Acaren found his voice at last. "If we are not your sons," he said stiffly to Athelin, his voice hoarse and rusty, "then pray tell, whose sons are we, and who are we to you?"

Athelin leaned forward. "I'm sorry," he said. "I could find no gentle way to break this news to you. I—that is, Dorlaine and I—have been putting off telling you because we didn't know how we could do it even though it had to be done. This must seem cruel and abrupt to you. I beg your forgiveness. Truly, I do."

"But who are we?" Acaren said, a note of desperation creeping into his voice.

"You are both my nephews," Athelin said. "Sons of my sister, Iowen, and her husband Davigan Harper."

"I don't understand," Acaren said. "How—?"

"I think a better question is why?" Rowan asked, speaking for the first time. He felt light-headed and a bit giddy, and he had the most disconcerting feeling that he already knew what Athelin's answer was going to be. He thought of his harp, still in its carry case on his bed back in his chambers, where he had left it when Cynric came to fetch him to the solar. He ran his thumb across the calluses on his fingers, the mark of a harper, then looked up at Athelin. "Acaren will never be Champion now, will he?" he said softly. "Nor will I be Kaith."

Athelin turned to look at him, his face grave. "No, Rowan," he said quietly. "You're absolutely correct. Acaren won't be Champion. And I highly doubt you'll be Kaith."

A shattered expression spread across Acaren's face. "I'm not to be Champion?" he said, a catch in his voice. "But whyever not? Surely an accident of birth is a small barrier—"

"In your case," Athelin said gently, "the accident of birth is an overwhelming barrier. You won't be Champion, nor will Rowan be Kaith, for one reason. And that reason is who Davigan Harper was."

"I'm confused," Acaren said. He sat down as if his legs would no longer hold him up. "Does this mean that Rowan and I won't go to the Continent to raise an army? Or that we won't go to Skai to find the lost swords?"

"You'll leave for Tyra in the morning as planned," Athelin said. "Forgive me. I'm not saying this well. You need to know who Davigan Harper was. I know you've heard all the tales told. Davigan was a bard who came to Skerry Keep from Skai when Gabhain was five. He was an excellent bard. I've never heard anyone play the harp as well as he could. In his hands, it laughed and cried as if it were a person trapped in a harp's body. That would be where your talent with the harp comes from, Rowan. When my sister Iowen heard him for the first time, she fell in love with both the man and his music. They consummated their love at the Beltane fire the next evening." He glanced at Dorlaine and smiled. "They did more than just pledge their love for each other at the Beltane fire," he said. "They bonded as bheancoran and prince. As Dorlaine and I are bonded. As my father Gareth and my mother Lowra were bonded."

Rowan's heart made a thudding leap in his chest. He leaned forward, his attention focused intensely on Athelin's words. "A bond like that . . ." he said more to himself than to anyone else. "But that would mean . . ."

Athelin looked at him, then smiled. "Yes," he said. "A bond like that would mean that Davigan was of the Royal House of Skai. Which he was. He was descended, as I am, from Red Kian of Skai. But where I am descended from Kian's eldest son Keylan, Davigan was of the line of Kian's second son."

Acaren stared at Athelin in disbelief. "Kian's second son," he said. "But—but Red Kian's second son was Tiernyn."

"Yes," Athelin agreed. "Tiernyn was Davigan's grandfather. His father was Tiegan, Tiernyn's son."

Acaren took in a long, deep, shaky breath. He looked at Rowan, then back to his father. "That's preposterous," he said explosively. "That means that I—I am *King*?"

"Yes, Acaren," Athelin said. "It means that you are uncrowned King of Celi."

Rowan realized that his mouth hung open. He closed it and sat back in his chair. If Acaren were uncrowned King—and the truth of the declaration rang like a chime in his heart—it also meant that he himself must be the enchanter of the legend. His mouth went dry and his heart beat so loudly that everyone in the room must surely hear it. He looked down at his hands. His empty hands.

Despair washed through him. How could he be the enchanter of the legend—how could he be any enchanter at all—when he could not control the magic.

19

When they were nine years old, Rowan had been chasing Acaren in some childish game that involved a lot of shouting and running and tussling for possession of a leather ball stuffed with millet seed. Acaren had snatched the ball and had run, shouting gleefully, into the orchard. Rowan had not been watching where he was going, intent only on catching Acaren and seizing control of the ball. He ran full tilt into the low-hanging branch of an apple tree, giving himself a fearful whack across the forehead and knocking himself to the ground. For what seemed like months, he had sat in the long, summer grass beneath the tree, feeling disoriented and far away and vaguely detached from the entire world. He felt a little like that now.

Across the room, Acaren sat stunned in his chair. Rowan thought bemusedly that his own face must mirror his twin's in its blank expression of bewilderment. Acaren shook his head and managed to find his voice.

"But why?" he asked. "What happened? Why were we never told this before?"

"For your own safety, of course," Gabhain said, as if it were perfectly obvious. He got briskly to his feet and went to the sideboard with characteristic practicality. He poured wine from a tall decanter into the goblets standing ready. Valessa moved gracefully around the room, distributing the goblets as Gabhain filled them. Rowan took his gratefully. The tart, astringent taste of the wine on his tongue went a long way to clear the fuzz out of his head.

"Gabhain's right," Dorlaine said. "It was for your safety.

But you have a right to know what happened the night you were born. You needed to know before you went to the Continent."

"What actually did happen?" Rowan asked.

"We have never told the whole story of how Iowen and Davigan met," Athelin said. "Nor have we ever spoken about the night you were born. We did nothing to correct the fantastic stories the bards came up with, like the one Mioragh told the other night about Daigwr and Ganieda, because we thought they were the best protection you two could have. If the Maedun ever heard any of those tales, most of them contradicting the others, they would pay little attention to them. We had to keep them as far away as possible from the truth."

"And what is the truth?" Acaren asked.

Athelin looked down at the goblet he held, swirling the wine and watching it as if it held all the answers. A small furrow of pain creased his brow above his nose, and his eyes glistened for a moment before he blinked away the suggestion of tears.

"My parents and my sister Iowen went to Tyra shortly after Autumnal Equinox for the investiture of Taggert dav Cynan dav Malcolm, Sixteenth Clan Laird of Broche Rhuidh. Our kinsman, as you know. Distant now, but still a kinsman. They were caught by unexpectedly bad weather and had to stay over the winter. The winter storms that year were exceptionally bad. Venturing out onto the sea would have been suicidally foolish, even for the little Tyran courier boats, and they've been known to sail in some completely hair-raising weather." He looked down at the wine in his goblet again, then took a sip and put the cup aside.

"Assassins disguised as Tyran clansmen found them in the practice field one morning. My father was murdered where he stood, as well as my father's aunt Brynda, who had been bheancoran to Prince Tiegan. My mother, because of the bond she shared with my father, died shortly after he did. Iowen survived and came home carrying Whisperer, Brynda's Rune Blade."

"Whisperer had once belonged Red Kian's bheancoran, hadn't it?" Rowan asked. "To Kerridwen?"

"It had," Athelin said.

"Where is it now?" Eliene asked.

Athelin smiled briefly. "Safe," he said. "In fact, it will certainly be in your hands before you leave for the Continent."

"Mine?" Eliene paled. She glanced quickly at Valessa. "No. Surely not. But why me and not Valessa? Valessa is bheancoran to your heir."

Athelin glanced at Valessa, who smiled back. She turned to Eliene.

"Because you can use a sword and I can't," Valessa said to Eliene. "I'm more than content with my bow. It was certainly good enough for Lowra, and it's enough for me. The sword should be yours. You are, after all, bheancoran to the uncrowned King of Celi."

Eliene started to say something, then stopped, her eyes widening. She looked at Acaren as if she had never really seen him before, then sat down on the upholstered bench beside him.

"I hadn't thought of that," she said faintly. "Oh, I'm sorry. I've interrupted. Please. Do go on."

Athelin paused for a moment, as if collecting his thoughts. Then he nodded. "Iowen returned from Tyra shortly after Vernal Equinox. Just before Beltane, a bard calling himself Davigan Harper arrived from Skai. They fell in love instantly. At least that part of Mioragh's tale was true. Iowen and Davigan, or Daigwr and Ganieda, did really meet at a Beltane fire. But it was Dorlaine who pointed out to me that the bond was more than simple love. My sister had become Davigan's bheancoran, and there was only one man who could have claimed her services like that."

"The king," Gabhain said, his eyes alight with excitement. "Tiegan's son himself."

"Yes," Athelin said. "Shortly after they bonded, there was a raid on Skerry Keep. More disguised Somber Riders. Assassins. They had a magic-seeking Tell-Tale stone with them. They murdered my brother Adair and his wife, but we defeated them, and none of them returned alive to the main island. But Iowen and Davigan were afraid that Hakkar had more Tell-Tales, and that the Tell-Tales were attuned to him. They wanted no more raids on Skerry Keep. So they went to Skai, seeking the swords of Wyfydd Smith. Davigan said he wanted to find them for his son."

He looked expectantly at Cynric, who was sitting in a hard, armless chair, his arms folded across his chest, his legs thrust out before him and crossed at the ankles. Cynric frowned at the floor by his feet, then looked up to meet Athelin's eyes. A small, flickering smile of understanding passed quickly between the two men, and Cynric nodded.

"That's where I met them," Cynric said, his voice softly filled with memory. "I was with two Saesnesi men named Wykan and Kier. Wykan was the grandson of Aellegh, who was the son of Donaugh, and also the Celwalda of the Saesnesi of the Summer Run when the Somber Riders invaded Celi. Wykan was killed by a band of Somber Riders disguised as Celae. Kier and I had tracked them down in revenge, but before we could kill them, they had attacked your mother and father. Kier and I helped your parents, and we managed to fight them off. Kier was wounded." He reached out and picked up his goblet of wine, holding it cradled against his chest. He glanced up, met Athelin's eyes again, then looked first at Acaren, then at Rowan.

"Your mother was convinced the swords were in danger," Cynric continued. "That something was draining them of their power, something that would eventually destroy them. The four of us, Davigan, Iowen, Kier, and I, eventually found the swords. Iowen was right. The Tell-Tales that Hakkar had been using to track the magic of the swords grew in the cave where the swords were hidden—"

The exclamation of surprise burst from Rowan before he could stop it. He had dreamed that. Dreamed it as clearly as if he had been there to watch. A vision of a young man in a red cloak picking up a sword from a crystal or ice altar rose before his eyes. "A cave deep in the side of the mountain beside the sea," he said quietly, almost breathlessly. "And the swords on an altar and a man come to claim them. And when he picked up the sword, its shadow felt as real in my hand as the sword did."

Both Athelin and Cynric stared at him in shock.

"You were only just conceived—you and your brother— and carried deep in your mother's womb," Cynric said. "How could you remember seeing that?"

"I dreamed it," Rowan said. "Not long ago. I dreamed it and went to Mioragh with it. He said he wasn't sure what it meant."

Athelin's hand gripped Dorlaine's, the knuckles pale. "Iowen dreamed the same dream," he said. "Just before she and Davigan went to Skai. She told me about it." He managed a crooked smile. "Mayhaps your magic is strengthening, Rowan. Otherwise, how could you have dreamed something your mother dreamed the morning after you were conceived?"

Rowan looked at his hands, then wiped his palms on the thighs of his breeks, leaving a damp smear on the fabric. "Mayhaps," he muttered. "Mayhaps it's my magic."

Athelin nodded, a speculative expression in his eyes. "Aye, it could be," he agreed. "It very well could be."

"Your father died outside that cave," Cynric said, an odd tone in his voice. "He died because I could not kill the man who killed him. The captain of the troop of Somber Riders. He was—" He stopped and took a deep breath to steady himself. "He was my father, and I could not raise my sword hand to him." He looked away, a dusky color suffusing his cheeks, his mouth twisted in pain. "Iowen eventually forgave me my lack, but I've never forgiven myself. . . ."

"Your only other choice was to become a kinslayer," Dorlaine said softly. "Davigan would never have asked it of you. Not even Iowen would have demanded it."

"But I let my king die—"

"It's done and in the past," Athelin said gently. "You know Iowen didn't blame you. And if she ever did, you've more than redeemed yourself, Cynric my friend."

"Thank you, my lord," Cynric said. He paused for a moment, as if to collect his thoughts. "Horbad was there after Davigan died. We took great care to let him think that Davigan was Prince of Skai, and that Iowen, his bheancoran, had died with him. Iowen had destroyed all of the Tell-Tales in the cave. We tried to make sure that no more Somber Riders would come looking for her, or for the Prince of Skai. Then I brought her home, and Kier went back to his people. I believe he stood Regent for Wykan's son Devlyn until Devlyn attained his majority and could step into his role as Celwalda."

Acaren made an impatient gesture. "But what happened the night we were born?" he asked.

Athelin gestured to Cynric. "Your story, I believe," he said. "You were constantly with her after you brought her home."

"If you insist, my lord," Cynric said softly. His face became remote and austere as he looked again into the past. "Then, as now, we were constantly plagued by raiding parties. Iowen very often had warning of them through dreaming true. I remember her standing by the window in her chambers, great with child, gazing calmly out to the southwest with one hand resting always against her belly as if she were protecting the child—or children—she carried there. On the morning of Imbolc Eve, she came to me, troubled and worried, and told me to tell Athelin to send soldiers to the small cove at the north foot of Ben Aislin. Athelin sent a troop, but they found nothing. Iowen told him they needed to wait."

"On Imbolc Eve?" Acaren asked, aghast. "On the eve of a holy night? A fire feast?"

One corner of Cynric's mouth quirked in dour amusement. "The Maedun don't follow our ways," he said. "Imbolc is just another late-winter day to them."

"And did they come?" Gabhain asked, his eyes wide. "Did the raiders come?"

"They came with the coming of dark," Cynric said grimly. "And they very nearly fought their way past the troop of our soldiers."

Dorlaine put her other hand over Athelin's, where their clasped hands rested on the arm of his chair. "I was also with child," she said. "But my child wasn't supposed to be born until at least a fortnight after Imbolc, and mayhaps even two fortnights. We weren't sure, exactly. Shortly after the fighting began, Iowen was brought to bed with her children—" She smiled wanly at Acaren, then Rowan. "The two of you. I summoned the midwife. It was a long and difficult delivery. She was exhausted by the time Rowan was born only eight minutes after Acaren. Then someone brought news that Athelin had been killed in the fighting. The messenger said he had seen him fall." Her hand went to her belly as if she still had a child there to protect. "After the strain of Iowen's delivery, and the fighting, the news was too much for me, I fear. I should have known Athelin was not dead. I could still feel the bond between us as strong as ever. But I began labor far too early. Iowen told me she was resting comfortably and sent me with the midwife to my own chambers. By the time Athelin came to me and I knew the messenger had been mistaken, it was too late. The damage had been done. The child was coming, and we could not stop it from being born."

"I went to Iowen," Athelin said. "She lay so quiet and still in her bed, holding the both of you against her, and smiling. She sent me back to Dorlaine. She told me she was well and I should not worry, nor should I send the midwife to her, but see to my wife. By the time any of us realized she was bleeding heavily, it was too late to save her. We had no Gifted Healer among us. None but Meaghan, who was with Dorlaine."

"Did she know?" Rowan asked. "Did our mother know she was dying when she sent you to—" He hesitated momentarily, then said the word anyway. "—Mother?" He would always think of Dorlaine as his mother, would be unable to think of her as anything else. She had certainly been the only mother either he or Acaren remembered.

"I think she did," Cynric said, an odd tone in his voice. "I was with her when she died. She made me promise to watch after the two of you, then died with such a look of joy on her face that even now, I'm moved to tears when I remember. I think she knew she was going to join Davigan. She died peacefully and—I swear it—happy."

"If she was bheancoran and going to her King, she would of course be happy and content," Valessa said softly, looking at Gabhain and not at Cynric. "You were right, Cynric. Once she had made sure the twins would be looked after, she really did die happy."

"Her death nearly slew Athelin with grief," Cynric said. "He lost his beloved sister that night, and I lost the woman who had become my spirit and my soul." He looked at Dorlaine, pain clouding his dark eyes. "And the lady Dorlaine's child died of being born too soon. It was truly a sorrowful night for all of us at Skerry Keep."

Dorlaine smiled at him, understanding glowing in her eyes through the remembered grief. "I told Athelin to bring the boys to me," she said softly. "In all the uproar of the raid, nobody noticed Meaghan slipping down the corridor to fetch Iowen's babies to my chambers. When things became a little more settled, we announced that Iowen had died in childbed, together with a stillborn daughter. And that Prince Athelin had two more fine, strong sons."

"To hide you from Hakkar," Athelin said. "We had kept Iowen hidden from the time she returned from Skai with Cynric. We could take no chance of any word of her or her children making its way back to Hakkar. Skerry would have been overrun and all of us destroyed if he had even so much as an inkling that she had survived, and had borne sons to the man who was uncrowned King of Celi."

"So the twins became my sons," Dorlaine said. "Mine and Athelin's. We could not tell you before this because we still had so much that needed to be protected."

Athelin looked first at Acaren, then at Rowan. "You were raised as your father wished you to be raised," he said. "He himself had been raised in a Tyadda fastness. You know the Tyadda are not a warlike people. Davigan and his older brother Daefyd never learned to be soldiers. Daefyd died in Skai when he slew Horbad and saved my mother and father. Davigan had never trained to be a soldier. He was a bard. He knew he could never be a king whom an army would follow. He wanted his sons raised to be men to lead an army." He smiled, the ragged edge of grief still quivering at the corners of his mouth. "I believe both of you to be men like that. And with the swords of Wyfydd, I think you and the army you raise in Tyra and among the free Celae in Skai, can rid the world of the Maedun sorcerers."

Rowan clenched his fists on his knees. Acaren would,

indeed, make such a king. But would he himself become the enchanter the legend said was necessary to overcome the sorcery?

Early in the morning of the day they were to leave, Mioragh called them to his chambers. The sun had just barely lifted above the eastern horizon when they gathered in the spacious outer room. Athelin was already there, standing by the window watching the sun rise.

"You will all need protection," he said. "I believe this will help." He gently laid four black stones on the small marble table in the center of the room. He arranged them carefully, then stepped back. Athelin crossed the room and stood frowning thoughtfully at the four stones.

"We're ready, my lord," Mioragh said.

"I don't know if I can do this, Mioragh," Athelin said hesitantly. "My father could weave the sunlight. He showed me once how to do it, but I don't know if I can remember correctly."

Mioragh lifted both hands in a resigned gesture. "If you cannot, the charm I work without it will do well enough to protect them for a short time. It will have to do."

Athelin nodded. "We must try," he said. He stepped back and reached out his hands into the stream of sunlight pouring in through the window. His brows drew together above the bridge of his nose as he concentrated.

At first, very little happened. The golden light thickened slightly and fell through his fingers like water to dissipate before it splashed on the floor by his feet. He drew his hands back, rubbed them against his thighs, and reached out again.

Very slowly, the light solidified in his hands. A thin film of sweat formed on his brow as he drew it out like strings of honey and began weaving it into a complicated, intricate knotwork pattern. Twice, it wavered and melted around his hands. Twice, he caught it and rewove it.

Finally, he held a glowing, lustrous pattern, solid and firm as beaten gold in his hands. He stared into its radiant heart, concentration making his face nearly devoid of expression, and slowly and carefully turned to face Mioragh.

"Now," Mioragh said quietly.

The magic flowed out and away from Athelin. Mioragh raised his hands, held them over the four black stones on the table. The woven pattern of sunlight left Athelin's hands and floated through the air to hover over the table.

Suddenly, it expanded to fill the space above the table, bursting into luminous incandescence too bright to look at.

Mioragh closed his eyes. Athelin felt the surge of magic burst out and away from him. The woven brightwork of the sunlight pattern shimmered, then dissolved. Slender threads of light arrowed down from the dissipating pattern toward the four stones on the marble table. The stones flashed and disappeared into a blinding burst of dazzling light.

The blaze gradually faded. On the table where the four black stones had been lay four water-clear crystals, each with a tiny iridescent sun at its heart.

Exhausted, Athelin sank down into a chair. He looked up and met Rowan's eyes and saw the bleak despair there.

"I should have been able to do that," Rowan whispered. "I'm so sorry, Father. I'm so sorry."

Part 3

Paean of the Swords

20

Cloudy skies and misty drizzle followed the Skai Seeker *on the voy-*
age to Tyra. Rowan spent his time in the bow of the ship,
waiting for his first glimpse of Tyra. Acaren and Eliene joined
him occasionally, but weren't as eager to reach Tyra. Cynric
had remained behind on Skerry and would not join them
until they were on their way to Skai. While they were in Tyra,
Cynric would be scouting the southern rim of the Verge,
gathering what information he could glean.

The sun came out the morning they made landfall in
Tyra, and by midmorning warmed the air enough to begin
melting the ice coating the prow of the ship. When the mountains of Tyra rose above the horizon shortly before noon, the
ice was completely gone.

He had heard all his life about the gray cliffs of Tyra, but
when Rowan saw them rising, sheer and forbidding, out of
the sea, soaring to a height that could easily be a furlong
straight up, he was nearly speechless. North and south for
leagues in either direction they marched in tortuous patterns
of pinnacle and crevasse, as far as the eye could see. Ice
carved into fantastic shapes by wind and water and sun clung
to the rocks, sparking rainbow glints back into Rowan's eyes.
The sea hammered and burst against the base of the glistening granite. Shattered, foam-flecked spray crashed high into
the air to descend like salt rain. From far out to sea the thunder of sea meeting stone rumbled like the beat of a hundred
hundred bodhrans, as if he listened to the slow, steady heartbeat of the world itself.

Rowan scanned the splintered heights of the cliffs with

their burden of twisted and frozen cataracts. He had no trouble understanding the truth behind the tales that Broche Rhuidh had never been attacked by sea and never would be. Surely no ship, friend or enemy, could find safe harbor among those murderous spires.

Just at that moment, the master stepped onto the quarterdeck and began to shout orders. The ship changed direction. To Rowan's untrained and horrified eye, they seemed to be heading straight toward a solid section of cliff. The prevailing winds working against the natural current and the tide set up a seething maelstrom at the base of the cliff. Rowan could see no way through or past it. Then he realized that part of the confusion was caused by waves breaking on a low spit of rock that curved out from a broken pinnacle of rock. Just before the *Skai Seeker* heeled over on her port side and slid neatly past the shoal with inches to spare, Rowan saw that the low-lying rocks were a natural breakwater, and behind them lay a reasonably calm harbor hidden among the cliffs.

Rowan let out the breath he hadn't realized he'd been holding in a long, sighing whistle. Beside him, Acaren laughed in nervous relief. Eliene relaxed, allowing herself to smile.

"For a moment," she said a little breathlessly, "I thought for certain we were going straight onto those rocks there."

"It did rather look like it, didn't it," Acaren said. "I think that was the reef they call the Hook." He pointed to the top of the cliff. "Look. Up there. That should be Broche Rhuidh, I think. You can't see much but a bit of wall that almost looks like more of the cliff."

"How does one get up there?" Eliene asked, looking upward. "It all looks like sheer cliff to me."

The master joined them where they stood near the bow. "There's a road leading from the back of the harbor," he said. "Doubtless there'll be horses or other transportation arranged for you."

Rowan could not tear his gaze away from that glimpse of forbidding gray wall above the cliff. Mayhaps an army waited there for Acaren to lead it to victory over the Maedun, but something else entirely awaited him. He couldn't explain the sudden conviction, nor could he explain how he knew. But the knowledge was there. It was as sure and certain as if he had come on a specific invitation. His heart beat a little faster and a little harder in his chest.

The master sent the *Skai Seeker* scudding across the relatively calm surface of the harbor, gradually slowing until the ship ran out of momentum just as it nudged up against the side of the wooden pier. Rowan glanced over his shoulder at the master, whose calm expression seemed to indicate that he had expected nothing less than perfect performance from both his ship and his crew. It was, Rowan thought in admiration, a showy piece of work, and he wondered if the master and his crew could pull off an arrival like that every time.

Men wearing the traditional kilts of Tyran clansmen appeared on the dock in a mad scramble that sorted itself out presently with the ship's hawsers neatly secured to the bollards, and the gangplank stretching the short distance from the ship to the pier. Rowan was suitably impressed with the efficiency.

One of the clansmen stepped away from the work crew and waved them back to the shelter of the hut at the root of the jetty. He came back to the pier and stood at the foot of the gangway, waiting as Rowan, Acaren, and Eliene gathered their scant baggage and disembarked. He wore a kilt in the Broche Rhuidh tartan of blues and grays and greens, a heavy shirt in a pale, creamy wool, and a bulky plaid wrapped around his shoulders over the shirt and secured by a plain, copper pin, all of it rubbed and worn and shabby but still warm and clean. He wore a blue knitted cap that hid most of his red-gold hair, but didn't cover the braid hanging from his left temple, or the dark blue sparkle of the sapphire on a delicate gold chain that dangled from his left ear. The brisk north wind had burnished his cheeks and nose with a high color.

Rowan followed Acaren and Eliene down the gangway. The clansman glanced from Acaren to Rowan and back to Acaren. He stepped forward to meet them.

"You'd be Acaren and Rowan, sons of Athelin of Skerry, I expect," he said, his Celae fluent and unaccented.

"Aye, we are," Acaren said, surprised. "I'm Acaren." He gestured toward Rowan. "And my brother Rowan. And my bheancoran Eliene al Saethen. How did you know us?"

The clansman grinned. Rowan thought he couldn't be that much older than he and Acaren, and remarkably self-assured and poised for a man who wore such shabby clothing.

"Who else would you be, a pair of twins that look quite a bit like the portraits of King Tiernyn and Donaugh the Enchanter that hang in our galleries?" the clansman said, still smiling. "I'm Donwald dav Rhuidri dav Comyn. I believe we are kinsmen. My grandfather and yours were cousins."

Eliene reached up and touched the hilt of the sword she wore in a harness across her back. "Comyn's mother was Brynda al Keylan," she said. "Wasn't she?"

"Aye," Donwald said. "She was."

"I now carry Brynda's sword," Eliene said. "The Rune Blade Whisperer."

One of Donwald's red-gold eyebrows quirked, and he grinned again. He made a small bow to all three of them. "You are all three of you well come here," he said. "I'll see you up to the Clanhold. Then I must come back and finish my shift here." He gestured to the small shelter. Two sturdy boats lay ready beside it. "We guard the harbor and rescue the sailors of any ship that doesn't manage to negotiate the Hook."

"That could be a chilly task in this weather," Rowan said.

Donwald laughed. "Oh, aye, it surely is," he said. "But it must be done. We've been fortunate this winter. We've lost no ships so far. The weather has been appallingly bad, and most ship's masters prefer to spend their time in a warm tavern with a mug of mulled wine rather than swearing and chipping ice off the rigging."

"I can see how the mulled wine and the hearthfire would be more appealing," Acaren said.

Donwald laughed again, then beckoned. "Follow me," he said. "We'll go by the road rather than the cliff track. It's an easier climb."

He led them briskly across the gravel shingle and

around an outcropping of jagged rock. Rowan looked in dismay at the road—more of a rough track than a road—that led upward along a small watercourse. He'd seen staircases with a gentler rise. He looked at Donwald, who appeared completely unconcerned.

"Uh, Donwald? Just what would you consider a difficult climb?" he asked dryly, eyeing the switchbacks and steep angles.

"Aye, well, straight up the cliffs, I fancy," Donwald said with a straight face.

"Of course. Shall we go, then?"

Rowan settled his pack and his harp more firmly on his shoulder, automatically adjusting the straps so they wouldn't interfere with his sword, and followed Donwald up the road. It was a long climb, and the muscles in the backs of his legs let him know he'd had far too little practice running up and down mountains during the cold and windy winter.

At the top, Donwald looked as much at ease as he had at the bottom. He grinned as Rowan, Acaren, and Eliene caught their breath, then led the way past a stand of winter-bare trees. The track followed the trees for nearly a furlong, then rounded a wide curve, and Rowan received his first glimpse of the Clanhold of Broche Rhuidh.

He had been expecting something out of legend, akin to the tales of lost Dun Eidon with its graceful towers and soaring balustrades. The Clanhold of Broche Rhuidh was large and turreted, but there the resemblance to legend stopped. Broche Rhuidh was stone-built, rising gracefully from the top of a small shoulder of the mountain. Behind it, the sheer face of the granite crag towered high enough to scrape the belly of the clear sky. The living rock of the cliff itself formed the back wall of the Clanhold. Crenellated towers stood at each corner behind battlements fashioned of the same rock, but the massive gates stood flung wide in the warm late-morning sunshine. Behind the walls, the Clanhold itself stood huge and graceful, solidly rooted in the mountain. Like Skerry Keep, the Clanhold was a fortress, but infinitely bigger and more imposing.

Above the Clanhold on an overhanging shoulder of the

mountain, Rowan caught a glimpse of the white columns of a shrine. If the Clanhold were laid out in the traditional way, a small circle of standing stones would lie beyond the shrine. Tyran strongholds were set up very similar to Celae strongholds. But then, legend said that the yrSkai of Celi and the Tyrs were one people once before a breakaway faction left Tyra to settle in Skai. Certainly both the Celae and the Tyrs followed the same gods and goddesses, and bowed to the power of the Duality who ruled above all.

The track from the harbor bypassed the massive front gates and wound around the smooth curtain wall to a smaller gate that opened onto a small courtyard bound by kitchen gardens to the left, the back wall of what Rowan thought might be stables, hung with the leafless remains of a vine of some sort, and ahead by the Clanhold itself. Donwald opened a small door and ushered them through into a long corridor with a polished flagstone floor. Doors led off to either side. Rowan caught a glimpse of a short rank of neatly made beds and concluded they were in the garrison quarters of the Clanhold guards.

"My sister will be sorry she missed you," Donwald said cheerfully, ushering them around a corner. "She said she had a feeling someone would be coming soon from the island."

Something prickled at the back of Rowan's neck, and a hollow sensation clutched his belly. "Your sister?" he asked cautiously.

Donwald laughed. "Your sister, too, I think," he said. "Ceitryn. My foster sister. She's years younger than me, but tries to treat me more like a son to be managed." He grinned. "She hasn't exactly succeeded yet. Now she can practice on you, too."

"She had a feeling we'd be coming?" Again, something churned in Rowan's belly. Not quite anticipation. Not quite fear. Not quite eagerness. "Is she a Seer, then? Has she magic?"

Donwald shook his head. "No, not a Seer. But every once in a while, she has a feeling something might happen, and it does." He shrugged and grinned again. "Good luck, mayhaps more than good Seeing."

"Where did she go?"

"Upglen yesterevening to help deliver a baby," Donwald said. "A difficult delivery, they told us. Ceitryn is something of a Healer. She inherited a small Gift from your grandfather. Hers is only a small Gift, ye ken. Not so great as the Gift your grandfather possessed, but a most helpful one in any event. Not one we have in plenty here in Tyra, believe me."

"I see," Rowan said softly.

Presently, the corridor decanted them into the bustle of the Great Hall. Fires blazed in the hearths at either end of the huge room, taking the early-spring chill out of the air. Servants hurried around setting up tables and pulling long benches from along the walls to place beside the tables. Others stacked dinnerware, cups, and utensils on a sideboard within easy reach of anyone entering the hall for the evening meal. Nobody paid any attention to Donwald leading three strangers through the Hall and up the staircase to the second floor. He stopped before a door in the west wing and knocked. A voice from the inside bid him enter.

Donwald opened the door into a study. Or a workroom. It was comfortably, if plainly, furnished. A long worktable stood before a window overlooking the harbor. On the wall adjacent to it hung a huge map of the Continent, the array of countries all color-washed in different hues—from the chill white of Saesnes in the north to the rounded gray bulk of Falinor thrusting down into the southern sea, with Tyra, a tapering green arrowhead running east from the coast, the blocky yellow shape of Isgard below it, and the sprawl of landlocked Maedun, blood red in the daylight, to the east. And far to the west, the pale tan shape of Celi against the blue indicating the sea. Rowan had never seen a more finely detailed map, except perhaps for the one Athelin owned, which hung in his own study at Skerry Keep. The one could have been an exact copy of the other. And probably was, Rowan decided, inspecting it carefully.

Three men stood looking at the map, their backs to the door, all three of them dressed in the traditional kilt and plaid. One of the men had the glossy, blue-black hair of a Celae. One of the other men turned as Donwald led his charges into the room. He was a tall, strongly built man of middle years, his kilt and plaid a tartan of gray, blue, and green, with a broad yellow stripe running through the weave. His hair, silvered only a little by the years, hung to his shoulders except for a heavy braid by his left temple. A brilliant red ruby hung from his left ear on a short length of delicate gold chain. His eyes were green, as green as the emerald in the silver pin securing his plaid at his wide shoulders. He stood straight as a sword blade, and bore himself with the poise and grace of a born swordsman.

Donwald sketched a quick bow toward him. "My lord," he said. "I have the honor to present to you three visitors from Skerry. Acaren and Rowan ap Athelin, and Eliene al Saethen, who is bheancoran to my lord Acaren." He turned to Acaren, Rowan, and Eliene. "My lords and lady, this is Brendon dav Taggert dav Cynan, Seventeenth Clan Laird of Broche Rhuidh of Tyra, First Laird of the Council of Clans, Protector of the Sunset Shore, Laird of the Misty Isles, Master of the Western Crags, and Laird of Glenborden." The string of titles fell easily from his tongue, as if he spoke them every day. Or had practiced a lot, Rowan thought in irreverent amusement.

"You are well come here," Brendon said formally. "As the sons of my kinsman Athelin ap Gareth, I would ask that you consider my home to be yours."

Acaren bowed. "Thank you, my lord Brendon. You are very kind, indeed."

The black-haired man turned slowly and stared at the twins, his eyes narrowed as if he had sized them up and found them wanting. He said nothing, but his expression was anything but welcoming. Rowan caught his lower lip gently between his teeth. He thought he should know the man, but he could not place him. Where had he seen him before?

Brendon gestured toward the two men by the map. "May I present my eldest son Fionh, and Caennedd ap Gareth. Your kinsman, I believe."

Caennedd smiled bitterly. "Your *banished* kinsman," he said softly. "Your uncle."

Acaren met his gaze coolly. "I remember," he said.

Caennedd raised an eyebrow. "Are you, then, banished as I am?"

"No," Acaren said shortly. "We've come to ask Brendon as First Laird of the Council of Clans to let us raise an army of Tyran clansmen to take to Skai and defeat the Maedun."

"I see," Caennedd said scornfully. "And what makes you think an army of Tyran clansmen might follow the third and fourth sons of an exiled prince?"

"They might not follow two men such as that," Rowan said. "But they might follow the first and second sons of Davigan ap Tiegan, the uncrowned King of all Celi."

21

Shocked silence filled the room as the echo of Rowan's words faded.
Brendon's eyes narrowed in consideration as he studied first
Rowan, then Acaren, but he said nothing. Caennedd's
expression moved quickly from incredulous, startled shock to
skeptical cynicism and disbelief. He would, Rowan thought,
be the most difficult to convince.

"It's here," Acaren said. He reached into his belt pouch
and drew out a letter. "It's all here. Athelin sent you a letter,
my lord Brendon. You recognize his seal, of course. He
explains it all for you. Our mother—our birth mother—was
his sister Iowen. Our father was Davigan ap Tiegan ap
Tiernyn, who was uncrowned King of all Celi. I am his eldest
son." He glanced at Rowan. "By eight minutes. I am his heir."

"The harper?" Caennedd asked, surprise plain in his
voice and his widened eyes. "That harper was the king? That
bard?" Surprise turned quickly again to skepticism. "I don't
believe it."

"Whether you believe it or not, the fact remains that he
was who he was," Rowan said. "We were raised as sons of
Prince Athelin and the lady Dorlaine so the Maedun
wouldn't suspect who we were."

The cynical half smile came back to Caennedd's face, but
Rowan saw a spark of fear behind it. As clearly as if
Caennedd had spoken aloud, Rowan understood that his
uncle felt as if his position with Brendon and Fionh was in
jeopardy. And he knew that Caennedd would do anything to
defend that position.

"I always thought that your mother was my half sister

Iowen," Caennedd said. "But I still say that your father was my half-brother Athelin."

Acaren went white. He took a quick step toward Caennedd, reaching for the sword on his back. Rowan put his hand to Acaren's arm to hold him back—a warning. Brendon stepped forward quickly, placing himself between Acaren and Caennedd.

"I'll have none of that in this house." Brendon's voice was quiet and calm, but held an unmistakable underlying tone of command that brooked no defiance. "I forbid it." He looked at Caennedd. "This conference is over for now. We'll discuss the placement of your company on the border later, after I've see to the comfort of my guests."

Caennedd stared first at Acaren, then at Rowan, and back to Acaren. "A Tyran army, he wants," he said mockingly. "Do you expect Tyran clansmen to follow an untried boy?"

"Caennedd—" Brendon's voice held a warning.

Caennedd turned to him, face bland. "I was merely about to suggest, my lord Brendon, that these two would-be warriors accompany me to the border tomorrow and get a taste of what it means to fight the Maedun Somber Riders."

The grim line of Brendon's mouth hardened. "I hardly think—"

"It's an excellent idea," Rowan said calmly. "Acaren and I have fought in minor skirmishes with small raiding parties, but we are, as our uncle Caennedd so correctly points out, untried in battle. Your army is renowned for its phenomenal success in keeping the Maedun out of Tyra. It would be an honor to fight alongside them."

"I think Caennedd's right, Father," Fionh said quietly, speaking for the first time. "I think Acaren needs to prove he's capable of leading men before any of our men would follow him. Before you can authorize him to raise an army to take back to Skai, you'll have to put it before the Council of Clans. They won't follow an untried leader."

Brendon's quick grunt of laughter was entirely without humor. "If it meant pushing the Maedun back into their own land, I'd lend half an army to the bluidy Ephir of Isgard, rot his soul." He nodded. "Aye, I think I agree with you. And with Caennedd."

"Then it's settled," Acaren said briskly. "We'll accompany Caennedd when he leaves tomorrow for the border." He grinned suddenly. "We won't have to pack, at least. We're ready to go now."

"After a good night's rest, be more like," Brendon said. "The sea at this time of year couldn't have been what in any way might be termed as restful."

Rowan stood on a high mound under a sky that glowed with a light that was neither dawn nor dusk, but some mystic, transitional interval out of time. At the foot of the hill, a vast plain stretched westward until it met the sea. Around him loomed a forest of standing stones thrusting up in stark silhouette against the luminous sky. He had dreamed true before, and understood that he now needed to come to this dream place.

The energy of the Dance flowed around him, filling him with its magic. He welcomed it with quiet relief. Mayhaps now, after all this time, his magic would come to him to fill his hands and his spirit.

Something moved behind him. He turned as the figure of a man stepped between the standing stones of a trilithon. Myrddyn looked exactly as he had the last time Rowan had seen him.

"You are well come here, Rowan Secondborn," Myrddyn said gravely.

"How did I come here?" Rowan asked.

"Does it matter?" Amusement tinged Myrddyn's voice. "You are here, and you are welcome."

"Did you call me here to give me my magic?" Rowan asked. "Is it mine at last?"

Myrddyn shook his head. "It was not I who called you," he said. He gestured to the standing stones behind Rowan. "Look, if you will."

Rowan turned.

She came to him through the menhirs, her red-gold hair gleaming in the fey light. Her feet passed so lightly over the tender young grass that the blades seemed hardly to bend. Her gown of pale green flowed about her body, clinging briefly to breasts and thighs, then rippling sinuously to outline hips and waist. She was so lovely, the back of his throat ached with his need and love for her.

"I called you here, beloved," she said. "As you called me."

He opened his arms and she stepped into them as if she had always belonged there. Mayhaps she had, he thought.

After a long time, she kissed his throat, then pulled reluctantly away and sat up. When he opened his eyes to look at her, she sat cross-legged beside him, pale green gown stretched taut across her knees. They rested in a small alcove in a formal garden, a high wall of sun-warmed stone behind them. A narrow herb border ran along the foot of the wall, the scent of savory, mint, and thyme rising like heat waves in the air. Overhead, the boughs of an apple tree, heavily laden with blossoms, stooped low above them. A few petals fell and caught in her hair like pearls. She reached up to brush them away, but he caught her hand.

"Leave them," he said. "They suit you well."

She looked up at him. Her eyes reminded him of the color of the tightly folded graybells that grew so thickly along the lower slopes of Ben Warden on Skerry. She reached up and plucked one of the gleaming red fruits from the tree and handed it to him. He bit into it. The tart flavor of the juice burst on his tongue like a flash of sunlight.

"Eat this and always think of me when you taste apples," she said teasingly.

"Beloved," he whispered. He took her shoulders in his hand and held her away so she could see what he did, then slowly sketched the sign for soul, and held out his cupped hands toward her. "My soul lies cupped within the palm of your hand."

Not smiling now, she faced him squarely and formed her hands into a cup to receive what he offered. Slowly, tenderly, as if she held something fragile and infinitely priceless, she closed her hands and pressed them against her heart.

"Your soul lies sheltered safe within my hands and my heart."

Rowan awoke slowly with the taste of apples on his tongue and the shape of a woman's heart imprinted upon his own. For a moment, he lay in the dark, uncertain where he was. The dream slowly shattered and dissolved into a glitter of drifting fragment. He lay in a strange bed, in a strange room. For a moment, disoriented, he lay staring into the darkness, wondering where he was. Then he remembered being shown to a guest chamber in the Clanhold of Broche Rhuidh.

He threw back the thick goose-down quilt and sat up. Only a faint gleam came from the brazier by the head of the bed, but the night's chill had not yet turned the air in the room frigid. Restless, he stood up. His clothing still lay neatly folded on the chest at the foot of the bed where he had left it. He dressed quickly and picked up his cloak as he went quietly out into the corridor.

Widely spaced torches burned along the corridor walls, sending dancing shadows stretching and contracting along the floor. Rowan made his way slowly by memory to the head of the staircase leading down to the Great Hall. Instead of going to the main doors, massive affairs of wood and wrought iron, he turned toward the smaller door Donwald had brought them through into the Clanhold.

A sentry posted at the door stopped him, then let him through as he recognized him. Another sentry outside studied him carefully in the light of a small torch so he would recognize him upon his return, then nodded him through.

The moon rode low over the crags to the northwest as Rowan stepped out onto the small flagstone terrace. To his right lay the road leading around the Clanhold to the track coming from the harbor. To his left, the terrace became a balcony, bounded by a waist-high stone balustrade, as the ground fell away beneath it. He set out to follow it. The shrine and the small dance of seven stones lay above the Clanhold. He thought there might be a set of stairs somewhere along the balcony that would take him to the track leading to the shrine.

The balcony curved, following the wall of a massive tower. The light from the sentry's small torch disappeared, leaving the darkness relieved only by the wan light of the moon. Rowan paused for a moment to let his eyes adjust, then walked on, his hand on the stone rail.

He had begun to think he had made a mistake about the possibility of a set of stairs when he found them. Steep and narrow, they led down to a footpath that was lost in shadows. He had just put his foot to the first step down when he heard something behind him. He turned.

Something smashed against the side of his head. Light

and brilliant color exploded behind his eyes, blinding him. He
pitched forward. It was as if he were a bird, launching itself
off a high cliff. The wind caught him and buoyed him up. He
felt light and airy and floating for a long, endless moment.
Then he crashed into something hard and unyielding. The
bones of his wrist snapped with a crack like a dry branch
breaking. Before he could wonder that it didn't hurt, he sank
down into the depths of a black sea.

There was no transition between unconsciousness and waking. Rowan opened his eyes and looked up into Acaren's anxious eyes. Relief swept in a wave across Acaren's face, and he
straightened up.

"Are you awake?" he asked.

Rowan blinked, then looked around. He had no idea
where he was. This wasn't the chamber he'd been shown the
night before. The bed was narrow and hard, and the room
was heated nearly to the point of discomfort.

"What happened?" he asked. His voice came out sounding rusty and hoarse, startling him. He tried to sit up, but
Eliene, who stood across the bed from Acaren, pushed him
back.

"Don't sit up yet," she said. "You've got a rather nasty
lump on your head, and your wrist is broken."

"What happened?" Rowan asked again. "Where am I?"

"In the infirmary." Brendon stood behind Acaren,
frowning. "The sentry found you at the bottom of the small
staircase leading to the shrine track."

"What were you doing there?" Acaren asked, his relief
clearly turning to exasperation. "When we found you at the
bottom of those steps, you frightened me half out of my wits."

Rowan closed his eyes and tried to remember. A dream?
Had he dreamed the woman with red-gold hair had called
him to the Dance of stone? Surely it was only a dream. But
he had awakened and wanted to go to the shrine. Or the
Dance of seven stones above it. He'd gone through a door
and past a pair of sentries. Then a swift rush of footsteps in
the dark and—

"Someone hit me," he said slowly, the memory blurred

and fragmented. "Someone hit me and pushed me down the staircase."

Both Acaren and Brendon turned to look at Caennedd, who sat in a hard chair by the wall. Caennedd lurched to his feet.

"You can't think I did it," he said, aghast.

Brendon said nothing.

Caennedd drew himself up. "I may be many things, my lord Brendon," he said quietly, "but a kinslayer is not among them."

His voice held the quiet ring of truth. Rowan opened his eyes. Caennedd was pale, but he seemed appalled at the suggestion that he would try to kill Rowan.

"He's right," Rowan said. "It wasn't him."

"How do you know?" Acaren demanded. "He was completely hostile to both of us yesterday."

"Mayhaps," Rowan said. "But he didn't do it." He looked at Caennedd. The truth of his denial glowed in his eyes. "No, not him. But if he has a servant, it might be an idea to question him."

Caennedd's eyes widened. Color rose quickly in his face. "Alyn," he murmured. "Dear gods and goddesses, Alyn. He's young Tadwyr's brother."

"Tadwyr?" Acaren asked. "Who is Tadwyr?"

"Tadwyr was his servant in Skerry Keep," Rowan said. "Don't you remember? He was killed in the Maedun raid just before Caennedd left there to come here."

"Say the word you mean," Caennedd said bitterly. "Banished. I was banished."

Rowan said nothing.

A wry smile twisted Caennedd's mouth. "Deservedly, mayhaps," he said. "But I had no hand in the attempt on your life. Aye, it might have been Alyn. I confess I ranted last night, and I might have blamed the two of you as the cause of my banishment. Alyn might have construed that to mean you were also responsible for Tadwyr's death." He straightened his shoulders. "Whereas it was entirely my own arrogant stupidity that the lad died. I shall speak to Alyn."

"Go gentle with him," Rowan said.

Caennedd looked at him, surprised. "Go gentle? You might have been killed!"

"But I wasn't, as you see," Rowan said. "And we need every yrSkai and Celae soldier we have."

Caennedd gave him a long, considering look. "I see," he said. "Thank you, my lord Rowan." He turned and left quickly.

Rowan looked down at his left arm. Someone had wrapped it from knuckles to elbow in linen soaked in ground boneset root. The linen had dried stiff and hard as rawhide. The tips of his fingers, fingernails a healthy pink, showed beneath the bottom rim. He made a sour face and tried to wiggle his fingers. They moved, but just barely. And his whole arm ached like a sore tooth.

"I'm certainly happy to see that you seem to be all right," Acaren said cheerfully. "But that wrist pretty much puts paid to the idea of you going with us to the border. We'll collect you here when we get back again."

"The Healer said to give you this when you awoke," Eliene said. She held out a goblet containing watered wine. "Go on. You're supposed to drink it."

Rowan took it. It left a strange aftertaste in his mouth that he recognized as poppy. Resigning himself, he closed his eyes and let the poppy take him away.

He awoke with the golden light of afternoon streaming across the bottom of his bed. A young woman sat on a chair beside the bed, a small book open on her lap. She looked out the window, her face in profile to him, her expression far away, almost dreamy. Her red-gold hair gleamed like newly minted copper in the sunlight. The light limned the soft, clean lines of brow and cheek and chin, casting peach-colored shadows in the hollows beneath her cheekbones.

As if sensing his gaze on her, she turned her head and looked at him, lips still curved in the soft smile. Her eyes, gray as smoke, gray as the sea in a misty dawn, looked deep into his. She smiled and something twisted in his chest. There wasn't enough air in the room to fill his lungs. His heart pounded wildly against his ribs.

He knew her. He had always known her. She had come to life out of his dreams and now sat beside him.

The air between them shimmered and sparked. Images of her flashed in the midst of the fizzing air. He saw her running through thigh-deep grass in a summer meadow, a wreath of wildflowers trailing from her hair, laughing as he pursued her joyfully. She reached up to touch his face as the apple-blossom petals drifted like sweet snow across her gleaming hair. They stood side by side in a large room, fingers interlaced, as flutes and pipes played in celebration of their joining. She held an infant tenderly in her arms, the curve of the child's head in her cupped hand echoing the rich curve of her breast. She sat on a cushioned chair, holding a child, while a bright ray of sun slanted through a high window and turned her hair to molten gold. And she stood beside him as a tall young man turned away from them to mount a warhorse while a troop of men waited.

He knew her, and she knew him. He had no idea if the images he saw came from past or future, or both, but he knew her. Their souls were bound, had always been bound, and always would be. They were two with one soul between them, perfectly joined, perfectly fitted.

Bound souls. He had always thought the stories of men and women bound throughout all eternity by the strength of passion, either love or hate, were but pleasant tales for a long winter's night. Bound souls, two sides of the same counter, together through all the lives of the souls, and forever before and afterward. But he recognized the woman just as surely as she recognized him, and he knew the tales were true. It had happened with Donaugh the Enchanter and his love Eliade. And now it had happened with him and this Tyran woman.

She had gone as pale as he felt. "You," she said. "I know you now. You've been in my dreams ever since I was a child."

"And you've been in mine," he said blankly.

"You're Rowan," she said.

"Aye, beloved," he said. "And you're Ceitryn."

An expression of horrified recognition widened her eyes. "Rowan," she whispered. "Oh, no. You're my—" She put her hand to her throat. "How can I feel like this. You're my *brother*. . . ."

He reached out and took her hand. "No," he said. "No, beloved. Not your brother. Only your cousin." He laughed aloud in relief. "Only your cousin."

22

The sun streamed through the window and lay slanting across Rowan's bed. He had no part of his attention to spare to notice the weight of it on his legs. All he could do was stare at the young woman who sat by the head of his bed. She stared back at him, her face filled with awed wonder and astonishment, an expression he knew must be a mirror of his own.

She was not a pretty woman. Her features were too strong for true beauty. But she was powerfully attractive, and each part of her was achingly familiar and loved. He had not seen her since she was an infant in Dorlaine's arms, yet he knew every detail of her face, the way her hair fell in curving waves past her shoulders, the sweet and clever articulation of shoulder, elbow, and wrist, the gentle incurve of her waist and the generous outcurve of breast and hip.

Echoes of all their pasts and all their futures flashed through his mind. All the lives they had lived together, all the lives they would live together, all the lives they had been forced to live apart.

"Not my brother," she murmured faintly. "My cousin."

"Aye, your cousin. Thanks be to all the gods and goddesses, your cousin."

She stared at him in wonder. "But how can this be?" she asked at last, her voice little more than a whisper. "How can it be that you've walked my dreams since I was a child, and I never knew who you were, yet here you are in my waking world?"

The question was impossible to answer. He smiled. "Do you mind?" he asked simply.

She drew back, startled. Then she smiled. "No," she said. She managed a small, delighted laugh. "No, I don't think I mind at all. Not at all."

The angle of the sunlight across his legs flattened as the sun moved almost imperceptibly down into the west, and he felt the weight of it shift. A thread of excitement shot through him, catching at his heart and breath. "Donwald told us you were a Healer," he said.

She nodded. "But my Gift is a small one. I've looked at your arm, and made sure the healing process is started. It will be a fortnight before you can use it properly again."

A wisp of memory tugged at his mind. The night she was born, he had crept into the bedchamber and huddled by the door. When Mioragh entered and bent his magic to Heal Dorlaine, it had drawn an answering surge of magic from Rowan. And from somewhere else. The combination was strong enough to pull Dorlaine back from the brink of death, to Heal her completely.

Rowan frowned, remembering, then held up his arm in its awkward wrapping. "Try to Heal my arm now," he said.

She drew back. "But I can't. I've done all I could for it."

"You must try again," he insisted, his voice hoarse with his urgency. He held his arm up again. The ache intensified into pain, but he didn't lower it. "Please, Ceitryn. This is very important. Try to Heal it completely."

Hesitantly, she put her hands to his wrist, then looked at him as if for guidance.

"Take off the wrapping."

"But your arm needs the support."

"Please. Take it off."

She took a deep breath, then turned to pick up a pair of heavy shears from the cabinet behind her. He grimaced with pain as she cut through the stiff wrapping. Alarmed, she paused.

"It's hurting you."

"Go on. Do it. This is important, beloved."

She applied the shears again. The wrapping came off, exposing his wrist, blue with bruising and swollen. The bone had not broken through the skin, he was pleased to note. A clean break, then.

"Now, Heal it," he whispered.

Again, she put her hands on his wrist. They felt cool and smooth against his bruised skin. She took a deep breath, then her face cleared as she concentrated.

Carefully, hesitantly, he reached for that quiet place deep within himself that Mioragh taught him to go to when he thought about his magic. He closed his eyes. Her hair felt like finest silk brushing against his wrist as she bent her head.

It happened in an unexpected rush. Suddenly, he was swirling deep in a life that wasn't his. Images that weren't his own flashed through his head, too fast to comprehend any of them. Mountains, tall and snowcapped even in the heat of summer. Placid blue lakes. White, boiling rivers. Gentle clear brooks. The sea breaking against the sheer faces of cliffs, throwing salt spume high into the air. Faces of people he didn't know. Pictures of rooms he didn't recognize. Voices singing songs he had never heard, never played on his harp. Jumbled, tangled images, all tumbled together without order, without sequence. And through it all, a sense of rightness, of belonging, of fittingness. Of absolute and joyous delight. Whatever this wild fusion was, it was something completely and utterly right.

He had come home. She had come home. They were finally together after too many lifetimes apart from each other.

In wonder, he saw the bones of his arm through her eyes. Saw them come together, knit into a clean, healthy whole, sensed her wonder and her incredulous, excited astonishment. When she dropped her hands to her lap, they both stared at the smooth, unmarred skin of his wrist.

He flexed his fingers, then bent and rotated his wrist. No pain. No stiffness. Just a perfectly working joint of bone and muscle and tendon.

"What's happening?" she whispered.

"I don't know. But I think—" He reached out to touch the ray of sunlight falling across the foot of the bed. The light ran through his fingers like warm honey. He willed it to firm and solidify and take shape, then watched in a wonder and delight that was tinged with disbelief, as it formed itself into a visible and tangible ball. For a moment, he held a globe of molten sunlight in his hands. Then it melted and sagged and flowed away like water, splashing onto the coverlet of the bed.

But he had held it. He had used his magic at his own will, even if only briefly. And he understood why it had never happened before.

He reached out to touch her face. A remnant of the globe of sunlight on his fingers streaked her cheek with the gleam of gold. "You're the other half of me," he told her. "Before now, I was incomplete. That's why I could never use my magic. It was waiting for you to make me whole."

Understanding suddenly glowed in her eyes. "And my Healing," she murmured. "The same thing."

"I believe so, yes. If we had not been separated when you were only an infant, this might have happened sooner."

She met his eyes gravely. "I wonder," she said. "Mayhaps not. Not if we felt this way about each other. We would think of each other as brother and sister, and be wracked with guilt. How can magic come of that?"

Startled, he stared at her. "Aye," he said slowly. "Aye, mayhaps you're right." He flung back the coverlet and sat up. "I must go to find Acaren."

"But he went to the border this morning with Fionh and Caennedd."

"Then I shall go to the border, too."

She stood up. "And I," she said. "I shall go with you."

He wanted to tell her she must stay here, where it was safe. But he could not bear to be parted from her. And for the first time, he thought he understood the bond between a prince and his bheancoran. If their souls were so intricately and completely bound, the death of one would tear the other in half. Little wonder his mother had died. The wonder was that she had forced herself long enough to give birth to Acaren and him. And if she were going to join her prince — her king — again, little wonder that she died, as Cynric said, with joy.

The Great Hall was nearly full of men and women. Light spilled from lamps, candles, and torches, as well as the blazing fire in the hearth. Rowan stood with Ceitryn before the hearth. The firelight glinted in her hair, making its color rival the fire of the hearth itself. Rowan thought his heart could not possibly contain his happiness.

They faced each other across a bowl of water, a stick of wood, and a large rock that had been placed on the floor at their feet. Behind them stood Ceitryn's foster father Rhuidri, her foster brother Donwald, and Rowan's kinsman Brendon.

"Ceitryn al Athelin ta'Rhuidri," he said, "I come to you to say that my soul lies cupped within the palm of your hand." He held out his hands, cupped as if he offered her something.

Solemnly, she cupped her hands to receive what he offered. Then she closed her hands gently and pressed them to her breast. "Rowan ap Davigan ap Tiegan, your heart is sheltered safe within my hands and my heart."

She held out both of her hands above the bowl of water, the stick, and the rock. Rowan reached out and took her hands in his. She smiled at him, her color high. Together, they stepped sideways so that the objects no longer separated them.

"Ceitryn al Athelin, I plight to you my troth," he said. "Not the sea, nor the forest, nor the mountains can come between us. We are part of each other. You carry within you my spirit and my heart, and we are one forever." He bent and pressed his forehead to the backs of her hands held firmly in his.

"Rowan ap Davigan, I plight to you my troth," she said, her eyes shining. "Not the sea, nor the forest, nor the mountains can come between us. We are part of each other. I carry within me your spirit and your heart, and we are one forever."

In the morning, they set out for the border. Ceitryn accompanied Rowan, smiling serenely and giving no sign that she had just won a short and vehement argument.

"You're not coming with me," Rowan said as he prepared to leave. "It's far too dangerous."

"Beloved, where you go, I go," she said. She was dressed in trews, shirt, and tunic, her bag of medications slung over her shoulder. "Eliene went to the border with Acaren. I go with you."

"Eliene's bheancoran. She and Acaren are soul-bound."

"Oh, I see." She slanted an oblique glance up at him. "And we're not?"

"Not in the same way. Eliene's nearly as good with a sword as Acaren is. Ceit, you can't go. I can't take the chance that you'll be hurt."

"I'm a Healer. I go."

"No."

She smiled blandly at him. "I fail to see how you can prevent me from coming," she said. "Unless you tie me to the bed rails, I'll follow you when you leave. So if you want to protect me, you'd better let me ride alongside you rather than trailing along in your wake, don't you think, beloved?"

He knew when he was beaten. "You're a stubborn woman, beloved," he said in exasperation.

"I'm a yrSkai who was raised as a Tyran," she said serenely. "How could you think I'd be anything but stubborn?"

"How indeed," he agreed.

They rode for five days to reach the border. Thick, gray clouds hid the sun, sending a thin, insubstantial drizzle drifting through the air. Ceitryn, dressed for practicality and riding comfort in trews and shirt, huddled deep into the folds of the plaid, and Rowan pulled his cloak close about him. The air wasn't cold, but the damp penetrated right down to the bone.

They heard the battle before they saw it. The jolting clashing of weapon against weapon, the harsh cries of men and horses carried in the damp spring air. Rowan had little experience with real combat. He had dealt with skirmishes with raiding parties of not more than a dozen or so Somber Riders, but never with a full, pitched battle. He could not tell whether fifty men fought each other beyond the hill, or a thousand. He reached up and gripped the hilt of the sword behind his left shoulder, then looked across at Ceitryn. She sat her horse, her eyes wide in her pale face.

"We might be too late," he said grimly. "Stay here while I go to see what's happening."

She turned her head to face him. "We vowed that we

would not be separated by sea or by forest or by mountain," she said with maddening calm. "Nor by a border war. I go with you."

"Ceitryn—"

She raised one eyebrow. "I'll be as safe as you are. We go together."

As they neared the brow of the hill, the hair on the back of his neck suddenly prickled erect. The faint stench of something he didn't recognize carried on the mild breeze. He paused, frowning. He had never smelled anything like it before, but he realized with a shock that it was the stink of blood sorcery. Whatever lay on the other side of the hill, part of it was Maedun sorcery. Either a warlock or a sorcerer.

They crested the hill and drew their horses to a halt. Below lay the shallow bowl of the valley with the winding glimmer of the river to the left. The bottom of the bowl seemed filled with a seething mass of men, struggling together. The air rang with the clash and clangor of weapon meeting weapon, and the shouts of men. Bodies of men and horses lay scattered on the trampled, bloody winter-dead grass.

The fighting was fiercest near the center of the valley. Rowan recognized Fionh's red-tower banner in the middle, carried by a standard-bearer hard-pressed to keep up with his lord. Little doubt that Caennedd was not far from Fionh himself, in the thick of the fighting.

On the hill, opposite where Rowan and Ceitryn stood, a man wrapped in a gray cloak sat a horse, watching the battle. A faint, black haze surrounded him, almost like another cloak. Even as Rowan watched, the warlock gathered his sorcery and sent it down into the valley. A Tyran clansman fell, pierced by his own dirk.

Rowan looked down at his hands. Around him, threads of magic, tangible as the rain and the mist on his face, ran like rivers through the ground beneath him, through the very air around him. But how could he use it to stop the warlock? What could he do with it?

His magic was gentle Celae magic—the same magic that gave Ceitryn her Healing power. It could not kill. Nor would it allow itself to be used as a weapon.

But there had to be a way to use the threads he could feel as plainly as if they were cords of rope.

Cords . . .

He took a deep breath.

Cords could be woven. . . .

Slowly, he drew the threads to himself, pulled them together. It felt like stretching and bending iron with his bare hands. Sweat broke out on his forehead, ran in rivulets into his eyes. Every muscle in his body burned with effort, but he slowly shaped the threads into a net.

When it was done, he gathered it and sent it wavering across the valley. Weak and shivering, he watched it. It moved slowly, haltingly through the air. Then abruptly, it shivered and broke into a scatter of shards that glittered like dust motes.

He let out his breath in a long exhalation that was nearly a sob. But threads *could* be woven. They could . . . He had done it before. He could do it again.

The memory—or fragment of a dream—flashed through his mind.

Even as Elesan raised the dagger to strike, Donaugh pulled his magic to him. He caught a strand of power from the earth beneath him, another from the air around him. In his hands, they became shimmering gossamer filaments. He wove them quickly, adding more threads, until the air around his hands glowed and sparked with the growing power. Like a glistening cloak, the web of magic wrapped itself around Elesan, arrested his forward surge instantly. Elesan's eyes widened in fear. He struggled against the enfolding magic, his breathing rasping and labored, but he could not move or cry out.

How had Donaugh done it? How had he fashioned his web of magic?

Pain broke through Rowan like a wave against the rocks as he pulled the threads of power to him again. Out of the air. Out of the ground. Wove them. Sweated with the effort, clenched his jaw against the pain.

"Rowan—" Ceitryn said in alarm. "You'll kill yourself. . . ."

"No," he muttered. "No. I can do this. Help me, Ceit."

Slowly, painfully, the net formed again. He wove it

tighter this time, knotted the threads more firmly. When he sent it across the valley, he thrust it fiercely from him, hurled it with all his strength. He tasted blood where he had bitten into his lip in his effort. He wiped the back of his hand across his mouth as he watched the net float like thistledown across the valley.

It enveloped the warlock like a cloak. A spiderweb wrapping a fly. The warlock struggled against it. Even from the opposite side of the valley, Rowan could see the man fighting against the enwrapping threads. The harder he fought, the tighter the threads held him. The warlock toppled from his horse and lay there, struggling feebly in the grass.

The men in the valley reacted instantly to the absence of the warlock's spell. A fierce shout went up, and the men under Fionh's banner surged forward. The Maedun, breaking from fighting stand to fighting stand, were pressed gradually back toward the river. The Tyrs followed them with steadily growing ferocity and triumph. Men began to run in behind the fighting troops to bring out the wounded and the dying.

Rowan slid from his horse and stood leaning weakly against its withers. He held out his hands and stared at them.

Magic. He had worked magic.

Finally. At last. He had worked magic.

He looked up at the mountains, tears of joy and gratitude flooding his eyes. "Thank you, Lady," he said. Rhianna could hear him here as well as she could in Skerry. These mountains were her domain as well. "Thank you, Lady." He turned, looked up at Ceitryn.

"And thank you, my heart."

23

Rowan and Ceitryn found Acaren with Eliene sitting exhausted at the edge of the battlefield. Blood spattered Acaren's tunic and trews, and soaked a corner of his cloak. He still clutched his sword in his hand, his blood-spattered knuckles white against the hilt. Eliene stood behind him, leaning lightly against him where he sat on a large, round stone. She wore a smear of blood across her forehead and down her cheek.

"It's just Maedun blood," Acaren said succinctly, as Ceitryn made an exclamation of dismay. "We're not hurt." He made a wry face, and laughed shortly. "Fighting Somber Riders in these numbers is rather more work than we bargained on, I think."

"They swarm like flies around a sheep byre," Ceitryn said distastefully.

Acaren grinned at her, his teeth startlingly white against the blood smearing his face. He glanced at Rowan. "Will you present me to the lady?"

"My lady Ceitryn, my brother Acaren. Acaren, this is our cousin Ceitryn al Athelin who—" Rowan grinned widely. "—is also my betrothed."

Acaren lifted one eyebrow and glanced quizzically from Rowan to Ceitryn and back to Rowan. "Betrothed?"

"A story for later," Rowan said.

"I should think so," Eliene murmured, but she smiled.

Fionh strode through the milling clansmen, Caennedd beside him. Both were splashed and spattered with blood, some of it their own. The right shoulder of Caennedd's shirt-sleeve hung in a ragged tatter down his arm, a huge red-and-

purple bruise swelling on the round of his shoulder. Fionh
had lost his plaid somewhere.

"The warlock on the hill," he said abruptly. "It was you
who blocked his spell." It was a statement, not a question. "I
saw you up there." He gestured with his chin. "Just after you
got there, the warlock's spell stopped. It was you, wasn't it?"

"Aye, it was," Rowan said. He glanced at Acaren, unable
to keep the glee from his voice. "I've found my magic. Ceitryn
did it. We—we meshed. I've not much control yet, but I can
learn now. I used a tangling spell on the warlock."

"A useful trick." Caennedd wiped his arm across his
sweaty brow, smearing more blood. He looked at Acaren in
frank appraisal. "Your swordwork—and the lady's—are useful, too."

The next morning, Fionh gathered his weary company to ride
back to the garrison fort camp. The rain stopped, the sun
struggled through the breaking clouds, and the company welcomed the meager warmth. They had sent the wounded back
to the Clanhold. The dead had been properly seen home.

Acaren and Rowan rode with Fionh and Caennedd,
none of them speaking. Rowan was conscious of Ceitryn's
presence close behind him, where she and Eliene talked in
quiet voices that hardly carried beyond the two of them.
Rowan ached in every muscle; his bones hurt. He had
dreamed of magic, and he had dreamed of the pain.

But the magic was worth the pain. Even through his
weariness, he nearly fizzed with the quivering excitement of
at last being on the threshold of fulfilling the promise of his
magic.

The track followed the course of a small river through a
wide glen that would soon be green and fragrant with the
coming of spring. The clear, cold water in the river bubbled
and swirled over the smooth stones in its bed as it tumbled
down the valley to join the River Lauchruch just as it flowed
out of Tyra into Isgard.

A small hook of uneasiness caught at Rowan's belly, sub-
duing the glee of discovering his magic. Frowning, he glanced
to his right, then his left. The hills to either side of the valley

were low and gentle, and the valley itself was wide. A league
ahead, it narrowed, and trees crowded down to the riverbank. But Rowan was certain it wasn't the narrowing ahead
that troubled him.

When the long ranks of Somber Riders appeared suddenly on the top of the ridge above them, it took him a
moment to realize what it meant. Then, even as the Somber
Riders began their charge and Fionh and Caennedd wheeled
their horses to meet it, Rowan had his sword in his hand.
Without conscious thought, he kneed his horse around and
seized the reins of Ceitryn's horse. Above all, he had to make
sure she was safe.

He swung his sword out sideways. The blade caught a
Somber Rider below the ribs and swept him out of the saddle.
Rowan didn't waste time watching him fall.

Ceitryn screamed. The reins he had been holding jerked
out of his hand. He wheeled his horse around in horror to see
her hurled from her saddle as her horse went down, an arrow
in its eye. Ceitryn scrambled to her feet, running toward
Rowan. He reached down, wrapped his arm around her
waist, and swung her up before him on the saddle.

Then they were clear. He let Ceitryn slide to the ground
and turned to see what was happening. He clung to his horse
and watched the battle below. He could distinguish very little
in the struggling mass of men and horses seething across the
meadow. At the edges of the battle, on the hill above the fighting, three men in gray sat their horses, faint black auras surrounding them.

Warlocks! Three of them. All with the ability to turn
weapons back on the user. In the meadow, Tyran soldiers
died by their own hands under the devastating spell.

Ceitryn clutched his arm. "Rowan, do something," she
gasped. "They'll all be killed—"

Acaren's hand ached from his grip on the hilt of his sword.
Tense and rigid in the saddle, he waited as the Somber Riders
charged down the slope. Eliene's presence on his left steadied
him. The bond between them thrummed and vibrated with
expectant tension, and he was unable to divide his own antic-

ipation from hers. He glanced quickly at her, found her watching him, her brilliant blue eyes dancing, strands of blue-black hair clinging damply to her forehead. Only a handspan shorter than he when they were standing, her head was nearly on a level with his as she sat her horse. She saluted him briefly with her sword and grinned.

Someone behind Acaren shouted, "Here they come!" The Somber Riders were nearly upon them. The Tyrs surged forward to meet them.

Acaren raised his sword high. The sun flashed from the blade and sparked brilliantly. For an instant, it was as if time had frozen into a crystal drop of ice. He had to remind himself to breathe.

A wild, shrieking war cry rose from the Tyran clansmen. To Acaren's left, Caennedd's sword slashed down and forward. The men of his troop moved as one man, sweeping out to meet the first rush of Maedun.

Acaren hesitated only a moment. He wheeled his horse to the right and plunged ahead, swinging around to catch the left flank of the attackers. He saw Fionh lunge forward with his men, thrusting around to close in on the right flank.

He lost track of Rowan and Ceitryn as a Somber Rider swung around to face him, mouth wide, lips drawn back in a snarl. The black-bladed sword in the man's hand flashed in the sun, but Acaren's sword met the brawny arm before the Maedun could bring it down. Blood spurted from the severed wrist. The black sword fell to the sodden grass. Acaren swung his sword again. The Somber Rider fell and disappeared beneath the hooves of the horse. Acaren turned to meet another attacker.

Maedun surrounded Acaren; he became lost in the fevered dance of the battle. High, piercing shrieks from the wounded and dying men blended with the agonized screams of horses. The clash and clatter of weapon against weapon echoed from the mountains. The air of the small valley seemed to shiver with the furious assault of sound. And above it all, Acaren heard the high, sweet, constant thrumming of the bond between him and Eliene assuring him she was close at his side.

Again and again, the sword in Acaren's hand rose and fell, the blade running red with blood. Eliene's voice cried a warning. Acaren ducked low across the neck of his horse as a black Maedun blade swept past his shoulder. He swung his own sword backhanded. The Somber Rider disappeared in a gout of blood.

Beside Acaren, a man fell from his horse, clutching at his belly in a vain attempt to hold in the entrails spilling from the gaping wound sliced by a Maedun sword. Eliene wheeled her horse, cursing, and the blade of her sword bit deeply into the Somber Rider's spine even as he was turning to look for another kill.

Something heavy landed on Acaren's horse behind the saddle. An arm, strong as a young oak, circled Acaren's throat, cutting off his breath. Acaren nearly dropped his sword as he reached desperately to grab at the sweat-slick wrist. A dagger blade flashed in a swift, descending blow toward his chest.

Acaren twisted in the saddle, pushing backward. The Maedun behind him lost his balance and slipped. His grip never faltered as he fell from the horse's back, dragging Acaren with him.

Acaren rolled as they hit the ground together. The Somber Rider's arm was still closed tightly around Acaren's throat, but he managed to stagger to his knees. Again, the Maedun raised the dagger to plunge it into Acaren's chest.

The sunlight, Rowan thought frantically. Today there's sunlight. . . .

What was it about sunlight?

He cast about frantically in his memory. Then he had it. Mayhaps another legend, but he had seen Athelin weave the sunlight into brilliant patterns. If it could be woven into patterns, it could be woven into something else.

He held out his hands. Sunlight poured into them, warm and rich as precious oil. Its weight and substance moved against his fingers like threads that could be braided or woven. . . .

Woven . . .

His hands began moving of their own volition. The sunlight spun out to form golden strands, and he brought them together into an intricate pattern. The pattern expanded into a long oblong that hung in the air before him. Like a shield. Or a mirror.

He had the way of it now. He left the first shield hanging in the air beside him and fashioned another, then another. When he had three of them, he flung them down the hill at the warlocks.

The bright shields moved swiftly, tracking straight as arrows through the air until each hovered before a warlock. Almost invisible in the clear air, they glinted softly like heat waves shimmering over dark stone in sunlight. Black threads of blood magic spun out from the warlocks' hands. Bright sparks shot from the mirrorlike shields as the black threads collided with the golden surface. The dark threads bounced back toward the warlocks.

One by one, the warlocks burst into flame.

Three columns of gray ash drifted away on the gentle breeze. The shields of woven sunlight shimmered for a moment, reflecting nothing but blowing ash, then dissolved and scattered like motes of dust.

Rowan gasped in pain and fell to his knees, giddy and weak. He didn't feel it when Ceitryn caught him and sank to the ground with him, cradling his head in her lap.

Acaren shouted and tried to twist aside. Then Eliene was there. She leaned far to one side in her saddle and her sword described a glittering and deadly arc as it swung at the Somber Rider. Acaren's faith in Eliene's ability was not disappointed. The wind of the blade's passing ruffled the back of his hair, and the Maedun's head flew from his shoulders, spraying a fountain of blood over Acaren. He staggered away from the crumpled corpse and tried to wipe the blood from his eyes.

Another Maedun leapt over the corpse by Acaren's feet, his sword held in both hands. Acaren flung his arm up, and his sword caught the descending blade squarely, deflecting the blow. Disengaging quickly, Acaren stepped back and chopped at the Rider. His sword bit deeply into the Rider's shoulder, half-severing the arm.

Eliene fought her way to Acaren's side, holding the reins of his horse. "All right?" she cried.

Acaren laughed breathlessly and nodded. He grabbed the reins and pushed the blood-matted hair from his eyes before he vaulted up into the saddle.

A cry went up from Acaren's right. He swung his horse around to see the clansmen fighting around Fionh falter and fall back. On the hillside, three men in gray stood, thin threads of black mist snaking out from their hands, reaching down into the valley. Horrified, Acaren watched as clansman after clansman struggled with their own weapons.

Then Acaren saw what he took to be three golden mirrors floating across the valley. Moments later, the three warlocks became nothing but three floating columns of ash. He swallowed hard against the rising nausea and raised his sword high.

"To me!" he shouted. "To me!"

A troop of clansmen gathered around him, and he pulled them back. As the Riders surged into the gap they had broken in the Tyran ranks, Caennedd plunged forward, leading his soldiers around to the rear of the Maedun company. Then, as the Riders charged again, Acaren shouted and set heel to the flank of his horse.

Eliene and nearly a dozen clansmen followed him. They scrabbled across the sodden grass and threw themselves against the Maedun. Acaren spurred his horse forward, Eliene close beside him. Blood turned the legs of his horse red as his sword glittered in a flashing arc around him.

Taken by surprise, the Somber Riders lost the momentum of their charge. Caught within a tightening circle of clansmen and deadly steel, they broke ranks and fled. Even as they turned, they found themselves facing Fionh's men, with Caennedd closing in on their rear.

That quickly, it was over.

Fionh shouted to the clansmen, breaking off the pursuit. Acaren drew back. He could not count the number of Tyrs still sitting their horses; there was too much confusion. There were far fewer than had set out that morning. One clansman, blood matting his hair, staggered to his horse, using his sword as a staff as he sagged to his knees beside the dying beast.

Fionh pulled free of the tangle of dead and wounded. He seized Acaren's hand. "You did brilliantly," he shouted, a wide grin splitting his features. "If you hadn't moved around to the front when you did, we'd have been lost for certain."

Someone raised a bloody sword high. "Acaren!" he shouted. Seconds later, others took up the triumphant chant. "A-*car*-en! A-*car*-en! A-*car*-en!"

Acaren was too tired to think. He managed a smile and raised his sword in acknowledgment. All he wanted was a hot bath and a week's sleep.

Only a single lantern lit the small tent. Caennedd sat on a stool facing Acaren.

"Is he all right?" he asked.

"Ceitryn is with him," Acaren said. "She says he's exhausted, that's all. He just needs rest."

"I saw those golden mirrors floating across the meadow," Caennedd said. "Then the warlocks just—just turned to smoke and vanished." He shook his head. "Incredible."

Acaren nodded. He, too, had never seen anything like that before. He wasn't sure he wanted to again, either. It was gut-wrenchingly disturbing.

Caennedd moved restlessly on his stool. "Athelin was right," he said quietly. "The time was not right when I wanted to lead the yrSkai of Skerry into Celi to throw out the black sorcerer. But if your brother can work that sort of magic against Hakkar, then I'm with you. My company will follow you."

"And half the Tyran army," Fionh said. Acaren hadn't heard him enter. "Rid Celi of Maedun, and the rest of the Continent will follow. You have your army, my lord King."

The burst of magic flashed across Hakkar's awareness shortly after midday. Strong enough to flare like a torch against a dark night, it sent a cold arrow of something that might almost have been fear into his bowels.

He was in the midst of a meeting with three garrison commanders, all three of them pompously and smugly assuring him that they had eradicated all traces of magic in the southwest of Celi.

Fools! They couldn't feel the white-hot wave that swept across him like a tide of fire and ice. Fatuous and complacent fools. The very ground beneath their feet pulsed with threads of this forsaken Celae magic. The air was thick with it; it clogged his throat as he tried to breathe it. The only way to eradicate it was to destroy the land itself. How could these idiots believe they had rid him of it? They had executed a few men or women who could use the magic, but it was still rampant in the country. And right now, it flared brightly enough to sear his mind.

He had to find out where that burst of magic had come from. So strong . . . How could there be someone on the island who could use magic that strong, and he not know before this?

"Thank you, gentlemen," he said, interrupting the last commander's comfortable report. He stood up. They all three scrambled to their feet with alacrity. He smiled briefly. "That will be all for now. You're dismissed." He gave them a curt nod and left the room, walking briskly but without unseemly or undue haste.

He climbed the narrow staircase to the tower room, still able to feel the heat of that burst of magic against his spirit the same way he felt the heat of the sun against his cheek.

So strong . . .

He flung open the door to the tower room. Three long strides took him to the pedestal where the Tell-Tale stone lay nested in black cloth. The stone glowed with the aftermath of the flare of magic. But he was too late to obtain any directional information from the stone. The surge was gone, the direction it came from undetectable. In fact, according to the Tell-Tale, the magic appeared to have come from the east, which was patently absurd. Only the Saesnesi of the Summer Run were northeast of Clendonan, and they had no ability to use the magic imbued in this island. Further east lay the Continent. The only magic on the Continent was Maedun sorcery.

No, the indication of direction must mean the surge had passed by and was gone from the west where it originated, and was now obviously fading to the east.

Hakkar glanced down again at the faintly glowing stone, then went to the window and looked west. Horbad was in the west now, ready to raise a campaign against the Celae again now that spring approached. Could he leave it to Horbad to investigate this latest manifestation of the wild magic? No, by the All-Father, he couldn't. Not after Horbad had assured him that he had extirpated the Prince of Skai and the whole of his line. If Horbad had really done what he claimed he had, where did that intense flare of magic come from? And once again, he cursed that taint of Saesnesi blood Horbad had received from his mother.

He would have to do it himself. He would have to go west. Into those miserable, wretched mountains, and take care of it himself.

The last place he wanted to go was to the western mountains. But he had to settle the bothersome matter of the magic—and the enchanter whose advent it might well herald—once and for all.

Mayhaps it was time to turn this whole accursed country into a crisped, sere plain of ash and cinder, akin to the Dead Lands. And let the rebellious, stubborn Celae within it wither with their island.

24

The Skai Seeker *made its way slowly around the north coast of Celi,* and entered Skerryharbor as the morning mist lifted from the water. Athelin and Dorlaine stood waiting on the jetty, and Rowan relinquished Ceitryn to the joyous reunion with her parents.

Cynric arrived with twilight, unshaven, dirty, and weary from hard traveling. Athelin insisted he take the time to rest and refresh himself before calling a Council of War.

Nine of them—Athelin, Dorlaine, Acaren, Rowan, Eliene, Ceitryn, Gabhain, Valessa, and Cynric—met in the small conference room.

"You have the promise of a Tyran army, then," Cynric asked.

"Aye, we do," Acaren replied. He glanced at Rowan and laughed softly. "Thanks to some rather spectacular magic Rowan produced."

"And thanks to your mastery of tactics and strategy," Rowan said in amusement. Humility was a new thing for Acaren. "But what news of Celi?"

"Hakkar is in the west," Cynric said.

"Hakkar?" Athelin repeated, startled. "We knew Horbad was there. But Hakkar? Whyever for?"

"Magic," Cynric said. "From what I could gather among the garrisons south of the Verge, he's convinced the enchanter of the legend has come."

Ceitryn looked at Rowan. "He has," she said softly.

One of Cynric's eyebrows quirked, and he smiled. "Let's hope so," he said. "At any rate, rumor in the garrisons says that Hakkar has sensed strong magic in the west and has come himself to deal with it."

"That might be good for us," Acaren said. "It will mean we won't have to go chasing across the island to try to ferret him out of his stronghold in Clendonan."

"True," Ceitryn said. "But it means we'll have the combined sorcery of both Hakkar and Horbad against us when we reach Skai."

Eliene glanced at Acaren, then at Rowan. "But their own prophecy says Rowan will destroy them."

"That's the point," Rowan said. "It's a Maedun prophecy. It may be as accurate as some of the legends and tales Mioragh tells about Red Kian of Skai, and Daigwr and Ganieda, or the 'Song of the Swords.' "

Acaren stared at him. "But they're only stories. Hardly any truth in them at all."

"Yes," Rowan said grimly. "Exactly."

The *Seeker* left Skerryharbor the following morning, carrying Rowan, Acaren, Ceitryn, Eliene, and Cynric. It skirted the rocky shores of Marddyn and sped, hull down, south toward the coast of Skai.

Early the next evening, the ship's master didn't have to tell his passengers that Skai lay off the port bow. They could smell the fresh, green perfume of growing things as the seabreeze turned to a landbreeze.

The soaring mountain peak appeared to be floating on the surface of the sea, blinding white against the sullen gray of the sea. Cone-shaped, shrouded with snow, it gleamed like a beacon against the cloudy sky. It was the highest peak on the Isle of Celi, the holiest place on the island to the Tyadda who had come to the island centuries before the Celae. The sacred places of the Tyadda, and the seven gods and goddesses of this island, were the high places, the mountain peaks and the high country, where they were closest to the endless expanse of the sky. Somewhere, just between the mountain and the sea, the Tyadda had built the immense circle of standing stones known now as the Dance of Nemeara.

The Tyadda had called the island Nemeara. They had

lived there in peace for untold generations, working their
gentle magic, living in harmony with the gods and goddesses
of the island.

The characteristic dark gold hair and brown-gold eyes
of the Tyadda tended to show up in the children of Tyadda
men and women who married the black-haired, blue-eyed
Celae. And their magic, too, surfaced, stronger for the mixing
of bloods.

Rowan's grandmother had been Tyadda. And his father.
The thought startled him. He was still not used to thinking of
Davigan ap Tiegan as his father, rather than Athelin ap
Gareth.

Acaren drifted across the deck to stand beside him.
Moments later, Eliene and Ceitryn joined them.

"Cloudbearer," Rowan said, knowing they all watched
the same thing he did. The mountain dominated the horizon;
it was difficult not to watch it.

Eliene bit her lip. "Daigwr fought Hakkar very close to
it, didn't he? Near the Dance, according to Mioragh's story."

"And died there," Acaren said. "Do you suppose it's true
that the flowers bloom red where he fell?"

"About as true as the rest of the story," Rowan said with
a smile. The smile faded as he watched Cloudbearer. He felt
suddenly a little dizzy. Ceitryn reached out and touched his
arm in concern.

"Are you all right?" she asked.

"There will be more blood spilled there," Rowan said, his
voice strained and hoarse. "More Celae blood spilled there
before the snow comes back to cover it."

Acaren stood in the bow, leaning on the rail, watching the
gray-and-white wave curl up along the planking of the hull as
the prow of the ship cut through the barely ruffled water of
the sea. He had learned that, by watching how high that curling wave cut on the curving white hull, he could judge the
swiftness of their progress over the water.

He had spent a lot of time by himself since boarding the
ship in the Skerryharbor. It was not a matter of his avoiding
the company of Eliene or Rowan or even Ceitryn and Cynric,

but merely that all of them seemed to have their own thoughts, which needed solitude to sort through. Acaren himself had a few things that he urgently needed to reassess.

One of those was his relationship with his twin brother.

It had shocked him indeed when Athelin told the true story of his and Rowan's conception and birth. He had certainly been struck speechless at the news that he himself would never be the Champion he had always known he'd be, but instead was the trueborn King of Celi. It wasn't every day in the year a man learned he was king.

Not that he didn't understand the need for the deception. It was Rowan's reaction that was puzzling. Oddly enough, Rowan had not seemed as startled as he should have. It was almost as if he had been expecting it, or had always known.

That fortnight in Tyra, though, truly needed sorting through. From the start, he had accepted the fact that Rowan had the gift of magic. The shocking and startling demonstration of that gift in Tyra, after all the years of mere potential had been—well, shocking and startling. Who would have known that Rowan could be so—so powerful! The image of the warlocks disappearing into a puff of ash and smoke still stood clearly and starkly before his mind's eye. And for the first time in his life, he looked at his twin and saw someone else besides an extension of himself, his other self, his twin.

All of his life, Rowan had merely been there for him. When he looked at Rowan, he saw someone so akin to what he saw when he himself looked in a mirror, he had never really been aware of Rowan as anything but that. Rowan had always been willing to follow his lead ever since he could remember. Everything he did, Rowan did. He was a willing partner in everything from childish pranks, to wild imaginary adventures where they were Anwyr and Avigus, or Tiernyn and Donaugh, fighting Saesnesi. Everything from a good companion on the hunt to a competent and challenging opponent on the training fields under Weymund's tutelage. Rowan had always, unfailingly stepped back to let Acaren be first at anything they did, because Acaren, after all, was the elder, even if it was by only eight minutes. And Acaren had always automatically assumed that, no matter what he did, Rowan would always be there beside him.

The only thing Rowan had ever done that he himself had not was learn how to play the harp. Without question, Acaren loved music, but he had never had any desire or inclination to learn how to produce it. And even as a small child, he had known he had no talent for it. When Rowan had first begun learning under Mioragh, it had made Acaren uncomfortable for reasons he had not understood. He now realized that it was because the harp made Rowan different from him, and he was not sure he wanted his twin to be different.

If he had been vaguely discomfited when Rowan took up the harp, he had been struck speechless when Rowan came abruptly into full control of his magic, at the sudden, blazing demonstration of that power. That suddenly made his twin very different from him, and it was no easy task to reconcile himself to that. He had thought he knew Rowan as well as he knew himself.

He had been wrong.

He realized with no little dismay that he did not know Rowan at all, and certainly not as well as Rowan knew him. It was a truly disconcerting revelation.

He remembered the afternoon the Somber Riders invaded the Keep, how both he and Rowan had rushed forward, clutching their small swords. He had been supremely confident of his own ability to defend himself even after Cynric was wounded and fell. He would never forget the cold, paralyzing leap of his heart when he had seen the terrifying figure of the Somber Rider looming large and dark between himself and the gate, and Danal falling limp and dead into the snow. Nor would he ever forget how, half-dazed, gasping and struggling for breath, he had watched Rowan kill the intruder. Rowan, who had been so afraid of the Somber Rider. He had never imagined there would be so much blood in one man's belly, and he had never thought so much of it could spurt so forcefully and for such a distance. It had drenched Rowan, turned him into a surreal figure out of a nightmare.

It wasn't until Gabhain, wistfully and marginally jealous,

said that he wished it had been he who killed the Rider that Acaren realized that he, like Gabhain, harbored the same wish. But because it was Rowan—his twin, his other self— who had killed the Somber Rider, it was almost as good as if he had done it himself.

Two seagulls, caught like flecks of ash against the luminous gray of the sky, drifted across his field of vision. He watched them for a few moments, his thoughts distracted, until they disappeared in the distance toward Celi to the east.

And now they sought the swords of Wyfydd.

As he had sat there at the table in the conference room in Skerry Keep, listening to Mioragh speak, he had almost been able to feel his hand closing about the hilt of the sword, a fierce, exultant glee filling his heart. The "Song of the Swords" spoke of a ruler and a seer. He had always thought his destiny was to be Champion, but he had not even dared to dream of finding and using the swords. That was for the king the song spoke of.

How very strange to think of himself as king.

The sun set with little fanfare behind the heavy cloud cover. Acaren remained where he was as a thin, wispy mist rose from the surface of the sea and blurred the outlines of the waves against the wooden hull. A gentle thrumming along the bond he shared with Eliene warned him, and he turned in time to smile at her as she came out on deck to join him. She stepped up to the rail and placed both her hands on the smooth, polished wood, then leaned over and looked down.

"Looking for answers there?" she asked.

He laughed softly and put his arm around her shoulders. At least this had not changed. She still shared his heart and his soul and his spirit.

She looked around at a small sound behind them. He glanced over his shoulder to see Rowan come out onto the deck, carrying his harp. He found a secluded place, not far from where Acaren and Eliene stood, and made himself comfortable, his back against the low cabin wall. Obviously thinking himself alone, he settled the harp on his knee and ran his fingers softly across the strings, plucking a simple

melody in a haunting minor key. Very softly, he began to
sing.

> *I am Rowan, lastborn son*
> *Bound to serve no man but one.*
> *In face and feature, form and limb,*
> *He like I and I like him.*
> *I the dark twin, he the bright;*
> *I the shadow, he the light.*
> *Two sprung from a single seed,*
> *I to follow, he to lead.*

Caught in the music, Acaren did not see Ceitryn until
she stepped out of the shadows beside Rowan. Rowan looked
up, saw her, and even in the dim twilight, Acaren saw his eyes
light with pleasure. Ceitryn's illumination was no less notice-
able than Rowan's.

"A strange song, that, beloved," she said.

Rowan glanced up, then smiled. "I claim neither credit
nor blame." He plucked a quick, sharp chord from the harp,
then quickly damped the strings with the palm of his hand. It
sounded almost like laughter. "Mioragh often says a bard's
awen is not always his to command."

She smiled. "Such a troublesome thing, an *awen*, at times."

"Aye, it is." He put the harp down and stood up. She
stepped into his arms easily and naturally. "The other gift
now," he murmured, "I owe only to you."

The strength of the bond between them shimmered in
the dusk, as tangible to Acaren as the mist rising from the sea.
Eliene obviously felt it, too, for she stepped closer to him and
put her head on his shoulder. A moment later, when he looked
back at the place where Rowan and Ceitryn had been standing, they were gone.

"What an odd song," Eliene said softly, then sang one
line. " '*I the shadow, he the light....* ' "

"You're right," he said. "It is a strange song." Once he
thought he might have been sure of the meaning. Now he was
uncertain. Now he realized that Rowan was not just his

shadow, but mayhaps someone very important in the events
to come. For the first time, he wondered about his own
importance. Who would become whose shadow? Which twin
the shadow twin now?

With the evening, came the sea mist again. It rose almost
imperceptibly at first, blurring the surface of the water.
Above, the thin crescent of the moon was still visible, scudding among the ragged tatters of high cloud like a Saesnesi
longboat through whitecaps with the Huntress Star as always
in pursuit. They trailed a scattered wake of stars. To the
north, the Nail Star burned clear and cold through the thin
cloud. The dark line on the horizon that marked the land disappeared within moments as the mist formed and took shape
around the *Skai Seeker*. Gradually, the mist climbed the sides
of the ship, then all at once, it was all around, an obscuring
blanket, hiding the masts and sails except as dim, indistinct
shadows from an observer on the deck.

The barest breath of wind blew from the sea to the land.
Taking advantage of this, and the concealing mist, the ship
crept closer to the rocky coast, moving like a ghost through
the enshrouding vapor. Finally, in hushed tones, the master
ordered the sails lowered and the sea anchor dropped.

Acaren, Rowan, Ceitryn, Eliene, and Cynric stood on
the deck, dressed in dark clothing, their cloaks wrapped
around them against the damp chill of the fog.

The master joined the small group. "Closer than this I
dare not go," he told them. "Ahead is a good beach below the
cliffs. There is a path to the top. You should have little difficulty finding it, even in the fog. You should have no problems
following the shore of the Ceg."

Acaren checked his pouch to make sure he had the map
Mioragh had provided before they left Skerry, then reached
out to grasp the master's forearm. "Thank you," he said. "You
brought us closer than I dared hope."

"Duality be with you, my lord Acaren," the master said.
"With all five of you. Adriel of the Waters guide your path
and grant you success in your search."

The hardest part was getting the coracle into the water

quietly. Once it was in the sea, paddling noiselessly presented very little problem with the muffled oars.

Acaren sat facing the bow of the coracle, peering forward through the mist, wielding his paddle carefully. He found his breath coming shallower and faster as they approached. He could hear the hushed wash of waves on the beach ahead although he could yet see nothing. He thought that the rest must surely hear the accelerated beating of his heart.

Skai. That was Skai ahead of them. Not only Skai, but the Ceg where the Eidon flowed into the sea, where the Princes of Skai had once lived in Dun Eidon. Acaren's mouth dried and he thought he could not bear the emotion that flooded through him. He would surely burst with its strength and power.

The coracle scraped against the gravel shingle. Acaren leapt into the knee-deep water, grabbed one side of the solid wood frame of the bow. Cynric took the other. Together, they dragged the small craft up onto the beach. As Rowan, Ceitryn, and Eliene brought the carry-packs, Acaren stood on the shingle with the soil of Skai solidly beneath his feet. He breathed deeply, drawing in the scent, the very essence of Skai. Cedar and new leaves and damp soil and snowberry blossom. His heart filled until he thought it would burst; tears of joy blurred his vision.

Home. He had come home. After four generations in exile, the Royal House of Skai had returned.

Rowan had not been able to sleep. He wrapped his cloak about him against the cool night air and got quietly to his feet. He moved noiselessly away from the hollow where Ceitryn lay sleeping, and went to stand beneath a tree overlooking the sea. Clouds had again covered the sky, blocking out the moon. The air felt chilly and damp. It would rain before morning.

They had not dared light a fire for fear it would be seen by the Somber Riders and investigated. Instead, they had found shelter in a shallow depression beneath a broken slab of overhanging rocks and made camp for the night. It would be some protection from the rain, but it was going to be unpleasant traveling in the morning.

He heard a soft footstep behind him, but did not turn. "Are you wakeful, too, Acaren?" he asked.

Acaren came to stand beside him and leaned a shoulder against the seamed and weathered trunk of the tree. "How did you know it was I?"

Rowan smiled. "One could almost hear you fizz ever since we sighted land."

"Call it excitement," Acaren said. "Or call it something else. Mayhaps it's just the air of Skai that smells so different than the air of Skerry. I hadn't expected it to be green down here. We're still barely above sea level here."

"I think it must be for the same reason the low country in Venia is still green," Rowan replied. "It makes it easier for us, in any event."

"I wonder if the spell that dulls the mind is active. I don't feel anything. Do you?"

"Nothing. But we have the Tyadda magic, and we have Mioragh's charm."

"Still, you would think we would know if there was a spell. I remember how cold the air felt when we went to the Verge."

"I didn't try to touch the air as you did. As for the spell, who can tell?"

Acaren was quiet for a moment. Then he said, "On the ship, while we watched Cloudbearer, you had another Seeing, didn't you?"

Rowan nodded.

"Do you remember what you saw?"

Rowan shook his head, a troubled frown drawing his eyebrows together. "Not really. Just that I saw blood on the ground. Celae blood."

Casually, almost indifferently, Acaren said, "Our blood? One of us?"

Rowan turned to look at him. "I couldn't tell," he said. "But it frightened me."

"We'll never win back Skai without the spilling of Celae blood," Acaren said. "To win it back, if we were certain of victory, I wouldn't mind so much if it was my blood." He grinned. "It would make for some colorful flowers, don't you think?"

"It isn't something to jest at, Acaren."

"I know," Acaren said. "Do you remember what our father—I mean Athelin—said when he took us to see the Verge?"

Rowan nodded. "He said, to die to free one's country is a sad but noble thing. But to throw one's life away for nothing is a shameful and shocking waste."

Acaren laughed. "Exactly," he said. "Never fear, Rowan. I'm not a man who puts up gladly with waste, shameful and shocking, or otherwise. Such an ignominious end to a fine adventure."

25

Acaren stood on a tumble of broken rock above the shore and stared eastward at rank after serrated rank of mountains stretching eastward to the barely risen sun. The thick black-green of fir, cedar, and pine mixed indiscriminately with the still-bare oak, silver-leaf maple, beech, and alder. The river valleys at this distance were little more than vague folds and seams in the flanks of the mountains. The whole of it appeared to be as impenetrable as the wall of a fortress.

"All my life, I've imagined Skai as a place of tall, soaring mountains," he murmured. "It would certainly seem that I was right."

Cynric rolled up his blankets and strapped them to his carry-pack. "Aye, you were," he said calmly. "Now get down from there before some passing patrol of Somber Riders sees you and bags you like a rabbit."

Acaren jumped down to the coarse sand and rolled his own blankets. Rowan and Eliene had already packed theirs and were helping Ceitryn sweep all trace of them from the campsite.

Acaren looked up again. The track along the River Eidon at the head of the Ceg was the quickest way to the valley where the exiled Saesnesi had built their hidden village.

Starting their trek from the ruins of Dun Eidon at the mouth of the River Eidon would have saved them at least a full day's travel, but the master had been unwilling to risk sailing to the head of the Ceg, even with a skiff of mist to hide the ship. If daylight caught the ship still in the inlet, there was no guarantee there would be no Somber Riders to see them.

Acaren could appreciate the master's concern, but he regretted the extra time. And the extra work for their feet.

"Give us a hand here, Acaren," Rowan said. "Jump lively there."

They had risked a small fire just before dawn to heat water for tea. Acaren raked sand over the remnants of the ashes and bits of charcoal, then looked up again.

"I had also," he said judiciously, "imagined Skai as a place of wide, green valleys."

"They're there," Cynric said. "Farther inland in this area. Closer to the sea in the north."

"Are we going to be able to get through that nasty tangle of forest?" Eliene asked. "It looks discouragingly thick."

"It's mostly new growth," Cynric said. "There's still a track or two through it."

"Dun Eidon's up there, isn't it?" Rowan asked thoughtfully.

"Aye. Abandoned, and tumbled to ruin."

"We'll rebuild it when this is over," Acaren said. He grinned. "Gabhain will bustle around telling everyone how to do their jobs and get in the way, and in the end, have everyone working so much harder than they thought they could."

Cynric laughed. "Gabhain does that very well." He got to his feet and hefted his carry-pack. "Are you ready?"

Acaren slung his own carry-pack over his shoulder. "As ready as we'll ever be, I fancy," he said cheerfully. "Lead on." He reached up and settled the sword across his back more comfortably.

Cynric looked at him. "There will be no fighting," he said grimly. "If we see a patrol of Somber Riders, we will hide like field mice when a hawk is overhead. Do you understand that?"

Acaren started to protest.

"Acaren, this is very important," Cynric said. "If something happens to us— If we're careless and run into a patrol, and we're killed trying to fight them off, there will be no army of Saesnesi and Celae here to meet the Tyran army when it arrives."

"But we can't just hide like craven—"

"Rabbits?" Cynric interrupted. "We most certainly can. The Somber Riders never ride in troops of less than a dozen, or even twenty. You're very good with that sword of yours, as are Rowan and Eliene, and I'm not so bad with mine, but odds of better than three to one aren't odds I'm comfortable with in this instance."

"But—"

"But nothing. Remember what Athelin said about the foolishness of throwing away a life for nothing."

Acaren smothered his exasperation. "Aye," he said. "I remember. And he's right. As you are. Let's go find those Saesnesi hiding in the mountains."

Shortly before evening, they paused on a ridge overlooking the mouth of the River Eidon where it flowed into the Ceg. The river water was brilliant turquoise in the strong sunlight. Glacier-melt water, Rowan realized. Spring was slowly turning even the high mountains green and shrinking the rivers of ice among the high peaks.

Rowan dropped his carry-pack and wiped the sweat from his forehead with the sleeve of his jerkin. He had long ago rolled his cloak and tied it to his pack. He looked down, and a hook of sorrow caught fiercely at his heart.

"Dun Eidon," he said softly. Acaren and Eliene stepped forward and followed his gaze. Ceitryn slipped her hand into his and put her cheek against his upper arm.

Cynric came to stand beside him. "Yes," he said. "Dun Eidon. What's left of it."

Below them, Rowan could just make out the ruins of a building. One of the towers still stood tall above the weeds and sapling-choked tumble of stones that had once been a beautiful palace. A raw scar in the young trees indicated that a tower had fallen just recently, within a year, probably. The crumbling outlines of the courtyard were barely discernible, its shape blurred by bracken fern, nettles, and tangled wild roses. If the yrSkai didn't return soon and rebuild the palace, the forest would take it back into itself.

"Do you suppose the ghosts still walk there?" Ceitryn asked softly.

Cynric looked at her, unsmiling. "Iowen asked the same thing," he said. "There's a sorrow and a sadness about the place. It could very well be the spirits of the slain still wandering there."

"Poor sad ghosts," Eliene murmured.

Cynric slung his pack across his shoulder again. "Our way lies through there," he said, pointing eastward up the valley. "There's an old track there. It used to lead to the palace, but it's nearly overgrown now. I don't know if it's patrolled or not. I'd advise keeping to the forest along the side of the track."

Acaren made a face. "And hiding like field mice if a patrol of Somber Riders shows up."

Cynric grinned. "You'll learn yet, my lord Acaren," he said.

Acaren shouldered his carry-pack and laughed. "You should treat your king with more respect."

"You are not," Cynric said dryly, "crowned yet."

Four more days saw them well into the mountains. They still followed the track along the River Eidon. The track was obviously well traveled. Where possible, the forest had been cut back a bowshot length to either side. In places, the track had been hacked out of the living rock of the mountainside, leaving a precipice on the one side and a sheer drop to the water on the other.

They kept well into the trees as much as they could. Twice, they saw a patrol of at least a dozen Somber Riders on the track. One of the patrols was accompanied by a man in warlock's gray. Grimly, Cynric pointed out the warlock.

"That's a bad sign," he said quietly. "It means that they're trying to reestablish their legend of invincibility."

"Wouldn't it take a powerful warlock to work his spell here in the mountains?" Eliene asked. "I thought their sorcery didn't work in the high country."

"It didn't, once," Cynric said. "But their sorcery is getting stronger. Besides, a warlock would only have to turn an arrow back once to reestablish their myth of invincibility."

"Not a myth if they can actually do that here," Acaren said quietly.

Cynric glanced at him, then nodded. "Exactly."

Rowan shuddered and watched as the troop of Somber Riders rounded a corner and disappeared.

Eventually, they came to a place where an old landslip had come tumbling and roaring down the side of the mountain. The edge of the track had crumbled under the weight of the falling stone. When the track had eventually been cleared, for nearly a furlong, it was barely wide enough for one horseman to pass. Stumps of trees torn up by the sliding scree still thrust broken spires out of the rock, tangles of dried and dead roots beneath them.

Cynric stopped just before the landslip and looked around. "I remember this," he said. "The track up to the Saesnesi valley is around here somewhere." He pointed. "Up there on the other side of the landslip, I think."

Rowan looked up. The steep slope looked dangerous. Even as he watched, a pebble rolled under the weight of an alighting bird and skidded down to the track.

"I don't fancy running around on that," he said diffidently.

"Neither do I," Cynric said. "If I remember aright, the old path led off the track to the east of the landslip. I think if we can find the little burn the Saesnesi called the Clearwater, we should be able to find the valley. We can't follow the Clearwater. The last furlong or so before it joins the Eidon is nearly straight down. But we should be able to make our way through the forest to the creek bed farther up. It's not an easy climb."

"None of this has been easy," Acaren said resignedly. "Why should this be any different?" He looked up again. "You would have to choose the steepest and most rugged bit of mountain around here, too, wouldn't you?"

Cynric shrugged. "We can only hope that bit of mountain has done its work and kept the Saesnesi safe these last twenty-odd years."

The path, when they found it, was barely recognizable as such. Had he been on his own, Rowan would have dismissed it as merely a game trail. Branches overhung it, too low for a man to walk beneath without constantly ducking to prevent cracking his head.

Cynric moved confidently along the track, the rest in his wake. The narrow little trail wound up the side of the mountain, meandering gently. To either side of the track, the first green of spring had already begun to show among the dead leaves and pine needles. Patches of grainy snow still lay thick in patches of deep and abiding shade, but the brilliant green of snowberry grew thickly around the edges of the tired snow. Where the sun reached, the branches of alder, oak, and silver-leaf maple held heavy buds, almost ready to open into tender leaves. The air smelled of damp and new growth and the thick, sweet scent of snowberry blossoms.

A small flock of starlings fluttered out of the trees and crossed the path ahead of them, twittering and calling to each other as they celebrated spring. Rowan smiled, but Cynric froze.

"Stop," he said, putting out his hand to catch Acaren's arm. "Don't move."

"What—?"

Rowan stopped, bringing Ceitryn and Eliene to a halt with him. Cynric slowly held out both hands, arms extended to the side. He turned his hands palm upward then downward. Acaren watched him, puzzled.

"Whatever are you doing?" he asked.

"Be quiet," Cynric snapped. "Do exactly as I say. Hold out your hands. Empty. Make sure they look empty."

Acaren shrugged, then did exactly the same as Cynric was doing. He extended his arms to the side, straight out at shoulder level, and turned his hands over. Suddenly sure he knew what Cynric was doing, and why, Rowan held out his hands, nodding to Ceitryn to do the same.

Cynric called out something in a language Rowan didn't recognize for a moment, then realized it was Saesnesi. The birds. Of course. The birds had alerted Cynric that men had moved into position on the side of the track.

"We come as friends," Cynric said again in Saesnesi. "We've come on an urgent mission to see your Celwalda,

Devlyn Wykanson. We bring a message from Athelin, Prince of Skai."

Rowan tried to study the trees to the side of the track without appearing to do so. He saw no sign of any men. Nothing moved. Not even the birds now. But someone spoke from the shelter of the rocks and trees.

"Lay down your weapons."

Cynric glanced at Rowan and Acaren. "Do as he says." He carefully drew his sword from its scabbard and bent to place it gently on the ground. He unslung his bow and placed it beside the sword, then stepped back away from them. He raised his hands again to show they were empty.

"Do as he says," he said again to Acaren.

Reluctantly, Acaren slipped his sword from the scabbard and placed it beside Cynric's sword. Still unable to see anyone in the trees, Rowan followed suit. He carried no bow, but he wore a dagger on his belt. He dropped it beside the sword and stepped back.

"Put out your hands," Cynric said very softly. "There are about six of them, and they all have arrows nocked and ready."

Rowan held out his hands and repressed a shiver. Below his left shoulder blade, a cold, scratchy patch seemed to be waiting for an arrow to pierce it. He stepped closer to Ceitryn, trying to shield her body with his own.

A man stepped abruptly out of the trees onto the path, separating himself from the shadows surrounding him. He held what Rowan recognized as a Saesnesi longbow with a black-fletched arrow ready to let fly. He was young, not much older than Rowan himself. A big man, powerfully built, but lithe and supple. He wore a small, double-bladed ax at his belt, a handy size for throwing or hacking off a hand. Or cleaving a skull. His hair was the color of corn, and was long and bound into a tail at the back of his neck. Gray eyes, narrowed and alert. Face held nearly expressionless. *Not at all friendly,* Rowan thought, *but with good reason*.

Cynric studied the man, then finally smiled. "You favor your father, Devlyn Wykanson," he said.

"How do you know my father?" the Saesnesi asked.

"I was with him when he died," Cynric said. "I and his kinsman Kier."

Another man stepped out of the trees. He, too, carried a longbow with an arrow nocked and ready. Taller than Devlyn by three fingers, as powerfully built. His white-blond hair was cut raggedly just above his shoulders, and his pale blue eyes were as cold as the glacier ice that fed the Eidon.

"Don't believe him, Dev," he said. "He's Maedun."

"But I'm Celae," Acaren said. "I'm yrSkai." He gestured to Rowan, Eliene, and Ceitryn. "As are we all. We've come from Skerry in the north. My name is Acaren. My foster father is Athelin ap Gareth ap Brennen, Prince of Skai."

Devlyn turned his attention from Cynric to study Acaren. Rowan read the unmistakable skepticism in the gray eyes.

"So you say," he said. "Mayhaps the Somber Riders have found themselves some tame Celae as pets."

Another man came out of the trees. He was older than the first two, his hair streaked with gray. He spared Acaren only a glance, then watched Cynric.

"I'd say it was more like the Celae found themselves a tame Maedun," he said. "Or the strangest Saesnesi I've ever seen."

Cynric slowly held out his left arm and pushed up the sleeve of his shirt, exposing a thin white line of scar tissue stretching across the blue veins of his wrist. "I've bled for my Celwalda, Kier," he said. "Have you?"

The Saesnesi grinned widely and turned over his own left wrist to expose a similar scar. "Only once," he said. "It was enough." Then he grinned. "I had thought you dead, Cynric. It's good to see you're not."

"I knew you'd still be alive, Kier," Cynric said. "You're too stubborn and ill-tempered to let them kill you." He laughed. "It's good to see you, too, my friend."

26

They made a small procession moving single file through the dripping
forest. The man Cynric had addressed as Kier led them up
the side of the mountain. Cynric followed Kier, Rowan and
Ceitryn walked behind Cynric, and the young Saesnesi called
Kley followed him. Devlyn walked behind Acaren and
Eliene. Rowan fancied he could feel Kley's suspicious, hostile
glare piercing the cold, clammy spot under his shoulder
blade, sharp as the head of an arrow. The Saesnesi had them
well boxed in.

Kier seemed to be leading them straight at the blank,
rocky face of a cliff. Then, just when a collision appeared
inevitable, the path swung around an outcropping of rock,
and a valley opened up before them. Rowan stopped in
amazement, and Kley nearly trod on his heel.

The valley hung on the edge of a high, steep embankment above the river, surrounded on three sides by soaring,
snow-covered crags. Near the embankment stood a stone-
built house that might have once been a hunting lodge. A
scatter of smaller houses lay beyond the lodge.

Someone had taken the care and the trouble long ago to
plant a small orchard along the south wall of the house, where
the trees would catch the first heat of the sun in spring. The
pleached and pollarded trees stood stark and bare, reaching
their entwined branches up into the early-spring mist, but
gave the promise of bursting into blossom at the first hint of
warmth from the sun.

At the edge of the small orchard, three tall cairns stood,
covered now with the dead remains of wild rose and oxeye

daisy. A smaller cairn had been raised beyond them, well within the shelter of the trees.

"I know this place," Rowan said in awe. "It's in all the tales. This is the mountain lodge of Donaugh the Enchanter."

Kier turned and looked at him. "Aye, it is," he said. "Or it was. The enchanter himself is beneath that first cairn over there. After Mikal slew him, the Tyadda came out of their fastness beyond the River Eidon and buried him with honor."

The flagstone of the floor cold beneath his body, blood cooling rapidly as it flowed onto the stone. Someone held him in her arms. A young woman with red-gold hair, her hair in a long plait across her shoulders. She wept, and her tears fell onto his face, the only warmth he felt. And beyond the walls of the house, two more lay dead in the lush spring grass. . . .

Rowan shivered. "And his two apprentices lie beside him?" Ceitryn slipped her hand into his. The pressure of her fingers offered comfort, and the memory of joy.

"Aye. And Devlyn's father, my kinsman Wykan under the apple trees beyond them."

"Not just a legend, then, any of them," Acaren said slowly.

"No," Kier agreed. "Not just a legend. Follow me."

Kier led the way to the largest house, the hunting lodge. He showed them into a large kitchen, where a fire blazed on a hearth. Cynric looked around, and the corner of his mouth slipped up into a little half smile.

"It hasn't changed much," he said.

"No," said Kier. "Things don't much around here, one way or the other."

Devlyn came in with a young woman who bore an uncanny resemblance to him. The same features that on him were rugged and masculine had on her been softened by her femininity. But she looked as fit and strong as her brother. Or Kley.

"My sister, Liana," he said abruptly.

Liana smiled and turned first to Ceitryn, then to Eliene. "You must be tired," she said, her voice low and pleasant. "Please come with me. I'll show you where you can refresh yourselves."

"I'm fine as I am," Eliene said, and edged closer to Acaren.

"Well I'm not," Ceitryn said. She smiled at Liana. "I need a hot bath and a change of clothing."

Eliene made a wry face and sighed. "So do I," she said.

Rowan watched them go with mild envy. A hot bath sounded like paradise.

Devlyn ushered them into the Great Room of the lodge, and they sat at a sturdily built table, Acaren, Rowan, and Cynric facing Kier and Devlyn across the scrubbed and polished wood. Kley stood behind Devlyn, arms folded across his chest, his face grim, his eyes cold. Cynric glanced up at him, then at Kier.

"Your son, I take it," he said, a glimmer of amusement in his voice. "He's very like you."

Kier laughed. "I raised both of these young men," he said. "Just as Devlyn's father and I were raised as close as brothers."

Cynric nodded. "Have you told them about what happened the last time I was here?"

"A little," Kier said.

Cynric nodded. He looked at Devlyn. "I knew your father, Devlyn Wykanson." He bared his wrist again and laid it on the table. "I spilled my blood for him and vowed to serve him. My mother was Saesnesi from the Summer Run. I count myself as Saesnesi as you are, and I'm as proud of my blood."

"You are Cynric, then," Devlyn said.

"I am. Do you know who Davigan ap Tiegan ap Tiernyn was?"

Devlyn leaned back and clasped his hands on the table before him. "He was uncrowned King of all Celi," he said softly. "Kier's told us how he and you helped him. And how you took his widow home when he was killed by the Somber Riders near Rock Greghrach."

"His wife was Iowen al Gareth, sister to the Prince of Skai in exile on Skerry," Cynric said. "My lord Celwalda, may I present to you Acaren ap Davigan ap Tiegan, and his brother Rowan, nephews of the Prince of Skai. Rather than send emissaries to you, as you see, your king comes to these mountains himself."

Devlyn was quiet for a moment, studying Acaren, measuring him man to man. "I see," he said, and turned to Rowan. "Are you then an enchanter? Are you the enchanter of the legend who would come to destroy Maedun?"

"I have magic," Rowan said evasively. "Whether I am the enchanter of the legend remains to be seen." He had yet to learn complete control over his magic. But surely the sword Heartfire or Soulshadow would make him powerful enough to defeat Hakkar's spell.

"What do you want of us, then?" Devlyn asked.

"An army," Acaren said. "An army of Saesnesi to fight alongside an army of Tyran Clansmen that will come from Tyra."

Devlyn fingered his jaw thoughtfully. "Saesnesi and Tyran clansmen," he said. "But what about Celae? Surely if this is to be a war to free Skai and Celi, there must be Celae fighting, too."

"We must rely upon you, my lord Celwalda," Acaren said. "You have lived here in these mountains. A man of your capabilities must surely have made contact with bands of free Celae, living much as you do here. They would rally under your banner to fight if it meant ridding Celi of Hakkar and his Somber Riders."

"And what would be your contribution?"

"We have an army in Skerry and Marddyn. Not large, but well trained and well armed. They would come, of course." Acaren smiled. "One would be hard-pressed to hold them back from coming."

"And the spell?"

Rowan drew in a deep breath. He glanced at Cynric for support, but Cynric merely sat, gravely watching him.

"We would not, of course, expect any man to fight the Somber Riders while the spell still hung over the land. We will make sure the spell is lifted, one way or the other, before we commit any army to battle."

"Surely an ambitious plan."

"It is," Acaren agreed. "But the swords will help. Heart-fire and Soulshadow were made for this. They were made to free us."

Devlyn nodded. "I can gather mayhaps a thousand men, mayhaps a few hundred more, both Saesnesi and Celae," he said slowly.

"And once the spell has lifted, I've no doubt every man in Celi will find a weapon to use against the Maedun," Acaren said. "The Tyrs will not come ashore until they know the spell is lifted. If you could signal them when it's clear, I truly believe we can drive the Maedun back into the sea."

Devlyn was quiet for a long moment. He glanced at Kier, one eyebrow raised in inquiry.

"Old Gordan said a king would come out of the west," Kier said. "Your father believed him without question. I believed him, too."

"Acaren is that king," Rowan said softly. "He truly is that king."

Devlyn studied Acaren in frank appraisal. "If he proves to be that king," he said, "then he will have an army of Saesnesi at his back, and I myself will lead them."

Acaren woke to a light touch on his shoulder. He opened his eyes to see Devlyn standing over him. Outside, the sky had barely begun to pale toward dawn.

"Come with me," Devlyn said softly. "I've something to show you."

Acaren followed him. Devlyn led him out of the valley, higher into the mountains, then stepped out onto an escarpment looking out over the mountains as they diminished to the east.

He stood there on the ridge, high up on the Spine, looking out to the east to where the morning sun would rise soon. "A small ceremony," he said softly. "A reminder of what we have lost. Begun by my grandfather Cynric, who remembered the lush green fields of the Summer Run between the River Gliess and the sea. My father Wykan continued the watch after the old man died, and I carry it forward in memory of them."

Below them was the sharp line of demarcation that signaled the limit of power of Hakkar the Sorcerer of Maedun. It showed plainly, even in the half-light before dawn.

"The spell can't reach us here," Devlyn said to Acaren. "But Hakkar's Somber Riders can, if they saw us."

Devlyn turned away and looked east, far beyond the horizon toward the fair meadows of the Summer Run. "Out there somewhere lies the land I was born to rule. The Summer Run. I've never seen it." He glanced at Acaren. "My grandfather came up here to this ridge in defiance of Hakkar, in defiance of the Riders. As they did, so do I." He lifted his head and his voice to the dawn and told the tale again, as his grandfather had first told it, and his father after him.

And in those days, Tiernyn the Young, High King of the Isle of the Celae, vanquished Elesan the Celwalda of the Saesnesi in the battle of Brae Drill. In surrender, Elesan bowed his knee but not his head to the victor. "I am beaten but not defeated," quoth he to the king.

"Truly," said the king, "we are both men of Celi. For six generations have your people lived in the east, and for six generations have our people fought bitterly. This day it ends. Swear fealty to me, Elesan, Celwalda of Celi, and to you and your descendants forever will I grant the Summer Run so that you may live there and flourish for the rest of your days, and our people might live in peace and understanding each with the other." And thus saying, he raised Elesan to his feet and bestowed upon his cheek the kiss of brotherhood.

Then did Elesan the Celwalda fall to his knees before Tiernyn and bend his forehead to touch the king's feet. "Bear witness," he cried to the assembled Saesnesi and Celae, "I give in honor and respect to this man what he could not take by force of arms. My life and my loyalty I give to him, and my sons' to his sons until the last days."

And he rose and took his people home.

Devlyn's voice rose to soar above the crest. "And I shall take my people home." The echoes rang off the mountains around him, rebounding boldly until his voice became a chorus of voices raised in defiance.

He turned to Acaren and went to one knee. "As my ancestor swore allegiance to your ancestor, so do I swear allegiance to you, and my sons' and my sons' sons after them. Thanks to you, and to your brother, I truly shall take my people home after all this time."

27

They followed a steep, narrow game trail that wound through the trees high above the main track. In the lead, Devlyn set a brisk pace, despite the chill of the fine drizzle. Cold and uncomfortable, Acaren had managed to keep up, but it was a struggle. He was beginning to think that all three Saesnesi—Devlyn, Kley, and Kier—were part mountain goat. Tireless mountain goat. Or ducks, if one took into account how little the rain seemed to affect them, Acaren thought sourly.

Rowan and Eliene weren't much better. Or Ceitryn. If the swift pace was difficult for them, they didn't show it overly much. And as for Cynric— Cynric was as always as imperturbable and impervious as the granite cliffs themselves.

Up one side of a mountain, down the other. Certainly the shortest route back to the coast, but just as certainly the most difficult route. But if Cynric and Kier, both of them old enough to be his father, could keep up the crippling pace, so could he.

Devlyn and Kley exchanged a few words now and again, speaking Saesnesi. Acaren couldn't understand them without concentrating, and right then, he needed all his concentration to prevent himself from putting a foot wrong on the slippery rock of the trail and tumbling straight down to the river below.

Once when Mioragh had set him to learning Saesnesi with Gabhain and Rowan, he had complained that the language had naught to do with him. Mioragh had merely raised one eloquent eyebrow.

"Why would you object to learning a language in use in your own country?" he asked.

Irritated, Acaren said, "There are no Saesnesi in Skai."

"No, Acaren, you misunderstand," Mioragh said with maddeningly exaggerated patience. "Skai is only your province. Celi is your country, and the Summer Run and its Saesnesi are a part of that country just as surely as is Skai and its yrSkai."

Acaren had given in with rather bad grace, if he remembered correctly, and learned the language. So had Gabhain and Rowan. Acaren had never spoken Saesnesi with anyone other than Cynric and Mioragh before, but he found the practice stood him in good stead. When he concentrated, he had little difficulty understanding the three Saesnesi and could speak the language fluently enough. Mioragh had been right. But then, Acaren had long since discovered, often to his chagrin, that Mioragh usually was.

At the top of the ridge, Devlyn stopped for a short rest. Ahead, the mountains fell away in a long, steep, downward curve that faded into the soft rain. Through a break in the mist, Acaren caught a glimpse of Cloudbearer's soaring cone and, beyond it, the white-streaked gray glimmer of water.

"Cloudbearer," Devlyn said. "The Dance of Nemeara lies in its shadow. We'll leave you where the track forks about a furlong from here. But there's a shallow little cave near the bottom of this ridge where we can eat our midday meal. We should be able to light a fire, if we can find enough dry wood."

Acaren drew his cloak around him. It was of good, oiled wool, but the persistent rain had soaked through it. He shivered. "A fire," he said. "I feel as if I'll never be warm again."

Kley grinned at him. "All the walking should keep you warm," he said. "Good for the muscles."

Acaren grinned back. "I'd sooner be riding a horse and let the horse worry about keeping its muscles warm."

Kley made a face. Devlyn laughed. "Kley isn't much of a horseman," he said. "Come to that, neither am I. None of my people are. Our feet have always taken us where we wanted to go." He hefted his pack again and started out down the track.

The trail descended the side of the ridge, dropping swiftly toward the level of the main track that traversed the coastal plain from north to south. Acaren kept his head down, watching the path. He paid little attention to anything else until Cynric swore softly and stopped so suddenly, Acaren nearly trod on his heel.

"Get down," he said in a low, urgent whisper. "Somber Riders coming."

Devlyn, Kley, and Kier had already disappeared into the cover of rocks and bushes, Rowan and Ceitryn with them. Acaren and Eliene dropped into a crouch beside Cynric. He peered carefully through the tangled stems of leafless briar rose and yarrow. He saw nothing on the track and turned to Cynric, about to speak.

Cynric made a sharp, abrupt gesture, and cocked his head as if listening. Then Acaren heard it, too—the unmistakable sound of bridle metal jingling and the metallic clink of many shod hooves rattling against stone.

A moment later, a troop of men appeared through the mist. Acaren counted twenty Somber Riders, an officer, a standard-bearer, and two men in warlock's gray. The sodden standard, a flying black raven on a field of white, sagged dispiritedly at the top of the banner pole. The troop rode past so close, the scent of sweaty horse and wet leather floated strongly in the air.

The officer in the lead looked neither left nor right. He rode with one hand on his thigh, his back regally straight. He gave every indication of ignoring the drizzling rain, as if it were too petty and negligible an annoyance to notice. His narrowly handsome face was pale, as if his skin seldom saw the sun, and his heavy, black eyebrows nearly met above the bridge of his nose. Two deep lines curved down from his nose to bracket his mouth, which was set in a small, sardonic smile. There was something about him that sent a hard, cold shudder skittering along Acaren's spine.

Involuntarily, he drew back. Eliene drew in a sharp

breath, then shrank down deeper into the brush. Cynric clamped a hand on Acaren's arm and shook his head, not taking his eyes off the officer. Acaren huddled down into his cloak and closed his eyes, still shivering.

When finally, the troop had passed out of earshot, and the clank and clatter and jingle no longer carried in the air, Cynric climbed to his feet and swore softly.

Devlyn materialized like a forest spirit from behind a thatch of willow scrub. "What is it?" he asked.

Cynric looked in the direction the Riders had disappeared. A sharp, troubled furrow creased his forehead. He put his hand to the hilt of his sword, the knuckles white against the worn black leather. "Hakkar," he said. "That was the black sorcerer himself."

Acaren reached up and gripped the hilt of his sword, his mouth firming into a thin line. "You're sure?" he asked.

Cynric nodded wearily, as if he had given this assurance far too many times already. Rowan knew in his bones that Cynric was right. He had smelled the taint of blood sorcery when the officer rode past. And the sight of the banner had raised his hackles as if he were a wolf spying an intruder. The rumors Cynric had heard were right. The black sorcerer was here in Skai.

"I'm sure," Cynric said. "It was Hakkar himself. I tell you, I recognized him."

"You recognized him?" Acaren repeated. "How could you recognize him?"

"I spent five years working as a courier out of Clendonan, out of Hakkar's fortress there. Quite often, he handed me the dispatch pouch himself if it contained secret papers he didn't want his aides seeing. I know him all too well."

"But it's been twenty-five years," Acaren insisted. "Surely he'd have changed. Mayhaps it was Horbad."

"It was Hakkar," Cynric said with dogged perseverance. "I couldn't mistake him. He hasn't changed in twenty-five years, and he hadn't changed in the twenty-five years before that. He uses his sorcery to keep himself young. It will work until he's over a century old, and when he dies, it will be suddenly. That's the way it is with sorcerers. Every Maedun knows that."

"He's come to stamp out the last of the magic in Skai and Wenydd," Devlyn said. "We hear things indirectly from the Celae under the spell. The men who serve in the strongholds are under the spell, but they aren't gagged. They talk to others in the villages, and the villagers talk to us. There've been stories about Hakkar coming here for the last fortnight."

"And now he's here," Rowan said. "I can't say I like it overmuch, though."

Devlyn nodded, then turned to Acaren. "What would you have me and my people do, my lord? We are yours to command."

"As I told you, an army of Tyran clansmen has pledged to support me," Acaren said. "They'll be coming on Tyran ships to the old harbor at Dun Llewen where there's easy landing for boats. They'll wait for a signal from shore that the spell has been broken before they land. Will you bring the army you gather to meet the Tyrs here and give the signal?"

"I will."

"What about the Celae now under the spell?" Ceitryn asked. "Will they be any assistance?"

Devlyn shrugged. "I would think so. Once the spell is broken, every Celae in the mountains will follow us. The spell prevents them from harming the Maedun. It can't prevent them from hating them." He gave Acaren a hard, sharp, predatory grin. "You'll have your army of Celae counted in thousands of men, my lord King, if you can lift the spell. If they have no other weapons, they'll use their hands."

"How will you lift the spell?" Kier asked. "Do you have a plan in place?"

Acaren glanced at Rowan, then back to Kier. "We'll have the swords of Wyfydd Smith," he said.

Devlyn nodded slowly, thoughtfully. "The 'Song of the Swords,' " he said. "Old Gordon was right. The time is now, then."

"We think so," Eliene said. She glanced at Rowan. "Aye, we think it's time to bring the swords to the use Wyfydd intended them."

"But do you have a plan?" Kier asked.

"The plan depends much upon where the swords will lead," Acaren said. He, too, shot a glance at Rowan. "And, too, we have my brother's magic."

Rowan looked down at his hands. Magic. Aye, mayhaps. He turned his head and looked into Ceitryn's gray eyes. She met his gaze levelly, unsmiling. Now that, with her, he was complete, mayhaps his magic might be enough.

Devlyn slung his bow and quiver of arrows over his shoulder. "We'd best get moving on it, then," he said. "You may count on your army of Saesnesi and wild Celae being ready when your Tyrs arrive, my lord Acaren. We'll see to it straightaway."

The late afternoon sun hung low over the peaks to the west when Rowan saw a plume of smoke rising straight into the air in the valley ahead of them. A moment later, the trees thinned and he found himself looking down onto a farm. But an odd farm, surely. The farmhouse, large and stone-built, stood to one side of the main track winding through the valley east and west, and the stables and paddock lay on the other side of the track. The paddock contained ten or twelve horses, but he could see no cattle, no poultry, and no byre to house them.

Wiping the sweat from his forehead with his sleeve, Cynric stopped well within the shelter of the trees and followed Rowan's gaze down to the valley. "Posting station," he said.

"Posting station?" Acaren said. He peered down into the valley. "Horses. We could do with a few of those." He swore softly and vehemently, then leaned against the trunk of a cedar tree and pulled off his left boot. Still muttering to himself, he up-ended the boot and shook it, producing a small shower of gravel. "I thought I had half the mountain in there," he said, and shook the boot again. "This is taking too long," he said. "At this rate, we'll never find the swords before Fionh brings the Tyran army."

"I doubt we'd get far just walking in there and asking politely for the loan of five horses," Eliene said.

Ceitryn glanced at Rowan, one eyebrow raised in speculation, then down at the posting station. "I wonder," she said thoughtfully. The bond between them quivered pleasantly and he thought he caught a glimmer of what she was thinking.

"Do you have an idea, my lady?" Cynric asked.

"I think so." Ceitryn turned to Rowan. "Could you hold a masking spell over us so we looked like something else entirely as we went down and—" She hesitated.

"Borrowed some horses?" he finished for her.

"Exactly."

He bit his lip and looked down at the posting station again. "I don't know." The bond between them pulsed gently with the beating of his heart. With her help, he had already done things he had once despaired of ever accomplishing. A masking spell should not be nearly as difficult as weaving sunlight into mirrors. "I can do it," he said firmly. "*We* can do it."

"Will we go in looking like Somber Riders, do you think?" Acaren asked.

"No," Cynric said. "Nor couriers. The schedules are rigid. Couriers come at fixed times. And if a troop of Riders needs replacement mounts, the arrangements need to be made well in advance. If we show up out of nowhere as soldiers asking for remounts, it'll take a fortnight for the kerfuffle to settle, and the station commander is liable to complain loudly enough to be heard in Clendonan. Not couriers or Somber Riders."

The shadow of the mountain crept swiftly across the valley floor as the sun sank lower. Rowan watched it for a moment, then nodded.

"Light and shadow," he murmured. "We can hide in the play of light and shadow."

Ceitryn glanced up. "Aye," she said slowly. "Aye, that would work."

He reached for her hand. "Stay close to us," he said, then turned to lead the way down into the valley.

Drawing the threads of power from the ground and air, Rowan wove a cloak of shifting, glimmering color and light around all five of them. From within the shelter of the spell, it appeared they were surrounded by shimmering heat waves.

From the outside, he knew they would seem like nothing more than a breeze rippling across the grass, or through the new leaves on the trees.

The bond he shared with Ceitryn trembled as her strength streamed into him, reinforcing his magic. His spirit and hers mingled and flowed together, until he wasn't sure where he ended and she began. The exhilaration made the breath too light in his chest and his heart beat faster in its soaring joy.

The aroma of cooking food came from the house, and the clatter of crockery and utensils. Dinnertime, apparently. Rowan hardly spared a thought for the Maedun, concentrating only on maintaining the spell.

He felt as if he drifted across the clearing, like a wisp of smoke trailing from Ceitryn's hand. A decidedly odd sensation. He could only watch as Acaren, Eliene, and Cynric caught five of the horses, then brought tack out of the stable for them.

They were leading the horses away when the door of the station house slammed. A hostler came out into the yard, glancing westward as he made his way across the track to the paddock. He looked directly at Rowan, and Rowan's heart made a creditable effort to leap up into his throat. The threads of magic he held began to dissolve in his hands. The hostler frowned and took a half-step toward Rowan.

"Go gentle," Ceitryn whispered. "He can't see us."

Rowan took a deep breath, and the spell steadied. The hostler shook his head, and continued on his way to the paddock. By the time the pounding of approaching hooves announced the arrival of a courier a few minutes later, Rowan had firmed the spell again, and they were well up the side of the mountain, deep in the trees and safe.

28

The horses were smaller and stockier than the horses Acaren was used to, but they were well muscled. They showed the depth of chest and sharp delineation of haunch that meant speed and endurance, if not carrying capacity.

It was the work of moments to saddle the horses. They mounted quickly and turned north and west, toward the towering cone of Cloudbearer. The overgrown trail followed a little river that plunged precipitously down the slope toward the coastal plain.

Ceitryn followed Cynric down a track so narrow they could ride only in single file. Rowan rode behind her, and Eliene behind Rowan. Acaren rode last in the file, trying to watch in all directions at once.

The branches of the trees intertwined above the trail, but the buds and tiny new green leaves offered no protection from the drizzle sifting down again from the clouds. The track twisted and turned, following the contour of the mountains above the tumbling river.

The noise of the rushing water masked the sound of the horses' hooves on the soft ground. Acaren rode leaning forward intensely, senses alert for the first sign of trouble, aware of the accelerated beat of his heart, the shallowness of his breathing.

The Somber Riders fell upon them with no warning at all. More than a dozen of them burst out of the trees ahead, swords drawn. Acaren had just time enough to realize there was no man wearing warlock's gray with them before the Riders were on them.

Then Acaren's sword was in his hand, raised above his head as he dug his heels into the horse's flanks. He charged into the center of the dark-clad Riders, his sword weaving a deadly arc about his head and shoulders. Eliene moved with him as if she were attached by invisible threads. He could no more lose her than he could lose his shadow.

Rowan shouted something to Ceitryn and drew his sword. He hacked his way to Acaren's side, grinning fiercely. Beside him, Cynric calmly swung his sword, guarding Rowan's right as fiercely as Eliene guarded Acaren's left.

Acaren shouted wildly as his sword flashed first left, then right. He felt the solid connection with bone and flesh, drew back the blade red with Maedun blood. His eyes alight, guiding the horse with only his knees and his body movement, he whirled to face another Somber Rider behind him. In the back of his mind, he was aware the Riders outnumbered them at least three to one, perhaps even four to one. But they had the momentary advantage of surprise. He hoped it would be enough.

One of the Riders charged straight at him, sword raised and ready. Acaren spun to meet him, but the Rider suddenly fell forward, blood spouting from his nearly severed neck, and Acaren found himself grinning at Rowan across the empty saddle of the Rider's horse. Rowan grinned back fiercely, then spun to face another opponent, his sword blade dripping red. Acaren laughed and whirled about to parry the thrust of a dark sword that came at him from his left.

Cynric disappeared behind a small knot of Somber Riders. A moment later, his horse plunged riderless into the trees above the track. Acaren could not see Cynric anywhere, but had no time to spare any more than a quick glance.

Rowan spurred his horse toward Cynric, who was surrounded by Somber Riders. To his left, a Somber Rider surged forward and swung his sword. Rowan met the blade with his own, but as he disengaged and chopped down across his body with his sword at his attacker, another Rider lunged forward and thrust the point of his sword at Rowan's side. Rowan twisted but could not bring his sword around swiftly enough to counter the thrust. The point of the sword went deep into the meat of his thigh, and he fell, yanking his dagger from his belt. The Somber Rider fell with him, trying to pull his sword out of Rowan's thigh. Rowan's dagger sank into the Rider's chest, piercing his heart.

Out of the corner of his eye, Acaren saw Rowan go down beneath a knot of Somber Riders. Her face the color of chalk and twisted with purposeful intensity, Ceitryn flung herself from her horse. She cried out in rage and fear, and snatched up the sword of a fallen Somber Rider. Fiercely, she brought it down across the back of one of the Riders who stood over Rowan's prostrate form, sword raised for the killing blow. Acaren spurred his horse toward the place where Rowan lay, lunged forward in the saddle. His sword point took another of the Riders at the base of his skull, severing the spinal column. Ceitryn barely glanced at him. She spun around to meet another Somber Rider. She might not have had the training with the sword that Eliene had, but Acaren thought she looked fiercer than a she-panther. He was just as happy he didn't have to face her.

Four Riders broke from the confusion and caught their horses. They moved purposefully toward Eliene, cutting her off from Acaren's side. She spun around, swung her sword. It caught one of the Riders across the chest. Before she could raise her sword again the three remaining Riders overwhelmed her. One of them swung his sword. His hand, clenched around the hilt, slammed into her head just above the ear. She slumped forward across her horse's neck. Before she could fall, another Rider swept his arm around her waist and snatched her off the horse and across the saddle of his own horse.

Acaren swung around, shouting Eliene's name. He spurred his horse toward her. Two more Riders bracketed him as he tried desperately to get to her. As he turned to swing at the Rider on his right, the Somber Rider on his left swept the flat of his blade against his chest. Unbalanced and winded, Acaren fell backwards. As he hit the ground, one of the Riders leapt to the track beside him and kicked him in the back of the head. Acaren curled himself into a protective ball and lay dazed and unmoving, unable to focus his eyes. The

Rider bent, grabbed him around the waist, and flung him across the saddle of a horse and sprang up behind him.

Rowan heard Acaren shout and looked up in time to see the Rider sling his twin across the saddle of a horse as if he were nothing more than a sack of flour. He groped for his sword and staggered to his feet. His wounded leg nearly buckled under him, and the pain sent waves of nausea churning through his belly. He shouted, but he was powerless to help Acaren.

Ceitryn cried out, and Rowan spun around. She was surrounded by Somber Riders, fighting desperately for his life and her own. He lost count of the number of men around him. The same skill that had turned his sword into a glittering mirror around him in the practice field held the Riders at bay as he whirled and danced. But if they could not get close to him, he could not get away from them as the five Somber Riders sped down the track with Eliene and Acaren.

One of the Riders came too close. Rowan's sword sliced through his chest, and he fell writhing to the ground. He parried the thrust of another Rider, spun to face a third. Beneath his feet, the track was sodden mud, slick with blood. He went to one knee in the slimy mud, raising his sword to meet the descending blade of yet another Rider. The Rider staggered in the bloody mud. Ceitryn leapt to one side and swept her blade backhand, cutting the Rider's leg out from beneath him.

There were still six Riders around them. Despairingly, Rowan knew he and Ceitryn could not last much longer. He was out of breath, the air rasping painfully in his throat. He was sure his leg would give way under the strain at any moment. The sword in his hand felt as if it were made of lead, and he wondered bleakly how much longer he could muster the strength to lift and swing it.

He heard a startled grunt behind him. One of the Riders fell forward, a black-fletched arrow protruding from his spine. Seconds later, Devlyn and Kier appeared, bows drawn and ready. Another Rider fell to Kley's arrow.

There were only two Riders still ahorse around Rowan and Ceitryn. On foot on the track between Ceitryn and the three Saesnesi, Cynric sliced his sword through a vicious arc and swept one of the Riders from the saddle. Another black-fletched arrow took the second through the eye. The man swayed stiffly in his saddle, already dead, but did not fall.

Rowan dropped his sword as a wave of dizziness washed over him. He fell to the ground, shivering and cold. Blood loss, he realized vaguely. The wound in his leg must be bleeding badly, and he'd paid little attention to it in the fighting. He hardly noticed when the last Somber Rider toppled from the horse and fell across his legs.

Barely conscious, Rowan looked up to see Ceitryn, moving as if in a dream, fall to her knees beside him in the track. She was disheveled, but appeared to be well. Only a small smear of blood marred the perfect curve of her cheek. With a strength he had not known she possessed, she seized the Rider's body and flung it aside.

Rowan tried to tell her how pleased he was she was not hurt, but she touched a finger to his lips.

"Don't talk, beloved," she whispered. "Save your strength."

Blood soaked Rowan's clothing. He wondered how much of it was his from the leg wound and how much of it was Maedun blood. Dizzily, he tried to touch the wound on his thigh, but couldn't find it. Ceitryn took his hand and placed it on his belly.

"Quiet, beloved. Just rest. Please."

Cynric and Devlyn dropped to a crouch beside Ceitryn. Cynric wore a hastily applied bandage around his arm just above his right wrist. Congealed ropes of blood stained the back of his hand. Rowan stared at him, then at Devlyn, and had to close his eyes to ward off the nausea as their shapes wavered, too bright and too close.

"Is he alive?" Cynric's voice echoed hollowly in Rowan's ears.

"Aye, he is," Ceitryn replied. "Hold him. The wound's a bad one. He's lost a lot of blood."

Cynric slipped his arms beneath Rowan's and held Rowan's back tight against his own chest. Ceitryn put both her hands over the wound on Rowan's thigh and closed her

eyes. The gentle flow of power in the ground, in the air, intensified around Rowan. He felt as if he had been caught in a
flood tide, or a gale. The air around her shimmered as the
power poured into her. It coalesced like ribbons of light and
shot from her hands into his thigh. Rowan convulsed in Cynric's arms, his face contorting, but he made no sound. When
she moved her hands and sat back on her heels, her face pale
and drawn with fatigue, no trace remained of the gaping
wound.

"Is it done?" Cynric asked. His voice sounded as if he
spoke from the bottom of a well. "Is he all right?"

"He will be soon," Ceitryn said. "But he can't travel farther today. He must rest to regain his strength. I've Healed
the wound, but he's lost a lot of blood, and I had to use some
of his own strength to Heal him."

Rowan looked up at Devlyn, who stood with his bow in
his hand, an arrow between his fingers ready to be nocked.
Light glowed in a nimbus around him. Rowan blinked, and
the light faded.

"You saved our lives," he murmured. "Thank you. But
why did you come back?"

"We saw that lot," Devlyn said, nodding at the sprawled
bodies of the Somber Riders. Kley and Kier walked among
them, gathering bows, quivers of arrows, and daggers. "I had
a thought that you might run across them and need help."

"You were right," Ceitryn said. "And now we have to
find where they took Acaren and Eliene."

"Rock Greghrach is the nearest fortress," Cynric said.
"The Riders will take them there."

"Then we'd best get after them." Devlyn slipped the
arrow back into his quiver. "We'll help you."

"No," Cynric said.

Devlyn turned on him, anger and shock twisting his
face. "No?" he repeated. "What do you mean, *no*?"

"Just that," Cynric said. "No. Two or three people might
have a chance to slip unnoticed into the fortress. But not half
a dozen. And certainly no one who possesses no resistance to
Hakkar's spell could take the chance. Kier was adopted by
the Tyadda, but you, my lord Devlyn, and Kley have no

resistance." He glanced at Ceitryn. "Neither, my lady, do you, I'm afraid."

"My grandmother was Tyadda," she said. "I inherited my grandfather's Healing Gift. Mayhaps I've inherited the Tyadda resistance, too."

"Let's hope so, my lady," Cynric said.

"I'm willing to take the chance," she said grimly. "I won't leave Rowan."

Rowan had not even considered Hakkar's spell. He reached up and fumbled for the little talisman he wore about his neck. Cynric had not forgotten, though. And he was right.

Devlyn made a disgusted sound with teeth and tongue. "You're right," he said, his reluctance thick in his voice. "But—"

Cynric interrupted him. "Devlyn, no. You, Kley, and Kier must gather the free Celae and the Saesnesi to meet the Tyran army when it arrives. That's imperative. We're running out of time too quickly. We shall rescue Acaren and Eliene."

"Can you do it yourselves?"

"We'll have to, won't we?"

Devlyn made the sound again. Cynric laughed shortly without humor. "As soon as Rowan is well enough to travel, we go after them," he said.

"He should be strong enough to ride tomorrow," Ceitryn said.

"No," Cynric said again. "I'm sorry, my lady. He must ride now. It's imperative that we go at once. He can ride in front of me if he can't sit a horse by himself."

Ceitryn put her hand to Rowan's forehead. Her fingers were cool and smooth against his skin. "Sleep, beloved," she murmured. Waves of darkness washed over him, one after the other. He could fight them no longer. He closed his eyes.

"We must go," Cynric said.

Rowan struggled to open his eyes and looked up groggily. "Do we ride after Acaren and Eliene, then?" he asked.

"Not yet," Cynric said quietly. "We go first to the Dance of Nemeara."

29

The great stone Dance stood on the wide, flat coastal plain at the foot of Cloudbearer. To the west lay the Western Sea, gray and silver in the wan light of early dawn. The clear sky gave promise of becoming blue, but the only color in it yet was a pale silver-blue just a shade beyond gray. The stones themselves stood massively gray against the mist that clung to the wet grass.

Gray stones, gray sea, gray sky, gray mist. And the gray-white plumes of their breath hanging in the crisp chill of the early-spring morning air.

Rowan pulled his cloak closer around himself and drew in a long, quivering breath.

He had awakened that morning in the predawn grayness to find himself with Ceitryn and Cynric on the lower slopes of Cloudbearer, less than an hour's ride from the Dance. He felt remote and detached, as if his spirit weren't firmly anchored in his body, but he had no idea why he might feel like that. For a while, he was content to drift there, halfway between waking and sleeping.

A vision of Acaren lying still and lifeless on the track brought him out of sleep, gaspingly wide-awake. He found himself tangled in his cloak and a blanket, tucked into the protection of a jutting overhang of granite and screened by willow and hawthorn bushes. Beyond the trees, the first hint of coming dawn lit the land, not quite bright enough for color definition. For a moment, he sat in confusion, wondering where he was and how he had come to be there. All he could remember was Ceitryn's worried face close to his as she put her hand to his forehead. Her hand had been cool and soft.

He pushed his hand through the tangle of cloak and blanket. His fingers met the torn fabric of his breeks, brittle with crackly flakes of dried blood. But no soreness. No torn flesh. No wound.

Healed.

Of course. Healed. Ceitryn would not let him die of the wound. Or remain in pain if she could help it.

As soon as he saw that Rowan was awake, Cynric had insisted they break camp, such as it was, and make haste to the Dance. He wanted to arrive before the sun rose behind the shoulder of Cloudbearer. He had subtly hurried them out of the cold camp and onto the horses. They had pushed the horses to a brisk canter and arrived at the edge of the coastal plain just as the rising sun was painting the eastern sky with streaks of pink and azure and gold.

Rowan had heard all his life of the Dance of Nemeara, and thought he knew what to expect. But the reality of the tremendous, smoothly carved stones nearly took his breath away. A triple ring of stone stood starkly defined on the wide plain. The outer ring, a series of capped trilithons, was more than a hundred and fifty paces across. The second ring, huge menhirs joined all around by capstones, stood slightly higher than the trilithons. The inner ring was not really a ring at all, but a horseshoe of seven stones surrounding a low altar of smooth black stone, polished until it shone like jet.

The Dance radiated power the same way a blazing hearth radiates heat. The strength of the power vibrated along his nerves and tendons, through the bone and muscle and blood of his body, as music sped along a plucked harpstring. It crackled at his fingertips, set the hair on the back of his neck stirring, and made the breath too light in his chest. It buffeted against him like a strong west wind in spring, and he felt he could lean into it as he could lean into the wind.

Ceitryn moved closer to him, slipped her hand into his, visibly quivering under the mesmerizing influence of the stones. She said nothing. But she didn't have to. He felt her awe of the massive Dance as easily and intensely as he felt his own.

Only Cynric appeared unmoved, impassive. He stood a little apart, watching the Dance calmly, his face expressionless. Finally, he turned to Rowan.

"Do you understand now why we had to come here first?" he asked. "Do you see?"

Rowan managed to tear his gaze away from the stones. "I see," he said. "We had to come here before we went after Acaren and Eliene. You were right."

"I've been here before," Ceitryn said softly, wonderingly. "Or I've dreamed it. I know this place."

Rowan said nothing. He squeezed her hand slightly. She had echoed his thoughts. He'd been here before, too. Many times. In dreams for certain. But, he thought, in more than just dreams.

She shivered and ran her hands through her hair. "But, now that we're here, what do we do?" she asked.

Half of Cynric's mouth slipped into a little half smile. "You go in there," he said.

Rowan took a pace back. "Go in there?" he repeated, his voice hoarse. "Surely not."

"Surely yes," Cynric said. "Both you and Ceitryn. Especially you."

"But why?" Ceitryn asked.

Rowan thought he knew, but he waited for Cynric to reply. Cynric looked at him, and spoke to him rather than Ceitryn.

"I've been here twice," he said softly. "The first time, I waited here with Kier and your father while your mother went into the inner circle where she had a vision of the swords. When she came out, we followed her vision to Dun Eidon, where the swords were forged, and then to the cave by the sea where the twin swords lay hidden but in grave danger from Maedun blood sorcery. And the second time I was here . . ." His voice trailed off to silence, and he took a deep breath and closed his eyes, as if he were trying to prevent tears from spilling over his lower lashes.

"And the second time?" Rowan asked gently.

For a long moment, Cynric didn't reply. He watched the Dance as if he could still see those pictures from twenty-five years ago. Finally, he turned again to Rowan. "The second time I was here, your father was dead. Killed by a man Horbad had set on his trail like a hound to a deer." The Dance drew his gaze again.

"Your father," Rowan said quietly.

Cynric glanced at him quickly, then back to the Dance. "Yes. My father. Kier brought Iowen here after Davigan died. I followed and caught up to them shortly after they arrived. Kier and I waited while she went into the Dance. She took both the swords with her. They weren't with her when she came out."

"She left them in there?" Ceitryn asked.

"Aye, she did."

"But why? Why didn't she take them with her to Skerry? Surely they would have been safer there."

Cynric held out both hands, palms up. "She told me that they were forged to free Skai," he said. "They could not leave Skai until their purpose was fulfilled. As far as I know, they're still in there."

Ceitryn stared at the Dance. "But surely, after all these years—" she said.

Cynric smiled wryly. "The Maedun don't go into the Dance," he said. "They tried once to bring the stones down, but the stones protect themselves. Even I feel uneasy and ill this close to the Dance."

"The swords are safe in there still," Rowan said with sudden, certain knowledge. "The Maedun haven't found them. The swords take care of themselves, too."

"And you must go in there and get them," Cynric said. "We can't free Acaren and Eliene without them, I don't think."

"I'm not sure I want to," Rowan said. "Go in there, that is." He shivered.

"Aye, my lord Rowan," Cynric said. "You must. And you must, too, my lady."

Visibly startled, Ceitryn stared at Cynric. "I?" she said, placing a hand on her chest. "Surely not."

A troubled frown drew Cynric's heavy, dark eyebrows together above the bridge of his nose. "Someone has to retrieve the sword for Acaren," he said.

The Dance seemed to float on the thin drifts and swirls of ground mist. Rowan nodded slowly. "Yes," he said. He glanced at Ceitryn, let a small smile of amusement play around the corners of his mouth. "You have magic. You're of the Royal House of Skai. You may take one of the swords."

"I'm neither 'the King's own seed,' " she said, "nor 'Royal blood and royal breed.' "

Cynric glanced over his shoulder at the eastern sky. Rowan looked. In only a few minutes, the sun would be peering over Cloudbearer's shoulder and flooding the plain with brilliant light.

"Now," Cynric said urgently. "You must go in now."

Ceitryn took a deep breath, and looked at Rowan. She lifted one shoulder delicately in resignation. "Very well," she said. "I'll go in if you're going."

"I'm going," Rowan said.

She moved closer to him. "Then I shall go with you."

Acaren slowly became aware that he lay on something hard and cold, something harsh and gritty that abraded the skin of his cheek and temple, and the fingertips of his left hand. He lay on his right side, half-curled. He could not feel his right hand, caught somewhere beneath his body. Pain pounded and throbbed in his head, causing bright sparks and pinwheels to explode behind his closed eyelids with every beat of his pulse. The crushing agony made it quite impossible to think. He had no room in his mind for anything else.

For a long time, he simply lay wondering what had happened to him. It hurt his head to try to concentrate. He kept losing the thread of thought every time the pulsebeat sent fresh waves of pain flashing through his head. It was far easier just to let himself drift. Somewhere in the back of his mind, he was vaguely aware of a sense of danger nearby, of mortal peril, but he could not concentrate long enough to pin it down to any particular source. Perhaps Rowan would know and could tell him — Rowan who had the Sight. Rowan, who lay on the track bleeding beneath a half-dozen enemies. . . .

Acaren lurched up to a sitting position as memory came

back in a rush, then nearly fell over as a wave of nausea and
dizziness swept through him. He remembered seeing Rowan
fall under a concentrated attack of at least six Somber Riders.
And he remembered leaping to Eliene's aid.

He brought his hands up and pressed his fingers against
his temples to try to ease the pain, his eyes squeezed shut.
Cold, sick grief closed around his heart, and he groaned with
its strength. He had abandoned his brother on the track.
Rowan had very possibly been dead already when Acaren
spurred his horse toward Eliene in response to her desperate
cry. Even then, he had been unable to help her as the Somber
Riders overwhelmed her.

Acaren let his hands fall to his lap. He opened his eyes. It
was all but lightless around him. He sat huddled on a damp
stone floor. A faint glimmer of light reflected off wet stone
walls. The air smelled fetid and dank, an indefinable stench
thick around him. And it was bitterly cold—the deep, chilling, bone-breaking cold of a cave far underground.

Or a dungeon, he thought wryly. It would make sense if
he had been thrown into a dungeon to contemplate his grief
and his guilt at abandoning his brother in the midst of a battle.

He closed his eyes again, still feeling sick and dizzy.
There must have been over a dozen Somber Riders. Far too
many to fight off. But even as the thought formed, Acaren
knew that running would have been just as futile as fighting.
Their horses would have tired quickly, and the Somber Riders could have easily run them down in relays, resting their
own horses between spurts.

Something moved in the darkness near him. A faint
rustling noise came out of the gloom around him, a scrabbling
sound of something brushing against the gritty floor. He
could see nothing, but his first thought was of rats, and he
shuddered with revulsion as he remembered stories of people
being bitten horribly by the vicious rodents. He gathered
himself into as small a huddle as possible, his hand groping
automatically toward the sword at his back. It wasn't there,
of course. Whoever had dumped him so unceremoniously
onto the dank stone floor had also removed his sword and his
dagger. He had no weapon left but his hands. Instinctively,

his hand went to his throat and found the thin gold chain that held the crystal. At least they had left him that.

The sound of movement came through the darkness again. Something scraped on the gritty stone floor. It seemed to come from his right. He turned slightly toward the sound, tensing his body against an expected assault.

"Who's there?" It was Eliene's voice. Acaren slumped in relief.

"Eliene?"

"Acaren!"

He reached out, found her arm as her hand groped for him. Almost instantly, she was in his arms, her head pressed against his chest. He held her tightly, rocking slightly.

"Oh, Acaren," she whispered brokenly. "Acaren, my head aches so abominably."

"I think they hit you with the hilt of a sword," he said. "One of them kicked me." He laughed softly and tried to make light of it. "It's a wonder our heads aren't broken to tiny, brittle little shards. I'm afraid to shake mine in case I can hear it rattle."

She shuddered. "Don't make jokes, Acaren. I thought you might be dead. I couldn't even feel your presence through the bond until you woke up. Where are Rowan and Ceitryn? And Cynric?"

The grief mixed with guilt clutched at Acaren's heart again. "I don't know. I saw Rowan go down. The last I saw of Ceitryn, she was fighting more than five Riders."

Eliene shivered. "Then they all might well be dead?"

"I fear so."

"Ceitryn, too?"

Reluctantly, Acaren said, "She's not trained to the sword as you are."

"Oh, sweet Deity," she whispered. "But then why are we still alive?"

"I don't know. I wish I did. But as long as I am alive, I'm going to find some way to avenge Rowan. I swear I will—"

"Where are we?"

"It might be a dungeon. One of the Maedun garrisons, mayhaps."

"Acaren, I feel so odd. It's so hard to think . . ."

"They hit you rather hard, Eliene."

"It feels like something is trying to stuff my head with quilt batting." She lifted a hand to her head and pressed closer against him. "Do you think it might be the spell?"

Acaren's hand went again to the crystal at his throat. It felt warm against his fingers. He glanced down and saw that it glowed very faintly in the dark. He looked quickly at the crystal Eliene wore, saw that it, too, glowed. His heart gave a sharp, painful lurch in his chest, and his fingers clutched tightly around his crystal.

It *was* the spell Eliene felt. He was sure of it. Even with Tyadda blood and the crystal, they had only limited protection. Bleakly, he wondered how much time *limited protection* meant, how long they had before both he and Eliene succumbed to the enchantment of Hakkar's spell.

30

Together, hand in hand, they crossed the soaked mixture of sodden winter-killed grass and slender shoots of new spring grass. The low-lying mist swirled and eddied like water around their ankles. Overhead, a lark rose to the pale dawn sky, pouring its sweet song into the windless morning air.

Rowan was conscious of Ceitryn's quickened breathing beside him, her hand cool and dry in his. She matched his strides, her gaze unwaveringly straight ahead. She paused for a moment before stepping through the entry trilithon and looked up.

"How could mere men raise something as huge and massive as this?" she murmured.

"By music and magic," Rowan replied. He glanced up at the gray bulk of the carefully shaped and fitted capstone above his head. "Aye, and by muscle, too."

Stepping through the entry trilithon was like passing through a doorway into a hushed and silent room. The song of the lark was gone, as was the soft, heartbeat rhythm of the sea. Even the whisper of the breeze in the grass was muted. They slipped between the stones of the second ring and stood, side by side, at the open end of the horseshoe of seven menhirs, facing the polished altar.

On the short, velvety grass of the inner circle, the altar stood no higher than mid-thigh, not quite as long as Rowan was tall, and a little less than half that wide. It was empty. The polished surface of the top held no more than the silver-blue reflection of the dawn sky. There was, of course, no sign of anything resembling a sword. Rowan could see no place

within the circle to hide anything. Unless Iowen had buried
the swords, they certainly weren't there.

The equinoctial sun lifted suddenly over the shoulder of
Cloudbearer, and light flooded through the Dance. Shadows
rushed across the grass and fell in dark, sharp-edged bands
across the altar. The reflected light dazzled Rowan's eyes,
stinging. For a moment, he thought he saw the shadows moving, as if they were alive. He closed his eyes briefly against
the glare. When he opened them again, a man stood facing
them across the gleaming surface of the altar.

Ceitryn's hand tightened convulsively on Rowan's. She
drew in a sharp, startled breath. Rowan knew the man. The
Guardian of the Dance had visited his dreams when his
dreams called him to the Dance.

"My lord Myrddin," he said softly in greeting.

Myrddin inclined his head in acknowledgment of the
greeting. "So you have come at last, Rowan Secondborn," he
said.

"Aye," Rowan said. "I have. The time is here at last, my
lord Myrddin. We've come for the swords."

Acaren had lost track of time. In the darkness of the cell, he
was uncertain whether it was day or night. He and Eliene
might have been locked up for several hours, or several days.
He had no way of telling. He had been trying to test himself
for signs of the spell beginning to manifest itself, and watching Eliene closely. But he was unsure of what he should be
looking for. He had been unable to detect any signs of the
spell working on him — or at least he thought he could detect
nothing. He was not sure about Eliene. She seemed half-
dazed and listless most of the time, but that might be simply
from the blow on the head she had sustained. The crystal at
her throat gleamed with a soft, golden radiance in the dim-
ness. Surely the glow would be gone if the spell had overcome
the warding charm.

He sat with his back against the damp stone of the wall.
He was cold to the bone. Beside him, Eliene lay sleeping,
wrapped in her cloak. He had tucked his own cloak around
her when he had noticed her shivering. She had slept for most

of the time they had been in the cell. Her periods of wakefulness seemed to be becoming longer though. He hoped that meant she was recovering.

They had been ignored since they had been thrown unceremoniously into the cell. Twice in that time, someone had opened the cell door just long enough to thrust a wooden bucket of water and two bowls of thin, rancid soup into the cell. The water was cold and sweet, but the smell of the soup turned Acaren's stomach. Neither he nor Eliene had reached the point where they were hungry enough to eat the slop.

Acaren had seen nothing of the men outside the cell but shadows. They had taken no chances, given him no opportunity to try for an escape. The fact that they were very careful indicated to him they knew he was not under the spell, and gave him something else to ponder. It was small comfort, but it was tentatively reassuring.

Beside him, Eliene stirred, then sat up and reached for his hand. She gave a small cry of dismay.

"Acaren, your hand is like ice," she said. "I told you not to give me your cloak. Here. Let me help you get warm." She took both cloaks and wrapped them about him, ignoring his protest. When she had finished, she curled herself into the shelter of his arm against his side, and rested her head on his shoulder. "There. Now we can keep each other warm."

"Are you all right?" he asked.

She considered her answer. "I think so. My head isn't aching anymore at any rate. How long have we been here?"

She seemed more lucid than she had before. He tightened his arm around her shoulder and tried to look at her in the dark. The glow from her crystal faintly illuminated the soft curve of her throat and chin, but he was unable to see much more of her face.

"I don't know," he said. "A day? It's difficult to say without being able to see the sun." He grimaced. "I am sick unto death of being in the dark."

They sat together for a long time, not speaking. The warmth of her breath moved against his throat in a gentle rhythm. He closed his eyes and thought about the fight on the narrow track. Again, the guilt assailed him. He should have been able to help Rowan. The guilt ignited a bright spark of anger, and he swore softly.

"What is it?" Eliene asked.

"This whole thing," Acaren said. "We've been such fools. All of us. We set out on this as if it were a lark. I didn't even take the battle on the border in Tyra seriously. We thought it would be so simple. And the first thing we do when we land in Skai is get captured by the enemy. So much for my glorious destiny to become king. I'm sorry for getting you into this, Eliene."

She laughed softly without humor. "As if you stood a chance of keeping me away," she said. "I'm your bheancoran. I go where you go, and that's flat."

"I was so eager to prove myself," Acaren said bitterly. "What a fool I was."

"No, that's wrong," Eliene said. "Our reasoning was logical. We ran into trouble because we were careless. We thought we were safe because we had seen no Somber Riders, and the track was so little used and overgrown. It wasn't your fault, or Rowan's or Cynric's. It was all of us. We should have been more careful."

"And Rowan may be dead because of it. . . ."

"Do you really think Rowan's dead?" she asked. "Or Ceitryn?"

He and Rowan had always shared a subtle bond. The twin-bond, forged in the shared womb, had always made Acaren aware of his brother. When he tested that awareness, he found it intact. The knowledge of Rowan's presence was faint, but it was still there.

"No," he said at last. "He's still alive. But he was hurt the last time I saw him."

Eliene shook her head. "I don't think either one of them is dead," she said slowly. "Cynric either." She put her hand to her throat and touched the crystal with one finger. "I think we'd know if they were. It has something to do with this crystal, with the charm Mioragh conjured for us. It's almost as if it's connecting all of us in some way. Can't you feel it?"

Acaren frowned and reached up to touch his own crystal. "I don't know. . . ."

The door to the cell opened. Startled, Acaren and Eliene scrambled to their feet. A man carrying a torch entered. Behind him stood two Somber Riders, swords in their hands. Another man wearing a dark gray robe came into the cell. He made an imperious, beckoning gesture.

"You will come with me," he said in thickly accented Celae. "The captain wishes to interrogate you."

Rowan looked around at the towering stones, the short grass barred by bands of light and shadow. A chill rippled down his spine, then a quiet, peaceful sense of familiarity.

"I've been here before," he said. "Not just in dreams. I've stood in this very spot before."

Myrddin met his eyes gravely. "Aye," he said softly. "You have. Many times and under many names. All of them leading up to this moment."

"Many names?" Rowan let the familiarity settle over him like a comfortable cloak. The memories were there, as clear and sharp as his recollection of other times, other lives, other names, all spent with Ceitryn. If they had been soul-bound throughout all time, surely this place—this imposing and wondrous Dance of stones—had featured prominently in those lives.

The sacred circle of birth, life, death, and rebirth was as real as the stones around him. He had always known that. Most people did not remember past lives. But most people were not soul-bound, nor were they Gifted by Rhianna of the Air or the *darlai* with magic.

He glanced sideways at Ceitryn. She stood serenely watching Myrddin, a small smile curving the corners of her mouth. His words had come as no surprise to her.

"Aye," Rowan said slowly. "Aye, I suppose I have."

"You tell me you've come for the swords of Wyfydd Smith," Myrddin said. "Then I must challenge you to tell me what gives you the right to carry a Rune Blade?"

"I've carried one before," Rowan said with more calm than he felt. "If my blood and my lineage don't give me the right, then no man nor woman may carry one."

Myrddin smoothed his beard and nodded once. "I

accept that," he said. He turned to Ceitryn. "And you, my lady. I believe you've carried a Rune Blade before. Would you carry one again now?"

Ceitryn's grip on Rowan's hand tightened, the only sign of nervousness he could detect in her. "I am not trained now," she said. "I once was, but not now." She smiled. "And besides, are not the two swords only one until they rest in the proper hands?"

Myrddin smiled and raised an eyebrow again.

"Will you give us the swords then?" Rowan asked.

Myrddin held out his hands, palms up. "I have no swords," he said. "As you can see. If you would take the swords, Rowan Secondborn, then you will prove yourself a proper successor to Donaugh the Enchanter, and find them where they lie hidden."

A shadow passed across the Dance, a small cloud scudding across the sun. When the shadow was gone, so was Myrddin.

Ceitryn let out her breath in a long sigh, as if she had forgotten to breathe for too long. She looked gravely at Rowan. "Truly," she said in a mild, conversational tone of voice, "if I weren't convinced this had to be a dream, I should probably be sobbing helplessly with fear right about now."

"It's real," Rowan said breathlessly. "Very much real."

"I was afraid of that," Ceitryn said. "Oh dear. But what of the swords? Where are they?"

Rowan tilted his head back and closed his eyes. He let the bond he shared with Ceitryn wrap itself more firmly around his heart and his spirit. The magic of the Dance flowed through him, as water flows through a pipe, thrumming like a plucked harpstring along the bond. The energy of it fizzed and tingled in his blood, crackled in his bone and flesh and sinew like the charged air before a thunderstorm. It filled him to overflowing, taking his breath, quickening his heart, singing in his ears. Slowly, he opened his eyes and looked at the high, vaulting, infinitely blue arch of the sky.

The bond holding his spirit in his body broke with a wrenching twist, and he tumbled dizzily, breathlessly into the sky. He watched the stone Dance recede as he flew upward in a rush of wind. The two figures standing near the altar became little more than tiny specks, insignificant and unimportant. He turned away from them and opened his spirit to the wild rush of light and music.

Below him, around him, the vast tapestry of the Isle of Celi lay like a green jewel in the blue glitter and sparkle of the sea. The Spine of Celi ran in an immense, curving white-tipped jumble along the north and west of the island. As if it were a map, he could see plainly each of the provinces—Venia in the north, Wenydd and Skai in the west with the mountains curling around them, Brigland tucked between Skai and Venia, Mercia and Dorian lying somnolently along the south with their rolling pastureland, and the Summer Run to the east. Wide bands of dead, burned land lay like open sores along the east slopes of the mountains and forming a noose around the throat of the island in the north.

The sight of the Dead Lands brought tears to Rowan's eyes. The sorrow of the island, its sickness, cried out to him for succor. As he watched, he thought he saw the shape of a woman within the land, her face contorted with pain, her body twisted in agony. The *darlai*. The Spirit of the Land itself. She opened dark blue eyes and stared at him with a sadness too deep for comprehension. He turned away, unable to bear her tormented gaze.

A flicker of light caught his eye, and he looked down at himself. A silver thread spun out from his chest, stretching to the far distance. And along the thread, like beads, danced the men and women who had gone before him, connecting him surely and securely to the past. An intricately woven web. Iowen and Davigan, his parents. Gareth ap Brennen, his grandfather. Brennen ap Keylan. Keylan ap Kian. And Red Kian of Skai himself. And from Davigan, the thread wound to Tiegan ap Tiernyn. But the filament that should have connected Tiegan to Tiernyn was not there. Instead, it went from Tiegan to Donaugh the Enchanter, then back again to Red Kian of Skai.

Fascinated, Rowan traced the thread. To Donaugh the Enchanter. And he heard a woman's voice whispering, "Three sons for you, Donaugh Secondborn. One son your bitterest enemy, one your staunchest ally. And one to seed a line of kings forward into the time when these stones will crumble back to dust."

The shimmer of magic ran along the silver filament, from Donaugh through Tiegan, through Davigan, to Rowan. And as Donaugh and Tiernyn had shared a womb, and shared blood and bone, so Rowan and Acaren shared. Donaugh had been gifted with magic; Tiernyn had been gifted with kingship. Rowan sensed the fittingness, the rightness of his role and Acaren's.

He drew the web about him and found the connectedness comforting. As he turned back to the green jewel of Celi, he caught a glimmer of the thread moving beyond him, out into the blue void of the future. Shadowy figures danced on the wind, seed of his seed, into the future.

"Until these stones crumble back to dust," he whispered. Smiling, he closed his eyes. The bond with Ceitryn tugged gently at his spirit, reminding him where his duty lay.

When he opened his eyes again, he lay on the ground before the polished altar in the center of the Dance, his head pillowed in Ceitryn's lap.

"Are you all right?" she demanded, her voice quivering with fear.

"I have never been better," Rowan said. "I'm just a little dizzy."

"Where did you go?" she asked through stiff lips, her worry still etched deeply into her face. "You weren't here. You were gone for a long time. Where did you go?"

Rowan looked up. The sun stood high overhead. Each stone stood in its separate little puddle of shadow. The polished altar itself reflected back the sunlight like a mirror.

"I've been looking for the swords," he said quietly. "I believe I know where to find them now." Slowly, stiffly, he climbed to his feet.

He stepped closer to the altar. The blinding dazzle of the reflected sun glared out of the stone. Carefully, gingerly, he reached out, thrust his hand into the blaze. His fingers closed about the unseen hilt of a sword. He drew it out and held it up to the light.

A plain sword, unadorned, but beautiful in the way that any well-crafted weapon is beautiful. The hilt, fashioned from translucent horn, glowed softly in the sunlight with a soft, amber gleam. Runes spilled down the shoulder of the blade. He traced them with the fingers of his free hand, but could not read them. He sheathed it, then turned to Ceitryn.

"Heartfire," he said. "Will you hold it? It should not lie on the ground."

She visibly started, then straightened and reached out to take the sword, caressing the plaited leatherlike grasses of the scabbard.

Rowan turned back to the altar. Once more, he reached into the dazzle and brought out the twin to the sword Ceitryn held. Again, he traced the runes etched deeply into the blade. *"I am Heart and Soul of Celi,"* he whispered. He looked up, met Ceitryn's eyes. "Soulshadow . . ."

She shivered, then handed him Heartfire in its sheath. As he took it and held it beside the other sword, Soulshadow's outline shimmered. The two swords blurred, then merged until Rowan held only one sword, sheathed in a scabbard that looked like plaited and gilded leather.

"If we're finished," she said, "I'd just as soon be quit of this place, if you don't mind."

Rowan laughed softly. "We're done," he said.

The dazzle on the surface of the altar faded. He turned away, ready to leave.

"Wait," Ceitryn said suddenly. She tugged at Rowan's hand and swung him back to face the altar. "Look! Another sword!"

The sword lay in the middle of the altar, its plain, leather-bound hilt stained by the sweat of the man who had last held it. The pommel bore a crystal, clear as water, big as a plover's egg. Runes glittered like the facets of a gem along the blade. Ceitryn picked it up and held it out to Rowan.

And Rowan recognized it.

"Kingmaker," he said. "That's Kingmaker."

31

For his very rare visits to the western territories — he refused to dignify them with the term provinces — Hakkar of Maedun had built an elegant and luxurious annex to the fortress known as Rock Greghrach. The annex, built atop the armory, stood within the curtain wall, with its back against the fortress, facing out to sea, not toward the peaks and crags of the mountains.

Hakkar stood on the small balcony in the chill of early dawn, his hands resting on the stone balustrade, and watched the never-ending surge of the sea. It never ceased its landward motion. Even when the tide was receding, wave after wave came curling and crumpling in to dash itself into spray on the rocks. So different from the lakes in landlocked Maedun, where he had spent his youth so many long years ago.

Behind him, behind the fortress, out of his sight, loomed the vast, untidy heap of the mountains of Skai. Arrogant and brooding, they glowered down at him, always and forever defying his sorcery. He was gaining strength every year, widening the area under his spell, but even now his strongest blood magic could not force its way very far into those towering, defiant rocks.

A fingernail on his left hand splintered as he gripped the stone. Irritation and annoyance swept through him. He should not let those accursed mountains bother him so much. There was a way to defeat them more quickly. There *had* to be a way. In time, he knew he could do it, but time was a commodity in short supply now, he thought. If the enchanter of the legend was truly come . . .

If only he could find a way to utilize all the magic that lay inherent in this land. It was all around, in the rivers, in the air, in the ground, in the very trees and grass. He could reach out and touch it, but he could not bend it to his will. Not yet. He had to find a way to use it. Use it against the Celae themselves. A fitting irony, mayhaps.

In the meantime, he needed to subdue the rebels in the west. He needed—

The flare of magic swept out of the northwest, eddying and swirling around him like a wave breaking on a rock. Strong and clear and bright, it washed up against the walls of the fortress, sparking and fizzing as it met the sorcerous defenses his spell had ringed about the fortress. It seemed to last forever—an eternity of held breath and jarring heartbeats—then receded as quickly as it had come. In only moments it was gone, leaving nothing behind but a few residual sparks to show it had ever really existed.

A flicker of real fear touched Hakkar's belly. That was no emergent talent for magic. That was someone fully come to power, someone who held strong magic, built into bone and blood and spirit, who wielded it with accuracy and knowledge.

But how could it happen that someone that strong had been hidden from him all these years? His warlocks had spent nearly a lifetime tracking down and destroying all traces of emerging magic. How had they missed this? How had *he* missed it?

He turned away from the view of the sea and strode back into his chambers, calling for Horbad.

The commander of the garrison looked up in distaste as the warlock entered the room. He remained seated, deliberately choosing not to rise. He was careful to conceal his mild satisfaction at the flash of annoyance in the warlock's eyes. He was equally careful not to show his revulsion as the warlock seated himself heavily in the only comfortable chair in the room, and the vast sea of flesh beneath the gray robe wobbled and quivered with the abrupt motion. One day, he vowed, he would puncture that greasy belly and let all the arrogance of the man spill out.

"Have they succumbed to the spell yet?" the captain asked.

The warlock shook his head. The movement set all three of his chins in motion. "No," he replied sourly.

"It's been two days, Voerdric," the captain said mildly. "Surely—"

The warlock waved an impatient, doughy hand. "They have some sort of immunity," he said. "It feels the same as some of those wild Celae we have been chasing through these All-Father-forsaken mountains these last fifty years, but stronger it seems."

"Are they sorcerers, then, Voerdric?" the captain asked, coldly and pointedly polite. "Warlocks, perchance? Enchanters?"

The warlock shot a malevolent glance at him from beneath lowered brows. "I can find no trace of magic in them. Not the slightest glimmer. Just the protection against the spell. Kill them now, Zerad, and have done with them."

Zerad raised one eyebrow. "Kill them before we discover how such a small party of wild Celae managed to overcome a company of Maedun soldiers? I think execution would be somewhat premature at this point, don't you? We should find out what became of the others. Their bodies were not among those on the track."

"Then the bodies were taken by other wild Celae," Voerdric said acidly. "These two are not worth keeping alive. They have no magic. They cannot be the ones the Lord Hakkar seeks."

"The woman carries a sword," Zerad said. "Does this not strike some spark with you?"

Voerdric grimaced. "A woman carrying a man's weapon. All the more reason to execute her immediately. Execute them both and have done with them."

Zerad raised an eyebrow. "You have no curiosity about a man being served by a warrior-maid? No, Voerdric, those two have much to tell us, I think."

Voerdric smiled grimly. "The wild Celae grow bolder," he said. "Give them these two as an example of what happens to Celae who attack us. Show them two heads on poles, and we will not fear for the safety of our patrols any longer."

"You could ride with the patrols, Voerdric," Zerad suggested in a deliberately neutral tone.

The warlock stared at him with blank astonishment. "I?" he said. "Ride with a patrol?"

Zerad smiled and allowed a trace of malice to show in it. "You," he said. "Ride with a patrol. Perhaps you might remind the Celae that our spell is still able to turn their arrows back on them. They seem to have forgotten that."

Voerdric meticulously arranged the voluminous folds of his gray robe around him. "You know my duties keep me here. Daily, I have to renew the spell on the tame Celae. It takes most of my energy."

"Of course," Zerad said smoothly. "I understand, Voerdric. These mountains—" He waved his hand in an expressive gesture. "So difficult—"

Voerdric's eyes narrowed above the fatty mounds of his cheeks, but he said nothing.

"You will have the two brought to me," Zerad said. "I would see them immediately. And Voerdric, you will attend the interrogation, please." He reached for a dispatch that had arrived by courier during the night, clearly dismissing the warlock.

Zerad was young for his position, and he knew the warlock resented his youth, feeling it was demeaning to take orders from a man so much younger. Hakkar had promoted Zerad to lieutenant after the raid on Skerry seventeen years ago, then to captain as he had proven his ability. And Hakkar himself had given Zerad command of this garrison because it was in the midst of a problem area. Nearly a hundred soldiers had been lost in the west since Winter's Death, murdered by the wild Celae. Zerad had come to put a stop to it. If he did well here in the turbulent west, there was no limit to how high he might rise in the hierarchy of power. More than anything, Zerad wanted power.

A man wearing an elegantly fitted uniform of unadorned

black stepped out from behind a large banner hanging behind
Zerad's desk. Zerad rose and bowed to him.

"You heard, my lord Horbad?" he said.

"Indeed." Horbad crossed the room and took a seat in
the chair the warlock had recently vacated. He reached for a
goblet and the decanter of fine Falian red wine on the small
table by his elbow and poured himself a glass. "Did the
woman have her sword with her when they brought her to
the fortress?"

"No," Zerad said. "Nor was it near the site of the battle.
It seems that the same band of wild Celae who made off with
the bodies also made off with the sword."

"Pity." Horbad smiled sardonically. "Having to put up
with an incompetent warlock like Voerdric is a challenge. But
you seem to be handling it well enough. My father is not
pleased with Voerdric."

"If Voerdric spent as much time and effort doing his job
as he spends satisfying his belly and his other unwholesome
appetites," Zerad said, "the problem with the wild Celae in
this territory might have been stopped almost before it
began."

Horbad held the goblet of wine up against the light and
admired the rich color. "Voerdric is fortunate that warlocks
are not easy to come by, and even a fat and lazy warlock was
sorely needed," he said mildly enough.

"For now," Zerad said.

Horbad smiled and sampled the wine. "As you say," he
agreed. "For now."

"You will stay for the interrogation, my lord?"

"I will. But you will not say who I am."

"Of course not."

"This is very good wine."

"Thank you. My father has been given a vineyard in the
south of Falia for his service to the Lord Protector of Falia.
He sends me several casks a year."

"Very good, indeed. Carry on as if I'm little more than a
secretary."

Zerad laughed. "Such a secretary as you, my lord, no
man ever had."

Zerad had nearly finished dictating replies to the pile of dispatches when Voerdric returned with the two prisoners. He closed his fist in anger, crumpling the document he held. But the insolence in the delay the warlock had contrived in obeying the order to bring the prisoners was not lost on Horbad. Voerdric might well be coming to the end of his usefulness.

Zerad straightened behind his worktable and merely waved the warlock to a seat without looking away from the two young Celae flanked by two guards in the doorway. Behind them stood Voerdric's gray-robed young apprentice, Crom, looking ill at ease.

The two young Celae stood blinking in the bright sunlight streaming through the windows, their eyes watering after being confined for so long in the dark of the dungeon. They were rumpled and extremely dirty, but both of them stood proudly and defiantly erect. The woman made no attempt to cling to the man for protection, which Zerad found oddly disturbing. Maedun women were not known for their proclivity for defiance or independence. Nor would any Maedun woman ever wear man's clothing of breeks and boots. Or carry a sword, for that matter. A most unusual woman, this.

He glanced quickly at Horbad, who sat quietly in his chair. Horbad's face was expressionless, but his eyes were narrowed as he, too, studied the woman.

The prisoners piqued his interest, Zerad realized. Mayhaps he had a powerful tool in his hands. He turned back to the prisoners.

Their eyes, one pair as blue as an autumn sky, the other a strangely clear golden brown, showed no trace of the dulling effect of the spell. Nor was there any slackness to their features. Only once before had Zerad encountered a Celae immune as these two to the spell, and that one had claimed himself to be of Tyadda blood. As Zerad remembered, he bore a slight resemblance to the young man who now stood before him.

The captain rose in a slow, languid motion and came out from behind his worktable, his hands clasped loosely behind him. The young Celae man's gaze had not faltered, meeting his own squarely and levelly. *The defiant bravery of youth*, Zerad thought, mildly amused. *The* foolish *defiant bravery of youth which has yet to encounter real pain*. This one would soon learn what price defiance, and pay dearly in the coinage of pain.

"Where is the interpreter?" Zerad asked irritably, turning to Voerdric. "Or am I expected to converse in sign language?" He was rewarded by the slight paling of Voerdric's bloated cheeks. He motioned to one of the guards. "You. Fetch Llan here. Quickly, man." Zerad spoke the barbaric Celae language reasonably well, but did not wish to reveal the fact. The appearance of needing an interpreter was for him a convenient subterfuge.

The guard turned and fled into the corridor. He returned moments later, dragging a tame Celae with him. Curiosity flashed briefly across the faces of the prisoners as they glanced at the interpreter, then faded as they looked back at Zerad.

"Ask them who they are," Zerad told the interpreter, and waited as the question was repeated.

The young man looked at Voerdric, then spat deliberately on the floor by his feet. Voerdric drew back his foot, grimacing. The woman didn't bother to try to hide her smile.

Zerad stepped forward and brought the flat of his hand hard across the young man's cheek. The force of the blow snapped his head to the side, but he turned back quickly to meet Zerad's eyes again, a small trickle of blood oozing from the corner of his mouth.

"Fool," Zerad said calmly. "There is little good in dramatics or stupid heroics."

"It made me feel better," the young Celae said diffidently.

Zerad slapped him again. The young man deliberately spat a mouthful of blood at his feet, then looked at him again, his face impassive.

Zerad turned to the guards. "Take them both away and convince him of the error of his thinking," he said. "Then bring him back to me after the midday meal. I will talk with him again when he has learned some manners." He paused.

"He *will* be capable of conversation when you bring him back, won't he?"

"Yes, lord," one of the guards said.

Zerad smiled. "Very good."

Acaren regained consciousness choking and coughing as someone dumped a bucket of ice-cold water onto his face. He rolled away, the murderous hatred in his heart stronger than the pain infusing every muscle, every sinew of his body. He lay on the stone floor, gasping for breath, his hands clenched into fists, and willed himself not to attack his tormentors. Dying now would serve no purpose. If he bided his time, if he let them think they had won and he was thoroughly subdued, sooner or later an opportunity might well present itself.

He let himself go limp as the two guards hauled him to his feet, let his chin fall forward onto his chest. The fat man in the gray robe asked him the question again. "Do you still insist on not answering my questions?"

Acaren pretended to be too dazed, in too much pain to answer. The man in the gray robe made a disgusted sound, and said something to the two guards. Inwardly, Acaren braced himself for more pain, but to his surprise, the guards dragged him into a corridor and to a small chamber where a man who was obviously Celae waited with an air of vacant patience. The guards let Acaren fall to the floor and said something to the servant. Acaren waited until they had gone, then got stiffly to his feet.

"What did they say?" he asked hoarsely.

The servant regarded him with dull eyes, his lean face incurious and expressionless. "They said to clean you up before you go again before the lord captain Zerad because you stink and you would offend him," he said in a listless monotone.

Acaren wiped away a trickle of blood from the corner of his mouth. "The lord captain Zerad offends *me* with his arrogance," he muttered.

The servant did not react. He merely stood motionless, watching Acaren. Like a patient animal, Acaren thought in distaste.

"Where is my companion?" Acaren asked. "The woman who was captured with me?"

"With the lord captain Zerad," the man said.

"She has not been harmed?"

"No. She is well."

Acaren looked more closely at the servant, saw the life-less eyes, the slack mouth. He shuddered, and his hand went without conscious volition to the crystal at his throat. Its warmth gave him some comfort. He had wondered what the spell did to a man. Now he knew, and it sent a coil of cold fear and revulsion twisting through his belly.

Something flickered on the servant's face, some slight hint of awareness. Acaren looked deeper into the dull, blue Celae eyes, thought he saw something glimmer faintly for an instant before it was gone, and the servant grimaced with pain.

"What are you called?" Acaren asked softly.

"Jordd," the man replied apathetically.

"Do you know what they've done to you, these Maedun with their black sorcery?"

Jordd opened his mouth to reply, but no sound came forth. His face contorted in agony, then he nodded once abruptly.

Acaren watched his eyes. Again, something flickered in the lackluster depths of the servant's eyes. "Jordd, the time is coming soon when the Prince of Skai will return and wrest Skai from these accursed Somber Riders," he said slowly and deliberately. "The seed of Tiernyn is alive, and there will be a high king and an enchanter come to free all of Celi. This I promise you. Do you understand me?"

Again, the spark in the dulled eyes, a shadow seen through deep and murky water, a flicker so faint Acaren was not entirely certain he had really seen it. But that grimace of pain crossed Jordd's face again. "Will you be forced to tell them what I said?"

Jordd shook his head.

Acaren nodded. "I will say no more to cause you pain," he said. He had learned enough for the moment from the brief one-sided conversation. His concern for Eliene's safety was still uppermost in his heart, but he believed Jordd. He did not believe the servant could lie under the spell. "Show me where to clean up, please." He smiled grimly. "The guards were right. I *do* stink, and I mislike it."

32

Rain fell out of a dead black sky. Piled masses of thunder clouds, blue-black underneath, tops laced with livid white, raced across the sky above the mountains before a driving wind that sent needles of rain slashing nearly horizontal across the sodden ground. Thick, jagged ropes of lightning stabbed out of the bellies of the tortured, roiling clouds to the ground, and the accompanying thunder made the mountains tremble.

Rowan drew his waterlogged cloak closer around him and flinched involuntarily as another flash of lightning rent the sky, and the simultaneous crack of thunder shivered the ground. The horse beneath him quivered with barely contained terror. He reached out a hand to pat the rain-slick neck, calming the animal expertly and gently. Ahead of him, Ceitryn made a startled exclamation as her horse shied, nearly unseating her.

The morning had dawned bright and sunny, but by midafternoon, the clouds had piled up high against the Spine. The full fury of the storm struck in the late afternoon. Until then, Rowan had merely wondered miserably if he would ever be warm and dry again. When the downpour began, he had given up dreaming of being dry and warm and simply hoped he might not drown in what appeared to be a solid wall of water sheeting down from the sky.

As they drew closer to the fortress of Rock Greghrach, an uneasiness grew in Rowan's chest. The spell gnawed at his heart and belly, even with the protection of his Tyadda blood and Mioragh's crystal talisman, threatening to dissolve his courage and determination in its acid wash. He tried to imagine how bad it would be to an unprotected Celae, and shuddered.

Cynric drew his horse off the track into the shelter of a wide-spreading oak and dismounted. Beneath his cloak, he wore the uniform of a Maedun officer, but instead of the black sword of a Somber Rider he wore his own, fashioned from good Edge Steel. Rowan thought he looked far too convincing in the somber black relieved only by the silver captain's insignia on the sleeve of his tunic. Cynric led his horse deeper into the trees while Rowan slid out of his saddle and reached up to help Ceitryn. The branches of the tree provided a minimum of protection from the slashing rain.

Rowan adjusted the scabbard so that it hung low on his back and arranged his cloak to hide the hilt of the sword. Heartfire/Soulshadow vibrated softly against his spine, and their voices whispered in his mind, just below the threshold of audibility. He glanced at Ceitryn. She wore the Rune Blade Kingmaker on her hip, her plaid wrapped shapelessly around her body, hiding both the sword and her figure. Rune Blades had a reputation of refusing to fight for anyone not born to wield one. Kingmaker did not sing for Ceitryn as far as Rowan could tell, but neither did it protest.

"Up ahead there," Cynric said, pointing. "Do you see the fortress?"

Rowan wiped the water from his eyes and peered in the direction Cynric indicated. Through the trees, part of a wet, black wall gleamed in the wan light, appearing vitrified under the water streaming in sheets down it. He could see no sentries posted along the battlements atop the crenellated wall, but any sane guard would remain snug in the turrets in weather like this.

Cynric turned to Rowan. "Can you use your magic to find Acaren and Eliene in there?"

Rowan looked at the gloomy wall and frowned. "I've never tried to call up the Sight before," he said. "I'm not sure if it will work." He stared at the dark gleam through the trees and concentrated. The misery of being wet and cold faded as he lost himself in the search for his twin. But no sense of

Acaren's presence filtered into his mind. Finally, he shook his head.

"I can't find him," he said. "Either this Gift won't come to my bidding, or Acaren and Eliene are no longer there."

"Are they still alive?" Ceitryn asked quickly.

"I think so," Rowan said. "I'm sure I'd know if Acaren were dead. We've always had a twin-bond between us."

"Aye, well," Cynric said. "Then we'll have to go in and find them. Are you ready to play prisoners?" He reached up to the glowing crystal on its chain around his throat and took it off. "You'd best take this, my lady," he said to Ceitryn. "I was told I have a high level of natural resistance to the spell even though I'm only half-Maedun. You'll need this more than I will, I think."

Ceitryn drew back. "I can't take your talisman," she said. "You'll need it —"

Cynric shook his head, then stepped forward and slipped the chain over her head. "I'll be fine without it," he said. "You might not be." When she started to protest and tried to take off the chain, he put his hand over hers to still its motion. "No, I insist, my lady," he said. "Please."

She acquiesced gracefully. "Very well," she said. "Thank you, Cynric."

"I have this," he said. He took an armband from his saddle pack and slipped it over his sleeve. The badge depicted a flying black raven on a circle of white. "Hakkar's insignia," he said. "Only those in Hakkar's service are allowed to wear it. Hakkar himself gave this one to me when he took me into his personal courier service. I kept it thinking it might come in handy one day."

"If it gets us into the fortress," Rowan said, "and out again, of course, it will be very handy indeed."

Cynric's fleeting grin flashed in the murky light. "Let's try this, then, shall we?" he said.

The first thing Acaren saw as the two guards dragged him into the chamber was Eliene sitting stiff and erect on a hard chair near a window. She wore an unbecoming gown in an ugly shade of dull green, ill fitting and shapeless. Her glossy

black hair, still damp from a hasty bath and limned by the
light behind her, glinted with blue sparks in the cool room.
He saw with relief that she seemed unhurt.

The guards gave him a vicious shove, which sent him
stumbling to his hands and knees. Renewed pain sent off
small explosions of pinwheeling light behind his closed eyelids. He barely prevented himself from sprawling facedown
on the floor at the captain's feet.

Eliene gave a small cry of dismay, but the gray-robed
man behind her clamped his hand down on her shoulder, preventing her from running to Acaren. She flinched away from
the touch, but remained in the chair.

Acaren managed to push himself upright, but had to
catch his breath before he could attempt to stand. He made it
look as if he were hurt more severely than he was, but it was
still an enormous effort to climb to his feet. He stood with his
shoulders slumped, his head bent as the captain regarded him
impassively from behind the worktable.

A movement in the shadows at the far side of the room
caught his eye. Without raising his head, he glanced sideways. A man sitting in a chair nearly hidden within the folds
of a draped banner crossed his legs and leaned back. He wore
a uniform of unrelieved black that blended with the shadows.
The black eyes that looked like two more pieces of shadow
were fixed intently on Acaren's face. Acaren took a deep
breath to control the suddenly accelerated beat of his heart.

Horbad. The man in black had to be Horbad.

Acaren did not see the obese warlock enter the room.
Too late, he heard a footstep behind him. Even as he turned,
the warlock's fist caught him in the midsection. The breath
knocked out of him, he toppled helplessly to the floor. The
crystal on its chain spilled out of the open throat of the coarse
shirt he wore.

The warlock gave a startled cry, then was on his knees
beside Acaren, shouting something, his hand reaching for the
crystal. Acaren tried to jerk away from the grasping hand.
The warlock seized his hair and slammed his head into the
stone floor.

• • •

Rowan and Ceitryn walked beside Cynric's horse as they
approached Rock Greghrach. Both kept their heads bent as
they walked. Ceitryn had put on the mask of a bespelled
Celae so well, it made Rowan uneasy to look at her. She had
let her lower jaw go slack and kept her eyes downcast so the
keen intelligence in them was not apparent, and she moved
with uncharacteristic awkwardness, her feet shuffling
through the muddy surface of the track.

Cynric had described the fortress as built to the same pattern as every other garrison fortress he had ever been in. The
outer wall, over three man-heights tall, loomed huge and square
in the wide clearing among the dripping trees. The massive
main gate, constructed of local oak and at least two hand-
breadths thick, stood open in the gray light of the afternoon. To
Rowan, the fortress looked square and squat, crouching on the
promontory above the sea like a predatory beast. Few windows
broke the coal black walls of the massive building within the
walls. Dark and hulking, it sent a chill shivering down his spine.

Cynric dismounted and handed the reins of the horse to
Rowan with a curt order to hold it. Two guards challenged
them from the shelter of a small hut just inside the gate. Cynric flung back the left side of his cloak to reveal the officer's
flash. The guards stiffened and bowed, then stepped back to
let them through.

Impassively, Rowan watched the faces of the guards.
They glanced at Ceitryn, then leered and chuckled. Ceitryn's
face gave away nothing.

Cynric ignored them. He took the reins of the horse from
Rowan and handed them to one of the guards. "Take it to the
stable and see it gets a good rubdown and feed," he said. To the
other guard, he said, "Take me to the quarters for visiting officers. My servants will accompany me."

The guard hesitated for a moment. He glanced quickly
at the insignia, prominently displayed on Cynric's sleeve, then
shrugged and led the way through the sodden mud of the
courtyard to the main building.

The guard escorted them to a small suite of rooms that
seemed little different to Rowan than some of the officers
quarters in Skerry Keep. Cynric dismissed the guard with a

diffident arrogance Rowan had never seen in him before.
Rowan waited until he was sure the man was gone before he
spoke.

"What do we do now?" he asked.

Cynric went to the hearth and held out his hands to warm
them over the flames. Before he could reply, the door opened
and a man entered. He turned quickly. Rowan noted the man
wore a lieutenant's insignia on his black uniform. He dropped
his gaze and stood, shoulders slumped, by the wall. Ceitryn
did her best to fade into the wall behind her, pressing her back
against the rough plaster.

The lieutenant clicked his heels together and made a
small, abrupt bow. He straightened and opened his mouth to
say something. Then his eyes narrowed and he frowned as he
studied Cynric's face.

"Jonvar?" he said incredulously.

Cynric inclined his head, unsmiling, and stepped forward to meet him. "How pleasant to see you again, Murbat,"
he said calmly.

In one swift, fluid motion, he drew his dagger and
plunged it into the lieutenant's chest. He caught the body as it
fell and dragged it away from the doorway, kicking the door
closed with his heel. Rowan leapt for the door and slid the
bolt home.

"The wardrobe," Cynric said.

Ceitryn snatched open the doors, and Cynric dropped
the lieutenant's body inside. He swore softly, retrieved his
dagger, and wiped it on the lieutenant's shirtsleeve.

"He was my father's executive officer," he said. "I didn't
think he'd ever paid any attention to me. Bad luck his being
here, and even worse luck that he recognized me. He'd know
I have no right to wear this uniform." He resheathed the dagger and closed the wardrobe doors, hiding the body from
sight.

"Will they come looking for him?" Rowan asked.

"I'm afraid so. He's probably the garrison captain's executive officer."

"Then we haven't much time before they start a search,"

Rowan said. "If they find him here, they'll be looking for us immediately."

"Aye, they will." Cynric went to the door and opened it, taking a quick look to either side down the corridor. "It's clear. Let's go. Just follow behind me, keep your eyes down, and shuffle your feet."

The hardened leather heels of Cynric's boots echoed in the long corridor. The walls, fashioned of undressed, unadorned stone, bounced the sound back and forth between them until Rowan thought they sounded like a small army advancing down the passageway. Once they passed a woman with dead eyes and a slack expression. She carried a basket of what looked like clean bed linens. As they approached, she ducked her head and moved so far to the edge of the corridor, her arm scraped the stone wall.

They came to an intersection, and Cynric turned unhesitatingly to his left. Two Somber Riders stood exchanging gossip quietly outside a half-open door. They stopped talking when they caught sight of Cynric. One of them stepped forward, raising a hand. Cynric made no attempt to slow his pace, gave no indication he even saw the soldier. He merely reached up and touched the raven badge as if to flick a speck of dust from it. The Somber Rider dropped his hand and moved quickly out of the way. Rowan averted his eyes and hunched his shoulders as he shuffled past them.

The air of the fortress felt thick and heavy in Rowan's lungs. Something—the spell?—plucked at his guts as a scavenger bird pecks at a carcass. He glanced at Ceitryn, saw her raise a hand to touch the glowing crystal at her throat. Mioragh had said the crystal would provide limited protection from the spell. Rowan wondered suddenly how much protection that would actually be.

He hoped it would be enough.

Cynric took the next turning to the right into a narrow, ill-lighted passageway. In less than a hundred paces, it dead-ended at a battered, ironbound door. A heavy iron ring on a swivel hinge, flaked with rust, hung from the wood above one of the iron bands. Cynric reached up and banged the ring against the plate four times.

They waited.

Cynric had just raised his hand to use the door knocker again when it opened. Rust might have attacked the door knocker, but someone took good care of the hinges, Rowan noted. The door made no sound at all as it swung smoothly back.

A guard holding a naked sword stood in the open doorway. He looked up at Cynric in surprise. "What do you want?" he demanded.

"I come from Lord Hakkar," Cynric said. "He wants to see the prisoners. The Celae man and woman. Bring them up to me immediately."

The guard shook his head. "No," he said. "Can't do it, sir."

Cynric drew himself up to his full height and stared down at the guard. "Did you hear me?" he demanded. "I come from the Lord Hakkar. You would disobey his orders?"

The pupils of the guard's eyes contracted in anxiety. "I haven't got the prisoners, sir," he said. "That fat warlock— Voerdric, I think—took them off to Lord Captain Zerad's workroom about an hour ago." He smirked. "The woman was a tasty-looking morsel. The lord captain Zerad might not want to be disturbed for a while."

Cynric's expression froze the guard again. "I'm sure the lord captain Zerad appreciates your efforts to ensure his uninterrupted pleasure."

The guard smirked again. "Not so much the captain," he said. "They say that Lord Horbad is with them, too."

Rowan's heart jumped in his chest. He glanced up at the guard, then at Cynric. The skin around Cynric's mouth paled slightly, but he gave no other sign of anxiety. He turned, beckoning to Rowan and Ceitryn, and began to retrace his steps.

"We'll join the lord captain Zerad," he said, quietly enough so that only Rowan and Ceitryn heard him. "And the lord Horbad."

The sword on Rowan's back quivered gently against his

spine. He reached up and touched the hilt. It was as warm as if it had been held in the palm of a man's hand in the heat of battle. The sword's voice, chiming like harp, bell, and flute combined, rose to an eager murmur in his ears.

33

Hakkar put down his pen and pushed the parchment aside. For a
moment he sat staring down at the smoothly polished surface
of the wooden worktable, his head cradled in his hands, a
frown creasing his forehead. The disquieting sense of unease
batted at his consciousness like a fly against a windowpane.

Something, somewhere was wrong. But he couldn't tell
what it was. Or where it was.

He got up abruptly, scraping the chair across the pale,
satiny gloss of the parquet floor. He went to the window and
watched for a moment as the rain sent shimmers of light and
shadow skimming across the surface of the sea. It was early in
the year for a thunderstorm. Not yet a fortnight past Vernal
Equinox. Spring had so far been more wet and miserable
than usual, completely unlike the Maedun spring he remembered from his boyhood, where the sun shone from a brilliant
blue sky and the warm southwest wind could melt the snow
in a matter of days. In Maedun, thunderstorms were a sum-
mertime phenomenon, occasionally accompanied by the
dreadful, twisting funnel winds.

But he had never seen a funnel wind in Celi. Nor was
this storm violent enough to produce one. It wasn't the storm
that was causing his uneasiness.

But if not the storm, what?

The weight of the mountains behind the fortress seemed
more than usually oppressive today. They were filled with
magic—frustratingly unusable magic. . . .

He turned quickly away from the window and went
back to his worktable. A small, carved soapstone box sat near

316

the inkwell. He reached for it, hesitated, then picked it up and opened it, expecting to see nothing there but a small gray-green stone, rounded and smoothed as if it had been immersed in running river water for centuries.

The harsh, blue-white glare seared his eyes and nearly startled him into dropping the box.

Magic! Celae magic. So close the Tell-Tale vibrated furiously with it, throbbing and blazing.

He snatched up the stone, half-expecting it to scorch his fingers. But it was cold—colder than a Maedun winter. He dropped it into his pocket and crossed the room in four long strides.

The guard in the corridor snapped to attention as he yanked open the door. "Fetch Horbad to me," he ordered. "Send my son to me immediately."

The guard flinched away from the anger in Hakkar's voice. "My lord, he's with the lord captain Zerad," he said, staring fixedly at a spot just above Hakkar's left shoulder. "Interrogating the prisoners."

"The prisoners?" Hakkar repeated softly.

"Yes, sir. The Tyadda man and the Celae woman."

Hakkar felt suddenly as cold as the Tell-Tale stone in his pocket. "Did the woman carry a sword?"

The guard cut a swift glance at him, then immediately looked away, back at the spot on wall. He nodded.

"You're certain?" Hakkar asked sharply.

"Yes, sir. At least, so they say."

Hakkar took a deep breath to stem the rising tide of fury within his chest. "Why, then," he asked in a voice too calm and too quiet, "was I not informed of the presence of these prisoners in the fortress?"

The guard turned white and took an involuntary step backward. He opened his mouth, but no sound came out. Hakkar raised his hand and willed a globe of sorcery to form. He flicked it at the guard and stepped aside as the searing red Sphere splashed against the man's chest. Not sparing the dead guard a glance, Hakkar strode along the corridor, looking for Zerad's workroom.

• • •

They came in twos and threes, in small groups of a dozen or less. They came from all through the wild mountains of Skai, from the hidden valleys, from the gaunt, rocky forests below the snow line. Celae men—and no few women—armed with spears made of fire-hardened oak, tipped with razor-sharp steel, or swords kept honed to a keen edge and polished bright and handed down from father to son since the last days of Tiernyn. Some of the women carried swords, but most held lethally efficient little Veniani recurved bows, or versions of the deadly Saesnesi longbow. Carefully shaped arrows, fletched with brightly colored feathers, crowded into quivers worn at shoulder or hip.

Slowly, they filled the hollows among the widely spaced trees on Cloudbearer's western slope. For the most part, they said little, merely reporting to Devlyn or Kier with little more than, "You sent. We have come."

They weren't an army drilled and trained in the arts of war, but they were an army that would fight with grim ferocity that asked and gave no quarter. Their numbers climbed toward the thousand that Devlyn had promised Acaren, then topped it. Gathered in small groups, they made cold camp and waited.

Devlyn counted them again in satisfaction, then sent twenty of them higher up the slopes of the mountain to build a signal fire that might be seen by any ship lying hove to several leagues offshore. Only when the black sorcerer's spell shattered and broke would anyone put a torch to the piled wood. Devlyn looked forward with fierce and pleasurable anticipation to striking flint to steel himself to light the torch.

As Devlyn watched his people building the signal fire, Caennedd ap Gareth stood on the deck of a Tyran ship. Gray-and-blue sails belled out to catch the southwest wind as the ship tacked swiftly north, following the west coast of Celi. The creaking and rustling of the masts and rigging, and the hissing bubble of water beneath the hull spoke eloquently of a ship proceeding at speed under full sail.

In a neat line behind Caennedd's ship followed more than twenty others. They carried clansmen from the coast of Tyra to the inland scarpland near the border with Maedun.

Two hundred clansmen to a ship, all of them pledged to follow Fionh and Caennedd, all of them eager to deal a killing blow to the Maedun.

Two days hence, the fleet was scheduled to heave to and ride the sea anchors where they were able to see the snowy cone of Cloudbearer, and wait for the signal that meant the Maedun spell was lifted.

Caennedd sat on a neat coil of rope and drew his sword, smiling grimly. He brought out his whetstone and an oily cloth and set to sharpening and cleaning the blade. After all these years, he was finally doing what he had sworn to do when he was just eighteen. He was on his way to help lead the army that would free Skai—and all of Celi—from the Maedun.

In the north, Athelin gathered his army and saw them take ship for the coast of Skai. He and Dorlaine boarded the *Skai Seeker* with half the army; Gabhain and Valessa took the other half aboard the *White Falcon*. The two ships carefully negotiated the channel between Skerry and Marddyn, and turned their prows south for Llewenmouth, where they were to rendezvous with the Tyran ships.

Athelin stood watching the *White Falcon* off the *Seeker*'s bow as it dipped and swayed gracefully in rhythm with the sea and wind. "It's happening, Iowen," he murmured, speaking aloud to his dead sister. "Everything you and Davigan died to bring about is happening now. May the Duality be with us all."

"That jewel!" Voerdric cried. "That's the magic. I must have that jewel—"

Horbad reacted instantly. He leapt from his chair and vaulted the worktable as Voerdric fell to his knees and fumbled for the crystal. It glinted with its own light as it spilled from the shirt collar of the unconscious Celae man. But even as the warlock touched it, he cried out and jerked his hand back, and Horbad saw the blistered and charred welt on the palm of his hand. Voerdric pulled the dagger from his belt.

The Celae woman cried out, struggling violently with Crom. Horbad didn't know whether Voerdric intended to use the dagger to snap the slender gold chain around the Celae man's throat or free the chain by removing his head. But he knew he could not let the warlock have that jewel.

"Don't touch that," he shouted.

Voerdric turned on him, snarling, blind in his rage. "Who are you to tell a warlock in Hakkar's service what to do?" he cried, obviously mistaking Horbad for Zerad in the dim light. Spittle flew from his lips in his incoherent fury. "You come here and set yourself up over me—me! A warlock! You dare to usurp my authority, my power—"

"You have no power, you fat pig," Horbad said viciously. "You've dissipated your power with gluttony and debauchery. For the last year, Crom's maintained the spell because you were incapable of it. Why do you suppose my father sent me here in the first place?"

Voerdric brushed a hand across his eyes and stared hard at Horbad. He recognized him and went white. Then he howled and lunged at Horbad with the dagger. Horbad drew his sword and plunged it into the warlock's belly. Voerdric's eyes and mouth made wide, startled "O's" and he crumpled at Horbad's feet, whimpering and gasping.

Wild elation poured through Horbad. In spite of what he'd said, he knew Voerdric still possessed a powerful store of magic. If he used Hakkar's secret ritual, he could claim all that power for himself.

"Crom, to me," he cried. He dropped to his knees before Voerdric and snatched up the fallen dagger.

"Yes, my lord," the apprentice murmured. He left the woman to Zerad's care and fell to his knees by Voerdric's head. He put his hands to either side of the warlock's temples and nodded fearfully at Horbad.

Horbad plunged the dagger into Voerdric's abdomen and ripped it viciously upward. As the steaming entrails tumbled and spilled out onto the floor, Horbad thrust his hands into the warlock's belly.

"Now!" he cried to Crom.

A black mist rose thickly from the tangle of guts around his hands. Slowly, it circled his wrists, climbing inexorably along his blood-splashed arms. It began to shimmer, softly at first, with faint colors barely visible in the black vapor. As it reached his elbows, the colors became brighter—reds and oranges and yellows, swirling and pulsing with sullen light, like flames twisting through sooty smoke. Horbad cried out sharply as the mist enveloped his chest, reached higher for his head. His face stiffened and contorted into a mask of orgiastic ecstasy behind the mist.

It was working! It was actually working for him. The power flowed into him, flooding through his body. He laughed aloud in amazement and delight.

Moments later, it was finished. The sense of absorbing something outside himself ceased. The strange colors faded around his wrists, then vanished completely. Horbad rose shakily to his feet and looked down at Crom, who still crouched by his dead master.

"Leave him now," Horbad said. "Call the guards. Have them dispose of this carrion."

He turned to meet the horrified eyes of the girl, who sat frozen in her chair. She looked as if she might be ill. Zerad looked little better. He swallowed several times, then sat down on the bench under the window. The young man still lay on the floor where he had fallen when Voerdric struck him. His hand had come up to grasp the crystal at his throat.

Horbad bent and slapped the young man's hand away from the crystal. The jewel glowed with a strange inner light. He reached a cautious finger toward it, but pulled back when he felt the heat.

"Don't touch it, Lord Horbad," Crom said hoarsely. "It's Tyadda magic. It is like the magic that stops our spell in the high country. It's dangerous."

Horbad nodded. He crossed the room to the woman, reached out and yanked aside the collar of her gown. Her crystal lay against her skin, glowing as brightly as the other.

"Do the both of you have magic?" he asked.

The woman leaned back, as far from him as she could get. Her mouth worked. Before she could spit at him, he slapped her, splitting her lip. She dragged the back of her hand across her mouth and wiped her hand on the shabby gown, leaving a smear of blood on the dull fabric.

"If you have magic," he said, and smiled coldly, "I shall have it from you." The stolen magic fizzed and seethed in his blood.

"I think," Hakkar's voice said from the doorway, "that it shall be mine rather than yours, Horbad."

Horbad straightened and turned slowly to meet the black, furious gaze of his father.

34

Rowan stared at Cynric in horror. "He'll kill him," *he whispered.* "Horbad will kill Acaren." A sharp lance of fear sliced through his chest. "If Horbad even once suspects who Acaren is, he'll kill both Acaren and Eliene. Instantly." A fist of ice closed around his heart, and he pushed past Cynric. "We have to hurry."

Cynric caught his arm and pulled him back. "Not so fast," he said. "And not that way. There's a back entrance to the workroom. That's how all the couriers come in. We can't go charging madly down the main corridors or we'll be dead before we can do any good at all for Acaren and Eliene. Calm down. Just follow me."

"Hurry," Rowan said.

"No," Cynric said. "Anyone running in a garrison fortress—especially a supposedly bespelled servant—is going to be stopped and questioned. Follow me and keep your heads down. Both of you."

Rowan lost track of the turns in the corridors as he hurried after Cynric. The bond between Ceitryn and him throbbed gently, a calming presence in his spirit. She didn't look at him as they walked side by side, but he knew she was as aware of him as he was of her.

Cynric paused at the intersection of two corridors. He looked left, then right, frowning.

"Are we lost?" Rowan asked, alarmed.

"No," Cynric replied slowly. "I think it's to the left." A wry smile tugged at the corner of his mouth. "I think. But it's been nearly twenty-five years since I was here, and most of these corridors look the same."

"Cynric, for Annwn's sake . . ." Rowan swallowed his impatience and took a deep breath.

"This way," Cynric said, and set off to his left. A few minutes later, he stopped in front of a door that looked no different from the other doors along the passageway. "I think this is it," he said. He put his hand to the latch and pressed the thumb piece.

To Rowan, the soft click was as loud as a log popping in a hearth. Cynric pushed on the door. The hinges were as quiet as the hinges of the door to the dungeons. The door opened silently, swinging inward to reveal a dimly lit, shadowy room. Rowan checked quickly right and left. No one in sight along the corridor. They slipped through the door and closed it after them.

They found themselves in a small anteroom, an alcove off the workroom. Rowan could almost touch both walls if he stretched out his arms. A counter ran the length of the small room to their left, holding a glimmering silver tray of crystal wine goblets and a tall decanter of wine that glinted darkly ruby red in the dim light. A teardrop-shaped green bottle, nearly an armlength high, stood at the other end of the counter. Probably holding a white wine, Rowan thought.

No door separated the alcove from the workroom. Instead, several banners hanging on poles stood in heavy metal stands along the opening. The light in the alcove was dim, filtering past the heavy fabric of the banners, and the banners themselves cast thick shadows through the alcove. Rowan crept to the entrance. Through the heavy folds of fabric, most of the room was visible.

The workroom was huge—at least ten paces by eight paces. The rain beat against a long bank of windows set high the walls, and the wan, streaming light fell across a floor of polished oaken planks.

Eliene sat in a chair below the middle window, held firm by a man in an officer's uniform who stood behind her. Acaren lay on the floor, huddled into a protective curl, his arms wrapped around his head. A fat man in warlock's gray lay on the floor no more than an armlength from Acaren.

Another man in warlock's gray knelt by the fat man's head and a man in black crouched in front of the fallen man.

Horbad, Rowan thought. The fist closed about his heart again. The man in black was Horbad. Then, incongruously, he thought, *He looks exactly like his father.*

Then he realized what Horbad was doing.

As Horbad ripped the blade of the dagger upward, spilling the fat man's entrails, Rowan turned away. He didn't realize he was shuddering in the chill shadow of the banners until his teeth began to chatter. He clamped his jaw as Ceitryn's hand came down gently on his arm. She stepped toward him, and he put his arms around her, bending his head over hers as she pressed her face into his shoulder. She quivered as violently as he. Unable to stop himself, Rowan looked up again.

There was so much sorcery in the room. Overwhelming. A hard, black aura surrounded Horbad and the warlock, blacker than a moonless night, black as the pits of Hellas. All the light in the world could not dispel the darkness around them. Rowan was mildly amazed that neither gave any indication of being aware of the quiet throbbing of the sword he wore on his back.

As the black mist rising from the fat warlock's opened belly curled up and around Horbad's wrists and arms, Rowan's skin crawled, and his very flesh crept across his bones, trying to retreat from the revulsion engulfing him. Chills and fever both raged through his body and he gagged and choked as the stench of the reeking mist reached him. Bile rose burning in his throat, and he thought he would be sick. Only with a supreme effort did he hold the bursting nausea back. Ceitryn made a soft sound of horror against his shoulder, and he raised his shaking hand to stroke back her hair. He closed his eyes, pressing his cheek to the top of her bright head.

Never before had he experienced anything so vile, so incredibly evil. He knew now what the legends meant when they spoke of blood magic. It was unspeakable terror, steeped in horror and pain, worse than any part of Hellas could possibly be, and for a moment, Rowan thought he might die through mere exposure to it. Weak and shaken, he pushed away from the wall bringing Ceitryn with him, and turned back to Cynric. Cynric himself was not unaffected, but it was the sheer horror of the act itself that turned him pale, Rowan thought, not the magic.

"It's over," Ceitryn said softly, her voice sounding as weak and ill as he felt.

Rowan turned back just in time to see Hakkar burst into the workroom. Hakkar shouted something. It took Rowan a moment to translate it in his mind.

"Get away from that man!" Hakkar cried. He pointed to Acaren, who still lay curled on the oaken floor. Blood from the fat warlock's ripped belly crept toward him in a thick, sluggish trickle. "Do you have any idea who he is?" He leapt across the room and slapped the young warlock out of his way. "He's mine. And the woman, too."

Horbad spun around and stared at Hakkar. The stolen sorcery fizzed and bubbled, sparking dull red in the black aura around him. He glanced quickly at Acaren—at the crystal glowing beneath his shirt collar—and snatched up the bloody dagger. Before Rowan could move, Horbad had launched himself at Acaren and thrust the blade of the dagger at Acaren's throat.

Rowan never remembered drawing the sword, but it was in his hands as he catapulted out from behind the banners, howling an yrSkai war cry. Behind him, Cynric swore vehemently, then followed him.

The shrill war cry pierced Acaren's fogged mind and he opened his eyes. Something moved just beyond his field of vision. He turned his head groggily to see Horbad lunging toward him, a bloody dagger held tight in his fist. The cold, sticky steel touched his throat and he jerked back convulsively. The blade snapped the frail gold chain holding the crystal, and the jewel bounced and skittered across the floor.

The door crashed open, slamming against the wall, and several black-clad guards burst into the room. Pandemonium exploded all around Acaren. He could not keep track of what was happening. Too many struggling bodies. Too many swords.

He rolled out of the way and came up hard against the flaccid body of the dead warlock. He twisted to his knees as Cynric leapt out from behind the cluster of draped banners, sword held high. The garrison captain behind Eliene spun about, his own sword drawn, to meet Cynric. Cynric swung his sword like an ax and caught the captain just above the hip. The captain went down like a felled tree. Cynric whirled about to meet the guards.

Eliene snatched up the fallen captain's sword and bounded over the body, skirts flying, and flung herself at the door, sliding the heavy iron bolt home. She turned back and thrust out a hand to pull Acaren to his feet.

"Rowan, over here!" she cried.

Acaren got his feet beneath him. Rowan spun around. Acaren stared, then shook his head to clear it. He thought he saw the sword in Rowan's hands split into two separate swords, one polished and gleaming, the other glimmering darkly in the stormy light coming through the high windows. Acaren blinked. There must have been two swords there all along.

Rowan flipped the bright sword into his left hand, held it high, then tossed it to Acaren. The blade flashed as it flew through the air above the heads of the struggling guards. Runes as sharply etched as facets of a gem glittered and sparked. The hilt fell into Acaren's hand as if he had called it to him.

The runes on the blade flared brightly. "*I am Blood and Bone of Celi* . . ." he read in a shaking whisper. "Heartfire!"

A high, wild keening sounded in his ears, and he knew it was the sword's own song. The music ran along his nerves, into his blood, and the sword became part of him. Then he had no more time. He ducked the wide, vicious sweep of a black Maedun blade, and let the rhythm of the sword take him.

He turned, caught the guard's blade with his own, then disengaged quickly as Eliene cut the Maedun's legs from beneath him. Cynric called a warning, his voice rising clearly over the clangor and tumult in the room. Acaren ducked, felt the disturbed air ruffle his hair as another blade barely missed him. He lunged sideways, brought Heartfire up in a quick, abrupt motion, and buried the length of the blade in the guard's spine.

A movement caught his eye. Horbad scrabbled on the floor by the body of the warlock, looking for the crystal Acaren had worn. Acaren raised Heartfire and leapt toward him.

"Acaren, your back!" Rowan shouted from amid a knot of guards.

Acaren plunged sideways, spun around. Hakkar himself, sword raised, lips drawn back in a fixed grin that held no trace of humor. Acaren turned his back to Horbad to meet Hakkar's attack.

Rowan and Ceitryn stood back-to-back, holding off four guards. Horrified, Rowan saw Horbad scrabble back from the crumpled body of the fat warlock and put his back to the wall. He brought his hands together in front of him, concentration twisting his features. A searing globe of red fire formed between Horbad's hands. Rowan had never seen a ball of blood sorcery, but he'd heard of them; they were lethal. Trapped by the guards, he could not break free. He could not stop Horbad from throwing the globe.

"Acaren!" he shouted, his voice cracking on his brother's name. "Acaren, down!"

Hissing and sizzling, leaving a trail of scorched air behind it, the horrifying ball slashed across the room. Sick and terrified, Rowan saw that it would take Acaren squarely in the chest.

Then Cynric was there. Shouting a frantic warning, he threw himself between Acaren and the blazing sphere. It splashed against his back, exploding like rotten fruit, sending searing drops of liquid fire spraying around the room. Cynric staggered to his knees, his face twisted in agony, his eyes wide in shock. He looked up at Acaren, lips parted as if he were trying to say something. Then the light faded from his eyes, and he slowly folded forward and collapsed.

• • •

Howling in rage Acaren swung his sword furiously. Hakkar leapt back over the body of a guard and raised his sword to meet Heartfire. Eliene spun away from Acaren's left, her sword taking a guard across the throat.

"I've waited a long time for this," Hakkar said, his voice quiet, but carrying clearly to Acaren's ears. "I shall kill you, Prince of Skai."

"Wrong on both counts," Acaren said. His wild grin held no trace of humor. "I'm not the Prince of Skai, nor shall you kill me."

Hakkar slashed first right, then left. Acaren leapt back, bringing Heartfire up to parry the black sword. He gave ground again.

"The wall," Eliene said breathlessly. "Behind you. Go left. To your left."

Acaren turned as Hakkar swung his sword again in a vicious arc.

"Who else but the Prince of Skai is served by a woman who can use a sword?" Hakkar demanded.

"You'd be surprised," Acaren said, panting with effort. "I'm not the Prince of Skai. He's my uncle. I—" He swept Heartfire around in a swift backhand curve. Hakkar leapt back, stumbled over the foot of the dead warlock. "—am the King of all Celi."

Hakkar's eyes widened. "You can't be. We made sure all the king's get were dead."

"You failed." Acaren swung Heartfire again, lips drawn back over his teeth. The blade caught Hakkar below the ribs. Hakkar staggered back and sprawled across the warlock's legs, the wound gaping open as his back arched in a shuddering death throe.

Rowan scrambled across the floor and pulled Cynric into his arms. Ceitryn dropped to her knees beside him and put her hands to his chest. Pale and shaken, she looked at Rowan and shook her head slightly. The wound was a mortal one—one no Healer could mend.

Cynric opened his eyes and stared uncomprehendingly up at Rowan. "Davigan?" he murmured.

"Not Davigan," Rowan said softly. "His son, Rowan. Davigan is long dead, Cynric."

Cynric nodded. "I remember," he said. His voice sounded faint as a wind rustling through dry reeds. "And Acaren? Not dead—"

"No," Rowan said. "Thanks to you."

A ghost of a smile tugged at Cynric's mouth. "Then I've redeemed myself," he said. "I couldn't save my king twenty-five years ago, but I could save him now."

"Yes," Rowan said.

"Iowen will be pleased." Cynric sighed, and Rowan felt his spirit leave his body, at peace. He let the body gently down to the floor and looked around.

Three guards threw themselves at Acaren and he and Eliene moved as a single unit to meet them. Horbad shrieked in rage and lunged across the floor. A swirling black mist rose from the bloody wound in Hakkar's chest. Horbad thrust both his hands into the wound. The black mist bubbled and seethed around him, and Rowan thought Horbad breathed it into his own body.

Eliene danced to one side, slashed the last remaining guard across the hip. Rowan leapt over the body of a fallen guard and slipped in a pool of blood. Before he could recover, Horbad had yanked Hakkar's sword from his dead hand and thrust himself to his feet.

"I'll kill you, Enchanter," he snarled. "I'll kill you, and Celi will be mine."

Rowan adjusted his grip on Soulshadow more firmly. The runes along the blade flared with a life of their own. *I am Heart and Soul of Celi.* Its voice shrilled in his head, fierce and exultant and wild. This was what it had been crafted for; its destiny was in Rowan's hands, as it was meant to be.

"You can try to kill me," Rowan said. "There's no guarantee you'll succeed."

The stench of blood sorcery in the room intensified. Acaren looked around just in time to see Horbad disappear. And Rowan and Ceitryn.

35

Valessa and Gabhain stood on a ridge overlooking the Verge. Behind them lay a still-growing army of Veniani tribesmen with their lethal little recurved bows. The Veniani, calling no man prince or duke, had gathered under their chieftains to Gabhain's summons just as their ancestors had come at King Tiernyn's call.

Valessa's father, Drustan of Dorian, had days ago set sail with Athelin of Skai, taking his warband with him. Gabhain had left Skerry Keep guarded by Weymund the Swordmaster and a determined army of boys too young and men to old to fight, and women archers. If the worst happened, there were hiding places already prepared high on the slopes of Ben Warden and Ben Roth.

Over a thousand Veniani waited in the camp below the ridge where Valessa and Gabhain watched. But they could do nothing to help Acaren and Rowan while the Dead Lands stood between them and the rest of Celi.

Valessa wasn't quite sure what she was expecting to happen. Athelin's ships were due to rendezvous with the Tyran fleet off Llewenmouth that same afternoon. If Hakkar's spell was not gone by the next afternoon, the Tyrs would have to turn away and return to Tyra. Then all would be lost.

Something flickered in the hazy air above the Dead Lands. Valessa couldn't swear she'd actually seen anything. She reached out tentatively and touched Gabhain's arm. He drew in a sharp, startled breath and pointed.

"Look," he whispered hoarsely.

The air above the withered and burned vegetation shimmered, then seemed to contract inward upon itself, writhing and twisting and heaving like a boiling current. Slowly, a handbredth at a time, like the tide receding from a wide beach, the harsh, scorched brown coloring ebbed down the slope of the ridge. As it sank, it left behind the soft, vibrant green of new spring growth.

Behind them, someone shouted. In moments, Valessa and Gabhain were surrounded by wildly cheering Veniani tribesmen, all waving their bows in the air in triumph as they watched the Dead Lands recede.

A hundred paces. Then a hundred more. New grass rose from the sere, wasted ground, and skeletal trees sent out green buds, stretching newly supple limbs toward the sunlight.

The sky flared in a garish display of crimson and orange. Neither sun nor moon lit the land caught between daylight and dark, a twilight neither morning nor evening. Enchanter and sorcerer faced each other across a wide circle of sand.

No, not sand, Rowan saw. But ash. The ash and cinder of the Dead Lands. No streams of power flowed beneath his feet here, nor in the air around him. The land was parched and dry, arid and barren of magic that should be there, the gentle magic of the Tyadda and the Celae. This was Hakkar's place of power — and Horbad had become Hakkar.

The hard, black aura of sorcery crackled around Horbad, shot with the searing dull red of blood magic, like flame in sooty smoke. It flared wildly as he moved. The sword he held absorbed the light and spilled chill darkness about both itself and the newly made sorcerer, as a broken ewer spills water.

Soulshadow quivered in Rowan's hands. Its voice came muffled and muted to his mind's ear. The runes gleamed dully in the fey light. This was not Soulshadow's realm, but the sword had not succumbed to the black sorcery.

Rowan was alone in the gritty ash circle with Horbad. He sensed Ceitryn's presence, but she was nowhere in sight. Behind him, off into the distance, stretched the fragile, attenuated silver filaments of the soul-bond they shared, a fragile web in this foreign place. If it snapped—

Rowan resolutely refused to think about what might happen if the threads broke. He would lose first Ceitryn, then his life.

Neither the Maedun prophecy nor the "Song of the Swords" said the enchanter of the legend would survive this encounter. Rowan took a firmer grip on Soulshadow's hilt and took a step closer to Horbad. The ash squirted from beneath his boots in a dry, lifeless cloud.

"You vowed to kill me, son of a mongrel cur," he said. "I invite you to try."

Ceitryn fell to her knees in the dew-sparked grass in the center of the Dance of Nemeara. The delicate threads of the bond she shared with Rowan spun out and away from her, disappearing into the distance. She saw no sign of him anywhere, but the webbing that connected them tugged and stretched as he moved somewhere beyond her field of vision. The motion nearly dragged her out of the Dance.

Frantically, she stabbed Kingmaker's blade into the soft grass and wrapped her hands around the hilt, using it to anchor herself. She looked up at the *darlai* stone, shining and glittering in the strong sunlight.

"Mother of All," she whispered. "Help us. For the sake of Celi itself, help us."

Acaren wheeled about to face another enemy, but found none. Only he and Eliene remained standing in the workroom. The oaken floor ran slippery and red with blood. Across the room, huddling against the wall, the young warlock shrank away from him.

Outside the workroom door, sounds of tumult and confusion filled the corridor. The heavy door muffled the uproar outside, but Acaren heard shouts and cries of both anger and pain.

Gasping for breath, he allowed Heartfire's point to ground itself in the bloody floor and leaned on it, letting his head droop with weariness. Eliene stepped closer to him and wiped the sleeve of her ill-fitting gown across her forehead. He raised his head and found he could still grin at her.

"It sounds as if we'd best get ourselves out of here," he said. "I'd bet the corridor out there is teeming with reinforcements."

Eliene glanced toward the door and nodded. "I'd bet you're right," she said. "But do you remember how to find the way out?"

He made a wry face. "I don't—"

"Acaren, look out!" Eliene's voice rose to a hoarse scream.

He turned and looked up in time to see a globe of that horrifying blood sorcery drift from the young warlock's hands. He leapt aside, dragging Eliene with him, but the fiery ball, leaving a trail of smoking, burning air behind it, turned and followed them. There was no time to get out of the way, and no room. He swore and reached for his magic.

The same magic that commanded the dice to show the faces he wanted pulled a battered silver tray from the wreckage near the captain's worktable. He sent it skimming and spinning directly into the path of the burning red globe.

The ball of blood sorcery hit the tray and bounced back. It retraced its path through the air, sizzling and spitting and hissing. The warlock screamed in terror as the ball flew toward him. It splashed against the wall just above his shoulder and rained fire across his head and left side. The scream bubbled in his scorched and scalded throat, then died as the glaring, searing fire consumed him. Flames licked at his gray robe, then at the fabric of the draped banners behind him. Greasy black smoke billowed up, thick as treacle.

Acaren gagged, and took a step backward, swearing. There was no getting through to the alcove and then out into the corridors through the back entrance. He glanced at the door that was still barred. Outside in the corridor, the tumult had died. There was only silence.

The fire took hold in the wreckage of the worktable and licked at the oaken floor and the paneling of the wall behind it. Enough heat to singe Acaren's hair burst from the flames.

"It's the corridor or nothing," he said quietly to Eliene. "If we stay here, we'll end up roasted like a Winter Solstice pig. Are you ready?"

She took a firm grip on the dead captain's sword. "As ready as I'll ever be," she said. "Let's go."

Horbad snarled and launched himself across the ashen circle, the obsidian sword held high in both hands. Rowan stepped lightly aside to dodge Horbad's wild swing and raised Soulshadow to parry the next cut. Around him, the silver web connecting him to Ceitryn flexed and stretched with his movements.

They circled each other warily. Rowan watched Horbad, trying to pick out small details of stance and pose that would tell him what sort of sword fighter he was. Horbad balanced easily on the balls of his feet, sword held in both hands. Dark eyes narrowed to slits, he studied Rowan as carefully as Rowan studied him.

Rowan sidestepped quickly to his right, searching for an opening. Horbad countered, his sword making small, purposeful sweeps before him. Rowan danced to his left, took a quick, experimental swing at Horbad's legs to test Soulshadow's balance and Horbad's alertness. Horbad parried the blow deftly and the blades met with a quick, whispering slither.

Rowan disengaged and stepped back, adjusting his grip on the translucent horn hilt. Horbad lunged at him, the black sword making a wide, sweeping arc toward his head. Rowan blocked it, then cut at Horbad's belly. Horbad parried the blow deftly, and jumped back out of reach.

Horbad feinted to his right, came at Rowan with a slicing cut from the left. Rowan swung Soulshadow down, blocked the black blade with a ringing clang, then carved another blow at Horbed's belly. Horbad leapt back, brought his blade up to parry Rowen's.

Again, they circled. Horbad attacked and Rowan lunged forward to meet him. Back and forth across the trampled expanse of ash, each step raising clouds of fine, powdery ash until Rowan's throat was clogged and each breath rasped like emery grit in his throat. But Soulshadow's fierce song soared around him, and he was blind to everything but the swing and slice of the other sword.

The sword in Rowan's hands vibrated with urgency. The smooth, translucent horn of the hilt fit his grip perfectly. Flaring light twisted around the blade, the runes glinting like gems. The sword's sweet, fierce song chimed around him and filled him with its soaring sense of power.

Horbad plunged forward, body tense, the black sword in his hands describing a vicious and deadly arc through the fey light. Rowan leapt back, bringing Soulshadow up to meet the obsidian blade. The two swords met with the crash of cymbals, and bright sparks shot up into the air around them.

Rowan let the sword take him deep into its own compelling rhythm. His magic sang in his veins, and the sword sang with it. He watched only Horbad.

Horbad disengaged and leapt back. Before Rowan could come after him, Horbad raised his hand and a globe of blazing blood sorcery spat from his fingers. It slashed through the turgid light, speeding straight at Rowan's head, leaving a trail of scorched and smoking air behind it.

Stark terror stabbed at Rowan's gut. There was no sunshine here to weave into a shield. No threads of power to fashion into a net. Nothing.

He twisted desperately, frantically aside and threw himself to the left, stumbling, falling to one knee. The searing, fiery ball sizzled past his head and exploded into the delicate strands of the web connecting him to Ceitryn.

Pain exploded through his whole body. He cried out in agony and fear.

Pain tore through Ceitryn's body as she knelt, clinging to Kingmaker's hilt. The bond—

Desperately, she reached out to seize the shreds that were all that was left of the bond she shared with Rowan. Beneath her hands, Kingmaker's blade flared incandescent white, sending glittering sparks of light around the stone circle of the Dance.

"Please," Ceitryn muttered breathlessly, not knowing

exactly what she was praying for, or to whom she prayed.
"Oh, please . . ."

The texture of the air around her changed subtly, and
she looked up. Her fear played tricks on her eyes. She
thought she could see the figures of men and women carved
in relief into the tall stones of the Dance—carved with such
clarity and precision, the figures seemed alive. Startled at
first, then frightened, she realized they were men and women,
and she recognized them. Rhianna of the Air, her long, moon-
silvered hair floating like a veil about her body. Cernos of the
Forest, with the tall rack of stately antlers rising from his
brow. Adriel of the Waters, carrying her enchanted ewer.
Gerieg of the Crags, with the mighty hammer he used to
smite the crags and shake the ground, spilling great landslips
down the crags. Beodun of the Fires, carrying in one hand
the lamp of benevolent fire and in the other, the lightning bolt
of wildfire. Sandor of the Plain, his hair blowing like prairie
grass around his face. And the *darlai*, the Spirit of the Land,
the Mother of All, smiling at her with compassion and tenderness.

Ceitryn stared at the *darlai*. "Help him," she whispered.
"Help him, please."

The *darlai* stepped from her place in the circle and glided
across the spring grass to Ceitryn. She put her hand gently to
Ceitryn's head.

"We made the sword he carries," she murmured.
"Through you, we shall protect it. And the one who carries it."

Acaren unbolted the door and flung it open. Eliene close
beside him, he leapt out into the corridor, Heartfire held
poised to strike. He stopped so suddenly, Eliene nearly trod
on his heels.

"By the seven," he whispered.

There were Somber Riders in the passageway. But they
lay crumpled in grotesque attitudes of death. One man bearing a sword spun around to meet Acaren, then checked his
swing and stood merely staring instead. He was dressed in
tunic and trews, now spattered with blood, but Acaren recognized him.

"Jordd?"

The Celae grinned, the expression contrasting starkly with the blood smearing his face. "Aye, my lord."

Acaren looked around in awe at the dead Riders. "What happened here?"

Jordd laughed with nervous excitement. "There were two Celae slaves for every Rider here, my lord. When the spell shattered, we attacked them." He swiped at a trickle of blood with his sleeve, smearing it across his forehead. "More than half of us died, I fear." Again, the wide, fierce grin. "But the rest of us are free. What would you have us do, my lord?"

Slowly, Acaren sheathed Heartfire. He glanced back into the workroom. The fire had taken the draped banners and had spread to the floor and the walls. "The first thing is to get out of here," he said. "And the second— Do you know where Llewenmouth is? North of Cloudbearer, where the Llewen flows into the sea?"

Jordd nodded. "I can find it, my lord."

"Then gather all the Celae you can and take them to Llewenmouth. There's an army waiting there to take Celi back from the Maedun."

"Will you be leading it, my lord?"

"Aye. I will."

"Then you can count on us."

A surge of energy flashed across the raveled threads of the bond and washed across Rowan like cool water on a scorching day. Soulshadow flared with radiant light, sending blazing sparks of blue and green and gold across the bitter ash. Rowan lunged to his feet. Soulshadow's voice howled in his ears.

Horbad scrambled back across the cinder and ash, another globe of fire forming in his hands, his face drawn into lines of strain.

High on the flank of Cloudbearer, Devlyn raised his head and an expression of wonder spread across his face. He leapt to his feet, shouting for Kley.

"The signal fire," he cried. "Light the signal fire. The spell is gone. It's gone!"

Rowan swung Soulshadow. Horbad dropped the half-formed globe of sorcery and snatched up his sword. Rowan saw the opening he so desperately sought. He leapt forward, taut with purpose. He swung Soulshadow in a short, backhand sweep. The glowing blade flicked under Horbad's guard and into the muscle of his belly. The black sword spun away into the dark. Shock and astonishment widened his eyes as he dropped to his knees.

Horbad lay crumpled on the cindery ground, ash clotting in the sweat on his face. As Rowan watched, gasping for breath, a dark mist rose from Horbad's body and slowly dissipated like morning fog. Horbad's body withered and shriveled until it was little more than a husk, frail enough for the gentle breeze to shred and fray.

Acaren and Eliene stood together in the shelter of a copse of hazel, watching the fortress. Flames leapt high behind the walls. The banner flying above the gatehouse, a black raven on a field of white, slowly blackened and charred as the fire raged. It crumpled and shredded on the wind, and was gone.

"That would seem to take care of that."

Acaren spun around at the sound of the voice. "Rowan!"

Rowan stepped out of the forest, his arm around Ceitryn. He was covered in pale, fine grit, his hair and clothing white with it. The rain had made sticky rivulets through the thick, powdery ash. But he was grinning.

"As ever was," he said cheerfully.

"By the seven, we thought you were both dead."

Ceitryn laughed breathlessly. "Not this time," she said. "We're all right." She stepped away from Rowan. "I have something for you, my lord King."

Rowan held out his hand. "But first, give me Heartfire."

Acaren drew back. "No!" he cried. "We haven't finished yet. There's still the island to be won back."

"That's not for Heartfire," Rowan said. He took Soulshadow from its sheath on his back and held it out across his palms. "Give me Heartfire."

Slowly, doubt and hesitation clear on his face, Acaren laid Heartfire across Rowan's hands beside Soulshadow. Then, even as he watched, the outlines of both swords shimmered in the watery light. Before he could protest, the swords vanished.

"You won't need them, my lord," Ceitryn said. "Their task is complete." She took the sword from her belt and held it out to him. "But this one—" She smiled. "This sword's task has just begun."

Acaren reached out and took the sword. Even in the rain, the blade glimmered with a vibrant light. Runes spilled down the blade, bright and sharp and clear. Acaren ran his finger across them, then looked up to meet Rowan's eyes.

"*Take up the Strength of Celi*," he whispered, his voice hoarse. "Kingmaker."

"Aye," Rowan said. "Kingmaker. Now we must ride to Llewenmouth and meet your army, my lord King. Celi lies waiting to be freed."

Epilogue

So it came about that Acaren ap Davigan ap Tiegan, great-grandson of Tiernyn ap Kian who was first High King of all Celi, took up the great sword Kingmaker and rode out from the ruins of the Maedun garrison fortress of Rock Greghrach. Following the instructions of the runes etched into the blade of King-maker to *Take Up the Strength of Celi,* he rode into legend. With him to guard his left rode his bheancoran Eliene al Saethen who carried the fabled Rune Blade Whisperer. To his right rode his brother, the Enchanter Rowan, together with Ceitryn the Healer. As they rode, the yrSkai liberated from the debilitating spell of the black sorcerer Hakkar came out of the hills to join them so that even before they met the army of Tyran Clansmen led by Fionh dav Brendon and the band of Saesnesi led by Devlyn Wykanson, the followers of the king swelled to thousands.

Some of the bards' tales would have one believe that the Maedun across the Isle of Celi and all through the Continent fled before King Acaren's armies as chaff blows before the wind. Not true. Four long years they campaigned before the Maedun were thrown into the sea and gone from the Isle of Celi. And another three years it was until the dark armies were beaten back into landlocked Maedun, and the last of the blood sorcery eradicated with the death of the last of the sor-cerers.

When the campaign was finally over, Acaren married Eliene, his bheancoran. When his first son was born, he read the runes on the reverse side of Kingmaker's Blade. *Now Lay Me Aside.* He gave Kingmaker back to the gods and goddesses in the Dance of Nemeara for the day that Celi might again need its strength. In peace with his queen and bheancoran Eliene, he reigned for many long years, and his son after him, and his son's son.

Athelin, Prince of Skai, and his son Gabhain returned to the mouth of the River Eidon where it flowed into the Ceg, and rebuilt the palace of Dun Eidon. Some say it is more beautiful now than the original palace that the Somber Riders destroyed. In one of the rose gardens that Dorlaine replanted stands a small cairn with three names carved into the pale granite—Athelin's sister Iowen, Iowen's husband Davigan ap Tiegan, and the name of Dorlaine's tiny stillborn daughter. Gabhain and Valessa's children and grandchildren played in the garden and scattered dried rose petals around the cairn every Imbolc morning.

Devlyn Wykanson kept his vow and took his people home. He and his kinsman Kley Kierson led their little band of Saesnesi down from the Spine of Celi and eastward into the Summer Run. Never a morning went by when Devlyn didn't give thanks as he watched his people settle back into a way of life they hardly dared dream of before Acaren ap Davigan came out of the west to them. Devlyn's children and grandchildren carry on the tradition even yet.

Rowan and Ceitryn retired to the little valley in the Spine of Celi where Donaugh ap Kian slept beneath his cairn in the orchard. The laughter of their children rang throughout the valley, and their children's children after them.

The *ðarlai* had promised Donaugh the Enchanter a line of Kings to rule over this land until the massive stones of the Dance of Nemeara crumbled to dust.

The stones stand yet.

Get ready for

EosCon IV

The original publisher-sponsored,
online, realtime science fiction and
fantasy convention

January 6, 2001

Meet your favorite authors online
as they discuss their work, their worlds,
and their wonder.

(Hey, it's the first sf/f convention
of the <u>real</u> new millennium!)

www.eosbooks.com

DISCOVER THE KINGDOM
OF KING ARTHUR
by *award-winning author*
DIANA L. PAXSON

THE HALLOWED ISLE
THE BOOK OF THE SWORD
AND
THE BOOK OF THE SPEAR
81367-X / $6.50 US / $8.99 Can

THE HALLOWED ISLE BOOK THREE:
THE BOOK OF THE CAULDRON
80547-2 / $10.00 US / $14.50 Can

THE HALLOWED ISLE BOOK FOUR:
THE BOOK OF THE STONE
80548-0 / $11.00 US / $16.50 Can